FEARFUL SYMMETRY

FEARFUL SYMMETRY

Morag Joss

Hodder & Stoughton

First published in Great Britain in 1999
by Hodder and Stoughton
A division of Hodder Headline

British Library Cataloguing in Publication Data

ISBN 0 340 71847 1

Typeset by Palimpsest Book Production Limited,
Polmont, Stirlingshire
Printed and bound in Great Britain by
Mackays of Chatham, plc, Chatham, Kent

Hodder and Stoughton
A division of Hodder Headline
338 Euston Road
London NW1 3BH

For my father

2nd September 1921 – 6th August 1999

The following is a list of music played by Sara Selkirk
in this novel:

Beethoven Variations in F on *Ein Mädchen oder Weibchen* from *Die Zauberflöte*

Brahms Cello Sonata No 2 in F

Dvorák Cello Concerto

Lalo Cello Concerto in D minor

Schnittke First Cello Sonata

Strauss Don Quixote, Variation 3, The Adventure with the Windmills
Variation 9, The Combat with the Two Magicians

BATH
city centre

AUTHOR'S NOTE

I suppose that Bath, being Bath, is bound to be harbouring some barking headmistresses, retired opera singers, ex-navy antiques dealers, Chinese students, self-worshipping composers, quack acupuncturists and wronged wives, and I would like to say to any of them who may read this book: *it's not about you*. I didn't walk around Bath thinking happy thoughts of homicide about real people, I sat at my desk and invented all the characters and events in this story.

I did, however, get out and about to consult a number of people for whose help I am very grateful. In particular I would like to thank Jan Snook of the National Autistic Society, Super-intendent Keith Shearn of Bath Police, Graham Kean, a gas fitter called Keith and a consultant neurologist who prefers not to be named. It was also helpful and enjoyable to read Tim Mowl and Brian Earnshaw's excellent *John Wood: Architect of Obsession*, *Autism and Asperger Syndrome* edited by Uta Frith, Baron-Cohen & Bolton's *Autism – The Facts* and Donna Williams' *Autism – An Inside-Out Approach*. And Margaret Campbell's *The Great Cellists* is a book I could not be without.

The nursing home which I believe is actually situated in the Circus in Bath has nothing whatsoever to do with the establishment in which Poppy worked; indeed I learned of the existence of the real one only after I had got Poppy the job. But I will own up to putting an extra house in the Circus, and to suggesting that it is not perfectly beautiful. I hope its fans will forgive this worrying lack of respect and believe me when I say that my enthusiasm for the architecture of the Circus is matched by my passion for all contemporary music.

Please don't go to Iford Manor to see the vegetables or the

rose garden because they aren't there. But (between April and October) do go – the garden is perfect as it is.

Morag Joss
1999

Part One

Music, when soft voices die,
Vibrates in the memory

Chapter One

It was most inconvenient of all for Miss Bevan, of course. Monday was her Oxfam day.

Although the shop would be shut because of the bank holiday, she was expected down at the stockroom at ten o'clock to look over some new things. She wondered how many bags there would be, and who from. Often as she picked things over she would try to imagine the frenzied domestic blitzes that produced most of the things that came Oxfam's way, but she never could. She kept her cupboards tidy and their contents current and consequently never needed to update her life in that sudden way, discarding books on invalid cookery and unfashionable hobbies along with macramé plant holders and clothing with ludicrous lapels. It occurred to her that real absent-mindedness lay less in losing things than in keeping them, because woeful inattention could be the only explanation for people hanging on to things like that for so long. But sometimes, and she fancied she could always tell, the bags were handed in not by triumphant turners-out of cupboards but by the slightly guilty relatives of someone 'recently deceased', and she had never got used to the smell that came from those bags whose owners, she felt, must have simply decayed carelessly away rather than actively died. And having died their overdue deaths, they left behind disembodied clouds of a stench like boiled wool sprinkled with damp pepper, which loitered above their empty clothes. No, it was not a job she liked, but when had she ever failed to do a job because she did not like it?

She preferred being out front. All you needed for that was confidence and a firm hand. Her mind wandered back to the previous week and how she had (as she had told the Oxfam Area Supervisor) averted a very undesirable incident. Mrs Silber, so tremulous and slow, was lucky that she had been there to take control of the situation. It was Alice Silber who had been on the till when the young girl and the youth had swept in and pounced on the raccoon coat that had gone on the rail that morning.

Alice Silber had said, first thing, 'Oh, Imogen, we can't put that out. They don't let us put any furs out nowadays.'

'That's nonsense,' she had replied. 'It's a perfectly good fur. Someone donated it. Yes, dear, I'm familiar with the arguments, but look how old it is. This coat was made before animal rights were even invented. I'm putting it out.'

So out it had gone. Out of consideration to Alice she had agreed not to put it in the window, but had hung it prominently on a rail just inside, visible from the door. The girl had simply marched in, grabbed it, dumped it on the counter and demanded in a loud voice that it be got rid of. Alice Silber, the silly woman, had opined that they should try to 'talk it through' (that phrase!). Fatal, of course, and pointless, because one cannot reason with these people. Then the young man had pitched in about being patronised and when she herself had come down from the steps where she had been rearranging Alice's hopeless display of woven baskets from Indonesia, Alice was actually saying that she had always felt sorry for the little creatures, too, and agreeing that perhaps an organisation like Oxfam should take an ethical stance on the fur trade. It was typical of Alice to cave in like that, but she was not going to be shouted down by a pair of arrogant hippies. They were not even clean. The row that followed had emptied the shop, but she had taken pleasure in showing them the door and putting the coat back on the rail. It had gone now, bought within days, so she rather hoped that the new stuff this morning would include another. Yes, it would be enjoyable to sell another, and win another victory for common sense and a bit of backbone.

Imogen Bevan braced herself over her second cup of breakfast blend and thought further into the rest of the day. Oxfam till one, then home for luncheon. She used the proper words for things, even in her mental lists. For luncheon she would have half of the mushroom soup in the refrigerator along with some wholemeal toast, a piece of smoked Orkney cheese and an apple. She pictured her neat little meal, wholesome, elegant, not at all fuddy-duddy. Somewhat like herself, really. Taking a pride. Maintaining her standards, which seemed even more important now that she had retired and no longer had to maintain a whole school's standards and see that things were done properly, the way a good headmistress insists they are done. And as long as she went on doing things properly, in the same way now at seventy-four as she had done at sixty-four, and in the same way in another ten years' time at eighty-four, she felt certain she could hold off any descent into that region of malodorous geriatric drift, whose atmosphere eddied around the clothes of those who had so disgracefully let things slide to the extent of shuffling off the mortal coil.

She ran some hot water into the sink, tied on an apron and carried her breakfast things over to the draining-board. As she mopped at her egg cup, she planned further. After luncheon she would rest with the *Telegraph* crossword for half an hour. Then she would telephone the cleaning contractors again, since there had been no response to the message she had left on Friday. It was all very well, she had told the answering machine, just putting a shine on the hall floor and rubbing the door furniture, but when she had had to stoop down to pick up the post (she was always first there) she had seen the state of the skirting boards. And they need not think that they could just flick a broom round when they came next Friday. She and her fellow residents at number 11 paid for a cleaning service for the common areas and she expected them round at once to do a proper job. There had been no response, but what could one expect from these people? She would leave another message this afternoon and call again first thing on Tuesday morning.

Had she really said 'fellow residents'? she wondered, sniffing. She had taken a tea towel with acorns on it and was now drying her saucer. A slip of the tongue, for she certainly could have no fellow feelings towards those homosexuals on the first floor. She supposed that what they got up to was their business, and simultaneously assumed the right to condemn it. And they seemed to have no qualms whatsoever. If she ran into one of them going in or out she would have to suffer the most breezy greeting, as if it were quite normal that they should be on proper neighbourly terms. She didn't welcome friendliness from that sort of person. Their flat was empty again. All the coming and going between Bath, London and Brussels because of work, so-called. Treating her like an ignoramus. She took a plate and wiped it vigorously. She followed the news. The foreign news reporting in the *Telegraph* was second to none and readers had not been spared the details of that disgusting Belgian business. The country was overrun by homosexuals, paedophiles and pornographers. Those two upstairs could even be dealers in that sort of filth; she had always been dubious about what they claimed to do for a living.

Now she was drying the cutlery, which had of course been properly rinsed. After her telephone call to the cleaners she had a letter to write to the spineless chairman of the Camden Crescent Residents' Association, to press upon him again the need for action about the nasturtiums in the window box of number 21, and to report again that the Londoners who had number 9a had brought their cat for the weekend again, in breach of the lease. That might take her up to teatime (Earl Grey). After that she would tidy up the plants and water the tomatoes on her back patio. Beyond that, there was an evening to fill with a little television, a lamb noisette and vegetables, some lemon mousse, a blouse to iron for the morning, and her bath. Very satisfactory, she thought, putting away the cutlery and thinking (incredulously, for it was the bank holiday) that she had just heard the postman.

She mounted the stairs from her flat up to the ground-floor hall. It was empty and echoing, its bare white walls and chequered floor almost chilly. She picked the package off the mat. She could tell by the size and weight that the plain Jiffy bag contained a videotape. She turned it over in her hands. Hand-delivered, of course, no postmark. Plain white label, name and address handwritten in black capitals. Sealed down, not just held with those clips you can get. Miss Bevan's heart began to beat faster. This would be just the way that kind of thing would start, one at a time. It would start so slowly you might not even notice it and then it would gather momentum and lead heaven knew where. She looked round the empty hall, and back at the package in her hand. She would know within seconds if it was something innocent, or not. If necessary she could reseal it with some tape of her own and just leave it on the post table. Nobody would know. That's if it were harmless, which it wouldn't be, and of course she wouldn't watch it, she would take it straight to the police. Really, it was a duty to open it. With a last quick look around the hall she tucked the Jiffy bag under her apron and made for the door down to her basement flat.

When she first held the package over the steam pouring from the kettle she almost scalded her hand. Then, turning the package over too late, she saw that it was the address label which was peeling away, while the seal remained perfectly intact. Worse, the lettering had not been done in fast ink, and had run into grey illegible streaks. She began to wish that she had never embarked on her private crackdown on crime. Rousing herself, she whipped the soggy label right off and tore it into grey shreds. She rolled the pieces into a damp little nugget and pushed it in among a mass of tea leaves and eggshell in the pedal bin. It would be an easy matter to write out another label in anonymous-looking capitals. She held the package over the kettle once more. The kitchen was filling with steam and still the seal would not budge. Obviously something much stronger than any standard envelope sealing had been used, and why would that be, unless to keep the vile contents secret while in transit? Certain of what she would find, she took the package in both hands and, with the strength of a holy warrior, tore at the wrapping.

So no, it was not convenient, it being not only the August bank holiday Monday but also the anniversary of Diana's death. The crowd, although smaller than expected, had been building up all weekend. A persistent swarm of thirty or so were intent on sleeping out in Parade Gardens, and there were bye-laws against that sort of thing. Others were encamped on benches in Abbey Churchyard. There were already twenty extra uniformed officers policing the abbey environs who expected that, among the many flocking to Bath intent on lighting candles, leaving flowers and praying prayers, there would be several dozen others who would manage to overcome their grief sufficiently to concentrate on parking illegally, thieving from cars, lifting from shops or drinking themselves to disorderliness.

Not a convenient day either for the Accident and Emergency Department of the Royal United Hospital, where the staff were waiting with weary fatalism for the admissions of keening girls, legs buckling from the combined effects of lager, sun and too long standing in sweaty crowds united in mourning. The poor air quality would bring in one or two emergency asthmatics and the temperature alone guaranteed a few heatstroke candidates as well. They could expect the heat to add to the domestic incident tally this year. There would, depressingly, be the usual bank holiday traffic victims. Then there would be the botched suicides, people too lonely and depressed to go out and get stung by swarms of bees, bitten by their neighbours' dogs or electrocuted by their lawnmowers.

It was not convenient for the police. It was not convenient for the hospital. Nor was it convenient for Mrs Maupesson or her granddaughter in the pushchair, whose progress along Camden Crescent was interrupted shortly after nine o'clock that morning by the appearance of Miss Bevan from the basement flat of number 11. She emerged from the area steps behind the railings, unusual in itself, because she generally came and went by the main front door to number 11 and thence by the door at the end of the hall which led down into her flat. Mrs Maupesson, coming out of number 27 without her glasses on, had at first thought it also unusual that Miss Bevan, normally reserved, seemed so animated. Really, she was babbling, and although Mrs Maupesson was too far away to hear clearly what she was saying, she seemed to be insisting with some urgency that Mrs Maupesson stop and accept, what were they? Handfuls of tomatoes? No, it was two rather limp bunches of flowers that she was holding out. She had one in each hand, twin nosegays of bright red, shiny, drooping peonies, petals falling and splashing everywhere. But then Mrs Maupesson drew nearer and saw that what Miss Bevan was waving at her were not bunches of flowers at all, but the remains of her hands.

All inconvenience to Miss Bevan came to an end at two thirty-five p.m. when her heart, affronted by the demands made upon it by trauma, anaesthesia and a sedated three-hour wait for a theatre, stopped on the operating table. Its determined resistance to all resuscitation attempts somewhat inconvenienced the surgical team. They had, having removed several bone shards, just succeeded in re-establishing a blood supply to the scant remaining muscle and tendon tissue, so that after further restorative surgery Miss Bevan might have been in with a chance of continuing her life with the aid of two quite serviceable claws.

Chapter Two

Detective Chief Inspector Andrew Poole took the call from DC Heaton and afterwards sat on at his desk, leaning across it with his chin cupped in one hand. He hoped he'd rung off with the kind of weary but purposeful authority that junior officers needed.

'Right, thank you, Constable. No point you hanging on there any longer. Still no relatives shown up? Better get on down to the woman's flat, then. DS Bridger's freezing the scene but we'll need to establish who's to be informed. Bound to be some family or friends of the deceased somewhere or other. And Heaton, when they've been tracked down: "cause of explosion not yet known". Same thing if there's any press there. All right?'

He was sorry Imogen Bevan had died, for her own sake. But he was almost sorry on his own behalf because, having posted DC Heaton at the hospital to await the remote possibility that Miss Bevan might be interviewed, while he organised the setting-up of an enquiry here at the Manvers Street station, there was now no excuse for him not to go back home, even though he was now in all probability investigating a murder. And he did not want to go home. The call informing him of the suspected letter-bomb explosion had interrupted the first turning of the meat on the barbecue and given him the satisfaction of handing over to Valerie the long tongs and the butcher's apron, with an insincere frown at having to leave. Now that Miss Bevan had died and he had officers at the scene of the explosion, there was nothing more, for the present, that he could do.

Lifting his head from his hand, he sat up and leaned back in his chair and looked round the empty Major Incident Room. That was something, at least, to have a designated room for this kind of work. Imogen Bevan would never know that hers would be the first murder dealt with here and she could hardly appreciate the honour, but it was progress. The last murder case he'd worked on, the death of the director of Bath Museums, had begun with the usual scramble to commandeer an empty room and purloin telephones, equipment and furniture from all over the building, wasting the better part of the first day. After that he had made a case to the District Commander for a permanent room. Now he had his Major Incident Room, with telephones, computer screens and consoles on a continuous line of desks which stretched round two sides, pinboards and large-scale maps on the walls, and even a microwave and kettle. Tomorrow morning they could get straight down to it, as soon as they had the PM report.

For now, he was free to return home to Oldfield Park where all three kids would probably be lying inside with the curtains drawn, glued to the bank holiday feature film. His three carelessly beautiful, maddening children, Benji, Dan and Natalie, whom he had discovered he could not leave. Outside, Valerie would be banging around in a penumbra of charcoal smoke, picking up from the scuffed grass the dirty skewers, knives, trodden bones, half-raw, discarded ropes of meat and ketchup-soaked napkins that reduced their semi-detached garden, post-barbecue, to something more like an abandoned field hospital. She would look up at him, her furious face smeared with sooty exertion, before barging past him with another bin-liner, pointedly saying nothing about the seventy concrete paving slabs and half-ton pile of sand that had been lying at one side of the garden for over a year, and that Andrew had still not built into Valerie's dream patio on which they could have proper civilised barbecues that would be rather less Crimean in their aftermath.

He should go back home. But instead, he allowed his chin to sink into the cup of his other hand and he leaned forward again, staring at his desk and trying, although not very hard, not to think about Sara, because that only made him feel worse.

Chapter Three

There was a certain tidiness, Sara thought, in being a woman alone in a room at night with a drink, a bath, a bed and a book. She had forgotten, or had not noticed in the first place, which floor of the hotel she was on. There might even be a view, but it could wait until morning. She did not have to look out at the New York nightscape to feel like an insignificant scrap of humanity, and she doubted if the city's energising buzz would penetrate the triple-glazed, unopenable window tonight, even if she were in a mood to receive it. She swallowed some of her whisky. She would be fine as long as she did not switch on the television. It was only when she switched on the television and talked back to it that she knew she was really lonely.

She was so tired of hotels. She was tired of stepping over thresholds into too-spacious rooms, tired of being called ma'am, tired of giving bright thanks and tips to someone with her luggage. Most of all, she was tired of the turning back, after the door closed, to the veneered surfaces wiped bare with chambermaidenly competence and the scent of acrylic carpet through which she fancied she could always smell a silence as heavy and over-generous as the swagged curtains and coordinating bedspread. It was nearly ten o'clock on Monday night. Waiting for her bath to fill, she thought of the now empty concert hall in Seattle where she had played on Saturday. The people in the audience, three hours behind New York time, would now be sitting down to dinner. They might now be reading the fulsome reviews of her performance in the Seattle press and disagreeing, the way some people liked to, with all the critics, indulging in a little recreational shredding of her reputation ('Didn't you find her Beethoven rather *jejune*?'). But there had been nothing mean-spirited about the Beethoven, despite how lousy she had felt during most of it, rather sick and light-headed. It was only afterwards, after the exhausting chats that well-meaning people got her into at the dressing room door, when she was trying to make her way out to her taxi with cello case, concert dress and hold-all, that she had given in to the fatigue and faint annoyance that she was now feeling. They had been so kind, these people, and she had signed a few programmes and answered the predictable questions.

'Well, I'm actually going on to New York tomorrow and meeting Herve Petrescu on Monday. Yes, a new work for solo cello, keyboard, percussion and pre-recorded tape. Oh, yes, a huge challenge. Yes, it's being written for me. No, I met him in Prague, a few weeks ago. Just a brief meeting, this time we'll be looking at his first ideas for the new piece. No, I haven't done much contemporary music. Yes, he *is* extraordinary. No, I'm not abandoning the classics. Yes, terribly challenging. Then I'm going back home to England. Petrescu will be coming over a bit later.'

She had first met Herve in Prague in early August, during the third week of her present round of engagements. She and Robin, her agent and manager, had waited for an hour at their outside table in the Old Town Square before he'd shown up for their lunch appointment. With him had been a much younger woman, leggy and mute. Whether she spoke no English or simply had had nothing to say never became clear because Herve, having tossed off her name by way of introduction, thereafter ignored her, except when he took a cigarette. He would take one from the packet, raise it to his lips and half turn towards her, his eyes still on the other side of the table. She, without fail, would have the lit match ready with a servile smile that Herve ignored and made Sara want to kill her.

'I herp you lakk my werk?' was the first thing he said to Sara and she, catching in Robin's eye a look that said *behave yourself*, had resisted the temptation to reply that she hoped he liked hers too and force him to apologise for not turning up the night before to hear her play the Dvořák Cello Concerto with the Prague Symphony. Probably too busy with Leggy Mute, she had reflected silently, feeling unattractively prim. And she did not mention that it was Robin who had insisted she accept the invitation to première the new work that Petrescu would be commissioned to write for her. (*It'll ginger you up, you might think about doing more contemporary repertoire. And he's very big.*) Indeed there had been little need to mention anything very much, since the purpose of the meeting, as far as Herve was concerned, was to deliver an enlightening tutorial about himself.

'Nineteen sixty-nine, my MA from Bucharest. Composition, analysis and formalised music. Then two years at Cologne and Darmstadt with Cage, Xenakis, Stockhausen and Ligeti.' He blew a long, tired plume of smoke across the table as if to emphasise how exhausting it had all been. 'You should know my opus 11: ULTIMATE SPACE INTO EMERGENT PLASMA for nine cellos from this period?'

Sara tried to express 'oh, yes, absolutely' with a lift of the eyebrows.

Herve leaned forward. 'You know? Where 4170 timbre-processes integrate the first forty-five spectral components of a C-fundamental – emanation of the emanation?'

'Oh, that one. *Love* it,' she had said, staring. Robin's lips twitched. 'No doubt, Herve,' she went on earnestly, 'as one of the, so to speak, mainsprings of the renewal of musical language this century, you are excited by the . . . the new, should one say, *well*spring of young composing talent in Europe?' From across the table Robin's eyes were frantically asking what the hell she was up to. She kicked him under the table. 'We all know that genius will out, of *course*' – she gestured sycophantically in Herve's direction – 'but it behoves one of your stature to encourage new talent.'

Herve smiled and turned to Leggy Mute again with a cigarette between his lips. Inhaling once, he removed the cigarette and waved it around. 'People come all, all the time. Like disciples, pilgrims, to my studio. Advice, lessons, I give all. Give, give, give.'

Sara rummaged in her bag and handed over a card. 'Just what I was hoping you'd say. Perhaps you can give someone this. These people here – this is the name and address – they need someone to write them a community opera. Perhaps you know someone who'd like the commission, one of your disciples. Someone able to write for voices, and able to live in Bath for a few months. Not much money though, I don't think, but then, it's not *about* money, is it?'

Herve was blinking at the card which she had thrust into his hands.

'Marvellous!' Sara said quickly. 'I'll leave it in your safe hands. Thank you, Herve, they'll be *so* grateful.' She picked up the menu and beamed round the table. 'Is everyone starving? I am.'

Afterwards, Robin had had to admit to some admiration of her nerve. But he was worried. Herve was a man who had to be taken seriously. Shouldn't she be making a little more effort with his music? She had reassured him that she would genuinely, wholeheartedly try to like Herve's music, without adding that it should be easy because she had found it all too easy if not to like him, then to find herself unable to ignore his huge, irresistible ego. To take seriously, at any rate, the fact that he was tall and interestingly fifty-something, and had the kind of agonisingly intelligent grey eyes, containing the right proportions of tragedy, brains and sexual promise, that she thought of as particularly and irresistibly east European. He would make a perfect dispossessed chess champion with four mistresses in a black and white film, she considered, but had merely agreed obediently with Robin that Herve was an extraordinary man, and it was only the effect of his complex, intense intellect that some people might mistake for vanity.

She wandered into the oversized bathroom, turned off the

taps and returned to the room, settling on the bed. Even the walk to the bathroom and back tired her. The useless doctor she had seen this morning had said she was suffering from stress. What a surprise, and how utterly New York of him that he should consider that 'some lifestyle modification' would lower her slightly raised blood pressure. She just needed to get home, she had said. Sure thing, and a little lifestyle modification, like getting tough with people who made too many demands, he'd agreed, and could he please have an autograph as a lasting memento? Sure thing, she said, how about this one here on the cheque? She had let him think she was joking.

In the afternoon she had met Herve in a high-up, wondrous New York apartment belonging to Herve's US agent and publisher, and she had almost laughed with excitement at the sight of New York literally at her feet. So it must have been jet lag or simple exhaustion that was at the root of her disappointment with what Herve had produced for her to play. She had gone through the 'sketches' diligently, but somehow she was not really seeing it yet; something was eluding her. When Herve joined her in England in ten days to start work in earnest she would have got to grips with what his stuff was all about. She had reassured him of that. She really ought to listen to the tape again and read the notes properly. She got up, pulled out her Walkman from her hold-all and fixed the headset over her ears. She found the cassette, loaded it in the machine and settled back again on the bed with the thick bundle of papers that Herve had given her that day along with the tape. There was nothing to be daunted about. Today it must have been something to do with the New York light that had made the whites of his eyes look a little creamy but still there had been an intriguing glint in them when he had said to her, 'I lakk to werk very clerse wiss my performer'.

The bath could wait. She would listen again to 'Visions: Revisions: Archetypes (1995)' for gamelan, percussion and synthesiser, and she would try again, by concentrating very hard, to understand the essay on Herve by some German musicologist, instead of being sidetracked into imagining him naked. Because that, she predicted, thinking ahead to the next few weeks of werking very clerse, might not much longer have to remain a job for the imagination, although any such development would be on *her* terms. She pressed the Play button and began to read.

Petrescu's music, with its strong emphasis on timbre, is thus founded on the notion of 'process', a technique allowing the transition from a given state to another within a directional continuum of sound (BONG*ONG* whee whee whee). His music is characterised by the entirely (BONG*ONG* whee broop shshsh) original oppositions it sets up between sound object and (pup *pup* prrup) transitory process (*whonk*), continuity and discontinuity, speed and stasis (*prrup*). The 'processes' are superimposed on one another, enabling the course of the music to include polyphonic or (*kssss!*) heterophonic constructions according to (WHONK*kssss*) articulatory (*aah kssss!*) principles (*wheee eee* eeep).

Jet lag. Or simple exhaustion. The New York light. Something. But please God, not her own limitations.

After her bath Sara pulled out the contents of her bag on to the bed and checked that her passport, wallet and ticket for tomorrow were in order. She rang the reception desk to order a taxi to the airport. It was time to go home, but by some conspiracy among airline schedulers she was stuck in this city for another seven hours. At last she was going home, but she felt afraid of what lay ahead. Reluctantly, she confronted a fresh line-up of anxieties, telling herself to be sensible. She was going home, in order to work quietly with Herve on the new piece, without distractions or interruptions. Circumstances like those were a privilege, and that was how she resolved to look at them from now on. And there was to be an open rehearsal of the 'work in progress' at Iford Manor in mid-September before its proper London première in December, and she'd always rather fancied playing Iford Manor. It was a tiny jewel of a place just outside Bath, an English manor house with an astonishing

Italianate garden where arcane but delightful concerts were staged every year. As it was ordinarily impossible to step off the international circuit to play such a venue, she was looking forward to it.

No, the thing that was worrying her was the question of Herve himself, and not just his so far impenetrable music. She forced herself to remember the embarrassing part of this afternoon. As she was leaving she had turned and asked him nonchalantly if he had found anyone to take on the commission for the community opera. His equally nonchalant half-nod had conveyed that he had taken care of it. And then, almost as if he had just thought of it, he had asked, with a penetrating look into her eyes and his hands gently on her shoulders, if one favour did not deserve another? She had met his look with what she thought was a smouldering one of her own. Now in her room she groaned at the memory of how she had risen to this dangling worm of sexual interest like the desperate old fish that he might now think her. She had swallowed it whole and wriggling and, with barely a gulp, concurred that one favour most certainly did deserve another. In that case, he had one to ask. He smiled. She smiled back. He needed somewhere to stay while he was in Bath. He hated hotels. Perhaps he could stay with her? As his hands massaged her shoulders, one fingertip reached over the collar of her cashmere jersey and just, only just, stroked the skin at the base of her neck. First, and simultaneously, Sara appreciated that it was a little late for dignified backtracking and that the pressure of his finger on her skin was delicious. Second, and more slowly, she began to think how nice it was to hear things like 'so exciting to work as closely together as possible' from lips so close to her own. The glacier of immense physical want that had formed deep in her body since Matteo's death was creaking dangerously.

It was only as he began to ask her murmuringly about her house, was she on e-mail, did she have only one music room, could he have his own private space, did she have any sound equipment, that she began to hear the klaxon going off in her head instead of the voice now very close to her ear: DON'T DO IT DON'T DO IT DON'T DO IT. She drew away, uncertain whether his

21

suggestion was refreshingly honest in its barefaced opportunism or an insult to her intelligence.

'We can work together at my house,' she said. 'It's perfect for working. But I'd better find you somewhere else to stay. To start with.'

And now she would have to. He appeared not to have thought about such practicalities for himself until that moment and now, probably because she was so damned susceptible, she realised furiously, it had become *her* responsibility, just as it had been Leggy Mute's job to light his fags. How? How had that happened? But she could see that if she did nothing, precious time would be wasted while he tried to find somewhere by himself when he arrived, or got peevish about not staying with her. Oh yes, and he hated hotels. 'Wanted: superior private accommodation for intense, foreign, possibly domestically helpless, rich and famous composer. Liable to emit, or cause to be emitted, loud, insane electronic noises.' She would have to deal with it.

And an even more immediate problem faced her tomorrow. She thought again of Medlar Cottage, concerned at how very intensely she wanted to be back in it and to move around all its spaces, feeling her body and mind rest into the embrace of each room. She pictured the furniture, standing undisturbed through a hundred comings and goings of daylight and dark, the stopped, waiting clocks and the propped-open fridge. Every uneven, well-known step of the stairs, every quirky door, each little draught and creak were marks of her house's own fragile familiarity, which by her absence she might have obscured into strangeness. What if she crossed her own threshold and instead of the private peace that she longed for, found again only the same smothering loneliness of a hotel? She had not been home in nearly two months, and now she could not face it alone.

She picked up the telephone and rang Andrew in England, where it was four o'clock in the morning.

Chapter Four

'Egg?'

'Sorry?'

'An egg. Want one?'

'Oh, yes. Thank you. Are you having one?'

'Am I, sorry?'

'An egg.'

'Oh. I don't think so. Thank you. Unless—'

Oh, Christ, Andrew thought, locking his teeth together. She is actually going to ask: *unless you mind having one on your own?*

'Unless you mind having one on your own?'

'Why does Daddy always get an egg now?'

Natalie and her brothers looked up from their bowls at the breakfast bar.

'Can I have an egg too?'

'Eggs are yuck. I want toast.'

'You've got cereal. Eat up. Then go and clean your teeth.'

The children resumed a subdued sucking on their honey clusters and some half-hearted kicking at one another's ankles, silently enquiring of one another whether that was the I Mean It voice or the Don't Bother Me one.

'Didn't I hear the phone last night?'

'Yes. About four o'clock.'

'Was it a call-out? I didn't hear you go out.'

Andrew lowered his voice and turned away from the children. 'Valerie, I thought the kids aren't supposed to know I'm sleeping in the spare room? How could you not know it was a call-out if the phone was still in our room?'

'Oh, it goes over their heads,' Valerie said, glancing over to the breakfast bar. The chewing children looked blandly back at her. 'You three. Teeth. And do it properly.'

'Why is Daddy sleeping in the spare room?'

'Is that why he gets an egg?'

'Cereal's yuck.'

'*Now,*' said Valerie, moving in and talking in unmistakable I Mean It.

They scattered, like little looters disturbed from the wreckage of their breakfasts. When they had gone she turned round to Andrew.

'So was it? A call-out?'

Andrew sighed. 'No.'

'Quite enough nastiness already, with that letter-bomb. Poor woman.'

'Hmm.'

'Quite enough, you being called in on your bank holiday off, without another call-out at four o'clock in the morning.'

'Yesterday was an emergency. The ambulance people twigged that a crime was involved, and the casualty doctor called us. A criminal explosion could be a terrorist bomb. You've got to act immediately.'

'Oh, don't emergency procedure me. Why would the IRA blow up a seventy-five-year-old spinster?' Valerie said.

'I didn't say political terrorists. We ruled that out quite quickly. But someone sent an old lady a letter-bomb that blew up in her hands, even if it wasn't meant to be fatal. I call that terrorism.'

'So who was it?'

'Dunno yet, unlikely to be a random nutcase. More likely a—'

'On the phone, Andrew. At four o'clock in the morning.'

'Oh. Actually, it was Sara,' he said, very nearly failing to sound neutral. 'She's in New York. She claimed to have forgotten the time difference, but you know what she's like.' His voice tailed away into a slight clearing of the throat. He remembered her tearful voice and felt like a disloyal bastard to be running her down. But Valerie must get no inkling of how he still felt about Sara. She was already making him suffer enough for their non-existent affair, the affair which he and Sara had never actually, but nearly (to his regret only nearly) had.

'So, no, instead of a random nutcase,' Valerie said, 'your little blip.' She turned to the cooker and set about boiling Andrew's egg.

Andrew sat down and opened the paper. To content herself with just that was a sign of new and considerable restraint in Valerie and he knew he should give her credit for it. Three months ago she had declared herself prepared to accept what he had told her all along, that the affair had never happened, and that when he had left to move into a flat it had not been in order to be with Sara. On that basis Valerie had allowed him to move back in but not to sleep with her because she needed her own space (her version). Seeing his children grow steadily more listless as the weeks of their separation went by, Andrew had given in to her demand that they try again, although he would take the spare room because he did not want to sleep with her (his). Like lots of couples, they were learning how to be kinder to one another. They had allowed themselves to grow apart, and Andrew's cello lessons with Sara Selkirk were not and never had been the issue. It was more a question of cultivating some shared interests and having fun together (theirs).

It was the new, fun-seeking Valerie who had signed them both up for the Circus Opera Group. 'I've signed us both up. They said singers and instrumentalists are welcome and no audition is necessary.'

'I hate musicals,' Andrew had said, lapsing into the style of the old regime, 'and I won't sing.'

'It's not a musical, it's an opera. A community opera. And you won't be singing. I'll sing and you'll play your cello. It'll be fun.'

Although it was a novelty to have Valerie not openly resentful about his cello-playing, the words 'community opera' were almost enough to send him running. He needed neither a community nor an opera, he needed only as much nineteenth-century cello repertoire as he could lay his hands on and time to play it. And Sara. But he knew that there could be no defence against the imperative that he and Valerie have fun. At the same time he calculated that he could use his working hours as a reason to keep himself safely away from most of the rehearsals. 'As long as I don't have to sing, then,' he said.

Valerie was now a 'key member' of the Circus Opera Group and often referred to Sara as Andrew's 'little blip'. Andrew had grown accustomed to locking his teeth together and allowing her to, calculating that the breezier Valerie became about her, the easier it would be for him to carry on seeing her, of course only for lessons, once she was back. It had even been Valerie's suggestion that Sara might be able to recommend somebody to compose the community opera. 'Isn't she supposed to know everyone? I'm sure you could persuade her to find us a nice young composer.'

Reluctantly, Andrew had mentioned it, just as she was leaving for the six-week block of engagements which was just ending. 'Well, yes, I do know people, but I thought the community was supposed to compose it,' she said. 'Look, I'm packing. I'll give it some thought.' Until last night, that was the last time he had spoken to her. He turned a page of the paper.

'Has she done anything about a composer?' Valerie asked, as if she had been tracking his brain. She was buttering toast viciously, as if trying to get something off it. 'The group's starting up again tonight, remember. It's getting desperate now.' The group had spent the three months before its summer break on part-songs and squabbles about the theme of the putative opera. Opinion was divided on whether it should be about Jane Austen or about the Romans and the hot springs. Andrew's contribution to the debate had been to point out that for one thing Jane Austen had disliked Bath and for another he hoped nobody seriously expected him to play the cello ponced up in a toga.

'I'm sure she has,' Andrew said, without lowering the paper. 'I didn't ask. We didn't chat, once I pointed out the time.'

He turned another page. 'She just rang to ask me to send a PC to check that Medlar Cottage was okay. Got herself in a state about possibly coming home to a burgled house,' he lied.

He looked at his watch. It was nearly eight o'clock. He had another twelve hours in which he had to act normally.

'And it was handy, in a way, her ringing. She knows the people who live above the Bevan woman. They're away, and of course we want to interview all the neighbours. And as it happened Sara had their other numbers.' He lowered the paper. 'Look, I'll try to make it to the rehearsal tonight. But this letter-bomb case will be coming first with everyone for a while. There's a lot to do. There are no obvious suspects. We need to interview a lot of people, and quickly. So I'll try, but don't count on me. All right?'

Valerie grimaced with understanding, for which Andrew felt a whole second's worth of guilt. But only another twelve hours until he would see her, until she would be stepping off her plane and coming through the Arrivals Hall. She would be tired out, laden with her luggage and cello case, but still the most beautiful woman in the whole building. And she would be a little lost, looking out for him, and as soon as she saw him the anxiety would leave her face and she would smile and walk towards him, because she had asked him to be there and of course he would be, waiting to wrap his arms around her and take her home.

'One fur coat isn't the issue. The issue is exploitation. Totally innocent animals are being exploited. I happen to believe

that's worth fighting for.' As she finished speaking Anna
Ward-Pargiter opened her eyes very wide behind her glasses
and took a deep breath, clenching her lips tightly as she did so.
This arrested, momentarily, the wobble that had started up in
her chin, but after a few seconds back it came, the involuntary
contraction that puckered up her lips and tightened her throat.
She grasped her chin tightly between a thumb and forefinger
and looked up at the ceiling. She tried to blink away the
moistness that was gathering in her eyes. Now there was stuff
wanting to come down her nose and invisible wires seemed
to be tugging down the corners of her mouth. Oh shit shit
shit shit shit – she was going to cry.

Andrew exchanged a glance with WDC Frayling, who
took the cue and said quietly, 'All right, Anna? Shall we
stop there? We can stop for a minute if you like – there's
no problem.'

Anna was now finding that it was impossible to leave off
gulping and sniffing. She didn't understand this. Bren had said
they were pigs. But these pigs were coming over all nice. She
took off her glasses, reached for a hanky, found none, sank
her head on to her arms across the table and bawled like
a three-year-old. Shit – now there would be stuff all over
her sleeves.

'Anna, it is quite clear to you, isn't it?' WDC Frayling
went on. 'You are being interviewed as a witness, not, so
far, as a suspect. You are not under arrest. And I know you
said you didn't want to, but you can still use a phone and let
someone know you are here. You're allowed to change your
mind, you know.'

Anna always collapsed the minute people were nice. From
the day Mum left and right through the divorce she had kept
a hold on herself. She knew it was only a question of winding
a part of yourself up so tight inside that it took up a very small
space, and then you could forget it was there, like looking after
your tights at boarding school. The small drawer you had was
fine when you rolled each pair into a hard little bumpy ball,
but a complete mess if you let them unravel everywhere. Her

brain told her that she was a statistic, another 'child of divorced parents'. It achieved nothing to blub about it. And that had been absolutely fine until her housemistress had wanted to see her about her bad marks and, instead of the rocket she was expecting, Anna had been asked gently how she was coping with it all. She had not even finished saying 'absolutely fine' before the tears had come. Now here she was blubbing again. Thank God Bren wasn't here to despise her for it.

At the sudden scrape of the chair she looked up. DCI Poole had stood up and was towering over her. He was very tall, strong-looking too. The lady policeman was leaning back in her chair, waiting. Now Anna understood. The man was reaching down into his pocket, probably for a truncheon. The floppy, unravelled part of Anna that made her cry tightened again into a hard, undetonated little land-mine of attitude. Shit. That warped bitch probably got a kick out of watching people get beaten up. This was what Bren had warned her about. Now she was going to get it. She jumped to her feet and shrieked through her sobs.

'I'm a minor! I have rights! You lay a finger on me and you'll see!' She was interrupted by a burst of astonished laughter from DCI Poole who, having finished searching in his pockets, had sat down again and was presenting her with a folded white handkerchief.

'Lucky I had a clean one,' he said, less to Anna than to WDC Frayling. 'Here.'

Anna sat down and took it, whispering thanks and burying her face. After several moments during which nobody spoke, she emerged from the folds of the hanky looking calmer, as if she'd had her nose plunged in a huge white flower. Then she found a clean bit of hanky, rubbed at her glasses, put them back on and looked up, sniffing, at DCI Poole. He had brown eyes, too. And something else about them, not just the colour, suddenly reminded her of Dad. Her face disappeared into the hanky again. How was Dad?

'Whether they're the issue or not, I want to hear again about the fur coat in the Oxfam shop. You went in there on Tuesday the twenty-fifth of August, at approximately ten fifteen, is that right? What happened?'

Anna swallowed. 'We were just walking past. I just had a peer in on the way past and Bren went on. Then I saw the coat and called out to him.'

Funny, Anna thought, how you can make it sound so uncomplicated, almost normal. It didn't matter to anyone but her that they had been walking along in silence because that morning Bren had been not speaking to her. Or that the night before, after he had rolled off her, she had lain awake, pleased that they had made love, even though it had happened in silence except for his quiet grunting into the pillow behind her shoulder. And that in the morning, when Bren was as aggressively silent as before, she realised she had been wrong to hope that the lovemaking signalled the end of this particular bout of 'not speaking'.

'Why won't you speak to me? What about last night?'

'What about it? You wanted it.'

It had shocked her into silence to hear him describe making love as 'wanting it'. It was about love. When they had first met at Glastonbury it had been falling in *love*. Why else would she have left home and spent all summer in one grotty room in Bath with him? He had been in love with her too, so much so that he had not even wanted her to ring home, although she had once or twice, telephoning when Dad was at work and leaving messages to say she was all right. It struck her for the first time that Dad deserved better than that, and then she knew it was pointless to try to stop them coming. She took off her glasses again and tears of the hot, unstoppable kind coursed down her face, while she sat there, shaking softly and making hardly any sound at all.

'So. The fur coat, Miss Page,' DCI Poole said slowly. 'Let's hear a bit more about the fur coat. Tell me about that, if you would.'

Instead of saying that she called out to Bren about the coat because she was desperate for his attention, she said, 'I

called out to him to come and see if it was real. We couldn't
believe it. We both feel really strongly about animal rights. I
mean, it's totally disgusting, killing innocent animals for their
fur.' Those had been almost her exact words to Bren, and she
remembered the flicker in his eyes as he had looked at her, as
if he hadn't been seeing her properly for some time. 'So what
you doing about it, then?' he had asked quietly. 'Just talking
about it, or what?' If there was sarcasm in the challenge, she
could not afford to acknowledge it.

'So we just had to do something. Make a protest,' she
told DCI Poole, 'on principle.' He nodded to her to go on.
'We went in and I grabbed the coat and went up to the
woman and told her it was just totally unacceptable. Only she
was completely useless.' For Anna's purposes the small, mild
Alice Silber had been useless, nodding courteously, showing
a willingness to hear what she had to say and putting up no
fight at all. And all the time Bren was behind her, watching
and waiting to see if she was going to go all polite on the
old bag and wimp out of the whole deal. That was when
the other one had come in, thank God, and given Anna the
chance to excel herself.

'Then the other woman came up and she was really
horrible. She started shouting at us. She insulted us. So we
shouted back. Okay, so I lost it. But she had no right to go
on at us like that.'

No, no right at all, but Anna kept to herself the fact
that she had been very pleased that she had. For the first
time in months, standing in that shop, everything she had
wanted to say had come straight out of her mouth with
beautiful, frightening clarity, not blunted into impotent tears
by soft-edged housemistresses or silenced into dumb worry
by Bren's fickleness. Accusations and insults had spilled from
her like the projectile vomiting of needles, purging her of a
stomachful of spikes.

'I want you to tell us again exactly what was said. As you
were leaving. Can you do that?'

Anna sniffed wretchedly. Just because the woman had been

killed a week later was no reason for her to be ashamed of what she had said.

'Miss Page?'

Anna took a deep breath. 'Well, she goes to us, all posh and really loud, "I insist that you leave these premises immediately. Get out now, before I call the police." She was horrible.'

Anna looked uncertainly at WPC Frayling. Then she almost whispered, 'And I went, "Drop dead, you stupid mad cow."' There was a pause before she added, almost inaudibly, 'And Bren goes, "I'll get you for this, you stupid . . . fucking cunt."'

To break the silence that followed, Anna snorted loudly into the handkerchief. Suddenly, what she and Bren had said did not sound like an understandable response to intolerable provocation, but ugly threats to a flustered old lady. 'I didn't mean it, neither did Bren.'

'And yet she did drop dead, didn't she? And presumably you do mean it when you say that animal exploitation is – how did you put it – worth fighting for? Is that what Bren thinks? Is that what he's off doing now – fighting the cause?'

'I don't know where he is,' Anna said. 'Honestly. I haven't seen him since before the weekend. Most of his stuff's gone, and the dog.'

'I see. And you really have no idea where he is,' DCI Poole said smoothly. 'He left no word, no message. And there are no friends, family, contacts that you know of. You're saying he just disappeared, on the Friday before the bank holiday weekend.'

Anna nodded self-pityingly as the full extent of her abandonment was set out for her perusal. 'And he hasn't left anything for the rent,' she whimpered, and started to cry again. She didn't give a fuck about fur coats any more. She wailed into the sodden handkerchief.

'I want my dad,' she spluttered damply. 'Please get my dad. I want to go home. My name's not Page. It's Ward-Pargiter. I didn't give you my real name. Please get my dad.'

There was a short silence before DCI Poole asked in his calm voice, 'As in, Judge Ward-Pargiter of the Western Circuit, would that be, Anna?'

Chapter Five

It wasn't plum anyway, it was more like raw liver. So standing there in it, in front of the mirror which certainly had some distorting kink in the top half and was making her breasts swell up and seem much bigger than they actually were, Poppy decided that the colour was ghastly. She wasn't going to take it because the colour was ghastly and she told the listless, lurking assistant so, shielding herself from having to admit that it didn't fit, and the assistant from having to point out that she had just tried it on in the largest size.

Back out on the street Poppy looked about, hating Bath and everyone in it. Did these women of about her age, cheerfully passing her by in their little nipped-in business suits, not realise that it was only mere historical chance that their poached egg bosoms and countable ribs were considered desirable, and not the rumpled landscape of her white thighs, with their suggestion of wadding just below the surface? Her brain began to bang like a fist on a table top. It was so unfair, she thought aggressively, how women are expected to have dynamic careers and dazzling sex lives and, by doing it on a couple of carrots and a mug of Bovril, have tiny little bodies as well, and the unfairest part was that so many of them seemed to manage it. She belonged to another age, one in which women did not aspire to look like egg-timers in Lycra. In the end, of course, body size simply did not matter. It was what was inside that mattered.

It didn't matter in the true sense, because Cosmo loved her for herself.

Poppy walked briskly past Gap and into Waterstone's, whose mild-eyed assistants would not care what she looked like and where books would never be unavailable in her size. Just the name – water stones – suggesting some timeless and restful lapping, appealed to her. Cool, black-shelved Waterstone's, where she knew herself to be not obese but Rubenesque and where, browsing among the art books, it seemed not unrealistic to think that the tea-gown could make a comeback, and in whose dark panelled tearoom you could read the papers, sipping tea and dropping bits of cake in your mouth and where Cosmo, who loved her for herself, would be waiting.

He came out from behind his newspaper when she arrived. 'Would you get me some more tea? This pot's empty.' Poppy deposited her cardigan on the back of her chair and joined the queue at the serving point. Looking back to their table she saw that Cosmo had disappeared behind the paper again. Sighing, she asked for tea and two iced ginger squares, anticipating that if she bought herself just one, Cosmo would end up taking half of it.

By the time she was halfway down her cup of tea Cosmo had almost finished his cake and had still not asked her if she'd found something to wear. So she launched into another subject, one of Cosmo's own and consequently of more interest.

'Tonight's the night, then.'

Cosmo nodded.

She went on. 'First rehearsal of Helene's little opera group after their summer break. You excited about meeting them? A bit nervous?'

Cosmo blew out his cheeks expansively, considering. 'God, no, I'm not nervous of this lot. The Circus Opera Group, I regret to inform you, won't have the first idea. Most of them won't even be able to read music. So I'm not really expecting them to begin to understand what *I'm* all about.'

'Well, no. Your music's not something you just fall into straight away, is it? It demands something of the listener. In a positive sense. But you'll be able to make them understand, I know you will. Just like you've made me understand.' Cosmo was staring somewhere into the distance and did not acknowledge her trusting smile.

'I'm not even attempting to give them anything to sing tonight. It'll just be an introductory chat – a getting-to-know-me thing. They might as well know who they're dealing with. And I need to assess how much they'll be up to. Not that I'm pandering to them, mind.'

'Oh, no. Of course not. I mean, Helene wouldn't want you to. She wants you to stretch them. Helene's on our side.'

Cosmo snorted, a little too productively. Wiping his nose on a shredded paper napkin he said, 'Oh, Helene. Helene's rather pathetic. Either pathetic or nuts.'

'That's not very kind,' Poppy said graciously, warming herself in the superior, contrasting glow of presumably being considered sane. 'When we're staying with her for nothing. When she gave you the commission. And after all she's had us for over two weeks already, so's you could get the feel of Bath and do some research before the group starts up again. We'd still be in horrid old London if she hadn't asked you to write her little opera. It's a start.'

Cosmo scowled at his plate. 'Okay, it's a start. But it's hardly Composer of the Year, is it? What's the point? I feel like giving up. There's no point, is there, if my work doesn't merit more recognition than *this* . . .'

'Than what?' Poppy asked hotly. 'What? What do you mean? "This" means being here, being together. You with a proper commission. What's wrong with "this"?'

Cosmo's voice tightened. 'Oh, come on, you know. A provincial little commission for practically no money. Having to take payment in kind, like rent-free accommodation, and ending up as the lodgers. With a third-rate has-been soprano who's nuts, and a daughter who's seriously nuts. And a *community* opera.'

Poppy watched him as he chewed sulkily on the last of his iced ginger square. 'Adele's not seriously nuts, she's autistic,' she said. 'Helene's had a very tough time with Adele. She could be very bright.'

Cosmo swallowed and said nothing. He regretted mentioning Adele. When he thought about her or her mother calmly, as he sometimes did at quiet moments, he usually found himself overwhelmed by the wish to be somewhere else.

'She *could* be, underneath it all.' Poppy sighed and changed tack. 'I really think it's going to be good for you, to be out of the fray for a while. Bath's calmer than London, better to work in.' Superstitiously, she hoped that by repeating this often enough it would become true. Cosmo's lack of productivity was becoming a worry, now that the opera project was the only thing on his immediate horizon. 'You'll get going again soon, I know you will.'

Cosmo's unchanging face told her she was not getting through and that he wished the subject changed. If she didn't break through soon, the shutters of a sulky depression would come rattling down on Cosmo's already weak motivation and would not be lifted for days. Ever since his return from Prague she had had to cope with these abrupt changes in his emotional weather, like the sudden clouding over of an anyway uncertain sky. The grey would be solid and slow to lift; he might not even try to work, and she could not risk that. She pressed her lips together. If only she could let him see what lengths she was going to in order to help him, he might set greater store by her efforts and reward her with a bit of effort in return. But she must not look for a return, not yet.

'Cosmo,' she said, leaning across the table. 'Cosmo Lamb, listen to me. This is a start. You are a professional composer. You're ambitious, and that's good. The next thing you do will be bigger. The next after that, bigger still. The South Bank maybe. The European Composers Series *next* year. Or something different – a musical. Theme music. It's how reputations are made. You've got it, Cosmo, I really believe that. You've got it. You'll get there. And you've got me. I'll support you.'

Cosmo looked at her with a doleful, doubting face, which

she mistook for concern. The thought that he might appreciate all that she had done for him suddenly made it all right. She beamed. 'You're not to worry about me. I don't care about the course, and the work on *The Magic Flute* would have finished soon anyway. I like working in the nursing home now. I'm getting to do almost proper nursing. They said one or two might even benefit from foot massages, maybe even acupuncture, so it's not as if I've had to completely give up on all my healing stuff. I don't care about not finishing the course. So you're not to worry. I'll support you right to the hilt, you know that, don't you? You've still got me.'

Cosmo nodded, and exhaled a deep, deep sigh. He seemed about to speak, but then hesitated. Poppy smiled expectantly. He was so reticent about expressing love, even gratitude, but clearly her sacrifice was making him feel guilty. Behind that sleepy, little-boy look, guilt was written all over his face. He was so insecure.

'Cosmo, I love you to little bits, you know,' she whispered encouragingly. She waited. After all this time, after all she did for him, he must love her by now. He had to say it back. Surely he was going to say it now?

'Hmm? What is it? Tell me. What, Cosmo?'

'Are you finishing that?' he asked, nodding at the half-eaten cake on her plate. 'Because if not . . .'

Chapter Six

She was wearing dark glasses, which struck Andrew as slightly ridiculous for around nine o'clock on a dull September evening in England. All day he had been picturing her tired but triumphant, coming towards him in slow motion out of some imaginary composite world of international airports, foreign cities and famous concert halls, in his mind all rolled into one vast, steel and plate-glass dream landscape. He had overlooked the fact that she was travelling from New York to Dublin and then on by the Cityhopper to Bristol Airport, which had all the chipped paintwork, buckled seating, vending machines and missing light bulbs of a popular casualty department, and about as much glamour. So he acknowledged that it was his own fault if the backdrop was a little disappointing. And although she was still the most beautiful woman in the building as well as the only one wearing lean, black trousers and a white T-shirt under a black leather jacket, the only competition was an assortment of stained business travellers, a few low-season tourists and a bewildered old lady from Dunshaughlin who did not know how to claim her luggage and was worried in case her daughter was not there to meet her. And Sara was obviously looking after her, taking charge and steering her towards the Information Desk and explaining her predicament at length to the ground staff, instead of looking vulnerably gorgeous and breaking into a slow-motion run before being swept up into the safety of his arms. He felt a bit daft.

In the car things seemed for a moment to get better. Sara, taking off her glasses and shaking her dark hair out from under a large silver clip said, 'Sorry about these. I saw a doctor in New York, he said lighting in airports was a major headache trigger. My blood pressure's up a bit. Probably just stress, he said acupuncture might help. I just need to get home. I feel fine *now*.' And then she turned on him a long, smiling gaze from her big blue-green eyes, so full of sleepy, relieved pleasure to be here with him instead of anywhere else in the world that he had been unable to look away, and nearly drove into the back of the car ahead.

'Watch!'

Andrew braked hard and dropped back.

'Christ, sorry. It'd be a shame if you got this close to home and copped it in the last twenty miles,' he said. 'Don't worry, I'll get you back in one piece.'

'I know you will.' Sara smiled. 'I just couldn't face going in on my own, without someone with me.'

Andrew stared straight ahead, trying to concentrate on the road. Someone? Anyone? Did that mean, not necessarily him? Just *someone*? He wanted to say that he was not 'someone', and that he was desperately, wildly excited to see her. What he did say, sulkily, was, 'You must be tired now, I suppose.'

'I think I'm perking up a bit, actually. How's Valerie?'

'Oh, she's, you know, she's—'

'Oh, look, there's a garage. Can we stop and get some milk?' she interrupted, making Andrew annoyed with himself for not already having thought of getting some for her.

When they reached Medlar Cottage Sara was chirpy and annoyingly independent. She darted about competently, switching on lights, drawing curtains, opening doors, dispelling the smell of cold dust in the still air of rooms. There was a lot of junk mail but no squatters, not a broken window pane nor a burst pipe, not even a dead bird in the fireplace. The pilot light had not gone out and the hot water came on, with a heart-warming WHUP, first time.

She sighed happily. 'I feel a bit of a fool for calling you

like that. I'm fine now. Of course I could have done this on my own, I shouldn't have bothered you. I've taken up your whole evening now.'

Andrew said no problem, and it wasn't, except that he was beginning to think that his being here was turning out to have been not worth lying to Valerie about. He began to wonder why he had lied, exactly. He would have claimed, even a few hours ago, that while it was not adulterous just to collect Sara from the airport, Valerie would jump to the wrong conclusion, and his lie about working late was just to keep her suspicions at bay. But it was more likely that he had been deceiving even himself and the truth was that if the chance to be unfaithful were to offer itself, he had every intention of taking it. Why else would he now be feeling so cheated?

He brought in logs and lit the fire. While Sara was wandering about outside trying to assess the state of the garden in the dark, he fetched the bottle of champagne which he had brought from the back of the car. When she came back in, clutching thick branches of rosemary from one of the huge bushes by the cottage gate, he had already found glasses.

'Welcome home,' he said shyly.

'Oh, Andrew,' she said, ducking from the pop and then the arc of the cork across the room.

'I'm so glad you're back,' he said, looking up from pouring.

She was still holding the rosemary. 'I must just get these in water.'

'Sara—'

'Back in a minute.'

When she came back she nestled into a corner of the sofa with her legs tucked up beneath her and asked, 'So, how's work? What was that about James's neighbour that you wouldn't tell me? Did you get him at the London number?'

Andrew did not want to discuss work, but nor did he want to appear provincial and boring as if, while she was jetting around the world playing in major concert halls, nothing had been happening to him. 'Oh, we handled a terrorist alert yesterday,' he said coolly. 'Fairly unpleasant. Someone sent a letter-bomb to the old lady who lived in the garden flat at 11 Camden Crescent. She died in hospital.'

Sara gasped. 'That's awful. *Awful.* You don't mean the bitch in the basement? That's what they call her. She's a monster. Terrible woman, apparently. They can't stand her.' She hesitated. 'Or couldn't, rather. Oh, but for someone to kill her, that's . . .' she added, shaking her head, unable to finish. She gulped from her glass and swallowed as if the champagne were a lump in her mouth.

'We're beginning to gather that,' Andrew said. 'Her other neighbours are polite about her, just. She was clearly a professional complainer. James's London number didn't help, actually. Answering machine's on. We've left messages there and in Brussels.'

'I'm pretty sure he's in Brussels,' Sara said absently. 'He's judging something. New works for piano. Tell me more about this old lady, though. D'you know who did it yet?'

'Got a pretty good idea.'

'Go on. Tell me more.'

Andrew shook his head. 'It's fairly cut and dried. The woman was threatened in public a few days before she died. A row with a couple of animal righters. One of them's harmless, just a spoiled twerp of a girl. But the other's got a record. Vicious little bastard, actually. We'll get him.'

'Animal righters? I thought they bombed laboratories and mink farms, not old ladies. Are you sure?'

'Sara, thanks, but this is *my* job.'

'And it'd be pretty stupid, killing someone *after* you've threatened them in public.'

Andrew smiled and shook his head at her.

She was smiling back, looking a little ashamed now. 'Sorry, sorry,' she said sheepishly. 'Mustn't start thinking I'm a super-sleuth, must I? Your department.'

'Well, your experience of murderers is a little specialised. It would be stupid to kill someone after you've threatened them, but actually, most murderers are. Makes my life easier. Intelligent murderers are so much harder to catch. Anyway, I am pretty certain about this one. He disappeared from his bedsit some time over the weekend of the bank holiday. He must have put the device together somewhere else, there's no trace of materials or equipment in the room. And he probably left town as soon as he'd delivered it. There's nothing mysterious about it.'

'But you said the other neighbours were barely polite about her. Maybe someone else did it, for some other reason.'

Andrew, intent on restoring an atmosphere of home-coming, was not going into the detail of the police search for Brendan Twigg or anything else. 'Sara. Sara, you're the cellist. I'm the detective, remember?'

Sara sighed, nodding. 'Sorry, Detective Chief Inspector. It's lovely to be back,' she said.

Andrew rose and topped up her glass, unnecessarily, and returned reluctantly to his chair. He tried to tease from her an indirect admission that she had missed him. 'So, what did you miss most, away on your own all that time?'

She thought. What she had missed was him, desperately, but she had driven out the longing by trying to picture him thoughtless of her and re-ensconced with Valerie. She had schooled herself painfully into the belief that he was not hers to miss, and so was not now going to let him know it.

'*The Archers*,' she said.

She would not settle, not even in front of the fire with her glass of champagne; the fire that he had lit for her and the champagne that he had brought to welcome her home and (he had to admit the possibility) also to engineer a mellow, sensual setting for what he had wanted for so long. Now she was not even drinking, just dipping one finger in the glass and sucking it almost unwillingly. He thought of proposing some toast, to 'Homecoming' or even 'Us' but it sounded so stupid. He was suddenly unsure of his ground. Perhaps in her absence he had been transforming their relationship in his mind until it was inevitable that the real thing should jar like this and he would feel as wrong-footed and disappointed as he did. And perhaps the reason for her corresponding slight awkwardness with him was that she had not thought of him once in all the time she was away.

She sighed. 'This is lovely, Andrew.'

'My pleasure.'

'It's really special.'

She drank thoughtfully from her glass. Her voice was very soft.

'Andrew? It's really lovely, but there's something I'd like instead. Something I've been looking forward to.'

She put down her glass on the floor. He rose at once from his chair and came to sit next to her on the sofa. She turned, uncurled her legs from under her and faced him cross-legged, serious-eyed, leaning towards him. He took her hands and kissed her on the lips, much more gently than he really wanted to.

'Andrew?'

'Sara, I've missed you so much.'

'No, but Andrew, the thing is . . .'

'What is it? You missed me, didn't you?'

'Andrew, I just meant, don't be hurt, but it's been such a long time . . .'

'What, darling? You're tired, I know, I know. We can wait.'

'No, no, no, I didn't mean that. Andrew . . .'

'Oh, Sara, let's not then. I want you so much.'

This time she returned the kiss, at length. His hands moved on to her thighs.

'Andrew, no. I mean, I wanted to ask . . .'

'What?'

'Don't be hurt. The thing is, there was lots of champagne on the plane. What I'd really like is a proper cup of tea.'

After Andrew had gone, Sara, guided by the light which beamed out across the grass from the back of the house, climbed the path to the hut at the top of the garden. She unbolted and opened the double doors. The dry spidery smells of old Julys which had been trapped inside spilled out upon the night. She found matches, lit one of the storm lanterns hanging in the roof and dusted off the old chaise-longue before sitting down. She stared out from the hut into darkness over and beyond the roof of the house below, a darkness unleavened by moonlight, and thought she could remember, without seeing them, the precise places of the six lime trees in the meadow across the valley. Tomorrow she would look out and see that their leaves, although still green, were sharper and crisp-looking, already curling back to show the undersides of branches. Before the green turned to yellow, most of the leaves would fall. She was wide awake now. But it was too chilly to stay out and too hazardous to start thinking about Andrew, Herve, the poor dead woman from Camden Crescent and her own feelings in relation to them all. She blew out the lantern, closed the hut and came back down the path to the house. She got ready for bed, glad to be back in her own room. Sinking under the duvet in the dark she thought it ironic that although she had now reached an age when she appreciated sleeping in her own bed, the combination of her mind behaving as if she were about sixteen and her body behaving as if it were noon would probably keep her awake most of the night.

Chapter Seven

Valerie scraped the remains of the children's mini kievs into the bin, holding the plates well away from her. She was dressed for the rehearsal, and a splodge of garlic butter on her jumper was not the effect she was looking for. She wouldn't be having to do this at all if Andrew were here as he was meant to be, but she squashed her resentment, knowing that it sat ill within the new tolerant scheme of things. Instead, she tried to feel sorry for him, for having to work on with the Bevan enquiry instead of coming with her to the rehearsal. When he had telephoned he had sounded already weary of the case, and she had believed him when he had said that the day had not gone well, although they both knew that he would never tell her otherwise by telephone and that she had just been taking a polite interest. So she loaded the dishwasher while Nicola the baby-sitter stood and watched and failed to say, *Oh, leave those, Mrs Poole, I'll see to them. Off you go, don't spoil your lovely cashmere jumper.*

It was actually only lambswool but she had brushed it up to make it look a little like cashmere and she had bought it in a larger size which she thought made it look better made and more expensive. The dark colour was good with Valerie's looks which were of that English kind which seldom ages well: nice hair which she now had to think of as dark blonde, and a pale, creamy complexion which, although still nearer to single than clotted, was yearly growing coarser. She was confident that the navy jumper with her big fake pearl earrings gave her the Hermès look, only without her having to buy the scarf, which would cost roughly the amount that she might spend on a winter coat. And the checked wool trousers and loafers added to the effect, because M&S were so good, these days, at doing things that didn't look M&S.

As she drove round looking for a parking space close to Helene's flat in the Circus, she wondered what Helene would be wearing. At the dozen or so rehearsals before the group had broken up for August Valerie had still not seen anything twice, although Helene's outfits all shared certain characteristics, like members of the same florid and slightly eccentric family. She went in for a lot of expensive knits, done in theatrical shiny yarns with bobbles and often with beads or ribbony bits, in colours like 'taupe' and 'avocado'; sludge brown and slime green if you were feeling ungenerous. They were invariably two-piece ensembles: a skirt made of knitted flared panels and the matching, much-embellished top which would drape floppily over Helene's boned underpinnings. Her shoes were high, usually decorated with gold buckles or monograms, and were too tight, so that the fronts of her feet swelled up like two pads of unbaked dough. She wore her dark hair loose and down to her shoulders in what she probably imagined were careless, tumbling locks, and although her jewellery was plentiful, large and inclined to chink it was real, and added to the impression that Helene was really a prosperous, protein-filled gypsy rather than a retired opera singer. Valerie considered that Helene was doing well for fifty-five but not as well as she herself would when it came to it in fifteen years' time, if she carried on doing the Rosemary Conlon video and stuck to her Nimble.

She parked in Queen Square and walked up Gay Street to the Circus, preparing the excuses she would have to give for Andrew and composing, partly for herself but mainly for the benefit of the other members of the Circus Music Group – Helene, Jim and Phil (Adele hardly counted in that sort of way) – the right facial expression for the patient, understanding chief inspector's wife that she aspired to be.

'No Andrew?' Helene was swift to conceal the splinter of annoyance in her voice. 'Oh dear, he is busy, poor man! Is it the woman in Camden Crescent? I saw it in tonight's paper and just shuddered. Poor woman. But you're here, Valerie dear!'

Helene, splendid in lace-knitted teal flecked with bronze and with toning eyeliner, pulled her across the threshold. 'Everyone's here. Come on in.'

Valerie made her way along the hall towards the drawing room door with Helene following and talking rapidly to her back. 'What a dear little jersey. You are lucky, you look so nice in simple things. I always look so dull in ordinary jumpers, but I expect that's just years of being on the stage. One always thinks costume when one should be thinking nice sensible clothes for the colder weather! If only I could wear classics! Go straight in! There's a surprise waiting!'

Damn her, Valerie thought, she didn't even give me a chance to say it was cashmere. From the doorway she took in at once that there were extra people here. Not Adele, who would probably be down in the basement kitchen preparing coffee. Jim was sitting in his usual place in the small armchair by the gas fire; Phil also was perched in his corner of the deep sofa. But beside Phil sat a new couple who were looking up expectantly. The woman jumped to her feet and advanced. The man rose sluggishly and stood behind her.

'Meet the surprise: our wonderful composer, Cosmo Lamb! This is Cosmo and this is his lovely Poppy,' Helene gushed. 'Poppy Thwaites. Cosmo is our composer-in-*residence*, I could say. They're staying here for the duration, they're almost family! This is our dear Valerie.'

She beamed round the room. 'Oh, this is a moment! Isn't it? Everyone? For the group? All of us, giving our talents, sharing the language of music. Joining together, giving whatever we can, whoever we are, that's what I love about it!'

Valerie tried to smile but her lips pursed instead into a pink little cat's bottom of disapproval. Helene was being at her most – *unreal* was the most generous way Valerie could think of it. In the face of exuberance like this something in Valerie invariably shrivelled up and refused to play along. She simply could not believe in it. A woman of Helene's age should not be saying these things. Helene knew as well as Valerie did that you do not go through motherhood, in Helene's case with its own very particular difficulties, and come out of it going tra-lah about anything much, not sanely or sincerely, anyway. Now the particular difficulty in person, Adele herself, was edging past with a loaded tray and shuffling over to the grand piano on the far side of the room. Valerie watched her serious face and the slightly tilted head as she stooped to deposit the tray on its closed lid.

Helene suddenly broke off from her eulogy and shrieked in a high-pitched sing-song, 'No, dear, not *there*! Wait, dear, the cloth's not down! Oh, goodness gracious, help! Someone? Cloth someone, cloth please!'

Quick-footed Phil darted at once to the piano stool where the folded cloth lay, whipped it out across the piano lid, took the tray from Adele and placed it down carefully, smiling at her uncomprehending face.

'No problem, see?' he said, smiling gently.

'It goes there,' Adele said, looking back at him seriously and talking at rather than to him. 'Tray goes there. That's where I put it.'

'But Mama puts down the cloth first, darling,' Helene said. 'Cloth then tray, only Mama forgot this once. Cloth then tray. Try to remember.'

Adele turned away and with her head tilted busied herself with pouring coffee, saying to no one in particular, 'No problem see tray goes there. No problem see tray goes there.'

Helene smiled wanly round and her eyes settled on Poppy, who returned the look.

'That's autism for you,' Helene said to the room. 'Her routines, you see. Poppy and Cosmo are quite used to it now, aren't you? And she's much better than she was. It's a matter of the right kind of environment for her. She must be in a caring group.' To Poppy and Cosmo she continued, 'As you know I really started the music group for her. I mean, of course it's for everyone, but with her in mind. As I've explained, she needs the right group. But you wait till you hear her sing. She has my voice.'

'Oh, how wonderful,' breathed Poppy, nodding. 'Wonderful of you. Isn't it, Cosmo? That gift. You must feel so *blessed*, I mean, despite the er . . . handicap. I mean not that it's, er . . . but the voice, *gosh*.'

While Phil took round the coffee, Adele sidled up silently with the biscuits. Arranged perfectly on an enormous plate were three circles, each made up of two different biscuits in an alternating and overlapping pattern. The outer one was of garibaldis and chocolate digestives, the next Jaffa cakes and lemon puffs, and the smallest, inner circle was fig rolls and jammy dodgers.

'Six kinds, three circles, two kinds each circle, one round, one square. Twenty-six. You can have a biscuit,' Adele intoned to Poppy. 'You can have a biscuit. You're allowed a biscuit.'

Poppy simperingly took a digestive and said, 'Oooh, scrummy. Thank you, Adele.'

'Adele doesn't mind you breaking the pattern.' Jim had risen and joined them. 'She used to mind a lot if any of her nice arrangements were upset, but she doesn't mind so much now. Do you, Adele?'

Adele looked up at Jim and offered him the plate. 'You want one. You're allowed a biscuit. Twenty-five now,' she said solemnly.

'Thank you, Adele,' Jim said, and took a garibaldi next to the space left by Poppy's digestive. Then he gently shoved the other biscuits in the circle round a little way, so that symmetry was restored. Then he gave Adele's shoulder a kind little squeeze. 'Well done,' he said.

Adele turned away with the plate and with the same tilt of the head made her way over to Phil, who appeared to be waiting for his biscuit.

Helene suddenly clapped her hands and waved everyone back into chairs.

'To the task in hand, everyone!' she called.

Valerie made her way quietly round the edge of the group, fetched her coffee from the tray and sat down on the piano stool to watch Helene resume her grip on the gathering. She judged that Helene, in broaching the question of Adele with Cosmo and Poppy, would have recited the same script as she had when Valerie, a new member, had come to her flat one afternoon for an 'informal little chat' about the group. The once-great Helene Giraldi had sat her down and confided her private tribulations to her, mere Valerie Poole. She had been flattered. Helene's only child was severely autistic. Years of useless treatments and regimes had been endured before the correct diagnosis was made, by which time her marriage had collapsed. Helene had done everything a mother could, including giving up her own career to look after the child who could not show affection, who communicated only sporadically and painfully and whose destructive rages, sleeplessness, irrational terrors and obsession with routines had ruled the household. Helene's handkerchief had come out at this point and her eyes had been dabbed, without disturbing her maquillage, in the unreal way that Valerie now recognised so well. And yet, and this almost made it worse, Helene had gone on, Adele had at quiet moments the power of total, absorbed concentration and displayed the most extraordinary gifts: an agile, pure, radiant soprano voice (she was her mother's daughter in that respect) coupled with a bizarre memory for music. She could also draw beautiful, stylised patterns of unerring symmetry, disdaining as subjects anything as imperfect and untidy as people, animals or landscape. My little changeling child, Helene had said, twisting her handkerchief.

Valerie had also heard that Adele, now aged twenty-five, no longer tore wallpaper or screamed daily, although her obsessive need for order and symmetry could still sometimes get the better of her and bring on a tantrum. She still made odd collections of useless things from which, for as long as the obsession lasted, she would not be parted. She could speak, but not well, and was most often silent. She had learned many tasks but could carry them out only by rote, remaining unable to vary her actions to take account of varying circumstances.

Valerie looked over now at Adele standing next to Phil who was quietly talking to her. It wasn't true what people said about Chinese people looking inscrutable. Phil was from Hong Kong but he had such a kind face. It was unusually patient, she thought, watching him speak, for someone as young as he was, no more than about twenty. Adele was looking somewhere past his shoulders, her face conveying nothing unless, perhaps, there was a sadness there behind the indisputably lovely blue eyes. With a slight movement she tilted her head to its usual angle and the light caught the gleam of the straight fair hair that poured down her slim back. She was beautiful, and Valerie was not sure that that did not make Adele's narrow life seem even sadder. She would never have a professional singing career – or any other career, come to that – because although the voice was a glorious, superior instrument, and she would know lines of music off by heart after one hearing, she would always sing like a mechanical doll. Whatever the song was about, it would be delivered in the same perfect tone, the words having no more significance than as vessels to carry the thrilling, singing liquidity of the gorgeous but meaningless notes.

Helene was back in charge. 'I am so excited, everyone, that I can introduce to you this evening our real live composer! I heard from this young man less than three weeks ago and I told him right there and then on the telephone that we'd love him to come and do our opera with us. So he came straight down from London with Poppy. He's got the most marvellous credentials but I won't embarrass him by telling you all about him – he can do that himself!'

Cosmo looked furtively round the group, blushing un-attractively.

'And the super thing is that we're to have Poppy, too. Poppy is to be our stage manager and will also oversee all the costumes and props, won't you, Poppy? Poppy's got a proper theatre background, haven't you, dear? Although she's been working in aromatherapy and massage more recently. And I know this will embarrass them but I'm going to tell you – that we're getting both Cosmo and Poppy but they're only accepting Cosmo's fee, which I think is just *so* marvellous of them and what it's all about, sharing and making music and not about money.'

Valerie, glancing over, caught Jim's eye and exchanged a look with him which said: *Helene's keeping the expenses down.* Valerie was grateful for Jim, whom she thought of as a sensible, organised kind of man, probably in his early sixties. He was a little too ex-navy to be exactly Valerie's type and rather starstruck with Helene which Valerie found unflattering to herself, but he brought a measure of bearded, modulated calm to the group which, under Helene's sole direction, was inclined to flutter.

'And for the duration of the project they're staying here with me. They've been getting to know our lovely city and Cosmo's been doing all his research. And Poppy's managed to get a little job as well. And the house is just so alive again! Which is so lovely, I do so love being surrounded by all their *creativity*.'

In another silent exchange Valerie and Jim agreed that, even for Helene, this was going a little far.

Poppy was now leaning forward with her round bottom firmly embedded in the back of the sofa cushions. She stretched up, straightening her arms and planting her hands on her knees, and looked round. Valerie noted how much Poppy would benefit from a thorough waxing, starting with the upper lip.

In a deep, unsmiling voice she said, 'We're totally committed to this project, Cosmo and I. We think it's just tremendously exciting as a project, and we've got tons of ideas. And of course we want to get tons of input from you too. After all, it's a community opera. And I've got lots of ideas about how we can really get the *whole* community involved. So, if I can kick off with a few logistics, I'm making myself available to the project on a daily basis, but please try to avoid Tuesday and Thursday mornings unless it's an emergency. You can access me at any other time, whatever, okay?'

She stared round in the silence that followed. What kind of emergency should we be expecting in a community opera? Valerie was wondering.

'I mean, please don't think I'm getting all kind of bureaucratic about it, but I'm actually working two nights a week on Mondays and Wednesdays and it's quite demanding and it might get kind of manic if I don't just set some boundaries now and I hope everyone understands, okay?'

'What do you do, Poppy?' Valerie asked pleasantly. 'Helene said you were in the theatre. Are you working at the Theatre Royal? Stage managing or something?'

Poppy closed her eyes and raised her thick eyebrows. Then she opened her eyes and looked languidly at Valerie, shaking her head from side to side slowly.

'No, actually. I was doing a bit in London, prop-making and stuff, just filling in while I was doing my course. But there's no real work in theatre these days, that's why I was doing this course. I mean, I'm practically a fully qualified acupuncturist and homeopath. Now we're in Bath I'm doing two nights a week in a care home for the elderly. The Circus Nursing Home, just along from here.'

'Right,' said Valerie, knowing she had just heard a prepared speech and thinking, Aha, so she can't get a theatre job, and they must need the money. She looked over at Jim who was stroking his beard, but his raised eyebrows told her that he hadn't clocked that one.

Cosmo was standing up now. The earlier unsightly blush that had spread over his face had settled back into an uncomfortable mottle over his cheeks. The rest of his skin looked too fine and white, and his lips too fat, red and petulant for a man. He was not even successfully boyish, since his long, downy hair was receding fast from his high pink forehead and looked like a thinning, damp, mohair shawl slipping slowly off the back of his head. His bulging eyes, crustily myopic, together with his narrow sloping shoulders, round belly and short legs, gave him the air of a viable but unpromising foetus, rather startled to find itself on its feet and wearing a Next linen-mix jacket and baggy trousers.

'Right, folks. I'm, ah, Cosmo. As you've heard.'

He was looking at the ceiling, resolutely addressing the air.

'I'm, ah, delighted to be here. Helene suggests kindly that you may want to know a little about me. Well, I've been involved in music from, ah, birth, you might say. My father's a musicologist, now retired, and my mother taught maths. I always say I got the best out of both of them, as I'm the only child! Anyway, usual stuff, degree in music, ah, composing since university, various things, choral, ensembles, piano. Some London performances, including Marthe Francis's debut recital at the Wigmore, some youth commissions, based in London, went to Prague earlier this year. And the reason I'm now in Bath is thanks to my teacher and mentor Herve Petrescu' – he paused to allow the name to impress them deeply – 'who was the reason I went to Prague. That's about it.'

He gave an embarrassed, slightly sardonic smile in Poppy's direction. 'It was hard to believe at first that the Circus Opera Group of Bath would approach Herve Petrescu in Prague for suggestions for their community opera maestro, but you did, and so there you are. And here I am.'

He gave a little mock bow to a little mock applause, led by the beaming Helene. Then, with an almost right-angled bend of the wrist, he pressed the back of one hand into the small of his back, took two or three steps away from the group and turned on his heel to face them. He raised his other hand, pressed his fingers and thumb together and, frowning at his fingertips as if they held something small, interesting and wriggling, began.

'My music, you see, depends on a degree of, ah, perceptive prominence so that the least identifiable or neutral processes mainly act on developments related to time, while the, ah, most identifiable, or marked processes are perceived as patterns.'

Poppy gazed at him rapturously and nodded encourage-
ment. Cosmo licked his lips.

'So conceptually, my music, my art, corresponds to crossing a new perceptive threshold, which takes on an almost
thematic, ah, function. Only almost.' He smiled, sensing that
his listeners needed that reassurance. 'But, and this will be
clear to everyone, this implies, I feel necessitates, a degree
of rethinking vis-à-vis the theme, apropos the principle of
textual, and contextual, integration.'

Adele, who had been sitting in the window seat with the
platter of biscuits on her lap, announced flatly with her mouth
full, 'Fourteen.'

Cosmo looked helplessly at Poppy, who addressed the
room earnestly: 'And that's why this process of consultation
is so crucial. So, right, are there any questions for Cosmo or
myself? Or can we take that as all agreed, then?'

Poppy and Cosmo exchanged a look across the silence.
Cosmo folded his arms and for the first time looked almost
relaxed.

'Great. Looks like everyone's happy, then. So, we're
not going down the Jane Austen route, right? And we're
definitely not having the Romans and the, ah, hot springs.
Great.'

'Thirteen,' came a slightly muffled voice from the window seat.

As Andrew came through the door Valerie yelled from the
kitchen, 'Andrew, get in here!'

Christ, how could she know? He entered the kitchen
tentatively.

She was bringing a little casserole out of the oven.

'Just sit down while I tell you. Here, chicken and rice.
You must be starving.' She put the dish on the table, lifted
the lid and plunged a fork into the steam. She began to stir
the contents round with such speed and ferocity that the fork
became a blur. But she was smiling.

'Gnash. Gnash. It's brilliant, isn't it? Come on, eat!' She

clanged the fork against the side of the dish and pushed it over.

Andrew, dumbly suspicious, sat down.

'Beau Nash. *Brilliant* theme. Good title, isn't it, *Nash*? Or maybe just *Beau*? Anyway, much better than anything on Jane Austen or the Romans.'

Andrew chewed and nodded, interrupting Valerie only to thank her for getting him some supper. 'It's very nice. Thank you. Especially since I had to miss the rehearsal. I'm sorry I was kept late.'

'Doesn't matter, eat up. I'll tell you all about it.'

Andrew had never seen Valerie quite like this. He managed not to groan when she told him that she had suggested that Cosmo write in a large solo cello part, and that Poppy had made a note of it.

'You've got to meet him. And Poppy too, of course. He's obviously brilliant, obviously going places,' she said. 'He's been studying with someone, not sure of the name, obviously the best, anyway. Harvey something.'

'Herve. Herve Petrescu,' Andrew said. 'Personally I think he's overrated. But sure, only the best work with the wonderful Herve Petrescu.' He could not share with Valerie the news he had heard from Sara that evening over the bloody cup of tea, about the new commission and Herve's imminent 'residency' in Bath. Nor could he share the moment when Sara had told him, apparently regretfully, that Petrescu would be taking up most of her time. Nor did he say that his first wild hope, that she was regretful because long rehearsals with Herve would prevent her spending most of her time with Andrew, had quickly died, because he had detected in Sara some considerable susceptibility where Herve Petrescu was concerned. And least of all did he mention the stomach-souring jealousy that he now felt at the very mention of his name.

'What does he look like, this Cosmo character?'

'Oh, he's young, younger than me. Than us, that's to say. Late twenties, early thirties. Not conventionally good-looking. Brown hair.'

'And the girlfriend?' Andrew asked, trying to steer his mind away from the thought of Sara and Petrescu together.

'Older than him, quite an organiser. Did stage management originally. She was doing a course on aromatherapy and stuff when they came here, now she's working in a nursing home. But a sweet girl, rather plain. I expect she mothers him, yes, that's what he'd need. A bit of mothering from an older woman . . .'

Andrew scooped up the last of the rice and managed to maintain his rhythm of placid chewing. Was it because, after his evening with Sara, he was better attuned to hear it, or was it his imagination that was making him think that in Valerie's voice he was now picking up just the tiniest edge of the same susceptibility?

Chapter Eight

'Please, James, *please*. I can't have him here. I just *can't*.'

'Sara, darling, isn't it a heaven-sent opportunity, to have him there with you? There's bags of room, isn't there? I can picture you both having a lovely creative time of it, a "period of intensive rehearsal", in your country retreat. And then you get your pinny on and cook a nice little supper and warm his slippers . . . and then after that, I mean after you've done the washing up, well . . .'

Speaking from Brussels, the mockery in James's voice travelled well.

'Don't! Yes, I'm sure *he'd* love it, I know all about his reputation. Yes all right, there are five bedrooms and an acre of grounds, that's not the point. It's so embarrassing. Of course I can't have him staying here. Please can he stay in your flat? Camden Crescent would suit him perfectly. *Puh-lease*, James? I mean, you won't even be there.'

'And he won't mind having an address that's a well-known scene of a recent serious crime? Possibly popular with terrorists? Probably on the open-top tour bus route by now? Yes, we've heard. Andrew Poole rang yesterday.'

'Oh, James, look, you shouldn't be flippant. That poor woman's dead. Anyway, Andrew knows who did it. *Thinks* he knows. What? Oh, because she had a row with someone in a shop. It could have been you or me.'

She could hear James giving a slightly guilty murmur

at the other end. Or was Tom giving him a shoulder rub?

'Look, the point is I can't have Herve at Medlar Cottage.'

'You've slept with him, haven't you?'

'No! No, I *haven't*! And you've got a nerve! I have *not* slept with him. And so what if I had, anyway?'

There was a muffled laugh, followed by a sigh.

'James, tell Tom to stop that at once. James? James, you are the limit. Stop laughing at me. Why are you so chirpy, anyway? I thought you were supposed to be exhausted and stressed-out with that new works for piano thing you're doing.'

'Oh, I am, I am,' James giggled. 'I can't think why I was asked to do it, after the things I've written recently about contemporary music, but there you are. Never again, though. I know now why they get someone different to do it every year: it's because nobody would do it twice. I've got to do all these programmes, four recitals featuring three new young composers each, but for God's sake, don't ask me if they're any good. I've no idea. In the end you might as well pick them out of a hat.'

Sara protested, 'Oh, come on, you must think they're good.'

'No, honestly, darling, what I've been through, trying to decide what to play. I got dozens of scores, mostly bollocks, and unreadable. And then you get all the misunderstood little wannabes ringing up, whining about the selection. There's no pleasing them. You've no idea what some of these people would do to get their stuff performed. So, what's Herve like in bed? You must have slept with him.'

'I have *not* slept with him! Look, I just want to borrow your bloody flat. Is that so difficult?'

'You haven't? In that case you're one of the few, from what one hears. Ah, wait, yes. Of course, I see. You're *considering* sleeping with him, and having him as a house guest would be awkward in case you do and then it doesn't work out. That terrible silence at breakfast. Yes, darls, I do see.'

'James, you are the most smug married bastard I have ever known. You couldn't be more wrong. I just want my house to myself. I never even actually invited him – he just kind of assumed.'

'Woah, woah! Stop! Plenty! What? No, sorry, babe, that was me talking to Tom. He's spilling. Trying to get me drunk.'

'James, let him have Camden Crescent, please. I mean, it'll be a bit of rent, won't it? And if I've got him somewhere else all lined up, it's a fait accompli, it lets me off having him here, don't you see?'

She could hear his obvious glee, even though he probably had his hand over the receiver, and some more conversation in the background.

'Are you there? Look, Tom says to say' – James's voice grew wavery with laughter – 'on balance, we don't mind taking Herve's money, he must be making plenty. So, sure you can have the flat for Herve until we get back. It's fine with us, as long as we get a blow-by-blow of what he's like. You know, in bed. We think it's *so* funny.' He dissolved into laughter again.

'Sometimes I hate you two, you big, ugly fairies.'

'Love you to bits, babe, you are such fun to tease. Big snogs from Tom. Bye!'

People who live in English cities are actually proud of how little they know about other people around them, Sara thought. She was sitting at the Lambridge traffic lights on her way to the flat and looking straight ahead wishing, if not pretending, that all the other cars didn't exist. Perhaps in cities everywhere it has become a virtue not to notice your neighbours. We didn't like to ask, people say, having overheard screams and blows from next door for months before the fatal battering. We did wonder, they murmur after the hospice ambulance as it bears away someone in their street who, they'd noticed, had recently lost a lot of weight and all his hair. We never really saw her is the boast of those so careful of their neighbour's right to privacy that they inadvertently uphold also her right to lie dead for weeks in a lonely house before either the stink or the buzzing eventually proves more compelling than the observation of good manners that forbade, at the point when it might have done some good, any concerned knocking at the door.

But by whatever means death comes, it is never long before prurience dressed in the clothes of shocked concern does come knocking as if, in expiation for neglect of the living, the wellbeing of the corpse can be enquired after. As soon as it is safe to go and have a good gawp, people do, demonstrating that it never was good manners that kept them away but a violent distaste for being thought nosy. And if nosy is what they are being now, well, it's not a vice of which they are going to hear themselves accused by the deceased, is it?

All of which, Sara thought, once she had parked at the far end of the crescent and was walking to within sight of number 11, made it hard for her to admit that she could not be altogether *un*curious about the basement flat. But probably her interest lay in the fact that a peep at the basement flat would also be a glimpse into Andrew's world, albeit one in which she had no more right of occupancy than she had in his marriage. And then, what was so morally superior about feigning a lack of curiosity about what happened to other people?

So it was galling that as she walked slowly past the railings on her way to the door there really *was* nothing to see. The windows of Miss Bevan's sitting room shone on to the still-watered plants in the area; through the polished glass Sara could see the feet of well-behaved furniture standing in the conventional places. She marched straight up to James's and Tom's place, reminding herself what she was really here for.

As she was preparing to leave, she looked round the flat, newly aired and spruced up for Herve's arrival. After making up the bed there had been little to do in the way of cleaning, because Peggy, who 'did' for James and Tom, was still coming in once a week. Sara had brought fresh flowers and filled two vases, one for the drawing room and a small one for the bedroom. She had stocked the fridge and brought one or two of her own illustrated books on Bath, a street map and the current issue of *Bath City Life*. The last, being a glossy monthly mag, did not carry the story of Imogen Bevan's demise in the flat below. Not that she would keep it from him should it crop up, but there was no need to shove it in his face moments after he had crossed the threshold. She left the books, map and magazine on the coffee table, along with a bowl of fruit and a bottle of champagne with a label saying 'Welcome'. Looking round, she bit her lip. Perhaps after all she had made the place look like a hotel. Dammit, she might as well go and fold the loo paper into a little point, she was so ridiculous. Locking up behind her, she very much hoped he would not think her corny. She hoped he would feel touched, and by her rather than by her efforts.

Coming down the stairs from the first floor Sara saw that the door that led down to the basement flat at the end of the hall was ajar. She approached it tentatively. It could be the police, although she thought she remembered Andrew saying that they had finished 'at the scene' the day after the death. Perhaps the place was being burgled. But surely burglars would have closed the door to get on with a quick burgle in peace? Could it be family? She knew also from Andrew that Miss Bevan had had none. Squatters? Whoever it was, it was plainly none of her business, and all the more irresistible for that.

She paused in the doorway and looked down a flight of empty crimson-carpeted stairs. Just then the sharp warble of a tremulous female voice intoning 'Nearer my God to Thee' floated up to her ears. Sara's first crazy thought was that this was Miss Bevan soliloquising a little hysterically, it being indisputable that she (and only she) could claim, since the afternoon of the bank holiday, to be nearer her God to Him. She shivered as the chill of the at least corporally unoccupied flat seemed to rise and tug at her shoulders. The wailing voice continued. Sara didn't believe in ghosts, but some people did.

Perhaps it was religious fervour that was edging this strange voice slightly out of control, and what she was overhearing was an exorcism. Sara had never been at an exorcism, but something told her that to announce herself from the top of the stairs with a 'Coo-ee! Only me!' in the middle of the opening hymn was unlikely to lead to an invitation. Instead, she tiptoed silently down the stairs and followed the voice through an open door on the left.

Standing singing in the middle of the very tidy sitting room, facing the window that looked out on to the front area, was a woman with hair of a wild red who was clutching a handkerchief tightly in one hand and a pair of spectacles in the other. She stopped singing and swung round, staring and open-mouthed, while benign but total incomprehension shone from her blinking eyes. She raised one hand and put on her glasses, through which she continued to peer at Sara. She looked quite irretrievably bonkers.

'But I've got your Beethoven,' she said, with the relief of sudden enlightenment. 'Haven't I? Good God. You're what's-her-name. The cellist.'

'Oh, er . . . er, no. No, but I look like her. I must do. People are always saying—'

'Sara Selkirk. Yes, you are. On Deutsche Grammophon. That really isn't you?'

There was a silence. Sara felt a complete fool. Should she own up, offer to sign something and just go?

'Are you sure? Well, you're very like her. Anyway, I'm Dotty,' the woman said finally.

Sara was not sure what to say to this.

'Dorothy Price. I'm the executor, I've got this lot to sort out.' She turned, swinging a little on her heels, and waved the hand still clutching the hanky around the room.

Turning back, her hand dropped and her face relaxed into a genuinely warm smile. 'I wasn't really expecting anyone just to walk in, least of all a cellist. Or a cellist lookalike, rather. It was all a little surreal for a minute there. Are you a neighbour? I suppose this is Neighbourhood Watch in action.'

Sara extricated herself from having to admit to pure, dumb curiosity by explaining about borrowing the flat upstairs and getting it ready for a friend. She found herself lying about coming down to see if whoever was down here needed any help, or tea. Or anything.

'I mean, I just thought, it must be upsetting, having to see to a person's things. Someone who's died.'

Dotty smiled sensibly and looked embarrassed. 'Well, yes, it is. You're right. Because it was such a horrible way to go. It did rather come over me when I first came in. That's why I was singing. I always sing a hymn. One of my favourites. That always stops me crying quicker than anything.' She shook her head and laughed. 'Although the way I sing might start everybody else off. Do forgive the row.'

Sara smiled and repeated her offer of tea. This wailing woman was almost certainly extremely sane. The eyes behind the standard, middle-aged, gold-rimmed glasses had a look of intelligent patience. She was wearing a belted dress of light wool, printed in floralish, dusty colours, and fashionless but good shoes of the flat sort favoured by English women who walk everywhere very fast. The springy red hair, although cut in a style designed to look after itself, appeared to have strong ideas of its own. Sara put her age nearer sixty than forty.

'Do you know, I'd love some tea. I did bring some bags and milk, but I forgot that the kettle's useless. So if we could use yours – but use my teabags, they're in the kitchen. Now if you wanted to do that, I could make a start on these books.' Not only was she sane, she was clearly used to organising people.

Dotty turned to the bookcases while Sara went into Miss Bevan's kitchen where, it seemed, any few minutes that had ever gone into the preparing of food had been insignificant in comparison with the hours spent cleaning up afterwards. A smell like coal tar mixed with Brillo pulsed out of every surface and archaic object, a smell as outdated and all-pervading as the belief from which it arose: that a thing was not properly clean until it had been scrubbed to oblivion. The enamelled cream bread bin, with BREAD painted on it in green, sat crumbless, alongside matching tins for TEA and SUGAR, on a cream worktop which looked clean enough to operate on. Opposite, a rack of painted shelves held a set of sky-blue 1950s china and two small biscuit tins. The stainless steel sink was unstained and gleaming despite its age, the draining board was empty, the brown plastic plate rack upended to dry off. A white cloth was folded over the polished arch of the cold tap and a metal scourer sat in a little green saucer on the windowsill next to a Cornish ware jug holding a washing-up mop with a wooden handle. Not only were the chrome rings round the four burners of the stove next to the sink perfectly polished, but not one trace of any burned-on anything spotted the coiled electric elements. This was a cooker on which not a single sausage had ever dared to spit.

Dotty's teabags and Tupperware container of milk stood in front of the bread bin next to the electric kettle, an old-fashioned and highly polished model. It looked from the outside to be quite serviceable, but following with her eyes the thick black snake of flex stretching from the back of it, Sara saw that the plug had been gnarled by fire into a melted little fist of black rubber. Traces of smoke from the single socket a few inches above the worktop lay in greasy grey licks across the wall, where the paint had begun to blister. Sara lifted the kettle lid. The crusted black element sat surrounded by flakes of burned limescale that had been seared off the insides.

'Found the bags?' Dotty was in the doorway. Her eyes rested on the kettle and she sighed. 'Awful, isn't it? I can't bear to think about it.'

'What happened to it?'

Dorothy Price sighed again. 'After the explosion she somehow managed to get out of the door here and up the area steps, and someone from further along found her right outside by the railings. She was hysterical, in the end she collapsed on the pavement. According to the police, she must have had the kettle on, because by the time the woman ran back in here to call an ambulance, it had boiled dry and a fire was starting in the socket. The kettle doesn't switch itself off, you see, it's so ancient. Luckily she managed to deal with it all right, apart from the mess on the wall. If poor Imogen had made it any further along the crescent and the woman had phoned from somewhere else, the whole place could have gone up.'

'You've had to clear everything up, then?'

'How do you mean?'

'In here. After the explosion, the fire and all the breakfast things, her teapot, whatever. It's all been cleaned up. It's all immaculate, except for the kettle.'

'Oh, no, that's just Imogen for you. The neighbour wiped round after the fire, I suppose. And the police came after that and cleaned up the worst of the, er, you know, the evidence. They went through everything, even the rubbish bin. All they found was breakfast debris, of course, and I don't see how that's supposed to help.'

'Well, I suppose they look at everything. But they haven't any idea who did it yet, I suppose?'

'No. Oh, no. Imogen fought plenty of little battles, but nothing serious. Or so I used to think. But, no, I'm sure it'll turn out to be a random thing.'

'How, random?'

'You know, like these nutcases you hear about. Like that fellow with a grudge against Sainsbury's, for instance. Setting off bombs. I think it'll be someone like that. Wait and see. Meanwhile, the police go through pedal bins.' She sighed.

Sara, for a reason she did not quite understand, decided to keep her friendship with the detective chief inspector to herself, even though it prevented her from defending him.

Dotty went on sadly, 'So she'd finished breakfast, and with Imogen that meant everything was instantly washed and dried and put away. She was like that. I worked for her, you know, until she retired. She was headmistress of Combe Down Academy, you know, the girls' boarding school? We've dropped the 'For Young Ladies' now, of course. I'm still there. Bursar now. I was just the admissions secretary in her day.'

'Is that when you became friends?'

'Heavens, no, I was much too young and scared of her then. No, it was long after she'd retired, about six years ago. I believe I ran into her in Waitrose. I got the impression she was a bit lonely. So I called in to see her from time to time after that, regularly.'

'I am so sorry. It must be awful losing a good friend, especially like this.'

Dotty prevaricated. 'Oh, well. Yes, and now there's the funeral to arrange, and one wonders what she would have liked. I've asked Canon Hart-Browne to officiate. Do you know him? Adam Hart-Browne, at Bathford. Not her parish, but he knew her years ago.' She sighed. 'Yes, it's hard, having to guess what she would have liked. I suppose we were friends, although I think I always thought of her as the headmistress. She had her faults, of course, who doesn't? We're not here to judge. I suppose we can all be difficult, can't we? You know, I should get back to the books. Are you getting us that tea?' She disappeared.

When Sara returned ten minutes later from upstairs with two mugs, Dotty flopped into one of Imogen Bevan's armchairs and rubbed her eyes. Neither her purposeful banging of dusty books, nor little exclamations over funny titles, nor her tidy, organised piles could dispel the air of redundancy surrounding the things that a dead person has no further use for.

'I'm not taking any of this away, of course. We haven't got probate yet, the valuers haven't even been in. I was just curious to see what there was. It's mine now, you see. She's left me all the contents.'

Sara looked round the room. The books, such as fill second-hand, rather than antiquarian bookshops, took up two bookcases. There was a nest of little tables, a small cabinet containing several paperweights of Caithness glass, a set of four cranberry glasses and one small decanter. There were ornaments of brass over the fireplace, two blue and white plates and one doleful Staffordshire dog whose broken ear appeared to have been glued back on with a small spadeful of toffee. There were a few fairly pleasant pictures, a practical clock. The matching furniture was well upholstered in disastrous sage Dralon, in excellent condition and unprepossessing. There were no sentimental reminders of a lifetime's teaching, no hideous, well-loved, handmade offerings from any one of the thousands of children who must have passed through her hands. Nothing in the room spoke of any quirkiness or irrational taste, no inspired or impulse buy, not a single crazy moment in seventy-four years when Imogen Bevan had said to herself, *Gosh! I must have that, and it will remind me of this wonderful day for ever and ever.* Sara felt sorry for Dotty. While there was nothing wrong with any of the stuff, it seemed to her entirely resistible, merely an unlooked-for responsibility. You just wouldn't want nearly all of it.

As if she had read her mind, Dotty said, 'I don't think I even want it. Poor Imogen. It feels odd, sizing up her things. I keep thinking she'll pop up and tell us off for our impertinence. She was quite a character.'

'She had her faults, you said.'

Dotty gave a resigned smile. 'Well, yes, but it's a little late for all that, isn't it? I think we all just accepted it when she was head; it was only afterwards I started to notice. She always had some complaint or other going with someone – with a shop, or one of the neighbours or the Oxfam lot. Always something. I think it kept her going, just like the school did before she retired. I suppose she needed to control everybody. I didn't come as often as I could, but I don't think anybody else came at all.'

'But she saw other people, didn't she? Didn't she do lots of things?'

'Oh, plenty. She did lots. But I don't think she had proper friends, except me. I was amazed when she asked me to be her executor. When I agreed to it, I had no idea what was in the will.'

Sara tried not to look curious and failed.

'Imogen left the house contents to me, but she's left everything else to the school. The lot, mainly the proceeds from the flat. It's to set up a trust for a sixth-form travel scholarship.'

Dotty's voice began to thicken. She fished out her hanky and pushed up her glasses, dabbing at her eyes.

'From her, of all people. A travel scholarship. But I suppose that's where her heart was, in her school. She wasn't easy, but the thought of someone harming her like that – it's so cruel. Imogen never meant to be cruel, she was just single-minded. They've got to catch him, whoever he is. He's got to be punished. Poor, poor Imogen.'

'Why would the kettle be on,' Sara asked abruptly, 'if she'd had breakfast?'

Dotty looked up, surprised. 'The kettle? What does it matter now? A little socket fire won't affect the value of the flat. Look, thank you for the tea, very welcome. I expect that was all Imogen was doing, making herself another cup of tea.'

Sara didn't think so. Imogen Bevan did not sound like a person who would have allowed herself unscheduled refreshment so soon after breakfast. But she thought, a little sadly, that she might easily have been boiling a kettle to attend to some pressing item of domestic control: clearing the sink with soda or scalding a colony of ants on the patio to assist them out of this world and into the next, perhaps. And she would almost certainly have been a cloth boiler. What an epitaph: Here Lies the Body of Imogen Bevan, Now She's Boiling Cloths in Heaven. But as she took her leave, Sara refrained from making this observation to soft-hearted Dotty, not because she seemed anxious to get on, but lest it provoke a new outburst of hymn singing.

Chapter Nine

The next day, Sara felt it was suddenly possible, even imperative, to talk to Andrew – her Andrew, not the near stranger who had met her at the airport. The need to hear his voice had nothing to do with the Bevan enquiry, less still to do with Herve's arrival in Bath in two days' time. Possibly it was just that: a need to hear his voice. She called him at work.

It was like having a second chance. It was so easy, so lovely, the way he had immediately taken her call and spoken so eagerly in his burry voice. She loved how he could be at once so relaxed with her, even when speaking from his office, as if nobody else existed and nothing else but his conversation with her were of any importance. She asked about progress in the Bevan case.

'There's a piece going in tonight's *Chronicle*. We're getting somewhere. It definitely looks like the animal rights brigade: a nasty revenge attack, though probably not meant to be fatal. We've got to find the guy and of course he's done a runner. Could be anywhere, but we'll get him.'

He was absurdly touched that she had rung. 'Thanks for asking. Sara, about the other night—'

She stopped him from apologising by trying to apologise herself. He wouldn't let her, so then she tried to stop him stopping her. They ended up laughing.

'All right then, it was your fault,' he said. 'All your big-cellist-superstar fault. Absolutely.'

'Oh no, you're the cellist. You're a great cellist. For a detective, that is.' There was a brief pause during which they both realised that he would be coming over the minute he could get away.

'Sara? I can make it in about an hour.'

'Good. Andrew?'

'Yes?'

'For a lesson?'

'At least.'

'At the very least.'

An hour later, the rush of excitement that had started with the telephone call had not subsided, in either of them. Hardly able to conceal his joy at seeing her, Andrew decided to play it for laughs. At seven o'clock he strode theatrically into Sara's house and dumped his cello case, while she stood aside in the doorway, her eyes shining.

'Cut that out, Poole,' she said. 'Cuts no ice round here.'

Andrew growled, swung round suddenly, grabbed Sara round the middle and swung her easily over his shoulder. Ignoring her shrieks, her not very serious kicks against his chest and her ineffectual fist blows on his broad back, he stalked off with her to the music room.

'Say sorry.'

'Never,' she said, her voice upside-down, her dark hair almost sweeping the ground.

He swung her round twice, very quickly.

'Say sorry.'

Buckling now under his own laughter as well, he swung her round three times.

'Say sorry, you overrated old tart.'

'Oi! Less of the "old".'

'Give in?'

She shrieked as he began another turn.

'Give in?'

'In a minute. Right now I'm being sick in your back pocket.'

He swung her down and set her on the ground in front

of him. Her arms remained round his neck, so while she, still laughing, got her breath back, he drew strands of hair off her face and out of her mouth. He bent to kiss her.

She slipped out of his grasp, saying, 'Sit there.'

Andrew sprawled himself on the black linen sofa in the middle of the music room and watched Sara, barefoot, as she crossed the pale floorboards to the shelves covering the whole of one wall. She pressed the play button on the compact disc player and turned. The volume of sound that blasted from the speakers behind her was so huge that Andrew almost dived across to cover her ears and save her from it. Then a ripple of sensation which started at the base of his spine began to spread up his back. The hair on his neck rose. Her eyes were on him. She seemed hardly able to move, but then walked almost unsteadily over to the armchair and unfolded herself across it, opposite him.

'Messiaen. Turangalîla-symphonie,' he mouthed. She nodded, a little disappointed. She had been hoping that this would be new to him so that she would be revealing a new delight. Andrew stretched out on the sofa and watched her. The music ripped at the air all around them and they stared at one another as if seeking safety, at the same time luxuriating in the wide-open danger of Messiaen's vast, harmonic fields.

It was too loud for talking and in any case they had always felt the same kind of response to such music. What was there that could possibly need saying so urgently that it would merit interrupting a sound like this, music that was also in its way speaking, and no less compellingly for doing so without words? Talking could wait. Long ago they had agreed that some music couldn't be kept in the background. There were pieces, and this was one of them, that reduced all talk to babble. So they listened.

But Andrew began to wonder if she was planning to play him the whole thing, which he calculated at around one and a half hours. He almost wished them back in the old vinyl and cassette days, because then Sara would have to get up to change the record or turn the tape round and he could then stand up, break the atmosphere somehow, make her understand how frantic he was for them to make love. Sara was trying to concentrate on the music but, not knowing how to read Andrew's face, was instead wondering why he seemed so relaxed. Shouldn't he be as excited as she was, to be lying here like this, with both of them knowing what would happen next?

Then it dawned on her that she'd blown it. That last time, when she had rejected him, she hadn't been thinking straight. But what Andrew was doing now was showing her there were no hard feelings, but that as far as he was concerned the offer was closed. For him, the moment had passed. Mixed with her dismay that for her the moment had arrived too late, was the pressing question of what the hell she should do next.

She got up and stopped the music. Silence rang around them. 'Right, let's be having you,' she said brutally. Andrew blinked. 'What have you been practising? You have been practising, I hope, when I was away?'

They both needed reminding that she was not a cello teacher. She was an international cellist. If he was gently making it clear he wasn't going to open himself up to rejection a second time, then she was making it clear, less gently, that he would not have to because she was certainly not desperate enough to lose any dignity over him. He was here for a lesson and that was just fine with her. He had wanted her, he had let her know it and she had rejected him. He did not want her any more, and she did not care.

Andrew rose, brought his cello case from the hall and opened it on the floor. Sara crossed the music room and arranged two upright chairs and music stands at the far end. Andrew carried over his cello and bow, sat down and began to tune up, as she glided over to the shelves which held her library of music. In the large room their silent choreography achieved their joint object, which was to avoid touching or looking at one another. She brought some volumes over from the shelves and placed them on the closed lid of the grand piano. As she leafed through them, Andrew played scales. He felt, even with his back to her, that all his disappointment and longing, mixed now with an unplaced fury that things were going wrong again, must somehow be beaming out at her through the back of his head. With her back turned, the only thing that Sara could have said with honesty was that it was wonderful to hear his cello in that room again. So she said nothing.

She placed four single sheets of music on the stand. Andrew looked at it, sat back sarcastically and breathed histrionically, 'Oo-err! Don't think I'll be up to *this*!'

Still furious, he screwed his face into a mocking, lugubrious leer and launched into 'Resurrections des Autres' by Herve Petrescu. Sara sat in the other chair and watched him, refusing to react. The look on his face now was that of someone with large fillings chewing on tinfoil. Why was he playing the fool now, when all she wanted to do was kiss him? She tightened her lips round an escaping smile. The music went on. Sara shifted in her chair and listened hard to Andrew's playing, trying to forget his mouth. 'Resurrections' was an early work which Sara had found to be, on first playing it, almost cheeringly comprehensible. But now Andrew was doing such things to it . . .

He began to concentrate on what he was doing. Sara watched him and listened, feeling mean for giving him this to play when he had quite clearly been working hard in her absence. His playing had anyway been technically fairly sound; now it was close to assured. The tuning, even in this chromatic, edgy stuff, was faultless. At one time he had tended not to shape his phrases sufficiently; now it seemed that he was bringing out of this music all the potential it held and at the same time showing that potential to be slight. Most of all, he had authority. Andrew's playing commanded attention, as if a voice running under the music were insisting that you stop and listen. He was a musician. He always had been, but now he played as if he really knew it, bowing with an artist's delicate strength, the tricky fingering simply an interesting test of agility for his long, powerful left hand. And although the achievement was his (and she was not a cello teacher) Sara felt a surge of pride.

Watching him, it seemed absurd that she had once tried hard to get rid of Andrew. He had contacted her out of the blue soon after she had come to live near Bath, and practically invited himself to her house. Then, for weeks, he had bombarded her with requests that she agree to give him lessons. Eventually she assented, his quiet determination having so impressed her, or perhaps worn her down. But had she, at the time, really believed that she was taking him on entirely on the grounds of his talent, or had she even then found his brown eyes mesmerisingly sexy? Had she just been sorry that despite his early and prodigious musical talent his unadventurous parents had forced him into a 'proper' career in the police? It had never quite been sympathy alone that was aroused by contemplation of his body, his long limbs astride his cello, his broad shoulders. Andrew's rapid promotion and success in the police force had been gratifying, but his frustrated musical ambition was still in quiet spate in him, like an underground river. His marriage added another clot to the thickening discontent in his life, and Sara was almost sorry about that, too. But after nearly three years in which their lives had been periodically intertwined to the point of confusion, whatever she and Andrew might or might not mean to each other now was not something she cared to analyse today.

As Andrew travelled on through 'Resurrections des Autres', Sara could hear that he was exposing the piece for what it was. He played quite artlessly, exploiting every phrase for what he could find in it, but giving the music no extra help with tone colour or dynamics as she almost unconsciously might have done. Very eloquently, his playing revealed that all that was actually there in the score was a succession of tricksy intervals between the highest and lowest notes on the instrument, adding up to banality in abundance. He reached the end of the piece, rested his bow on one knee and gave a patient sigh. There was silence.

He turned to look at Sara and in a faint, tired voice said, 'What . . . utter . . .' Sara looked back at him and together they intoned, '*balls.*'

Sara brought her Stradivari cello, the Christiani of 1700, from its case in the corner. After tuning it she began on the piece herself, seeking earnestly for the music's rewards, which must surely be in there somewhere.

After a moment, Andrew stopped her, serious-faced. 'It's not just us, is it? It really is balls. Quite pleasant, faintly interesting . . . balls.'

'Yes, I think so,' she said, sighing, laying down her bow. 'Poor Herve.'

'Doesn't bode too well for the protégé and his community opera. Your pal Cosmo Lamb. Is he any better?'

Sara's mystified face told him she had never heard of Cosmo Lamb. When Andrew explained she said, 'Oh, I don't take any credit for him. Or the blame, if it turns out that way,' she added quickly. She explained about leaving Helene's number with Herve in Prague. 'I thought he might have a student or someone who'd be interested. I'm glad he passed it on. Although he wasn't slow to call in the favour, I can tell you.'

'Well, I suppose we'll see what he's like. Valerie's certainly impressed.' The train of thought depressed him. 'Christ, a community opera,' Andrew said derisively. 'Why the hell did I ever allow myself to get caught up in it?'

Sara said nothing.

Eventually Andrew answered his own question. 'It's Valerie. I shouldn't have agreed. Then there's Helene Giraldi and the girl. I mean, it's not that I'm not sympathetic, but a *community* opera? Community balls, if you ask me. Not to mention all the rest of them.'

'Oh, now,' Sara said. 'Don't be snobbish about amateurs. Actually, Helene Giraldi was pretty good once upon a time. It can't be that bad.'

'No? Try this. The "community" opera is to be based on the life of Beau Nash. The "community" so far is nowhere in sight, so all the main parts are being sung by five people. "Current thinking" includes three costume changes for the chorus, once we find one, who come on every five minutes either as dishonest servants, pretentious Bath gentry or leprous invalids.'

'Could be worse,' Sara said, leaving unanswered the question of how.

'The chorus,' Andrew went on, 'it is anticipated, will consist of Boy Scouts and Brownies, none older than eleven. Beau Nash will be played by Phil.'

Sara raised her eyebrows.

'Phil is Chinese.'

She bit her lip. 'I see. And you feel perhaps Bath audiences are not yet quite ready for a Chinese Beau Nash?'

They both stared rather hopelessly at the music on the stand.

'Andrew, I was at James's flat yesterday. I met this woman, Imogen Bevan's executor.'

'Oh, yes. Red hair. Interviewed her. Nice woman.' Andrew sighed. 'Sara, please don't go on thinking about it. You're not really supposed to know anything about it, you know. I shouldn't even discuss it.'

'I know, but why was she so quick to get round there and sort out her stuff?'

Andrew closed his eyes and shook his head. 'You have such a suspicious mind. Dorothy Price works at a busy school. This is their busiest term. She wants to get on with sorting out the contents before half-term because come October she'll be flat out writing the school panto and what not. She asked us if it was all right for her to go in. I can promise you, Sara, there's no mystery here. It's just a routine police matter to track down Brendan Twigg and charge him.'

'Well, yes, if you say so. It's just − I don't know − I'd like to help somehow.'

Andrew shook his head again. 'You can't.'

He began a series of slow arpeggios. His cello was not a great instrument, but he managed to draw out the deepest, most chocolatey tone of which it was capable. Playing softly, he turned his head and spoke again, rather sadly.

'Just help me get through this damn opera without going mad or killing someone. They're pitiful, all of them. Oh, I don't mean I don't like them. They're nice people, all of them. Adele really is sweet. And Jim's all right, very straight, full of good intentions. And nobody could object to Phil. They've all got such faith in Helene, and she's got this ridiculous faith in Cosmo, although from what Valerie says he's been sponging off Helene for weeks now and still hasn't written a note.'

'Play me something. How about some Brahms?'

Andrew stopped. He had memorised the second sonata for her. In her absence, closing his eyes and playing Brahms was the closest he could get to seeing her, hearing her voice. He did not want to ruffle the air around them with an Allegro Vivace, so he began with the slow pizzicato notes of the second movement, the languorous Adagio Affettuoso. Sara seemed to understand that the mood should not be broken. At the end of the pizzicato he paused, his face sad with concentration, before drawing his bow gently down the strings and sending up a sound so warm that it seemed to rise and wrap itself around them. Over the music, he spoke slowly.

'Honestly, Sara, I do try not to be cynical about it. But it's farcical, all of it. Not just the music, but Valerie's little plan to bring us together. It won't work. It's just not going to happen and it's my fault. Nothing's changed, you see. I love you.'

For a few seconds Sara could not speak, for the sudden relief that was exploding inside her. Andrew was still playing and she was still cradling her cello between her knees. She rose, first to unencumber herself and then pull his cello away from him so that they could reach each other. The telephone rang. Andrew stopped abruptly.

'That could be her,' he said hopelessly. 'Checking up. She'll have got home by now and noticed that my cello's gone.'

'I'll say you've just arrived,' Sara said rather desperately, shocking herself by the ease with which she could connive to keep Andrew here for at least another hour. 'Start playing something, she'll hear it.'

They looked at each other, knowing that the duping of Valerie was beginning in earnest. They would be naked together within half a minute of Sara's getting off the phone. 'Answer it,' Andrew said firmly, starting to play scales as Sara picked up the receiver.

'Herve! Herve, how wonderful to hear you! You're still in New York?' Sara turned to Andrew and grimaced. Andrew raised his eyebrows and to Sara's horror stopped mid-scale and launched into 'Resurrections des Autres'. She shook her head and shooshed him silently. He ignored her.

'No, no, the line's perfect. Still arriving on Sunday? Yes, the sixth. Wonderful, I'm so looking forward! Oh, yes, I'd take a chauffeured car from Heathrow if I were you. Yes, I see. Uh-huh, the flat's all arranged. Why, Herve, don't you trust me? I faxed you the address and direc—Oh, good, you got them. What?'

Sara turned again to Andrew and gestured frantically for him to stop. He played louder, impassive except for raising one eyebrow at her.

'Yes! It is "Resurrections"! No, no, of course it's not me. I'm speaking to you. It's er . . . ah . . . um, er, it's just a recording.'

At that, Andrew made a deliberately loud and crass mistake, went back several bars and sawed laboriously, repeating the error over and over. Sara whirled round with a look of utter fury on her face. Andrew looked up mildly, amused at her powerlessness.

'Oh, no, only an amateur,' she said. 'Work in progress. Yes, very poor indeed, really quite ghastly,' she added triumphantly.

To this Herve clearly had much to say. As she listened, Andrew began to ham up the music, adding ridiculous pluckings, trills and eighteenth-century grace notes. Now and then he would add a line of his own, so that from time to time snatches of 'The Teddy Bears' Picnic', 'Ode to Joy' and

'In an English Country Garden' shoved their way ludicrously through Herve's atonal undergrowth. Andrew was enjoying himself hugely.

'No, Herve, please, there's no question of an *unauthorised* recording,' Sara was pleading. 'Well, yes, of course I understand the royalties issue. *And* the composer's own high standards; look, there's lots to discuss when you get here. Yes, yes, promise. No, you'll love the flat. Yes, I got your list of requirements. What? No, don't worry. Yes, you too. Right, *çiao* for now.'

She replaced the receiver and without drawing breath turned on Andrew. 'What the hell do you think you're playing at? What the *hell*, Andrew? Just what the fuck was all that about?'

Andrew seemed surprised by her rage. 'Me? What am I playing at? Well, I'll tell you what I'm not playing at. I'm not toadying up to some guy who I've just agreed writes crap music. It was only a bit of fun, anyway. Is he so bloody precious he can't take a joke? Why, suddenly, can't you?'

'Joke? A *joke*? Is that what it was? Look, I've got to work with this man. As a *professional*, Andrew. And he happens to be a very important composer. Oh, I see. Perhaps that's it. Jealousy. Is that your problem? How *dare* you behave in that childish way!'

'I'm not childish,' Andrew said. He was entirely calm. 'Or jealous. I'm appalled. I'm appalled at the way you can go along with it, pretending that you think he's so wonderful. You should listen to yourself. I couldn't believe all that "lovey-dovey wonderful" crap coming from you. Why are you even working with him, if you don't rate his stuff? Where's your famous honesty?'

'How *dare* you.' Sara felt now every bit as cornered by Andrew's questioning as she did by Herve's demands and the necessity to see the work with him through to its end. She was obliged to do it, whether or not the music held any conviction for her, and how would it help if she made her feelings known to Herve? She was dealing with an ego bigger and even more fragile than her own and she had to look after it, even if only to make sure of a premiere of which she would not be actually ashamed. Couldn't Andrew understand that? He was betraying her. He had claimed to love her, and yet the first time she looked to him for understanding of her predicament he attacked her, quite unfairly. She could attack, too.

She mustered the worst thing she could think of to say to him. 'You're an amateur. You obviously don't understand the situation. It's to do with professionalism, Andrew. But I'm not going to try to explain it to you.'

She swung on her heels and left the room. In the kitchen, she breathed deeply until she began to feel the return of her calm. Right, let that sink in for a minute or two, she thought. He'll see my point. She pictured him pacing the music room in remorse, considering. She opened a bottle of red wine, debating whether they should drink it now to seal the peace or later, after they'd made love.

But the silence following her words stretched out, lengthened and settled, and was broken only five minutes later by Andrew's angry slam of the front door.

Chapter Ten

Poppy knew better now than to press the freezing soles of her feet against Cosmo's thighs. She had tried it once and been told in the morning that he'd thought he was being attacked by two damp old fish. Not that he had reacted at the time, except to turn over in a sleepy huff and shuffle even further away from her side of the bed. So now, after walking back from the nursing home in the chilly early morning and entering the sleeping house quietly, she went to the bathroom and ran a basin of hot water instead of collapsing straight into bed beside him. Hopping uncomfortably, with her thigh muscles straining at the effort of keeping one leg raised and one foot in the basin, she would wash her feet, rubbing at the soles and toes to restore sensation and lathering them in Waitrose's oatmeal soap (four for the price of three) to remove the salt tang that so offended Cosmo.

It was only a little thing, really, the feet, which probably were a little whiffy after a night shift in shoes with manmade uppers. She shouldn't feel hurt. Cosmo needed his sleep. Creativity was very exhausting and when this project was over and he could relax a little he would realise what a support she was being. He would then see how uniquely aware she was of his needs and he would be happy to see how quietly indispensable she had become to him. She wouldn't jeopardise things now by insisting on recognition of her efforts, she thought sensibly, for all the research, for volunteering to do the costumes, for getting on with the community liaison. She would never remind him again that leaving London to come to Bath with him had meant giving up her diploma course on complementary therapies. Possibly Cosmo had not really understood how important it had been to her to find something she was really good at. Not his fault. He was so focused himself, or was usually. Prague was obviously still having its after-effects. Obviously, all the new ideas from Herve Petrescu were taking time to bed down.

Cosmo could not be expected to know what it had been like for her after college, going after job after job, eventually the most menial assistant stage manager ones, and getting nowhere. He hadn't even known her then. College had not been fun. First she had been thrown off the performers' course but, as her mother had pointed out, she could hardly be surprised at that since she had in the first place only scraped on with some vestige of an idea of becoming a character actress. If she couldn't find herself some confidence from somewhere, they had said, she had better transfer to stage management. That turned out to be an area in which she had also failed to shine because she simply had no appetite for it. Or rather, she went about it with every bone in her body aching with jealousy towards the pretty girls who got to go on stage, which prevented her from ever really involving herself. She hoovered from lectures to practicals and finally to idiotic projects, sucking in envy which then swelled up and filled her like a dirty bag in need of emptying. After three years she had mustered neither the heart to cooperate nor the imagination to care and, unaware of how completely she failed to conceal it, continued to show up hopefully at interviews in her one good jacket, with her mediocre degree in her handbag and her bitterness all over her face.

Repeated failure did nothing for a person's confidence, and she found that the less she had, the more she needed. When she had been five years out of college with her stage management degree and had only worked occasionally, Poppy began to wonder where she was going to find enough confidence just to carry on. Her parents had talked brightly at first about her being off their hands at last; gradually it dawned on Poppy that she bored them. How long, her mother asked with diminishing good nature, was Poppy planning to wait before she surprised them with some success at something? They could hardly be blamed, as the years went by, for giving so much more attention (and time, and energy, and money, and approval, and love, Poppy added silently) to Poppy's sister, who had produced a grandchild. It was her own fault, probably. But it began to matter that she could see no end to living in rented places in the bad, inconvenient parts of London, no end to the cheap food, the expensive, wearying bus journeys, the filthy tube. Worst of all was when she could see no end to being single, a kind of an emotional amputee – maimed and incomplete, and yet carting round with her everywhere, like an aching phantom limb, her longing to have someone to laugh it all off with.

Mincing quietly on fragrant tiptoe from the bathroom she folded herself in under the duvet beside Cosmo and tried to breathe silently. At least now, *basically*, she did have someone to laugh it all off with, so giving up the course was an easy sacrifice. So she would not insist on gratitude for the bit of money she was earning for them, or on affectionate tolerance for her tired old feet. Or on sex, for the time being.

Creative people should not exhaust themselves sexually when they needed to channel their energies into their creations. Cosmo needed her understanding as well as a little bit of handling. And with her to handle him, or help manage his career, Cosmo had a future which she intended to help him enjoy. She had sensed it almost the first time they had met at an unlikely dinner party given by Gemma. After college she had watched Gemma saunter into a job in stage effects at the Coliseum that she herself would have loved. Gemma had a perfectly tolerable partner who was a trombone teacher, and their two salaries had secured a very decent place in Tufnell Park which Poppy also would have loved. Gemma got Poppy round to dinner now and then in order to complain at length about all three: job, partner and house, but this particular party had yielded fruit. Gemma's Jeff was doing a new trombone piece written by Cosmo, who was employed as a project worker on a six-week community education project in Tower Hamlets, so what could be more natural than that he should be at dinner, too? She and Cosmo had got on 'terribly well' and swapped numbers. It was not that she had found him straightforwardly attractive but, as Gemma had remarked sniggeringly to Jeff later, Poppy was so desperate by now that she would probably give a second look, if not the benefit of the doubt, to anyone with testicles and a pulse.

Then there had been nearly six months of seeing each other in the courtship style of arty and impoverished Londoners: going out sometimes to films, never the theatre, and restaurants with ethnic food, never European, cooking each other one-pot suppers to which the other brought plonk and cheese and, eventually, staying the night instead of forking out for taxis home. It was one of the happiest periods of Poppy's life. There was still the bad accommodation, the tiresome travelling by public transport and the filthy food, but, sitting on the bus, Poppy knew herself for the first time in her life not to be entirely alone, and the knowledge made her brave. She got herself on to the complementary therapies course, negotiating the application procedures and the waiving of fees for 'the unwaged' with a sudden burst of courage. Her courage grew when she became almost the star student, soaking in everything about reflexology, acupuncture, cranial massage, aromatherapy and a clutch of other arcane practices with which she became acquainted. She had exceptionally good hands, the tutor told her.

Just as Poppy was beginning to feel confident enough to tackle Cosmo about their relationship being all a bit studenty and it being high time they got serious about a permanent base and some joint planning – concepts that privately she boiled down in her brain to their true essence: a mortgage and marriage – Cosmo succeeded in getting a grant to study with some famous composer in Prague. Or it might have been a loan, it was all a little hazy. They corresponded. Cosmo wrote of his rough rooms in Prague, the beer, his studies with the 'maestro'; Poppy wrote back with chirpy accounts of her triumphs on the course, later with outlines of plans for 'our' future.

As the months rolled by, she began to add the word 'international' to 'composer' when describing Cosmo to other people. She read a biography of Alma Gropius and began to see that Cosmo needed her to promote his work. Simply not enough people had had a chance to find out how good he was, and in his absence she set about putting that right, sending a few manuscripts around London to likely venues, reviewers and performers. She began to appreciate what a tough, cut-throat and unfair business it could be, and fancied that she could become Cosmo's shield. Of course things would not necessarily go swimmingly either every time or straight away, but with her determination and his talent, they would get there. She cleared out his bedsit and brought his stuff over to hers, and told him about it in a letter afterwards.

When he came back from Prague he had not minded. He had seemed rather frayed and displaced, and genuinely vague about things like his belongings and his address – in truth, also about her – so it was a relief that within a week of his return he had landed the project in Bath. She tingled at the memory of coming back one day to find him actually packing, having kept even the possibility of going to Bath together as a surprise. She was touched that he had not mentioned it, keeping it a secret so that she would not be disappointed if he had failed to get the commission. At her insistence they had gone to a good restaurant to celebrate and, a little drunk, toasted themselves: Cosmo and Poppy vs the universe. They were in it together. If Cosmo were to go down, so would she, hypothetically. But Cosmo was on his way up. Bath was only the beginning.

After Bath, she could see it going either of two ways. If Cosmo carried on writing the kind of stuff he was doing now they would, in a couple of years, be living somewhere at least picturesque if not chic, a university or cathedral town at the very least. Their house would be large and charmingly shabby. Cosmo would have enough work from commissions and a bit of university teaching to keep them fairly comfortably, as well as lots of little bits of broadcasting, reviewing, guest lecturing and so on to help build his name. She would have a battered Volvo and organise everything from the vegetable garden to the fridge magnets. Their two children, which she planned to have almost at once and close together, would be tousle-headed and precocious and called (for she would have a boy and a girl) Jasper and Juniper. The names would indicate to the world the sort of original and intellectually confident family they would be. Life would be so hectic and enjoyable that the weight would just drop off her. Her children would have all the clarinets, gerbils, clay, tree-houses and spaniels she could dredge up for them. Their little brains would be stimulated until their ears bled.

Alternatively, Cosmo could make a few concessions. She might be able to get him to see that it would not kill him to write something accessible, perhaps something for the West End. If he did a few of those then other doors would open, film music maybe. In that eventuality their house would have to be not merely large but charming minus the shabbiness, and cleaned by others. To her children's agendas she would add skiing lessons, drama coaching, ponies; to her own, private tuition in garden design and interior decor. Her and the children's day clothes would come from Agnès b and in the kitchen she would be organic but wasteful. She would be raucous when the mood took her and Bohemian enough to snarl at the staff if she felt like it because she was the one with the cheque book. There would be a third baby – Tarquin or Lupin – and a Norland nanny. She would have a studio built in which she would do nothing at all, complaining laconically to whoever their current friends were about the amount of time Cosmo had to spend in LA. Poppy would go often up to London in order to treat Gemma to lunch in places that Gemma could not afford and would prefix

'Gemma' with 'poor' all the way from the marinaded olives to the espresso.

But either future would do. Poppy hugged herself in bed and thought of people saying, *Oh yes, Cosmo's brilliant, but it's Poppy who keeps him together.* The world might prevent her from becoming a success in her own right, but she did not intend to be stopped from associating herself with the success of her husband, even to the extent of being credited with some of the responsibility for it. Never again would she hang back in the wings while people she hated pranced out past her on to the stage.

Her side of the bed was still chilly, so she warmed herself with the thought that Jasper and Juniper would never have to work as hard, or even know how much she was doing for them in advance of their births. Not for them the humiliating round of failure in a world that overlooked them. Sometimes it almost frightened her how passionately she wanted her children to grow up with an assumption that she had never been able to make: that when they ventured out grown-up and strong in her love, the world, should they have any use for what it offered, would be waiting at their feet.

Cosmo stirred and flopped over on to his back with his mouth open. It was almost daylight and Poppy could see a little trapeze of saliva between his top and bottom lips swinging to and fro in the breeze floating from his mouth. She lifted the duvet and peeped down to be gratified by the sight she was expecting. Yes. Cosmo was wearing them again, the expensive boxer shorts she had bought for him in Gieves & Hawkes's summer sale, less than half price because the pattern was slightly Christmassy. They were a ludicrous price for underwear, and a little on the tight side for Cosmo, but they were a symbol, a portent. Cosmo was going places where you could have any number of boxers just because you fancied the pattern, Christmassy or not. Yes! A dozen of those! Charge them to my account and have them sent! And she wouldn't have to wash them, or anything else, on the quiet in a nursing home washing machine, in the middle of the night, just to save on launderette costs. Bath was only the beginning. Thanks to her, Cosmo was on his way up. And she was going, too, soon to be joined by Jasper and Juniper and then, if she continued to handle their father in the right way, by their dear little brother or sister.

Herve paused on the pavement shivering, wondering if he had a chill coming on, if he had picked up something on the plane. He became so absorbed in considering this that he almost omitted to notice that he was now at the edge of the Royal Crescent in Bath, one of the most famous streets in the world. It was also one of the few famous streets of the world that he had not walked along before. The main reason for coming here at eight o'clock in the morning was to see the celebrated architecture with an empty foreground, free of writhing humanity, and now he had forgotten to notice it.

How tiresome of it not to attract him. He wondered whether he would bother to lie to Sara about it and agree that it was special in some way, since it was she who had described it to him in the first place with an enthusiasm that seemed less forced than her appetite for work. He thought not. She might as well know from the outset that he was not to be drawn in the ordinary way to ordinary beauty, nor was given to displays of enthusiasm. He closed his fists in his pockets and hunched his shoulders against the morning cold. It did not register with him that he was feeling the first nip of autumn because he did not think about seasons beyond taking the usual precautions, depending on where he was, against the extremest effects of weather. Most points between sunburn and snow-blindness he tended not to notice. He dressed for interiors, acquiring his outer layers of clothing only as the need arose, and his thin indigo jacket was not quite warm enough now.

Out of habit he walked on with his head down, before realising that this would not accomplish the object of his visit. Without altering his stride he looked up and dutifully scanned the façade, puzzled that the round-headed window in the dead centre, the only central feature, should be so inconsequential as almost to escape notice. It added to his dissatisfaction. Was there some point to all this architecture? He considered why this so celebrated city sat ill in his perception, not noticing that it was a necessity with him to look for, and if necessary to create, some complication in his responses to most things. Other cities that he knew provided him more obligingly with a sense of unease. To urban ugliness of the ordinary kind he could, indeed often did, respond in his music with strangulated screeches of alienation. It appealed to him, the picture of himself set against a barren cityscape, his music articulating the latest in the tragedy of the human condition, his the potent but lonely voice of a lost, post–industrial generation. All this pleasantness made that difficult here. It was all so understandable.

In the middle of the crescent he stopped. He could see right to the far end from here and it was obviously exactly the same as the end from which he had just come. Anyway, he was cold. He crossed the road and turned back in the direction of Brock Street. As he entered the Circus he could see that people were on the move, brisk ones with shoulder bags and mobile phones, and older, sleepier others with poop scoops and plastic bags, who shambled on the kerb while their vile dogs in the gutter made it worth their while. Herve hurried past and made his way down Gay Street and into George Street where the traffic was already heavy and the shops were open. Here the city's heart beat with a vigour that exhausted him. He was in no mood for the uncomplicated thrum of daily lives. Everywhere he looked he saw people purposefully engaged in their transparently innocuous business, going in and out and passing up and down in front of uniformly pleasant buildings. A mild optimism seemed to gleam from the stone itself and these unresisting people soaked up its message on their way and went about looking on the bright side. And Herve found this unsettling, being so much more at home with futility. Bath provided too little to complain of, as did Sara Selkirk herself, and that in itself amounted to a complaint.

He turned away, back into the ordered claustrophobia of the Circus with its inward-looking windows. Selkirk was a puzzle. When he'd heard a recording of hers he had been certain he was listening to a woman of depth, yet Sara herself was turning out to be quite frivolous. He was disappointed, too, that he was not having on her the effect that he usually had on women. In fact, he seemed not to be having any effect on her at all. It was most odd, not to say irritating, as was that unshakeable pleasantness of hers. They went together, she and the city, and burdened him with weariness.

This time he left the Circus by Bennett Street. He wandered up Russell Street and from the top of it saw almost what he had been hoping to find. Not a Catholic church, of course, but one which he hoped would provide the same kind of dark stillness where he could talk privately, if not in peace, to his mother. The door latch was heavy and noisy but he proceeded into the church as quietly as he could, in fear of being greeted by anyone. It was lighter inside than he had hoped and the noise of traffic reached him here as a high drone. He sat on the back pew, sensing with relief that he was alone.

Edesanya! Mother. If he closed his eyes he could imagine her kinder than she had ever been in life, as if this place were her natural home and he would be sure to find her here. *Mother*, he whispered. *Bocsasd meg a mi vetkeinket.* But would she, were it even in her gift to do so, forgive him his trespasses? Silence lay like dust across the wooden pews and rafters. She would not. Why would she forgive in death, having judged him with unvarying harshness in life? If he could only light a candle, would it help her to hear the sincerity in his confession? *I do try, Edesanya*, he pleaded. *I keep trying, but I need a little help. I am so alone!* Tears escaped from his closed eyelids and his shoulders convulsed in self-pity. *And I do no harm!* he whispered aloud, suddenly feeling petulant and reproachful. If she had not died in the first place none of this would be happening. Everything would be as it had been until two years ago, except that by now, had she lived, Mother

96

would surely no longer be able to treat his achievements with her customary faint incredulity. By this time, he would not still be failing to impress her with his successes. She would not still be throwing him watery congratulations and then turning back to her beloved Brahms and Beethoven, leaving him still starving for her praise. By dying, she was not only still withholding her good opinion but had robbed him of the hope of ever deserving it: *You certainly do not deserve it now, do you?* He could almost hear her voice. Herve rubbed his eyes and sniffed. *I do what I have to*, he hissed rebelliously. *What else can I do, if you have gone? It was all for you. How can I do anything now?* A self-righteous silence – either his or his mother's, he could not be sure – descended and filled the space around him. He got up and made his way down the aisle. At the open door he sniffed again. He was definitely going down with something.

As he made his way along Julian Road, Herve continued to fret enjoyably about his chill. He needed whisky and some proper sleep. With his hands jammed in his pockets and his arms pressed close into his sides he climbed the short distance up Lansdown Hill back to Camden Crescent. But because his eyes were fixed firmly on the pavement as he reached number 11, he felt no particular pleasure in his return from the unsatisfactorily empty church, and did not notice the troubled face of the woman with untidy red hair who entered the building just ahead of him.

Chapter Eleven

Andrew was too busy feigning his own surprise to be more than peripherally aware of Valerie's reaction, seated next to him on the piano stool in Helene's drawing room. He replaced his coffee cup in its saucer and looked round at the others, grateful that he need not find anything to say. With Helene in full flight, none of the other seven people in the room would be required or indeed able to say anything either, at least not for some time.

'I've got a teensy bombshell, everyone,' she had said. Adele had finished her mantra of 'Phil milk half sugar. Jim black no sugar. Valerie milk no sugar. Mama milk two sweeteners. Adele milk no sugar. Poppy milk no sugar. Cosmo extra milk two sugars,' and was doggedly taking the cups and biscuits round. Phil, as usual, was helping. Poppy and Cosmo, after nearly five weeks, were now on Adele's coffee list but Andrew, whose attendance at rehearsals had been sporadic, was still not included in her computations. Like all people, events or physical facts which were new or at variance with what she recognised, the presence of Andrew had yet to be accommodated somewhere in Adele's understanding, and until such time as it might be she would behave as if he simply were not there. He had risen quietly and poured his own.

'Never fear, it's a nice bombshell,' Helene went on encouragingly. 'And it is, tan-ta-ra – there will be no rehearsal tonight!' Feeling herself illuminated by the beam of everyone's attention, she went on, 'I thought that instead of yet more *preliminary discussions* about our own little creative enterprise' – she glanced at Cosmo – 'we should have an outing. The minibus will be here in quarter of an hour. I am taking you all to Iford Manor for a very special evening. You could call it a reunion!'

Again she glanced at Cosmo. 'At Iford Manor this evening, there is to be an open rehearsal with *Herve Petrescu*, our own dear Cosmo's inspiration and mentor, and the cellist Sara Selkirk. And we will all be there, to celebrate our own *creative selves* and the universal language of music that we all share! So, if anyone wants to spend a penny before we go, you know where it is, everyone!'

Andrew leaned towards Valerie. 'Or in other words,' he whispered, keeping his eyes on Cosmo and Helene who were at a safe distance, '"we've been coming here for nearly a month to start work on a non-existent opera but the guy who I'm paying to compose the thing hasn't yet written a note. So let's at least bugger off and have a good time instead of sitting around here and spending another bloody rehearsal talking about possibilities." Am I right?' Cosmo was sitting alone in an armchair and his face, cupped in one hand, revealed that his own interpretation of Helene's words might not be very different from Andrew's. It had changed colour from maggot white to earthworm pink. He was staring at the carpet, frowning.

Valerie tightened her lips into an exasperated line. 'Can't you just be positive for once? Can't you just try? I do – I try a lot.' She rose crossly and joined Helene. Andrew watched her go, feeling guilty but no less cynical. So she wants positive, does she? Right, he thought, let's be positive. Good idea. Let's all go off to a nice posh house in the country and listen to some pretentious bullshit presented by some megastar groovy composer, who's bloody moved in and taken over. Taken over Sara. *My* Sara. He swallowed most of his coffee in one gulp and made his eyes water.

He had not seen Sara since the evening he had stormed out

eleven days ago. He had not mentioned to Valerie that he had seen her at all, never mind twice, and Valerie had mentioned her about a week ago, only to ask with studied casualness if she was home safely. Andrew, knowing how closely he was being watched, had carried on wiping the sink, looking bored and said that yes, she had rung the police station to thank him for checking the house and now, was there anything else for washing up.

The thought of Sara made him feel like a foreign plant, stuck in the wrong garden and just managing to hold on with the wilting conviction that his own wife was a slow toxin which he was being forced to ingest through the roots. Sara was quite simply his climate, pure, exhilarating and utterly necessary for his survival, yet she seemed to be happily casting her healthful light elsewhere. On that pretentious Hungarian bastard, to be precise.

Valerie suddenly reappeared. 'Isn't she marvellous?' she asked with determined friendliness, standing over him with her cup and saucer and looking back over at Helene. 'She's marvellous, isn't she?' Just then she caught Helene's eye and smiled toothily. '*She's* always positive.' She turned back to Andrew. 'Did you know that Sara was playing at Iford tonight?'

Her scrupulously casual, gimlet eyes were upon him.

'She may have mentioned it when she rang about her house check. I didn't think we'd want to bother.' He smiled insincerely. 'Oh, but I'm meant to be *positive*. So sorry.'

'Listen. "There was a Roman settlement at Iford and there are still traces of Roman occupation on top of the hills. Iford, under the name of Eford, is mentioned in the Domesday Book." The Domesday Book, Herve, that's this er . . . book, you see . . .' Sara was trying to interest him in bits out of the visitors' leaflet, anything to shut him up about how this provincial audience would not appreciate his work unless he talked to them about it first. He had been fretting all afternoon. She had said, feebly, that she was sure that what they would want would be to hear some of his music, and perhaps ask questions. But they will not understand it, they must learn a little first, Herve insisted, so first he would talk. Not for long, perhaps only for forty minutes. Sighing, she had abandoned any attempt to talk him out of it. In a little over a week of working with him every day she had failed to discover any instance, important or trivial, in which he could be talked into or out of anything. Trying to admire his firmness of purpose, she stabbed at the leaflet again with one finger.

'Listen, this is fascinating. You see, we're standing in what is essentially an Italian garden, only it's in the middle of Wiltshire. Well, not the middle, it's almost in Somerset. In fact,' she said, looking back at the map over the page, 'it's nearly, but not quite, in Avon. It's right at the join, imagine.'

She looked up and around her, rather desperately. They were standing at one of the highest points of Harold Peto's garden at Iford Manor. It was five o'clock on a glorious autumn afternoon. It was so beautiful, or rather it would be so beautiful if she were here with someone just marginally interested in anything other than his own worries. Could he not at least pretend? But, she remembered, that would mean compromise, the diluting of his concentration on matters of trivia, and that would be true agony for him. He was not like other people and she had no right to expect him to be.

'Peto. Harold Peto,' she went on. Herve was looking at her sadly. 'Peto the architect, a friend of Edward Lutyens. This was Peto's house, you see. He designed the garden. All the paths and plants, the statues, the follies – all this. The little . . . er . . . garden buildings . . .' As she tailed off inadequately Herve smiled politely, not having heard of either Peto or Lutyens and considering the idea of follies not worth the intellectual effort of grasping.

'The audience, they are arriving when? Ah yes, at seven, still two hours to wait,' he said. 'I will talk first, yes, and then we play. Please we will check again the sound equipment. The tape I have here, yes. All is fine, but we check again, please.'

He looked down at her with intense, nervous eyes and Sara

smiled. When he looked like that, so troubled, so brilliant, yet vulnerable enough to need her, funny things happened to her insides. She touched his arm.

'You're ready. Everything's ready. We've worked hard, we know what we're doing and there's nothing to worry about.' She turned and set off up the path towards the cloisters, then turned back. 'Oh, come on then. We'll check it all again if you like. We'll check it all again and then we'll give ourselves a little walk in the garden, to calm ourselves down, all right?'

He followed. 'You are interesting woman, Sara. Always so calm, as if nothing is important. How is this, that you can be calm, now? Okay, we check, afterwards we walk.'

But after the checking Herve declared himself in need of solitude. He needed a quiet time alone to prepare mentally, and perhaps run over some of the percussion sketches again. Sara had smiled, nodding seriously, supposing she must make allowances for his nerves. He was a composer first and a performer only second and by necessity, since much of his work was deeply unplayable by anyone other than himself and the people with whom he would work to create it. It would then be recorded, usually at its première, and by a combination of listening to the CD and industrious study of the 'score', other musicians, ambitious for their reputations as interpreters of contemporary repertoire, would labour to learn it. Sara, who had studied his form in detail, had observed that Herve's CV listed an impressive number of prestigious commissions and world premières, but fewer deuxièmes or subsequent performances. And she knew that the list of Petrescu pieces that had found a place in the repertoires of soloists, ensembles and orchestras, except those few who chose to totter on the cutting edge of late twentieth-century music, had tailed off into insignificance. Reserving judgment, she reflected that in his day Beethoven had been reviled by all but a few, and that Herve still sold respectable numbers of recordings to a young, mainly European, university-educated following. Her trouble was she just lacked vision. And if she lacked a certain conviction about the music itself, there were other things, as a professional, that she would have to contribute: at the very least she would work to convey to her audience the pleasure she felt in performing. She could share that, even if the music itself remained a little puzzling to them all.

She had done several of this sort of open rehearsal, where the musicians work at a piece of music in front of an audience, talking to one another, stopping, discussing, trying it another way, all in the cause of demystifying the process. Sometimes it worked, if the players knew one another well and if they could put into words what they were trying to achieve in their playing and when, despite its being a rehearsal, they never quite forgot the audience's presence. Then it could work, and the audience could leave stiff with new insights and feeling slightly superior, like the privileged observers they were. Sara thought that she would still rather have her audiences leave feeling at the very least uplifted and restored in spirit, on a good night touched by joy, even ecstasy, but Herve seemed to want them to leave edified and better informed. Perhaps she was rather shallow, but she would rather delight than educate. She had begun to slip into the habit of wondering if she was rather shallow.

Leaving Herve to his mental preparation, pacing the floor in Peto's miniature cloisters at the east side of the garden, in which chairs, lighting and sound equipment were already installed for the evening's event, Sara wandered out along the high gravel walk that ran from the cloisters to the little summerhouse, past the chestnut trees on the lawn. She looked out towards the south, beyond the garden's boundary to the river below, tumbling under the grey bridge. On the parapet of the bridge stood a life-sized statue of Britannia, gazing down into the water as if incongruously frozen in a mid-eighteenth century moment of personal desperation, in the very act of gathering enough courage to jump. In the field on the far side of the river the bowed heads of a few Jacob's sheep swung languidly in the grass.

The high ground of the garden where she stood overlooking the field reminded her of her garden at Medlar Cottage.

Here too at Iford, the garden rose up the hillside behind the house embracing it like a collar. In this garden, too, were peaceful walks, shining ponds, purple autumn crocuses in the grass and dwarf cyclamen under the trees. Here too, glancing up from any point in the garden, you looked out and felt the secret safety of a valley, hiding and holding all the low houses, narrow lanes and slow-moving animals within the diocese of its hills.

As she stared out, a sudden slight wind gusting out of the north shook the leaves of the trees behind her with a sound like thin applause. She turned her gaze from the river and the sheep in the water meadow back to the garden and the direction of the wind, the steep hanging wood behind her where, a few feet to her right, a staircase made of logs rose up and was lost in the quivering foliage. Her own garden had hidden corners, beloved secret places and paths which disappeared into thick shrubs, but here Sara could not be quite sure if these log steps were an invitation to venture into the high wood, or a malevolent dare. The steps might fade into a harmless nothing on the bark floor between the dark trees or they might bring her to a new delight, another stone figure, a pool graced with waterlilies. But they might lead her on, away, out of the garden, where she would be lost. She could not see to the top. As quickly as it had arisen the wind subsided, and Sara wandered further along the gravel walk while the returning silence came to her almost like a voice through the garden, making promises and whispering of beneficence. Ahead of her, the low evening sun behind Peto's ruined columns cast daggers of shadow across the stones.

This is Italy, whispered the voice. Look, there's the bronze of Romulus and Remus with the she-wolf, between the colonnades of the Great Terrace. Nearby is a Renaissance figure of a prophet, and there's a Roman sarcophagus. Here are two pink marble Verona columns. Everywhere, by the walks and ponds, on the edges of the steps and across the terraces, Sara's eyes were beguiled by roundels, reliefs, urns, columns and figures, all speaking of the faded, mellow Italy of vineyards and villas, poets and emperors. She was wilfully escaping Herve's digitalised, minimalist, slate and chrome world and finding a wistful, slightly guilty comfort in noticing how the first fallen leaves of autumn were drifting in little piles on the paved terrace outside the pretty, low-roofed *casita*. She knew that the *casita*, like the cloisters, was another illusory Edwardian folly of Peto's, which looked reverently back to Italy and the time of the Renaissance, when people had been in turn looking further back still, to the classical, ancient world. She recognised a dubious, exquisite sadness about it and wondered about the psychological health of all this backward-looking melancholy. Must Utopias lie always in the past? Then reality will always push us forward and further from them. Our yearnings, impotent and unrealisable, descend into rootless nostalgia.

She sighed and looked round in annoyance. Why did she have to think about everything? She had broken the spell for herself and now could only gawp, undecided as to whether the garden truly was breathing with some eternal pulse of antiquity, or just resonating emptily with a series of dead echoes, reaching back and back and back. Perhaps after all the whole place was just a piece of Edwardian sophistry, a conceit by a man who belonged in an uncomfortable age that was also panicked by technology and as heritage-hungry as this one. Now she could see that among the cypresses and acanthus stood huge, lusty bushes of English sage and lavender. The stone hounds guarding the colonnade were stiff-jawed and German. Standing in among the red-berried berberis was Mozart's birdcatcher, Papageno, striking a stage pose. The figure of a pudding-fed boy and the façade of the faux-Romanesque cloisters had been designed by an Englishman, Grinling Gibbons. She smiled. It was beautiful, certainly, and about as Italian as a Wall's Cornetto.

Andrew was glad, when Sara caught sight of him in the audience, that Valerie was beside him and was at that moment looking in her direction. There could be no mistaking the look of genuine surprise on Sara's face. It was certainly not the look of a lover catching sight of the beloved, a fact that slightly depressed him at the same time as it pleased him that it would further divert any suspicions of Valerie's.

The open square of the cloisters had been covered over with a tarpaulin, at Herve's insistence, to shield the electronic equipment from any sudden rain. Sara sat in the centre, nursing her cello. Behind her stretched lines of cable, amplifiers and speakers, two keyboards and a expanse of percussion kit. There was nothing defensive in her body language, her playing posture was too engrained in her for that, but with a small but intent audience in front and on both sides, and all Petrescu's ironmongery behind, Andrew thought that something about her seemed to fear encroachment.

The next hour and a half were the longest in Andrew's life. Within two minutes his mind began to dwell less on what was happening and more on the supper that would be served afterwards down in the main house. After ten minutes he became less preoccupied with food than with the idea of thumping Herve Petrescu. When he had been droning on for about twenty minutes in his irritating accent, Sara had interrupted to break his flow and venture a remark of her own.

'I think the point you've just made is a very interesting one, Herve. Shall we try and illustrate that with an example?' she said, smiling at him with what seemed unnecessarily intimate warmth. 'What I understand you're saying is that a series of different sounds, with no apparent relationship one to another . . .'

Then had followed a few exchanges, interspersed with short bursts of music played on the cello, before Sara had encouraged questions and comments from the audience. The audience took her invitation as an opportunity, en masse, to impersonate rocks. Nobody, not even Cosmo sitting almost hidden at the back, broke the silence. Andrew was surprised, since the one thing Cosmo could do was *talk* about composing, and with as little clarity as Herve. Then, just before it all became too embarrassing, Sara had introduced the 'work in progress'.

So far, she explained, Petrescu had come up with four 'notions' (as he called them) which, following a nod from her, he played with one finger on the electronic keyboard in an unvarying, computerised *wung*. As far as Andrew could tell they were four tunes. Short, incomplete and bad, but tunes. He shifted in his chair with impatience and crossed his arms as if to contain the annoyance that heaved in his chest. Was that what notions were then, bad tunes? He could tell that that was what Sara thought they were too, because when she played through each of them in turn on the cello he could see that she was practically bursting with the effort of imbuing them with some sort of attractiveness, trying to pull out the meagre melodic possibilities of each one.

Then the audience was treated to the sight of the 'creative partnership' at work. Petrescu added percussion noises which sounded like crockery being smashed inside a grand piano in a swimming pool, and more synthesiser sounds suggestive of the outbreak of interplanetary war, while Sara battled with her four notions, trying to evoke from the grudging material something more rewarding for her listeners than the sound of sobbing robots. Andrew recalled the treacly, generous, smiling tone of which Sara's cello was capable when she played it as she wanted to, and felt again like punching Herve on the nose. From time to time Herve stopped with some remark about the cello playing. Once Sara shifted her line up an octave and embellished the last three notes with a little vibrato and an entertaining flourish of her own, but Herve considered the result too redolent of melody, too 'cadenza-like'. Sara only said meekly that she did feel that the cello was a melodic instrument, before dropping back into the sludge of the lowest register.

At last when it was over there was the mingling to be got through. Herve was immediately surrounded by several of the audience, mainly women in dark polo necks and glasses. He, towering above his entourage, moved outside. Others lingered in the garden or wandered slowly over the grass in a languorous procession down to the main house. Adele and Phil were slipping unobtrusively from the rest of the group and making their way to a bench further down on the path that bordered the top of the rose garden, facing across the valley. Andrew knew that Adele did not always feel comfortable in a crowd. He decided it would not be helpful to follow. Valerie and Helene, with Jim a redundant chaperone, were fluttering around the edge of Herve and his shoal of pilot fish. Andrew saw that Sara had disappeared behind one of the pillars of the cloisters to put her cello away in its case. She re-emerged a moment later, glass of water in hand, and came over almost shyly, smiling at him. With Valerie just yards away, he was able only to smile back and felt he would burst with the effort of not wrapping his arms around her.

'Well, now, that was . . . *something*. I . . . I don't know how to put it,' he blurted desperately.

Sara conveyed with less than a blink of her eyes that she knew what he was saying and would collude. 'Indeed it was. And neither do I. Thanks for coming tonight – most unexpected, I must say. Oh, look, here's Valerie.'

Valerie, again in her navy sweater and snug trousers, was making her way over, feeling very Hermès next to Sara's strangely coloured jersey which she did not recognise as actually cashmere and by Rebecca Moses. She was prepared to be gracious. Sara Selkirk need not think that she was anything other than completely relaxed about her marriage; consequently her greeting was full of unnecessary, unamused laughter. 'Hi! *Hi!* Well done, *you!* How *do* you work all your fingers like that? Aren't you clever!'

Sara played the game back so adeptly that it did not occur to her to feel sickened by Valerie's encoded hostility. 'Hi yourself! What's all this I hear about an opera? Can't *wait* to see you on the stage! It's *so* exciting!'

'Oh I *know!* And I'm actually *secretary* of the thing. For my sins! And thank you for bringing us Cosmo. Herve Petrescu's protégé! I never imagined we'd be so honoured!'

Sara's face was conveying nothing. She nodded, allowing Valerie to wade on in the classic manner of the socially uneasy.

'We feel so lucky. Helene feels that it was somehow meant. I can see her point, can't you? These things sometimes are, aren't they. *I* think so, anyway! I mean the coincidence! Cosmo, who happens to be English, studying in Prague with Petrescu just at the very moment when you arrive? And you're there to ask Petrescu if he can suggest a young up-and-coming composer for our community opera! And Cosmo's just on the point of returning to London and it just so happens he has space in his diary that coincides with our dates. And the rest, as they say . . .'

'I'm not sure it was absolutely, *quite* like that,' Sara said, weakly, lapsing into sincerity. 'I'm afraid I'm not familiar with Cosmo's work. Do you like it?' She directed the question to Andrew.

'We're not familiar with it either,' Andrew said roughly, 'because he hasn't actually written any yet. That's partly why we're here. Helene obviously thinks it'll stir him up a bit to hear a new piece by the maestro. Can't see it, myself, but it's better than another bloody discussion.'

Valerie interposed, levelling and wifely. 'Oh, that's just you. Cosmo's an artist. Andrew doesn't understand artists. And then men just don't have the same sort of feeling for these things as women, do they? I'm always telling him he's in just the right job, aren't I, my darling? Nothing artistic about being a detective chief inspector, I'm afraid, just thugs and crooks and too many late shifts, isn't it, my darling?'

For one appalling moment Sara thought Valerie was actually going to ruffle Andrew's hair and call him a silly-billy. Andrew shifted his weight away from his wife, and without taking his eyes off Sara said, 'No, of course not. After all, police work is all about bopping people on the head with truncheons. We don't have to worry about how people's *minds* work, do we?'

Valerie squealed and biffed him on the arm. Then she

pretended suddenly to feel the cold. She gave a stage shiver and looked up at her husband. 'Ooh, isn't it getting autumnal! Let's all go down to the house.' She linked both her arms round Andrew's elbow and held on hard.

They were interrupted by a commotion over by the path above the rose garden. The sound of two or three voices raised in anger or protest was followed by the sound of a sharp slap, a wail and more shouting. Andrew turned in time to see Adele running away from the group round the bench. Helene was now turning her wrath on the slight figure of Phil. Jim was also there, placing an appeasing arm on her shoulder. His low voice could be heard breaking occasionally through her breathy, high-pitched outbursts. As Andrew, Valerie and Sara watched, Phil turned calmly from Helene's tirade and simply walked away.

'Looks as though Helene's big night out isn't going altogether swimmingly,' Andrew said.

'It's Adele. A tantrum, I should think,' Valerie said authoritatively. 'I'm going to see what's wrong. Helene probably needs help.' She detached herself from Andrew and strode off across the grass to where Jim was comforting Helene.

'That, I take it,' Sara murmured, her eyes on Valerie's back, 'is the opera group. I thought I picked them out in the audience. You have my sympathy.'

For much of the evening, in the longueurs during Herve's explanations, Sara had been studying her audience, matching people to Andrew's descriptions of the Circus Opera Group. The young woman who was Adele had been sitting between the good-looking Chinese and her mother Helene. The contrast with the mother was remarkable. The girl was small-boned and seemed slender enough to slip unnoticed out of sight, even out of existence, so little space did she occupy, while the mother was most sculpturally and three-dimensionally present. Oddly, there had been more of a shared atmosphere between Phil and Adele despite the differences in their features and colouring, as if they had both been fashioned in cool porcelain by the same long hands. Helene was more of a large bronze, beaten out in a hot, *fin-de-siècle* foundry. Even Adele's straight pale hair was somehow slim, while next to her the statuesque woman's hair-do seemed to be not just waving but shouting. Veering now towards late fifties' handsomeness rather than beauty, Helene had sat as if someone just out of sight might be painting her. She kept her big features composed, the eyebrows proud and the jaw taut, so as to be looking her best in that eventuality. The bearded, well-preserved man on her other side, who Sara now knew was Jim, had from time to time glanced at her. Perhaps Helene's state of perpetual readiness with her best face was for him. But the girl had seemed oblivious of anyone around her or of her own smooth-faced beauty, possibly entranced by the music or possibly mentally worlds away. In every sense except the merely physical she seemed simply to have been elsewhere.

'There go Cosmo and Poppy now,' Andrew said, nodding towards the two new figures hurrying across the garden to join the party now forming around the gesticulating Helene. 'Not a lot we can do, I don't think. They don't need us.' He gestured down the garden towards the house. 'Are you having supper? Shall I walk you down? You must be hungry – it sounded like hard work, all that.'

They stepped out of the light from the cloisters into the softer glow of the fading daylight on the path. Sara said nonchalantly, 'So you don't understand how a composer's mind works? Well, I can't say I do either, after less than two weeks with Herve. But I can't come out and say so, you must see that. And I'm still hoping it'll come right in the end and I'll get to like it. He is still working on it, after all. I've got to stay with it. You do understand, don't you?'

Just as Andrew was opening his mouth to say that of course he did, they were caught up by a rather breathless Valerie. She seized Andrew by the arm.

'Adele's been *smoking*,' she gasped. 'Can you believe it? Helene had no idea, apparently. She's furious. Furious with Phil. They were just sitting there with a cigarette when she found them. She started shouting and Adele went hysterical.'

'Oh, is that all?' Andrew asked. 'Well, I'm glad it wasn't anything serious.'

'How can you say that? Of course it's serious!'

'But how old is Adele?' Sara asked. 'Can't she smoke if she wants to? It's her health in the end, she's an adult, after all.'

Valerie tutted with impatience. 'That's not the point, is it? She's *autistic*. And Helene's furious because of what it'll do to her voice. After all Helene's done to get the opera going, really all for Adele's sake, and now she's *smoking*. Honestly, you can see her point, can't you?'

'Maybe Adele doesn't care about the opera,' Sara ventured quietly, 'as much as Helene does.'

Valerie did not consider this worth responding to. She turned to Andrew. 'Anyway, look, she's gone off somewhere. Her mother slapped her to stop her hysterics and she ran off, nobody saw where to. And it'll be dark soon. We've all got to help look for her.'

'But why can't she go off on her own if she wants to?' Sara interrupted.

'I told you, she's *autistic*,' Valerie said. 'Come on, Andrew.'

She tugged at Andrew's arm.

'You go off,' Sara said. 'I'd better go and mingle. Adele doesn't even know me. Although I still don't see why she can't be by herself if she feels like it.'

Andrew allowed himself to be reclaimed for the search and Sara stood watching until he had been drawn out of her sight beyond the trees on the east lawn. Helene and Jim, and one or two others newly enlisted, fanned out down the paths and across the lawns and terraces. There was no sound from the cloisters. Voices dropped away. Quiet slowly wrapped itself around hedges, urns and columns, stole over the long grass and came to rest under the trees. It was not yet dark but the sky was glowing with a heavy indigo, a deeper, northern note that did not belong in a summer sky. Even now as she breathed, Sara sensed something, mingled with the night scents of grass and lavender, that reminded her of cold water. A couple of months from now and up there would be a winter rug of inky sky, weighting the air with the smell of ice. Already the evening's silence lay over the garden like a fall of snow.

Valerie had been too busy fixing Andrew in her uxorious armlock to bother explaining much about what Adele's being autistic meant, but Sara knew a little anyway. It still did not seem to her either extreme or serious that the girl might simply have wanted to find some peaceful corner of the garden in which to be by herself, away from the fuss and that rather overbearing mother. If indeed she had managed to hide herself away somewhere, it seemed almost a cruelty that Helene, or someone like Valerie (all right, not *like* Valerie, actually Valerie) would be breaking in upon Adele, blaming her for getting lost, shattering the fragile quiet in which she might be sheltering like a feathery Victorian ornament under a glass dome. Although she had opted out of joining the search Sara wanted suddenly to be the one to find her, so that it would be done respectfully. Looking round the garden, offering all its secret but obvious twisting paths and its charmingly deliberate hiding places, its randomness seemed contrived. If I were Adele, she thought, I should want to get right out of here.

Without thinking further Sara descended the garden, taking the path down the side of the manor past the lily pool and the conservatory. To reach the lane outside, beyond the garden boundary, she had to pass in front of the house and she did so cautiously, knowing that she was expected inside. Even less than usual did the prospect of achieving the precarious balance of plate, glass and polite conversation appeal to her. Through the lighted ground-floor windows she could see the thickening assembly of people from the audience at their buffet supper, swaying gently. Standing taller than any of them was Herve, now holding forth and waving his fork hand with agile authority to a sea of upturned, mainly female faces, as if conducting their adoration. Guiltily she tiptoed off the gravel and on to the grass under the grove of wisteria in front of the house. Two minutes later she had slipped round the main gates and reached the bridge across the river on the other side of the lane.

In the fading light the river ran like liquefied pewter under the eye of Britannia. Sara stood alongside. To her left, back across the lane and beyond the roof of Iford Manor she could see occasional slow-moving figures in the garden, no doubt searching for Adele. Gliding along the top path above the rose garden where earlier, in the sunshine, she had stood looking out, was a figure she recognised as Phil. He was stopping now, pausing and standing alone, allowing himself to be slowed to utter stillness by the sight of the river, the field and the valley, just as she had done. Sara turned and looked directly upstream. On the left bank of the river, between the river itself and the lane which bordered Iford Manor, was a massive high-walled garden. The only entrance to it, as far as Sara could see, was a narrow door on the river side, invisible to anyone who was not either standing on the bridge as she was, or actually walking the river bank. Another of Peto's beloved larger than life-sized statues had been placed along the top of the wall just above the doorway. From even as far away as the bridge, Sara could see that it was a classical male nude who, reclining on one side with one knee raised, was propped on one elbow and leaned down directly over the lintel of the garden door under him. He was incongruous, perched up there; probably a Narcissus plundered by Peto from the reedy edge of some Italian villa's pool and stuck up on a brick wall in Wiltshire to contemplate, instead of his reflection, the balding head of a bow-legged gardener stooping through the doorway on his way to hoe the brassicas. Without being aware of deciding to do so, Sara found that she was making for the doorway, and that her pace had quickened.

She halted just inside the door, on the threshold of a different country. Here was the stronghold of a kingdom of rectangles, squares and straight paths. In this orderly garrison, sections of the parade ground were marked out by red bricks, set into the edges of the earth beds in rows of tight triangles. The pebbles of the gravel paths which intersected the borders seemed not merely raked but counted. Within the borders were ranks of vegetables which appeared to understand that no slacking would be tolerated. There would be none of that pansy stuff here: no meandering or drooping or growing all over the place that might be all very well over the wall there, in that Italian set-up. This was the vegetable army and they had better buck up their ideas. She set off along a path, inspecting the insignia of flower, leaf and pod, all present and correct. It was oddly restful, Sara thought, like being a tourist at a piece of absurd military showing-off. She remembered how a little over a month ago she had taken a baking August afternoon off and gone up to the Presidential Palace overlooking Prague to see the changing of the guard. It had been hilarious in the most relaxing way, scores of men tightly dressed and stamping, stopping, stamping, with hundredweights of weaponry attached to them, bursting with the heat and precision and vanity of it all, while she had wafted about in white muslin eating ice-cream. She had now walked down the whole of one side of the garden and at the corner, just past a row of bean tripods of equilateral perfection, she turned the right angle to continue along the second side. Ahead, exactly halfway down the path in front of her, was a bench set back against the wall. It faced down another path directly to the very centre of the garden. Exactly in the middle of the bench sat Adele, gazing straight ahead. She held upright between one thumb and three fingers a cigarette which had burned to the tip.

Sara approached slowly and quietly.

'May I sit down?'

Without turning Adele said, with a distrust that reminded Sara of someone speaking into a microphone for the first time, 'May I sit down? Yes.'

Adele continued her gaze down the path and began to sing, so faintly and obviously to herself alone that Sara did not even smile but half turned and listened, hearing with surprise how clean, constant and true was the soft tone that emerged from Adele's barely open lips. But what was completely astonishing was that she was singing, over and over again, all four of Herve's musical notions. She sang them smoothly and unhesitatingly, despite their being atonal and unmelodic, and was also singing exactly the same notes, albeit two octaves higher, that she had heard played on the cello. Over and over again they came, no louder than a hum, but perfectly remembered and faithfully reproduced as if from some unerring machine. The voice was sailing through the unhelpful, alien-sounding intervals like a synthesiser, having clearly no need of the usual melodic reference points of western 'tunes', the implied modulations to related keys or the eventual return to the tonic key. Then she stopped. Before Sara could fill the pause with any remark, and she could think of none that would not be inadequate, the gentle sound began again. This time it was different. Another four little tunes, each one different, all a little strange but somehow easier on the ear than Herve's, and of about the same length. They came again and again, and still Sara could not say anything that would not sound patronising, so matter-of-fact was Adele's delivery, so *un*performance-like. As the singing went on Sara followed Adele's gaze down the central path and noticed that the planting here was completely symmetrical. Nearest the edges of the path were corresponding rows of parsley. Next to them on each side was a row of flat-leafed plants which might have been sorrel. Next on both sides was a wide strip of sieved earth where something had already cropped and every trace of it had been removed. Clearly, no late straggling harvests were permitted here. Further out were the next taller rows of peas which created the soft walls of a tunnel of symmetry which ran down to the point where four paths met in the dead centre of the square garden. Beyond the centre the path continued straight down to the opposite wall where in shadow, facing the one they were sitting on, stood an identical bench. It was weirdly empty, Sara thought, as if their absence from it, because they were looking at it from this one, created an asymmetrical jar on the sensibilities. By means of some metaphysical conceit there should lie, at the end of this knot garden of correspondences, the paradox of beholding yourself.

Just then a movement caught her eye. As Adele's murmuring went on, a peacock strutted into the intersection of the paths in the last of the light. The singing dropped to a sweet whimper which would have sounded like a charm had not the voice continued to inflect mechanically, communicating neither humanity nor magic. But suddenly magic happened. The peacock turned towards them and stopped. Up swept the blue-green arc of its tail, its light spraying the air with fire as the sun caught the jewels in the half circle of feathered eyes. Adele gasped. The peacock gave a little preening shiver with a sound like a breeze in tall grass. It moved round and a little closer. Now it stood, as if it knew, exactly at the intersection of the paths, in the dead centre of the whole garden. It must have been by chance that it stopped there, so that the mean, black eyes in the crowned head, mantled by the sapphire arch of shot silk feathers, stared back down the broad ribbon of path with its flanking green guard of honour, as if from their own dominion of perfect symmetry. But perhaps, Sara thought, glancing at her, it was not chance at all but some entreaty in Adele's voice or eyes which had brought it and held it here, while she stared back, an enrapt courtier, with a look on her face of pure happiness.

Chapter Twelve

By next morning Jim was still feeling wronged and indignant but, as in all such instances, he felt it privately. He clattered quietly down his spiral stairs into the basement kitchen, turned on Radio 4 and made the usual efficient breakfast of coffee and toast with Marmite. No smear of Marmite left in the butter, no thumping of the kettle, it wasn't his way. Were Helene to telephone at that moment he would pick up the phone and say, 'Helene, my dear, how are you? All present and correct? I hope Adele's better now? My dear, I feel I must make amends. I do assure you I meant no harm.'

Mildly, he considered that Helene would probably believe him, but would believe also that her forgiveness would not be worth the having unless she made him work for it a little. So she would say, 'Well, Jim, I'm getting over it of course, as I must. As I always do. But I'm going to be frank with you and say it has been a blow. Well, a double blow: first to find Adele with cigarettes and then to find out that it was you, Jim, who started her on the dangerous habit. A bitter blow, dear.' If she telephoned.

He would claim, again mildly, as he had tried to do last night for most of the journey home in the minibus, that he had simply left some cigarettes in his workshop one day and come down in the morning to the smell of burning and the sight of Adele puffing on one. Not that it had been altogether, absolutely, quite like that. But it was so long ago now that even

Adele had probably forgotten all about it. He had given her her first cigarette just after the little bit of fun they'd been having. He'd been having, rather, and only up to a point. And only now and then, and now not at all, because she really was on the skinny side and besides, he liked to feel a woman respond under him, not just stare up at him while he got on with it. The fun of it had dwindled pretty rapidly. It was the mother he wanted, really. He supposed it was just that Adele had been there, blonde, compliant and not unwilling, foisted on him by Helene, in fact, soon after Helene had made it clear that she was not looking for a relationship of that sort herself. So perhaps it had been revenge of a kind, but he was a healthy man and the girl hadn't come to any harm, he'd seen to that. And she was what, twenty-five now, so nineteen the first time, soon after she'd come home to live after her residential school. Hardly a child.

And now all this fuss about a few cigarettes! He smirked at the thought of what Helene would say if she knew that Adele's first cigarettes had actually been post-coital ones. She was altogether too protective. Of course he had not said as much last night, nor had he spelled out that he had every intention of continuing to leave his packet lying around so that Adele could carry on helping herself to one every morning as soon as she arrived.

'Dammit, Helene, just an old navy habit, I can't get down past ten a day. And don't think I've turned her into a chain smoker; she never had more than one a day. Just a bit of harmless copying, you know. 'Spect she felt grown-up,' he had said. He was quite sure she did not even smoke them properly; she seemed just to like to hold one and flick the ash. The others in the minibus had backed him up, too, while Adele herself had sat next to Phil at the back, staring out of the window and taking no interest. She had no grasp of how much others did for her. He would be tempted to point all this out, should Helene telephone. But she did not telephone. Jim poured his second cup of coffee.

Adele could get on today with that French chandelier of

Mrs Dyson's. If he was paying her to be in the workshop Wednesdays, Thursdays and Fridays, ten till four, he might as well get some work out of her. The rigid patterns and time-tables that ruled Adele's life helped him too, he acknowledged, and what had started as a favour to her mother had developed a momentum of its own. Business had never been so good. The shop's performance was still a little modest but steadier now than in all his twelve years of ownership. Because Adele got through so much work in the basement here, he could be at the shop more regularly. He was doing well, even now at the end of the season when he could not rely on Americans paying silly prices for fairly ordinary Clarice Cliff and damaged Staffordshire. If he bought cleverly at the ceramics and glass auction in Salisbury on Friday he could expect an excellent Christmas. Venetian glass necklaces, a lamp or two, wineglasses in pairs, those should go well. But it was the restoration side that was making the difference.

He would never forget the occasion, so distressing and embarrassing had it been. Sipping his coffee at the kitchen table, his mind went back to March, six years ago. The daffodils had been in flower under the trees in the Circus and the sun shining when he had set off with Helene on his arm and Adele doing her shuffle walk in front. Helene had worn gloves and what she called a spring hat. He had been rightly proud of the work he had put into that chandelier. It had occupied the whole workshop for weeks. Every single one of its thousands of crystals had been taken off, cleaned in soapy water and put back in its place among hundreds of loops and swags of glittering icicles. The day before he had watched as the whole wondrous thing was reattached to its ceiling chains and swung up gently into place above the tables in the Pump Room. A proud moment for an ex-navy, self-taught antique ceramics and glass restorer. So it was to be a celebration, treating Helene to tea and showing it to her. Helene loved the Pump Room teas, so it should have been perfect. But Adele, back from school and now living permanently with Helene, had to come too, of course.

As soon as they got to their table she had become distressed. Staring up at the chandelier, she had whimpered like an animal and stretched out her arms as if she were trying to reach it. Then she had begun to screech, and then she climbed up on the table to get nearer. Flowers, vase, cutlery and the beautiful white cloth all ended up on the floor. People stared. The screeching had grown louder and she had proved quite handy with her fists when he had tried to get her down. Eventually, with her hat knocked sideways, Helene had got her arms right round her – it was fortunate she was so much bigger than Adele – and got her out of the place. She had calmed down eventually in the Ladies, away from the chandelier.

One little crystal. One little crystal facing the wrong way, just one that he had put back the wrong way round during the reassembly. Adele had been aware of it immediately because, as Helene later explained, Adele had an extraordinary eye for anything symmetrical, but let it be wrong in any detail and she would spot it at once and become very upset.

He didn't understand it, the autism. It certainly brought more problems with it than benefits, but Adele's ability to tell if the symmetry of an object or pattern were disturbed was remarkable, he could see that. And it was an ability for which Helene, that day, had suddenly seen a practical application. Adele's thing with the chandeliers suddenly became what Helene termed 'such a blessing' because dear Jim had been persuaded (coerced rather) to employ her as an assistant in the workshop.

The restoration side of Jim's weedy antiques business grew buoyant. And he realised that, while paying Adele less than the rate for the job, he could still glow in the warmth of Helene's gratitude for the bit of extra time to herself, she being too genteel to refer specifically to the poor money. Adele herself, as far as anyone could tell, seemed to like going out to work even though it was only seven doors along in the Circus. She seemed to like the dismantling and cleaning of the crystals, manipulating the shiny pieces and reassembling them effortlessly from her perfect recall of their arrangement.

And she had seemed, if not to like, then not to mind Jim's skirmishes under her clothes and his short-lived pumpings between her legs on the workshop couch, and also neither to like it nor mind when they ceased. It seemed that on Wednesdays, Thursdays and Fridays from ten until four Adele entered a world that was tolerably understandable and within her control.

But still, this morning, he was a little indignant. After all, Phil smoked too and it was one of his Adele had been lighting when Helene burst in on everything. Still less was it Jim's fault that Adele had run off and got lost, and in any case he did not see that the frenzied search for her had been necessary. The woman who had been playing the cello had come across her, apparently. Then Phil had turned up after some lucky guess about where she'd gone, and the three of them had taken a stroll round the vegetable garden and sauntered back as calm as you please. Adele had not been upset in the least.

Recalling how he, wearing contrition like the imprint of a hand on a slapped face, had let Helene go on at him all the way home about how Adele was a constant worry to her and how she had thought he understood, Jim felt a Marmitey burp of anger. My God, did he understand. He understood that his courtship of Helene was a campaign that he would win only by attrition, as long as Adele stood in the path of victory. He remembered with strictly private resentment his first whispered suggestion that he and Helene might enjoy more 'intimacy', late one evening, after endless shared late suppers à deux. All evening she had been particularly open and relaxed, even affectionate, inviting. She had been warm, ample, delicious, at least in prospect, but at the suggestion of bed she had been suddenly overcome with self-denial. There was Adele to consider. 'But she's been upstairs asleep for three hours!' Jim had almost squawked, but neither that evening nor subsequently had Helene changed her mind.

He was probably an old-fashioned fool, but he had not given up hope that his cheerful loyalty, not to mention his tolerance of Adele, would eventually wear her down. After all, he was well preserved and straight-backed, still had plenty of hair and looked better than many in a camel lambswool polo neck and a tweed jacket. Only sometimes, on days like today, he wondered how much longer Adele was going to provide Helene with an excuse to keep him at a distance. Lately, he had begun to wonder if, at sixty-two, he was perhaps a little long in the tooth to be trusting so much to patience, persistence and the allure of Austin Reed.

He carried his breakfast dishes to the sink and paused, looking up through the low window. He could not see much, of course, just the wall and dustbin, the iron steps in front leading up from the area to the pavement and the two doors on the left at right angles to his window, one leading straight into his kitchen, the other one on the far side leading down the passage to the workshop at the back. He had taken in his pelargoniums already and the bare area was bleakened by their absence. Helene's advice, some weeks ago, had been to cheer it up with something evergreen, a myrtle or a miniature bay. She had even promised him a cutting of something. If he got a pot ready with compost and put it where she might notice it walking past, it might jog her memory. He had always been sentimental about flowers. It would be a particular joy to grow something she had given him, to water and feed it and keep the snails and the frost off it. He did not think she had said anything about its being a flowering plant, but somehow he could not imagine its not being. From Helene's little cutting he would grow a wondrous flowering bush and amaze her. People passing on the open-top buses would gape at it, forgetting architecture. He would nurture such blooms for her: huge, pollen-laden, jungle-hued, soft, petal-dripping blossoms like babies' heads in Lalique bonnets. He found himself hoping that she would ring so that with understanding words he could bathe her in his loyal adoration. So like dear Helene to offer him a cutting. She was so giving.

Sara had slept badly. At half past eight she woke up and debated whether to lie in bed a bit longer and then slop around in a bathrobe eating too many croissants, or to get up now, pull on her running kit and take herself off round the lanes for a few miles. Each felt like a kind of punishment, depending on which side of her nature – the infantile or the grown-up – was being consulted. Her baby voice complained that on top of her tiredness, she felt unloved and confused. She was being made to do things she didn't want to do (Herve) and not being allowed to do things that she did (Andrew). She was not in control; a state which left her petulant and inclined towards pleasure-seeking of a mildly self-destructive kind.

Alternatively she could summon her inner adult who ceded that all right, she was indeed tired and felt unloved and confused. Did that make her a victim? Would four croissants leave her feeling any more in control, or better able to withstand this unfamiliar feeling of not getting precisely what she wanted with either of these two men who, in different ways but equally irritatingly, exerted such power over her wellbeing? All right, four miles that she did not feel quite up to might not either, but she put on her running clothes and set off from the front door of Medlar Cottage before her Poor Me voice could raise a protest.

For the first few moments' trotting along the lane which ran below Medlar Cottage and through the valley Sara's body yelled for its bathrobe and croissants. She ignored it. She could just see across the top of the hedgerow towards the farms and meadows on the far side. There was a dank ground mist on the lower reaches of the valley this morning, all but hiding the straggly line of willows which bordered the stream at the bottom. Higher up, the six lime trees stood out like giant golden bushes, the black trunks masked in mist. In the fields around, other trees, a stone barn and a little copse where cattle had gathered, appeared through the mist like smudges done in faint pencil on foggy, soft paper, floating worlds as if from a Japanese drawing of a damp English morning. As she ran, Phil came to mind although he was, she knew, not Japanese but Chinese. Yet talking with Phil, she imagined, would be halting and difficult, in its own way like one of those drawings:

tottering from tiny floating world to floating world of speech, crossing the deep mists of silence in between by means of increasingly frail and desperate bridges of conversation. It was easier to establish a little duet of smiles and nods and venture no further. She supposed it was lazy but she didn't care.

Her body warming in the steady rhythm of her running, Sara's mind slipped into an easeful unthinking of the kind usually felt just before sleep. Past Radford Farm, Ivan's gun-dog kennels and Upper Northend Farm and still she was conscious only of the regular footfall of running, her plodding like the therapeutic push of kneading dough or the drubbing of clothes against a washboard. After half a mile she took the right-hand fork down to Oakford Farm and across to Marshfield on the other side of the valley, where the lane fell steeply past Wessex Water's high-fenced brick building, like a dolls' penitentiary, on the left. At the bottom of the hill, on the stone bridge over the stream, she stopped, flapping her arms and running on the spot. Not pausing to observe how rapidly the clear brown water spilled under the bridge after nearly two weeks of rain, she set off again, feeling now her body and mind wake up together with an exhilarating burst of energy as if an unexpected wave of laughter from somewhere inside her was gathering into a huge, tidal roll.

The energy surge liberated not just euphoria but also her not exactly righteous anger. How had she got into this state? Where was her independence? Where was her *mind*? While it had been somehow sidetracked or duped, first by Herve's wondrous reputation and then by Andrew's wondrous body she had almost, *almost* allowed herself to be quite grossly imposed upon. How had she been so blind and weak as not to recognise at once Herve's music for the facile, pretentious stuff it was, and say so? And just when had she allowed herself to become so weak and needful that she had almost overlooked the fact that Andrew was a married police officer?

She jogged on for another mile, and then turned back for home. By the time Medlar Cottage came into sight she felt restored to herself, the purity of her indignation substituting admirably for the clarity that was still absent from her mind. She would see this bloody horrible music through to its première in December, because she had to, but after that she would never play it again. She bloody well would not record it next year, as Robin and Herve were intending. And as for Andrew, well, she would not be lured into taking an interest in him or in his horrible cases, because that tedious dead spinster in Camden Crescent was not her responsibility. She did not care about the animal rights lunatic who had killed her. She didn't need anyone. Bloody Imogen Bevan. Bloody Herve. Bloody Robin. Bloody Andrew. Bloody men.

There was a message from Herve on the machine and she played it with a sneer. In his very personal brand of imperious wheedling, Herve asked her to ring him back without delay. He had to speak to her with 'very urgency' about last night's performance. There was so much that had not been right, so very, very much on which she had to be corrected, and with all speed.

She looked at her watch. It was nearly half past nine. He would be waiting for her to ring him back, unable to settle to work. She sighed happily and went upstairs to take a long, long bath, and to dress very, very slowly. Then, after some coffee which she most certainly would not rush, she might call him.

But after her coffee Sara decided that painting her toenails should take priority over returning Herve's call. As she was stretching out on the sofa in the music room with one leg raised straight in front of her to assess the effect of Prussian blue on the toes of one long tanned foot, the telephone rang again. Turning the foot this way and that, wondering about a second coat, she listened as Herve began to record his second agonised message. Abandoning her resolve to let him suffer, she sighed, reached behind her for the telephone and lifted the receiver. Power was making her magnanimous, perhaps also just a little devious. As Herve embarked on a detailed analysis of last night's shortcomings, she crooked the receiver under her chin, lay back, bent her other leg balletically to rest the foot on the other thigh and began, with the delicacy of a miniaturist, to paint her toenails. Smiling cruelly, she pretended she was taking notes.

'Hmm, that's a good point, Herve, hold on, I'm just getting that down . . .' she lied, stroking the brush over a toenail. 'Yes, yes. Just a minute.'

She had applied two coats to each foot and let them dry by the time he had finished. Just as she had concluded the last round of goodbyes and pressed the off button on the phone, she was startled by a deep laugh behind her. She turned round to see Andrew grinning in the doorway, his arms folded.

'My God, how long have you been there?' she gasped. 'You could have knocked.'

'You are a perfidious, unprincipled so-and-so,' Andrew said pleasantly, walking into the room. 'I did knock,' he said, still smiling, and flopping into an armchair. 'Very softly. Then I thought you might turn me away from the doorstep, and I wasn't having that. So I just came in. I could hear you were on the phone. Couldn't help overhearing. You've almost made me feel sorry for the man. As I was saying, you are a perfidious, unprin—'

'I know,' Sara said languidly, turning on to her side to look at him. 'But one uses what weapons one must.'

He stared back at her, appreciative of the long curve of her body that she was offering to him.

'I'm delighted to see you, but I wasn't expecting you. Why are you here?'

Andrew's face grew serious and he sighed, not sure how to begin. Instead of speaking, he stood up, crossed the room and crouched down beside her. He took hold of her face in both of his hands.

'Not to play the cello, for one thing. Or to apologise. I'm sick of apologising to you. You can tell me to go if you want. Only don't.' Sara opened her mouth to speak but he stopped her. 'I couldn't stand seeing you like that last night. So separate. Separate from *me*. I'm here because I can't stand it any longer.' His hands left her face and travelled down her shoulders, across her breasts and under her arms. Sara knew there was no need now for her to say anything at all. She was allowing him to raise her from the sofa. She did not take her eyes from his face.

'I just walked out of the office. I'm here because I'm sick of apologising when all we need to do to make things better is to make love,' he said. 'I need to. So do you, don't you? Now.' Sara's only answer was to lean forward, slide her arms round his neck and plant her mouth over his. She pushed her tongue between his lips, not gently.

'Oh, Jesus,' Andrew breathed, pulling away. His hand travelled down and started fumbling in the region of his groin. Sara, not understanding, reached to help him. He groaned. 'No, wait, don't. We can't. It's my phone. The fucking mobile.' He eased himself on to his feet, pulled out the phone, took a deep, laboured breath and answered. Sara had never seen him look so angry. 'Yes, *what*? That you, Bridger? What the hell do you want?'

She sighed, got up and walked over to the French window, opened it and stepped out barefoot on to the grass. She hesitated and turned. Andrew was still snapping impatiently at Bridger. 'Yes? So? So why aren't you just getting on with it? Yes, of course just get on and interview them, man! What?'

This was what it would always be like with Andrew. A ringing telephone would mean not just a sudden interruption, bad enough in itself, but also, from the second it rang, that she would no longer be the centre of his attention. She was no longer even important, while suddenly a corpse, a PM report, a new piece of evidence, would be. Two minutes later and she might have been lying naked. How would she have felt if he had got up and left her then? To be so abandoned, and then truly abandoned, would be intolerable. She wondered how often it had happened like that to Valerie. The ground was cold and, looking down, she saw that she would be unable to walk anywhere without getting her feet very wet and probably stepping on worm casts. Still, it seemed a more appetising option than returning to the house and listening understandingly to Andrew's excuses for having to leave. Sighing, she made off across the grass.

Part Two

Rose leaves, when the rose is dead,
Are heap'd for the beloved's bed

Chapter Thirteen

The next day, Valerie rang.

'Yes, this Saturday. Could you possibly? It's short notice, I know,' she said. 'But we've got a bit of a crisis. Andrew's hurt his back. But we can't possibly hold everything up just for him, you see?'

'How? What's happened?' She did her best to keep any hint of fear for him out of her voice. 'What's he done?'

Valerie responded in the tone of one woman talking to another when both know how ridiculous men are. 'Oh, you know, just being *ridiculous*. He came back yesterday in the most appalling temper. You know how they get. Goes storming out to play squash. He hasn't played for months so he was asking for it. Wrenched something and broke the racquet. He can hardly move now, let alone play the cello. So we're in a complete crisis situation. That's why I'm getting a few people round. Herve's coming.'

Sara was entirely at sea. What crisis? And why should it suddenly precipitate a little dinner party? But she felt that to venture further in pursuit of an explanation might be dangerous. It would be dangerous even to express too much interest.

'Right, well, er, yes, I think I can come. If Herve's going, then I suppose I don't need to keep Saturday evening free to rehearse. So thank you, I'd love to come.'

Difficult. What to wear to supper as the guest of your

incapacitated, almost-lover and his unsuspecting (please God), highly organising, highly strung, high-heeled wife, not forgetting the presence of the most self-obsessed charlatan in the music business for whom you have developed a distaste that amounts almost to an allergy? How to look sexy, unthreatening and unreachable all at once?

To Sara's initial relief, when she arrived in Valerie's 'lounge' on Saturday evening in a loose trouser suit of maroon silk and a pair of Manolo Blahnik shoes more like weapons than footwear, she saw that the toxic concentration of the evening was diluted by the presence of other guests. Poppy, Helene and Jim, along with nibbles and white wine, were introduced by Valerie who was exercising hostessy control from the vantage point of three-inch heels. Sara's were three and a half. Andrew watched in hideous, wine-dulled pain from a very straight-backed chair as the two women stepped and counter-stepped the offering and accepting of introductions, glasses, pretzels and a place to sit, in a carpeted but unmistakable flamenco of mutual disdain.

'And no Cosmo, alas. He's working. And no Herve, after all,' Valerie cooed through bared teeth. 'Not even when he knew you were coming. He's had to cry off with a headache.'

'What a shame,' Sara said smoothly, addressing the room. 'How very disappointing.'

'It is, isn't it? I do hope it's no more than a headache,' Helene said from the depths of the sofa. 'He is obviously a brilliant, sensitive man. I could see that at once when I met him at Iford. We just clicked, he and I. You are so lucky to be working with him. What a privilege.'

Jim, sitting beside her, opened his mouth and then closed it, looking glum.

Perhaps because their feet were hidden, it got better at the table. Sara, such was her praise to Valerie, seemed genuinely ignorant of the Marks & Spencer provenance of most of the dolled-up food. Valerie lightened up in the glow of her success in pulling the wool over the cosmopolitan sophisticate's eyes with little more than a sprinkling of ready-washed coriander leaves. But it was Jim who led on the food eulogies, paying soft-voiced compliments to Valerie and Helene (because Helene was a wonderful hostess, too) in which they both basked. It was, if deliberate, very skilful, Sara thought. Although he was not a large man he gave an impression of ageless solidity which, together with the sort of kind brown eyes which so often go with beards, exuded a quiet, approving warmth a bit like a human Aga. He even managed to include Poppy, who grew smiley and pink in his attention and chattered in reply to his compliments.

'Now, tell me, what would one call this marvellous colour you're wearing?'

'This? This top? Oh, I suppose it's, well, magenta or something. I made it, actually, just out of a remnant.'

'How skilled you are! Clever with your needle *and* a stage manager *and* practically a nurse. Why, we have Renaissance Woman here. What's your secret, dear lady?'

'Oh, I'm not! I've just always been more practical than brainy. I take after my mother for dressmaking and my dad for the technical things. I used to help him and he taught me a lot. I pick things up quickly, that's all. And I've got very good hands.'

'And what sort of line is your father in?' Coming from Jim, this was probably not an attempt to place her socially, but Poppy stalled. Sara saw one panicked blink of her eyes. 'He's a . . . a heating engineer.' Evidently she had spent too long with Cosmo, the progeny of a musicologist and a maths teacher as she had gathered from Andrew, to admit that Dad was a plumber.

'Another engineer! I was an engineer myself. Naval engineering was my line. Left the navy over ten years ago, they booted all us old fellas out early, you know.'

Bless him, thought Sara, smiling at Andrew. Andrew was silently blessing him too, because his skilful warming of the other women round the table left him free to look at Sara almost as much as he wanted to.

'Yes, do tell us how you manage to do it all, Poppy,' Valerie said, lining up the reply she wanted ('Oh, well, because I haven't got three children!') so that Andrew should be reminded of how much Valerie managed practically single-handed.

'Oh, well, because I get a lot done on my working nights,' Poppy offered instead. 'It's usually quite quiet once we've turned the residents. In fact, I get all our washing and ironing done because Jean lets me slip off and use the machines, and then I let her off later for a little sleep. That saves me hours in the daytime.' Valerie's face had grown glassy. Poppy, without quite knowing how she had disappointed, quickly added, 'Gosh, this is a lovely pud. I could never make lemon mousse. It's so . . . *lemony*.'

When the topic of what they were eating had been exhausted, and after Helene had sighed that Herve would have so loved the occasion and proposed a toast to absent friends, a little social panic began to shimmer over the polyester-clad table. Someone said something nice about Valerie's tight little arrangement of coordinating dried flowers in its centre. What next? Helene looked at Poppy, then Valerie. All three nodded.

'Now, I think, don't you?'

Valerie nodded again and glanced defiantly at Andrew. Then she turned to Sara.

'Sara, we hope you won't mind us asking you a little favour. Something you – only you – could do for us.'

'*Little* favour? I can't allow this. I said it was out of the question. Valerie, don't do this.' Andrew's voice was barely raised, but his fury was obvious.

Valerie raised both hands. 'No, I will be heard. She can always say no, can't she?'

As she turned her head away, Andrew settled on Sara a look of enraged powerlessness more than tinged with lust. It was rather how he had looked when Bridger's call had come. She smiled.

'Of course I can,' she said, trying to answer his look without seeming to. 'Don't worry, I don't mind. What is it, then?'

Helene was to be the chief petitioner. She pursed up her lips and clasped her hands in a gesture of supplication.

'Only you can do it.'

Sara looked at her in amusement.

'And it'd be just tremendous if you would,' put in Poppy.

'Only you,' Helene went on. 'Valerie's quite right. She agrees with me, and so does Poppy, and Jim sees it that way, too, don't you, dear? And Herve would too, if he were here. You see, with poor, dear Andrew laid up, and we don't know how long for, the whole project's in jeopardy.'

Helene, Poppy and Valerie all leaned seriously across the table, a War Cabinet of three. Jim waited benignly in the hope of being included again, while Andrew, whose eyes were on the ceiling, was wishing he were elsewhere. Anywhere, as long as it was with Sara.

'Because it's such a key role. Andrew's cello part. It's just crucial in every scene. We can't rehearse any of the singers without it.'

Sara tried to embrace the seriousness of the matter. 'Can't they rehearse with just piano and put the cello in later?'

'No, no,' Helene gasped. 'It's much too integral. You can't just fill in on piano. The piano, cello and voice, they're in every sense a trio,' she breathed. 'That's Cosmo's view, too. He'd be glad to explain it to you himself only he's rehearsing Adele and Phil this evening, and very kindly entrusted me with the task. And I think dear Herve would bear us out, if he were here. Musically speaking.'

'I see,' Sara said, not seeing.

'It wouldn't be very much playing,' Helene was saying, 'and of course nothing difficult, not for you. So if you could just stand in at rehearsals for Andrew, until he's better, well, you can see what it would mean to us . . .'

'And what with all the time you've given Andrew in the past, we know you're the *last* person to be above working with amateurs,' Valerie said slyly.

'Sara, I want you to know I had nothing to do with this,' broke in Andrew.

'Oh, but I'd be delighted,' Sara said.

'*What?*'

'I'd love to help. I'd enjoy the change. And by the time you're fit again, I'll know the music, so it'll be easy to help you with it. Though I expect we might need to spend a bit of time on it, just to get to grips with it, don't you? To get you fit for performance.' She managed, only just, to say it without glittering too obviously in Andrew's direction.

'Bravo!' cried Helene, clapping her hands.

'Oh, tremendous!' breathed Poppy.

'Wonderful,' said Valerie. 'Coffee, everyone?'

When Valerie brought coffee into the sitting room nearly half an hour later she was carrying a tea towel, signalling that as the main business of the evening had been accomplished there was clearly no reason to detain anyone too long or to delay starting on the clearing up. Andrew promptly offered brandy and raised himself slowly to his feet.

Jim cleared his throat, bartering a new topic of conversation in exchange for his glass of Armagnac.

'So, Andrew, the criminal fraternity making hay in your absence?'

He had not meant to sound flippant, but he was earnestly seeking a way out of music talk and what seemed to him Helene's unduly frequent allusions to Herve.

'Oh, they're keeping us busy,' Andrew said. 'I'm keeping tabs on things from here until I'm more mobile. We specially want to get this letter-bomb case wound up, but it's proving to be a tricky one.'

'What's the latest?'

'Well, the good news is it's certainly not part of a campaign. We're getting good cooperation from the animal righters, and we're quite confident it doesn't fit into any big plans of theirs, though we haven't ruled out a connection. In fact' – Andrew shot a look to Sara – 'on Wednesday four of them turned up at Manvers Street, volunteering themselves for questioning. Quite an interesting bunch, our main suspect spent the summer with them. They claim not to have seen him since Glastonbury. So we haven't got him yet, and these associates of his don't seem to know his other haunts. And we'll have to think about stepping down the enquiry soon. That's the way it goes with these things: if there are no new leads you keep it open, of course, but you have to step things down. There isn't the manpower to keep lots of people on it indefinitely.'

Andrew was saying nothing confidential. Sara almost opened her mouth to say, 'I still think you should—' But what? What did she think he should be doing instead? As Andrew had pointed out to her, there was no other logical line of enquiry and her vague feelings about the case were no use to him. She wanted to convey how sorry she was about Wednesday, that perhaps next time . . . But he would not look at her. Watching him as he spoke to Jim and longing to reach out and touch him, she could see in his worried but so kissable face all the despondency and frustration that were missing from the official version.

'An isolated incident, then?' Jim was asking. 'Not part of a campaign?'

'Oh, definitely just an isolated incident,' Andrew replied. His eyes were now on Sara, almost burning her. 'Ill thought-out, and badly bungled. The attempt won't be repeated.'

Chapter Fourteen

Cosmo could hardly stand it. He had never been handed so much on a plate in his life, at least never so much of what he wanted. She didn't exactly volunteer, but nor was she unwilling. She did only what she wanted to and luckily for him, she also wanted to sing. *Can you give me a trill, like this? On these two notes, a top A and B flat? Yes, that's it, lovely, lovely.* She simply didn't mind what he asked. She would just do it, then stare at him patiently, wanting his next instruction, only a little less eager than a spaniel waiting for him to throw a stick. That was it. It was her compliance that was almost off-putting. As a child Cosmo had learned to express his wants to his elderly parents by means of carefully veiled wheedling. Adele's naked, unconcealed wish to please was almost embarrassing next to his own perfected indirectness.

But then, he told himself, it must please her to please him or she simply would not do it, any of it. *Oh, yes. Lovely Adele, oh yes, that's lovely.* Still, it made him feel almost awkward, her being quite so pliable in her uninterested way, like a good-natured tart. He knew himself capable of exploiting her to an almost reprehensible degree although there was no question of force, none whatever. He was learning, too, that there was no question of her ever complaining, either (that had worried him rather, at the beginning). Still, perhaps in future he would call in at the workshop instead; it really was a little close for comfort doing it in the house. She *could* always refuse. Meanwhile, he had to assume she was enjoying herself.

The arrival of the little Chinese squit had eased his tension, a little. But after he'd taken them through their duet a couple of times there seemed little point in continuing and no point in his sticking around. There was no chance of anything else as long as Phil was here. He had not expected Adele to enthuse about the music, but Phil might at least have said something about it. But no, he had just frowned at the notes and concentrated on singing them, without referring once to the fact that this was Cosmo's own work. Not so much as a 'nice tune, Cosmo'. So as soon as he reasonably could, he had brought the rehearsal to an end. There was certainly no point in hanging around for conversation; Phil spoke almost as little as Adele.

And he did not suggest they come to the pub, too. The prospect of a Poppy-free night of steady drinking had been shining in Cosmo's mind since morning, when he had cried off from the dinner party because, he claimed, he had to work. 'When things start to flow, I feel I have to go with it. It's almost as if it's not quite *me* in control.' Then he had so succeeded in looking artistically troubled that Helene had graciously offered to ring Valerie herself to excuse him. 'Let me at least take that pressure away from you, Cosmo dear.'

Poppy had looked hard at him and offered him an aromatherapy massage, which he refused. Acupuncture? No, thank you. She must go to Valerie's without him and enjoy herself; he wouldn't mind. He so didn't mind that he had managed a kiss on her forehead to show her. So he was not going to waste this opportunity by taking a couple of mute, inscrutable dummies in tow. He was not going to be a bloody baby-sitter on top of everything else, and Adele and Phil were both adults, for God's sake. Adele certainly was well able to stick up for herself, in fact he wasn't at all convinced about the autism thing. It was a bit of a front. In the end Adele knew what she wanted, and got it. And anyway Phil seemed in no hurry to leave, so let him deal with her. He pushed off at half past eight. Helene and Poppy had seemed to assume that he would be working all evening. Let them, but he had never said that.

They made themselves coffee. They ate biscuits. They sat on the floor. They watched television but only for a short time, because the programme was something noisy with several people laughing a lot and being asked pointless questions. In the silence, they sat on the floor some more. After a while Adele stopped Phil from kissing her all over her face and neck and drew back to look at him. His hair fell from the crown of his head straight over his forehead like a blue-black waterfall. It halted abruptly just above his eyebrows, in a scissored, horizontal line. His eyebrows looked greyish because they did not grow thickly enough to conceal the skin beneath, but each blue-black eyebrow hair seemed to be matched by an identical one on the other side. It was wonderful to see. She smiled, but stopped Phil as he leaned forward to kiss her again. It was not that she minded the kissing – she knew about kissing – it was just that she hadn't finished looking.

His eyes were almost closed and they looked a bit wet. It was funny how people went wet in different places once the kissing started. She knew that, too. She saw the white web of skin that rose in an arch from the corner of one eye and noted with intense satisfaction its perfect equivalent on the other side of the bridge of Phil's nose. And the nose itself was straight, and was the same even colour as the rest of his face. Best of all, it came to a neat stop which did not draw your attention too much, not like some other noses which were mottled, bent and sticking out and had damp hairs waving at you out of the end. Her eyes travelled outwards and perused his right ear, around which the hair had been cut so that she might more easily admire it. It was a thrill to confirm, as she took his face in her hands and turned his head for inspection, that the one growing out of the other side was exactly the same, only its opposite. Phil was smiling now, and she could see how every tooth had its white counterpart. It was so exciting already, but she knew there would be more.

She quickly unbuttoned his shirt and found what she was

looking for. Shoulders, flat and straight and, just where they should be, in the middle of a smooth, even front, his two brown nipples, one on either side. Perfect. Phil seemed keen to see hers, too, which was all right as long as he didn't touch them; it would probably hurt. But no, it didn't, his fingertips were sort of nibbling at them softly and it was nice. Then he nibbled them properly with his mouth and made them tingle, so that they stuck out hard, just like his. There was more, she knew, and Phil knew too, because he wasn't stopping her from taking off his other clothes now. There it was. The ridges all the way down his front, the belly button, dead centre, and the other thing sticking up and that's when it all got spoiled. It wasn't the sticking-up bit itself that she disliked (funny how people went all wet in different places), it was the rest she couldn't take to. The two round bits underneath it, the two round things that she wanted to be like a pair of identical bristly lychees, weren't. One looked a bit bigger and sadder than the other and drooped down, like an exhausted older brother, and she wanted them to be twins. It was all spoiled. But Phil wanted her to have a better look. He was kneeling in front of her and she leaned forward to get closer. She could see it very well now, thank you, but, oh yes, here comes the part she had forgotten. The part when she's so close to it she's got to have it in her mouth and then he starts pushing her away with it. No, that was wrong; now she remembered. He wants her to stay down there so that he can jiggle longer with his key in her lock. His hands left the side of her head and stretched down her body. Now the clothes which she still had on were getting in the way of Phil's fingers (funny how people get all wet in different places once the kissing starts).

Chapter Fifteen

Stepping over the threshold into 11 Camden Crescent on Monday morning, Sara was aware of a sharpness reaching her nostrils, quite unlike the delicious scent of clean paint and flowers that she was used to in James's and Tom's flat. Herve moved aside to let her through the doorway with her cello case. She smiled, only with her mouth.

'You want coffee?' he asked unenthusiastically.

'No, thanks,' Sara said. The sharpish smell was coming from the kitchen.

'Have you got something cooking?' she asked, knowing that he wouldn't have, knowing from the smell that the bin under the kitchen sink would be a sordid installation piece overflowing with scraped-out cardboard trays, pierced film covers and discarded 'product sleeves' from ready-made meals, and the inside of James's microwave like a still from a spatter movie featuring a week's exploded dinners.

'No. I don't find pleasuring in kitchen,' he said. 'Peggy she comes tomorrow to clean. So I left for her, all plates and cups and so.'

Sara the cosmopolitan fellow artist closed her lips, while the contemptuous Scottish housewife within her was tapping on the inside of her head saying, oh, so being a genius gives him leave to be filthy in someone else's house, does it? She would have a quiet word with Peggy, pay her extra if necessary to have everything nice for James's and Tom's return.

Coffeeless, they began work. And it felt like work, as Sara embarked again on Herve's four notions while he whanged and whined and clashed around her on the electronic rig that had taken over the drawing room. Over and over again they came, all four repeating hauntingly, like bad curry. The telephone rang. Sara was surprised at first that Herve answered, until the tone of his voice told her that he had been expecting the call.

'Helene, yes! Hello! And a good morning to *you*,' he treacled. 'Oh, yes, my headache is quite gone. So sad, yes, about Saturday! I am quite well. Werking, werking, always werk in progress. Tired, of course.'

Sara placed her cello on the floor and wandered over to the window, looking out across the city with her arms folded. She had managed to get two hours' expensive parking a long way down Lansdown and had lugged the cello all the way up, all because he had been too tired this morning to bring a keyboard with him in a taxi out to the cottage in St Catherine's Valley. Or perhaps he had just not wanted to miss Helene's call. She was furious to find that this possibility made her jealous.

'Oh, thenk you, thenk you so much. Yes, perhaps you are right, it takes another musician to appreciate . . .'

How long was he planning to be? Whatever he wanted to do with his time was his affair, but was it fair of him now to squander hers? She cracked the joints of her fingers extravagantly and stretched her arms.

'Oh, yes, how interesting. Of course also creative. Where? Just to listen, listening only? Well . . .'

And meanwhile it was embarrassing, because although she could hardly help overhearing the conversation, she certainly wasn't going to go and wait discreetly in the kitchen and let the smell of old baked-on E numbers from a sinkful of washing-up get in her clothes and settle on her hair.

'When you say, tomorrow? In the evening? Oh, well, I think perhaps yes, is all right. Sara too? *Oh.* Yes, tomorrow. Good, yes, *goodbye!*'

Herve's smile followed Helene down the telephone as he

replaced the receiver. Oh, bloody marvellous, Sara thought, doing her lips-only smile again, as he explained to her that he had just accepted Helene's invitation to go to the first proper rehearsal of Helene's community opera, at which Sara herself would be standing in for Andrew.

'They would so like, Sara, so I say yes. Their little opera. Helene is interesting woman. I go, yes. To hear you too, is so *extraordinary* you agree to play for them.'

'Not at all,' she said, trying to sound breezy, succeeding only in sounding defensive. 'Just a favour for a friend. You'd do the same, I expect.'

'No, I don't think so,' Herve said thoughtfully. 'To do so is not . . . serious. You are perhaps not serious, Sara. Only for fun you play. You play for fun, with these little people.'

Sara opened her mouth, barely knowing where to begin her enraged defence of herself, fun and 'little people', but Herve said sharply, 'Werk! Come, Sara, back to werk. Already we waste enough time.'

When Sara rose from her chair an hour later and began to put away her cello, she glanced over at Herve. He was jotting something down, some detail to do with the music, half smiling to himself, absorbed and happy. Just then he looked up and smiled at her, and the rage she had been keeping warm inside her throughout the rehearsal cooled into sudden understanding.

'Here, Sara, here are today's sketches. New werk for you,' he said, holding out the sheets of music almost shyly. Suddenly she could see that perhaps Herve was lonely, after three weeks working in a rented flat in a foreign city. How callous of her not to have thought of that. That's why he had said he would be there tomorrow, his aloofness merely a pose to disguise his loneliness. She pictured Cosmo, Helene and the other fawning disciples in their grateful humility as their small, poor rehearsal was graced by the presence of the great man, and in the glow of her resolve to think more generously of him, did not suspect that that was exactly what Herve was picturing, too.

They said goodbye with an exchange of kisses, Sara

lingering just long enough to catch the scent of clean, male skin from his cheek and wonder if their kisses would remain indefinitely in the merely social category.

As she came down into the hall she heard the sound of banging from inside the basement flat and remembered that two of James's and Tom's china mugs were still inside. She had left without them that day, almost abruptly, with the feeling that Dotty's desire for company had been satisfied as swiftly as the tea had assuaged her thirst. In the ensuing days, nearly three weeks now, Sara had passed the empty flat several times and had begun to wonder if she was going to have to go to Rossiters and replace the mugs. Now at last there was someone inside, perhaps Dotty herself, so here was her chance, even though, cello case in hand, she might this time have to own up to being 'that cellist'. She leaned the cello case against the wall at the side of the door, knocked the knocker and waited. The banging from inside stopped. She waited some more. The banging resumed, more vigorously. She knocked again, harder, and again the banging stopped. After a long pause Sara heard the sound of someone coming up the stairs to the door. It was opened by a harassed–looking, almost hostile Dotty.

'You! Oh! Er, hello. Look, do excuse me, I was . . .'

'I am so sorry, it's just I left the mugs behind last time. I thought I should just . . . they're not actually mine, you see.'

'Mugs? Oh! Oh, the mugs, yes. Look, I'm awfully sorry. Would you just . . . hang on a minute. I'll get them.'

She left Sara standing by the open door as she disappeared back down the stairs. Bloody cheek, Sara thought, leaving me on the doorstep. Friendly enough when she wanted a cup of tea. She pushed the door open further and stepped in. From where she stood she could see down the stairs to the wide passageway at the bottom which led into all the rooms of the flat. But instead of an expanse of red carpet across the passage, there were bare boards. A large claw hammer sat on the bottom stair. Sara wondered why Dotty was having the carpet up. She couldn't be replacing it. Did she want it herself? Although it was in good condition the carpet was far from new, and was cut to fit the peculiar and not very large shape of the hallway. Strangest of all, why was Dotty herself doing the job, in what must be her lunch hour, and single-handed?

Leaving her cello case leaning on the wall by the door, Sara made her way down the stairs to the bottom and called out, 'Do you remember the ones? One was dark blue and the other one green; they had those big gold dots on them.' Not that she thought for a second that they would be easily confused with anything in Imogen Bevan's mug collection, but how else was she to get a closer look? But just then Dotty appeared from the kitchen with the mugs, one in each hand. Sara took them and put them in her shoulder bag.

'Thanks. Dotty, what on earth are you doing with the carpets?'

'Oh, nothing, nothing. It's nothing to do with the carpet. I'll be putting it back. It's the floorboards. They were just loose, one or two of them. Loose floorboards, that's all.'

'Oh, right. Well, I'll let you get on, then.'

She turned and climbed the stairs, with Dotty close behind, almost shooing her off. Sara retrieved her cello case and turned to say goodbye. Dotty gave a little exclamation of surprise.

'You *are* her! I knew you were.' She shook her head in disbelief. 'I *knew* it. Tell me, why did you say you were someone else?'

Sara looked at her and smiled sweetly. 'Tell me, why did you say you were fixing floorboards when you haven't got any nails?'

Dotty's shoulders fell. She stared at Sara, tightened her lips and looked back hard at her, blinking. 'I didn't say I was fixing them. I just said they were loose. I've lifted them because I . . . because I've lost an earring. I think it might have got down . . . somewhere . . . under the floorboards. I'm just searching.'

'Oh,' said Sara. She turned back just as Dotty was closing the door. 'Good luck with the search, then. For whatever it is.'

Chapter Sixteen

Although it was Cosmo who was talking it was Herve they were all looking at. Or almost all, for Adele in the window seat had turned over the sheets of music she had been given and was absorbed in drawing something on the back. Sara sat next to her, glancing down occasionally at the detailed snowflake pattern that was emerging. It was astonishing; six points like double-ended daggers radiated from a central point, each branch embellished with elaborate little darts, cuts and bladelike edges. As far as Sara could tell it was accurate and symmetrical down to the last detail, but being unwilling to interfere with the air of self-possession that surrounded Adele she did not ask to have a closer look. She wondered if Adele remembered the soothing garden of Iford with its squares and paths.

Herve had been installed in the large wing chair by the fireplace while Helene, having obviously conceded what was her habitual throne, perched slightly outrageously on the arm, marking her new possession like a self-appointed composer's moll. Jim, Phil, Poppy and Valerie occupied the other chairs and the sofa, which had been swung round towards the baby grand piano at the end of the room where Cosmo was intoning unhappily, trying not to notice that nobody was really listening.

'So, ah,' Cosmo said at last, taking his place at the piano, looking frightened. 'Ah, are we ready to start?'

Sara slipped off the window seat and went to her place slightly behind the piano where her cello and music stand were ready. She set the pitifully easy music on the stand and nodded to Cosmo that she was ready.

Sheets of music were rustled and throats cleared as the room filled with the nervous expectancy of amateurs about to sing in front of strangers. Helene stood up, planted her feet and took up a pose of exemplary magnificence, the professional showing a bit of form, guiding the timid. She looked round, smiling her oh-the-joy-and-wonder-of-music smile, pressed four fingertips into the tungsten musculature of her diaphragm, lifted her head and drew her lips back across her teeth. She was ready to sing.

> Gentlemen coming into the room in boots,
> where ladies are,
> shew little regard to them or the company!

The schooled voice was huge; there was something both lovely and quite unlovable in the sheer scale of it. It was steady and rich, sustained by solid technique and decades of marathonic training, which yet could not quite conceal the friendly, fifty-five-year-old wave in its timbre. She finished with a purse of the lips, smirked and turned to Jim with a look of quite inappropriate hilarity while he, jerking his shoulders convulsively, replied in a breathy but surprisingly round baritone:

> Except they have no shoes!

A frightened Valerie came in slightly sharp, in a tremulous soprano, with:

> Ladies dressing and behaving like Handmaids
> must not be surprised

and then, in three parts, Valerie, Jim and Helene sang

if they are treated as Handmaids!

although only Helene could be heard, very nearly louder than lovely.

Sara looked over at Herve, whose eyes were dancing over the ceiling. He had sucked both cheeks in tight and was puckering up his mouth, seeming to suppress a series of small explosions in his nose and throat. Helene turned, looked at Valerie and said in a loud, concerned whisper, 'Sneezing fit. He's *not* a well man.' Valerie nodded.

Cosmo rapped on the piano. 'If I may have your attention, please?' he said, and spent the next quarter of an hour schooling his singers in some of the finer points of the performance. None of his remarks involved Sara, so she merely sat sluggish and bored. The music was facile dross, far too easy even for Andrew, and she was inwardly wondering how it was that she had got herself involved with such no-hopers. At what point had she consented to be dragged down to such mediocrity? She felt as if she were braising in a lumpy stew of her own stupidity.

Herve, having arrested his fit of whatever it was, continued to sit in the wing chair, inscrutably gorgeous, his blue eyes suggesting the beautiful, serene recesses of his own assured genius, and the infinite depth of his patience with these members of a lower order of humanity. Jim and Valerie returned to their places and Helene announced that she was 'just popping down' to see to the coffee. Cosmo sweated at the keyboard as Adele and Phil made their way over to the piano. The pace picked up as Cosmo bashed out what sounded to Sara like a reasonably creditable tune, the kind of forgettable ditty that you feel quite affectionate towards on a first hearing, because it almost, but not quite, reminds you of something. Taking a deep breath, and with none of Helene's stage posture or Jim's shoulder twisting, Phil sang out in an easy tenor voice that made Sara think of a slim little yacht with a white sail going before a favourable wind.

> Immortal Newton never spoke
> More truth than here you'll find,
> Nor Pope himself e'er penned a joke
> Severer on mankind.

It was a natural, good voice, not a great one. Perhaps that added to the surprise. Because what then drifted out of Adele's mouth, as if just carelessly let go like a helium-filled balloon, was the most spell-binding voice that Sara had ever heard, a sound that made the hairs stand up on the back of her neck and sent a shiver down her spine. It was a creamy, effortless soprano of unearthly purity and strength.

> The picture placed, the busts between,
> Adds to the satire strength;
> Wisdom and Wit are little seen,
> But Folly at full length.

The obscure banality of the words was irrelevant. Adele took Cosmo's poor melody higher and higher, soaring and trilling over top As and B flats, carelessly playing her own voice like an instrument on which she had never needed a moment's tuition. When she stopped and looked round placidly, everyone was sitting a little straighter. Herve was staring, enraptured. Spontaneous applause broke out, to which Adele did not visibly react.

But, Sara thought, while the voice is beautiful, the singing is not. She merely replicated, with that exquisite instrument, the notes and words that she had been taught. While she sang perfectly in tune she gave no shape or dynamic shading to the music's phrases. She sang words clearly, but without seeming to understand or care for their sense. She had reached the end of her performance without apparently noticing that the opportunity to communicate anything had been and gone. This did not appear to bother Herve, who was on his feet, his eyes on fire with an enthusiasm that Sara had not seen before.

'Bravo!' he cried.

As the clapping subsided Helene appeared at the door with a large tray, smiling as if the applause had been for her entrance. Cosmo got up from the piano blushing, looking anxiously at Herve. To his apparent relief he was ignored by everyone except Poppy, who was beaming her amazed approval and squeezing his arm. Other people stood up and formed their customary twos and threes round the room, excluding Sara. Adele was back in the window seat. Poor girl, Sara was thinking, she probably doesn't understand what's going on, and made her way over to join her. But there was something about Adele, almost a hint of granite in the clear eyes, that defied pity, that gave the impression that she was not uncomprehending but rather infinitely discerning in her attentions. The grave stare that she turned on Sara as she sat down was oddly hurtful. She felt herself to have been assessed and found lacking in real interest, not a feeling she was used to. Just as she was wondering whether to speak, and risk further spurning by asking her if she remembered Iford Manor, Adele was on her feet again. Pouring the coffee was her job, and the compliant Phil who had been busy with the cups allowed himself to be quietly demoted to assisting her. Adele shuffled back to Sara with a cup and saucer, and as she handed it to her, met her look with nothing so obvious as recognition, only the merest softening of the eyes. Sara held her breath, feeling both immensely gratified and rather preening, absurdly like the peacock in the garden. The moment passed. Now Adele was turning and making her way round to hand cups to Cosmo and Herve. There she paused, looking from one to the other.

'Backward!'

She pointed first at Herve.

'Forward!'

Her finger swung round to Cosmo.

'Backward!'

She looked neither baffled nor embarrassed, in contrast to the two men.

'I know *all* about it,' she said.

'Now, Adele, we don't point, do we, dear?' Helene was at her side. 'Pointing's rude. You sang so sweetly, darling. I heard you from downstairs. Didn't she, everyone?' Murmurs rose. Jim appeared at Adele's other side.

'All right, Adele?' His voice was kind. Adele looked up at him and round at Phil, waiting silently behind her with the plate of biscuits.

'Backwards. Forwards,' she said, her voice rising. 'I know all about it. I go backwards. Twenty-five. You can have a biscuit. You want it, don't you?' She pulled the plate of biscuits away from Phil and turned to Cosmo, who shot Poppy a look that said *save me*.

'Twenty-five,' Adele informed nobody in particular, holding it out. 'You want it, don't you? You can have a biscuit.' She began to laugh at some hilarious private joke.

'Twenty-five?' Poppy asked appeasingly. 'Lovely.' Gently she took the plate from her and gave it back to Phil. Adele drew a hand up to her mouth and bit it excitedly, still laughing. Poppy quietly lifted her hand away and pulled it down towards Adele's dress pocket. The laughter subsided. 'Hands in pockets, Adele, that's right. No biting. There. Now, I think you've been doing more drawings, haven't you, Adele? May I see? Will you show me your drawing?' Adele turned and made her way back to the window seat. She did not look again at Sara. While Poppy oohed over the drawing Adele sat with her hands clasped under her throat and her head tilted, ignoring her completely. Her contribution over, there seemed to be nothing more she wanted to say.

Chapter Seventeen

The next morning Sara calculated peevishly that it was time to give herself a day off. Because of her recent tour, including the practice and other commitments before it and the work with Herve following, it had been months since she had allowed herself a full twenty-four hours in which to do exactly as she liked. She rang Herve and cancelled their rehearsal. Then she put on her running clothes and began this day all to herself with a gentle jog through the valley, gleeful in her selfishness.

She wondered what Andrew was doing. Probably trying to run the Bevan enquiry from the sofa, or even pretending he could walk comfortably to his car and drive to the police station. He would never permit himself to skive off as she was doing, and would probably be mildly shocked at the pleasure she was taking in it. In some ways Andrew's work was not so different from hers; they both understood about long, dogged hours that sometimes seem thankless and pointless, hers practising with Herve, Andrew's with routine, repetitive and unpromising enquiries. He had combed through the details of Imogen Bevan's life and found it morally blameless, sparse in events and essentially solitary. In Imogen Bevan's cupboards there had been not so much as a jar past its sell-by date, let alone skeletons. So Andrew was now pursuing the most, indeed the only sensible line of enquiry. Guiltily, she saw for the first time how exasperating it must have been for him when she, instead of really trying to help, had tried to get him to latch on to some sensational invention of hers about dastardly enemies of the dead woman. She had been using his work as some kind of attention-seeking recreation for herself and when, with that untimely telephone call from Bridger, Andrew had shown that he would not be distracted from the real job he had to do, she had flounced out. She stopped abruptly in the lane, hands on hips, winded less by the exercise than by the realisation that she had been behaving unforgivably. Remorse landed suddenly in her stomach and settled like quick-setting cement.

She walked on, head down, thinking, her body steaming gently. Poor Andrew. She pictured him, in pain, interviewing Brendan Twigg's friends, probably fruitlessly. None the less, he would stay with the enquiry, she thought guiltily, until the end. He would find some new line to take, something else to try, and it would be based on some actual truth about Imogen Bevan and the circumstances of her death, not some smart-arsed 'instinct'. How could you, after all, lie on your back in a cornfield when it was your job to track down the killer of a sweet, innocent old lady? An innocent old lady, then. Well, an old lady, certainly.

What had Dotty really been doing, going at the floorboards with a claw hammer? It crossed Sara's mind wildly that however innocent Miss Bevan's cupboards might be of skeletons, she might have had a corpse or two under the floorboards. What had she really been looking for? Sara mentally measured the hallway and concluded, a little disappointed, that it would have to be a dainty corpse to fit down there. She was conscious that she was doing it again, speculating largely for her own amusement, and suppressed the dangerous tingle of inquisitiveness. Perhaps Dotty had actually just been looking for an earring. No reason why ringless, unbraceleted Dotty, without so much as a locket round her neck, might not indeed have lost an earring. No reason at all.

After her shower she put on a narrow dress of heavy grey linen and black loafers, casting aside the utilitarian black trousers and white shirts that had become her habitual uniform for the joyless sessions with Herve. She felt different already. Having decided that she would not play at all today, she looked out from the drawing room window at the valley drenched in autumn sun and reflected that today might be her last chance this year to play up in the hut at the top of the garden. Very soon she would have to shut it up for the winter. Even if she just did an hour, she might make some sense of Cosmo's stuff and out of respect for Herve (and also to drive out the remorse which was still with her) she could work on the new sketches he had given her on Tuesday. But to her intense annoyance, after she had climbed the slippery path with both cello and music case, opened out the doors and bolted them back, dusted off the chair and tuned up, she found that the music was not in her case. Neither Cosmo's funny little cello continuo, nor Herve's monstrous rumblings was there. It was infuriating, but she was going to have to go back to Helene's to retrieve them because somehow, probably in her indecent haste to get away last night, she had managed to leave it all behind.

Parking was a nuisance, of course, and Sara's temper with the sheer temerity of all these other people who had the nerve to bring their cars into town did not sweeten the errand. Entering the Circus on foot, she marched with a scowling face round to Helene's door. Her welcome was so warm that Sara practically blushed at the uncharitable things she had been thinking about the opera.

'Just in time for a sandwich, dear! You'll have a bite and a cup of coffee with me, won't you? I'm on my own, Adele's at the workshop. You pop in and find your music – I expect it'll be somewhere near the piano, try under the window seat too – and I'll put the kettle on!'

The blasted music was nowhere. After quarter of an hour's searching she was interrupted by Helene, who came up from the kitchen with a tray.

'I expect Cosmo has it,' Helene said soothingly. 'He's got bundles and bundles of stuff all over the place. But we can't ask him now, he's gone off somewhere, for a walk, I expect. He doesn't get much exercise.'

They settled themselves in chairs at a low table with coffee mugs and smoked salmon sandwiches. 'It seems to be coming on well now, the project,' Sara said, unable to bring herself to call it an opera. 'Adele's so lucky, having you do all this for her. Oh, but look,' she added quickly, 'I don't mean that I think she's lucky in the usual sense. I mean, things can't be easy for her. It must be difficult.'

'Oh, thank you for saying that. It is difficult.' Helene sighed. 'Most people don't realise. Now they've all seen *Rain Man* people think it must be entertaining in some way. Well, they should see how entertaining it is to have your child in nappies until they're fifteen.'

Sara nodded. She could just, *just* imagine not minding too much for a couple of years . . .

'The way Adele is now, that's taken over fifteen years. It took for ever to get her diagnosed. Autism's so much rarer in girls, for one thing. She was at a residential school until six years ago. They worked wonders with her. Things that aren't a struggle with a normal child take years. Helping her over her irrational fears, tolerating noises, being touched, teaching her basic things like washing and dressing, never mind making coffee and so on. She can do all those, you know,' she added proudly.

'I've seen. Sometimes she seems utterly focused on one thing, sometimes she seems to be thinking of nothing at all.'

'Oh yes, she sort of tunes out sometimes. It's as if she can't take too much of the world all at once. She never really knows what people will do next because she can't imagine anyone else's thoughts or feelings. She doesn't understand people's reasons for things, and that can be frightening. When too much is coming at her, she'll either tune out or do something comforting, rocking herself or looking at something, or drawing. That's hard for other people to understand, but it's better than hysterics.'

'I saw the drawing she was doing on Tuesday. Is it one of those talents that autistic people have? Like doing maths automatically, or something?'

'Yes,' Helene said in a tired voice. 'Yes, just a thing she

could do. She can draw a symmetrical pattern instantly. I don't know how. It's as if she sees everything from the middle. Mirror-imaging, in a way. She loves the way patterns do that. But don't say what a marvellous gift, please.'

'I wasn't going to.'

Helene smiled slightly apologetically. 'No, you probably wouldn't. But it's amazing how often people do. They some-times think an ability like that must make up for it all. They're wrong.'

Sara nodded. Years ago, there had been a family in the same street in St John's Wood where she and Matteo had had their flat before moving to Bath. Her nearest neighbour had told her that the son was autistic. Sara had not really known them except to nod to and could not now remember their surname, only that the distant-looking little boy had been called Theo. Once she saw him having a tantrum in the street, writhing and screaming in his mother's one-handed grasp while she tried to keep the other on the handle of the buggy holding the younger child, a girl of about two. With one arm Theo was flailing at his mother while with the other he was clutching his ominously stained crotch. Sara, passing by in the car in a solid line of traffic, had genuinely been in no position to help. But what help, even supposing the mother did not resent the offer, would be appropriate? All she could see was the overwhelming difficulty of the poor, tired-looking woman. Theo, according to the neighbour, was a real whizz at train times, having memorised apparently without effort the entire Southern Region network. Well, how truly remarkable that was. But Sara had thought then that if she were in the mother's position, she would gladly trade a little ordinary intellectual dullness for the luxury of being able to assume that her child was not going to wet himself in the street at the age of nine.

Helene smiled and nodded. 'It doesn't make up for it at all. She can draw any symmetrical pattern from memory, that's all. It's a bit the same with music, she can remember anything she's heard. She's what's known as autistic savant. But there's not always a lot she can do with her gifts, because of her other problems.' She sighed. 'I'm fifty-five and I have a grown-up daughter as dependent as a child. That thought depresses me sometimes. I'll get old, won't I? Sometimes, when you think of the future, you can feel quite desperate, quite *un*motherly. Oh, look, but not for long,' she chuckled, looking up and nodding at the mantelpiece. 'Isn't she funny? You've got to keep your sense of humour.'

The hands of the carriage clock stood at six o'clock. 'She's always doing it. Doesn't like the hands actually telling the time, it's too untidy, too uneven. She goes round and puts all the clocks in the house at six o'clock or midnight. I've had to get a digital clock for the kitchen, otherwise I'd never know what time it was. You have to laugh, sometimes.'

Sara would have sat on and listened, sensing that Helene wanted to tell her more. She was even a little flattered to be shown this more private, honest, but no less warm side of Helene. But traffic wardens were afoot.

In the car she rang Andrew. 'I wondered if you'd be at home. I'm in town and I thought I'd come and see you if that's all right. I think I owe you an apology, really. And I *would* bring some of last night's community opera highlights to amuse you, only I can't find the music. I've mislaid some of Herve's too; it's somewhere at Helene's.'

'Thank God,' Andrew said happily, 'twice over. That you're coming to see me, and without the bloody music. Can you just get here? Right now? Valerie's out, but she's arranged for Poppy of all people to come round later. She's coming to give me relief. Only with her hands, of course.'

'*What?*'

'Yep, it's true. *Full* relief.' For a moment Andrew could not go on for laughing.

'*What?*'

'Acupuncture, my suspicious friend. Acupuncture. Poppy does acupuncture, for pain relief in my case. It was her own idea. She mentioned it to Valerie and Valerie took her up and arranged it for today. I'll try anything that might work. I've got to get back to that enquiry. So come now, before Poppy comes to relieve me.'

She found Andrew not nearly as better as he had sounded. He seemed a little smaller and paler, lying stretched on the sofa. Perhaps it was because of the back pain, but Sara fancied it was also because he was just in the wrong place. There was nothing actually wrong with the room or with the house. It was a roomy, pre-war, semi-detached example of Bath prosperity, like others in the wide street, and decorated Valerie-style in the kind of commercial good taste that can be bought off the peg by anyone with enough nous to find their way into a John Lewis and a Habitat. It was all so acceptable, and, like many reasonable and sensible choices, it was also pretty dull. There was just one little touch that spoke of Andrew and not of a compromise that satisfied Valerie's desire to have things neat and nice and the same as other people: on one wall hung a set of four sepia ink drawings of a nineteenth-century string quartet, on badly foxed paper, of erratic quality and with the beading on the ebonised frames broken in places. He had got them cheap, he said, because of their condition and because the artist was unknown. But Sara could see, as he had, that whoever had sketched them had captured here and there the glancing and swaying of people feeling the almost sexual energy of playing together as one. The drawings were the only thing in the room that anyone could feel strongly about. Overall, the house didn't seem his and didn't suit him, but there was no point in going into all that. There were bigger things to say apart from carping about paint colours, although Sara was not quite sure how to put them.

She tried to explain. 'I'm having a day off and I've been thinking. I feel stuck. I'm stuck in the wrong place with the wrong people, Andrew, and so are you. The damn opera group and bloody Herve, the whole thing. It feels like I'm working against my own nature all the time. I don't want to play contemporary music – not *this* contemporary music – and I just keep pretending. You're stuck, too, stuck in that enquiry that refuses to go anywhere, and stuck here. And it brings out the worst in us. I mean, why aren't we allowed to say what *we* want? It seems to me that other people do just that, all the time. And we just fall in with it. We shouldn't. We should have what we want.'

'Be selfish, you mean,' Andrew said. Sara was kneeling by him now and he gently stroked her indignant, earnest face. Her hair was full of such amazing colours, rich sparkling coppery strands among the shiny darker ones. There was the occasional white one as well. Thirty-eight now. She claimed she'd always been too busy to think of having babies. She said it had never been an issue all the time she was with Matteo, and now Matteo had been dead for over two years. So what about Sara's babies? Something in Andrew almost physically crumpled at the thought of her never having any. Almost immediately, it crumpled again at the thought that she might go off and have them with someone else who didn't already have three of his own. Three who needed him. So how was that for being selfish?

'Other people are. Why shouldn't we be?' Sara said.

'I suppose because other people somewhere will always, always be hurt if we are,' Andrew said hopelessly, thinking of Natalie, Benji and Dan and picturing, for some reason, not them but their silly pyjamas with cartoons and daft writing on them. How could he leave them? But how could he not be with Sara?

The doorbell rang. Sara started to move away from him to a safe public distance, but he detained her for a moment. 'Poppy. She's early. But we haven't finished talking about this. Stay. This won't take long, and there's more to talk about. Right now' – he heaved himself into a sitting position – 'we have to put up with being stuck a little longer. Literally, in my case.'

As Sara made for the door to let Poppy in, Andrew suddenly said, 'Oh, listen, Sara, I've just thought of something. A police officer having acupuncture? A stuck pig. I think that's rather good.' He felt like weeping, but he loved it when she laughed.

Poppy laughed too, before embarking on a laborious explanation of the efficacy of acupuncture and taking notes on the location and severity of Andrew's pain. She declared the sitting room an unsuitable place for Andrew to lie for the treatment, but the dining room would be fine. And although it was a little unorthodox, she did not mind Sara being present (since Sara explained that she had always been fascinated by acupuncture) as long as she said nothing and did not draw in her breath sharply at the sight of the needles going in. She bustled into the dining room to set up her folding table and unpack her bag, and a few minutes later bustled back in to check that Andrew's clothes were loose enough to give access to the relevant points on his body. Between them they helped Andrew to 'pop' himself up on to the table. Poppy was suddenly immensely likeable, Sara thought, like a nurse who knows what she is doing and was proud and happy in her skill.

Lucky Poppy. Sara had to curl silently into a chair in one corner and keep her hands to herself while Poppy was allowed to hover close, so close to Andrew that Sara wondered how on earth she resisted the temptation to climb up on the table beside him. She was almost jealous, but at the same time Andrew's pain was making him so unhappily fragile that she longed to see his strength return, even if it had to be under the healing hands of someone else.

An hour later Poppy tidied away her travelling acupuncture kit in a daze of happiness. She was quiet on her feet so as not to disturb even the air around her patient who was lying back now on the sofa, his eyes closed and on whose face was the peaceful, exhausted expression of one hauled in from a boiling sea of pain and landed safely on a dry shore. But she could move gently around the room without having to quell inwardly the jubilation she felt. Her power surged through and warmed her as it impressed others. Sara was looking at her now with a look of intrigued admiration. Hail, Poppy, Deliverer from Pain. But she would be gracious in her majesty, pink of face, bashful but delighted to be of use.

'Oh, well, they say you've either got the touch for it or

you haven't. I'm just lucky. My tutor says I've got very good hands,' she whispered happily. 'Of course, he'll need more than just one session. But he'll sleep for hours now. I must get off. I've got things to do at the library and I'm on duty tonight.' She gathered her things and gave a comfortable parting smile, like a little mother's, in the direction of the oblivious Andrew.

Sara followed her to the hall. 'You do work hard, Poppy. All the things you do. You should have a day off now and then.'

'Oh, I like to keep busy. 'Bye!'

Andrew opened his eyes when Sara returned.

'I've no intention of sleeping for hours, with you here,' he began, as his eyelids drooped heavily. 'Come here.'

Sara came and sat at the far end of the sofa. She looked at him carefully. 'Oh, yes, you will. You look exhausted.'

Andrew reached out and took her hand, pulling her towards him. 'Come here.' Sara allowed herself to be drawn closer. His fingers gently traced a line across her face and came to rest on her ear. He pulled off her jet and silver earring and his fingers returned to the naked lobe and squeezed it gently, sending warm shivers all through her. 'You're all velvety there,' he murmured.

Sara raised her head slightly from his chest. 'Andrew, you remember Dorothy Price?'

'Shh. Shh. Don't want to talk about Dorothy Price. Want to talk about you. Want to stroke your earlobe.'

'Dorothy Price was at Imogen Bevan's flat. She had the floorboards up, she said she was looking for an earring. Andrew, I don't think she was.'

'She should . . .' Andrew's voice was drifting. He yawned. 'She should report it to the Missing Earrings Bureau.'

'Andrew, I'm serious. There was something odd about her. Suppose it's something to do with the case? Shouldn't you ask her?'

Andrew smiled. His eyes closed again. 'Ask her what? All right, I'll look at it again. Sara?'

'Hmmm?' She rested her head lightly on his chest once

more. He lifted a thick strand of her hair and brought it to his lips, kissing it, loving its scent. They lay quite still. After a few moments Sara could feel, from the regular rising and falling of his chest beneath her cheek, that Andrew was, indeed, asleep.

Chapter Eighteen

The next day Adele put on her red T-shirt and struggled into the white jeans that she always wore with it. She went down to the kitchen, not for breakfast because she really did not want any, but to pick up her lunch SANDWICH BANANA BISCUITS in the Thomas the Tank Engine lunchbox PERCY AND THE FAT CONTROLLER and to fetch her keys from the tin on the dresser. Adele's own keys. Adele had a key for her own front door (KEY LABELLED NUMBER ONE) and a key for the side door into the workshop passage (KEY LABELLED NUMBER TWO) and a key for the workshop door at the end of the passage (KEY LABELLED NUMBER THREE). They were her own keys. When she had first been given them, her very own keys, she had carried them around with her for days, jangling them on the key chain. Then she had busily sought out three more key chains and linked them all together so that she had a really good long jangling key chain that caught the light and that she could clank around with, until her mother had stopped her. DON'T JANGLE THE KEYS, ADELE. *New Rule*: ONE KEY CHAIN ONLY, AND KEYS TO BE KEPT IN THE TIN ON THE DRESSER WHEN NOT IN USE. That was two. Two new rules, not one. Did they think she was stupid?

The keys were there. So was Helene, sitting in her bracelets and dressing-gown, looking that spongy way she did in the mornings and not talking so much. But she was doing her 'No breakfast again? Got your keys? Goodbye, darling!' And she was lifting one hand from the rim of her coffee mug but Adele had already turned and gone, so that her tinkling finger wave was given more to the swinging door than Adele's purposeful, departing back.

Turn left. *Rule*: DO NOT WALK IN THE CRACKS. Adele has keys and goes to work. *Rule*: GO STRAIGHT TO JIM'S. Sixty-eight steps to Jim's railings, through the gate down the basement steps. Jim's out today. Unlock (KEY LABELLED NUMBER TWO), open the door, go in, close the door. Down the passage. The door at the end, always locked, precious things inside. Use KEY LABELLED NUMBER THREE, ADELE. Jim's workshop. Jim leaves Adele's work out on the table. Sparkly crystals. Adele will fix the crystals. Apron. Rags for cleaning with. Jim leaves cigarettes and matches out on the table. *Rule:* DO NOT PLAY WITH MATCHES, ADELE. Big bottle of washing-up liquid. Funny slippery stuff. *Rule:* THIS IS NOT FOR DRINKING, ADELE. It is for cleaning the crystals. MAKE YOURSELF SOME COFFEE, ADELE. Adele's coffee. Wash mug, dry mug, put in coffee, dry milk. Adele white no sugar. HELP YOURSELF TO A CIGARETTE, ADELE. Fill kettle. In a minute. First get cigarette. Light cigarette, first put in mouth, get match out, strike.

Chapter Nineteen

'Oh, fab. Fucking fabulous. Another? Is that what you're telling me? What is this: Bath, the World Heritage City, renowned for its exploding basements? Is that it? Oh, yes, yes of course. Yes, all right, right away.'

Detective Sergeant Bridger replaced the receiver and tried to stir in himself some sense of urgency. Of late he had found it more and more difficult to do, and it had been a while since he had actually bothered to do his impersonation of a committed detective for anyone other than his superiors. The call from DC Heaton was not worth that effort; he would save it for DCI Poole. But he would have to get over to the Circus where, he had just learned from Heaton, it appeared that there had been another explosion. Animal righters again?

It took Bridger less than an hour at the scene to establish, to his relief, that there was no connection between the two unfortunate cases. What had happened here was an accident. After the fire had been dealt with, the gas people had shown up and made a preliminary inspection. The only gas appliance in the room, the cooker, was an old model, about twenty years old. The explosion and fire had been caused by a build-up of gas in an unventilated room, ignited by a flame, possibly an electrical spark, possibly a match. It appeared that the gas had been left on by mistake. The householder was not registered as a service customer, they were able to verify. They had shut off the supply and no gas was present now. The fire crew confirmed that the premises appeared to be structurally safe, although a proper survey would be necessary. An elderly couple on the scene, residents of the Circus, had given them the name of the girl they had seen going into the building, but the next of kin would have to identify her formally. The police surgeon had been at it, coming up with theories as to the cause of death instead of just certifying her dead and leaving the pathologist, whose job it was, to answer the question of how. They all did it, couldn't help themselves, but in this case the guy was actually right. The girl goes in, shuts the door and goes to light a cigarette or switch on the kettle. Combination of blast injuries and inhalation of fire gases sees her off. Looks like someone left the cooker on. Incredible she didn't smell it, but then people do do such silly things. Tragic.

At the dead girl's house, number 31, a constable ushered him down to the basement kitchen. The two tenants were sitting unkempt, almost as if they had slept rough, rather fearfully drinking coffee. Not tenants but house guests, they corrected him. The man, Cosmo Lamb, had been asleep. He usually did not rise until around half past ten, because he was in the habit of working long into the night. He had not heard the explosion. Poppy Thwaites had come in from her night shift at the Circus Nursing Home at seven thirty and got into bed beside him. She too had been fast asleep, but she was a lighter sleeper than Cosmo; the noise had woken her up. She had not gone to investigate because their bedroom was at the back, on the first floor. Helene's – Mrs Giraldi's – bedroom was at the front of the house overlooking the Circus, so she would have had to go in there to see what the noise was about, and so disturb Helene. Thinking it was probably nothing anyway, perhaps a car backfiring, she had drifted back off to sleep until screams from the street had woken them. They had got dressed quickly and rushed down. Helene had been in front of them, running towards Jim's flat. The gas people and the police had kept them all away, so they had brought Helene back here, and the policewoman had taken over. Poppy was so worried. Helene would need her. Poppy was here. If DS Bridger was going up to see her now, could he give Mrs Giraldi that reassurance? They would not dream of deserting her at a time like this.

The mother, Mrs Giraldi, was sitting passively with the WPO as if in a waiting room, as if she thought that if she just waited long enough someone would come and tell her what to do. Meanwhile, perhaps if she were patient and waited quietly, and even answered questions, eventually all this would turn out to be not really happening. She appeared to be concentrating hard on the task of just breathing in and out.

Bridger decided to get it over with, for both their sakes. She was lucid. Yes, she had been startled by the explosion, but being in her dressing-gown and this being the Circus, she had not ventured straight out to investigate. Her first thought was that Adele, who had just left, would have heard it too and be frightened and come straight back home. Adele was not able to tolerate unexpected things; she could react violently. Bridger was impressed at the way she managed to say her daughter's name almost without faltering. That was where a lot of them would have started to crack up. The noise, she went on, must have been an engine backfiring or something of that sort, she had assumed. So she had come up from the basement kitchen, expecting at any moment to greet Adele in the hall, who would have come straight back rather than continuing on her way to work. She had gone into the drawing room to look out for her and had seen several people running past her window. Then she had gone upstairs and thrown on some clothes – not quite enough, Bridger had been unable to stop himself thinking, taking in her bare legs in court shoes, the wobbling flesh under the jumper and skirt – and rushed down to the pavement, seeing only then that whatever had happened had happened at Jim's. She thought perhaps that it was then she had screamed.

'Excuse me, Mrs Giraldi,' Bridger interrupted. 'Please excuse me. Did I hear you say that you expected your daughter to come straight home instead of going on to *work*?'

Mrs Giraldi nodded, a little surprised. 'Yes. She works three days a week. For Jim in the workshop.'

Bridger cleared his throat. 'In that case, Mrs Giraldi, we shall want to speak to Mr Roscoe as a matter of urgency. Of course we'll need to see him in any case, but you see, if we're dealing here with a workplace accident, then that puts quite a different complexion on it. Quite a different matter, you see, in law.'

He might have been speaking in tongues for all this seemed to mean to Mrs Giraldi. She had already told the WPO that Jim had told her that he would be leaving the night before to go to an auction in Salisbury. He had done it before. He simply left two days' work out for Adele and it made no difference to Adele; she didn't much bother with people anyway. It had not been difficult to identify the auction house and local officers were apparently being sent round to find Mr Roscoe and break it to him that he no longer had either the workshop or the assistant he had had when he left home the day before. So Jim Roscoe would in any case be on his way back now.

Helene was struggling with the sense of what she had been told. 'Well, I'm not sure. Whatever it is, look, I'm not really following, I'm afraid. Jim wasn't even there when it happened. But you'll be able to talk to him when he gets here.' She looked at the WPO, suddenly tremulous and old. 'Jim . . . Jim will . . . he is sure to be here soon, isn't he? He is one of those people . . . since he came here, I mean . . . one feels one has always . . . Jim . . . he – he'll be so . . . he is sure to be here soon, isn't he?'

Time to go. She was losing it now, and having delayed her proper reaction since the accident happened, over two hours now, her collapse would be total and prolonged. Bridger, supposing he was getting soft in his old age, felt a reluctance to leave with his sympathy unsaid. He stood up, pausing after the WPO had reached the door. An exchange of looks confirmed that she knew her next task was to go back to the basement and get the tenant to call a doctor. This one would need sedation. He turned back to Mrs Giraldi. If he was quick, he could get it in before she lost control completely, although he still was not sure why he was feeling he had to.

'Death was almost certainly instantaneous,' he told her. It was one of the phrases he knew how to use. She nodded.

'It would have been very quick.' He cast a hopeless look round the room. He had to say these things, hadn't he? He remembered the last time he had done so. The near naked body of a chronic alcoholic had been found in her burned-out bedroom. It had turned out not to be arson. She'd started the fire herself by dropping a cigarette on the duvet and then passing out. Presumably the sensation of her own skin burning had woken her up. But the body had been found curled up half in and half out of the wardrobe. The PM showed that she had a sufficient quantity of whisky in her to mistake the wardrobe for the bedroom door, but too much to work out why it might be leading her into a cave hung with suffocating cloth instead of out on to the landing and into air she could breathe. *It would have been very quick*, he had reassured the family, keeping to himself not only the precise location of the body but also the fact that under her torn fingernails they had found splinters clawed from the inside of the wardrobe. *She wouldn't have known a thing about it*. He had to say these things.

Mrs Giraldi was looking at him. 'She wouldn't have known a thing about it,' he said. As he left, he had the sensation of leaving behind something so frail that it would collapse into fragments in the draught of the closing door.

Chapter Twenty

Andrew's GP turned out not to believe in miracle cures.

'But look, I'm practically mobile. And pain-free, well, almost. It's two days since the acupuncture. I've had acupuncture for it.'

'Yes, I know, you said,' Jenny Blum said.

'But I've got to get back to work. You just have to declare me physically fit. Please. I promise I'll be careful.'

'Physically fit? Sorry, no can do. Could you chase a suspect? Make a difficult arrest?'

'Well, no, but I hardly ever have to.' Andrew knew the argument was lost.

'Give it until next week. There's been substantial tissue damage and it needs time. Be as active as you can without being silly. All right?'

Actually he was getting on quite fast at home, even managing to keep up the momentum, such as it was, in the Bevan enquiry. But they were so desperate for a lead now that they were chasing up and interviewing people with the most tenuous of connections to the dead woman. One of the last things he had done before his back went was to interview the deputy editor of a national newspaper who had a weekend flat in Camden Crescent. Yes, he had admitted, he brought his aged cat with him from London for the weekend although the lease forbade it. 'He's an old cat. He can't be left in London all on his own.' How had he felt, Andrew asked, when Miss Bevan had written to the Residents' Association about it? The silver-haired man had turned on him a look of such friendly intelligence that he had hardly needed to go on to say that he wished he did have the time to get worked up about a petty complaint from a provincial harridan whom he had never, to his knowledge, actually met. 'But next time I bring Andreas, I'll be sure to take his collar off before I let him out. Thanks for the tip-off,' he said, winking. As he left he had given Andrew a pitying look, with a slight shake of the head, which conveyed that he understood that Andrew was scraping the bottom of the barrel in the hope of progress.

Part of him was in no hurry to get back to work and confront the Giraldi case, about which he was being kept informed. He had already extricated himself from the front line of the investigation on the grounds that he was too close to those involved, but it was still painful to know that Jim might find himself up on a charge of corporate manslaughter. The enquiry was only just starting and it would be some months down the line, if he knew anything about the speed of progress within the CPS, but it was bad enough. Adele's death was in one sense a tragic accident, but if a case could be made that Jim as an employer had failed to maintain a safe workplace then that case would have to be answered.

It was Friday now; by this afternoon it would be forty-eight hours since he had seen Sara. Yesterday she had not answered his call. He had wanted to tell her himself about Adele, but more than that he had simply wanted, since he could not see her, to hear her voice.

Playing cello to Herve's percussion had begun to feel to Sara like a habitual row between two people who, having abandoned long ago any thought of winning the argument, carry on rowing all the same. Only occasionally did she catch glimpses of the Herve she had first found attractive and it was only those slight smiles or the sight of his face in repose that kept her faith. Where the music itself was concerned she was braver about expressing her opinions. This seemed to be having no effect whatsoever on how the work was shaping up, she was beginning to realise, as she persevered to manifest meaning out of the new sketches and notions that Herve continued to deliver.

After bunking off on Wednesday she had intended to work especially hard on the Thursday, partly to convince herself that her enthusiasm had been renewed after her little break, but mainly to dislodge thoughts of Andrew. It had not helped that she had had to confess to losing two sheets of music, but Herve had been surprisingly sanguine about it and had simply written the notes out for her again and handed the sheets to her at the end of their rehearsal. For the rest of the day back at Medlar Cottage she sulked over the music, defying it to say something to her. She switched off her answering machine, let the phone ring and went to bed early and depressed.

By Friday morning she woke up acknowledging two things: failure – nothing in Herve's music could renew enthusiasm that had never been there in the first place, and a craven need for Andrew – the sound of his voice, the sight and the feel of him. She got through the morning's rehearsal by focusing on the coming afternoon when the first of her agonies, Herve and his music, would be over for another week. For the Andrew problem she had no solution and felt the bleakness of the coming weekend, the forlornest time of all for women in love with married men. At one o'clock she drew her bow for the last time over the bottom string with the depressing creaking noise that Herve wanted. It would have been the moment, working with any other partner, to suggest a friendly bite of lunch together somewhere, but from Herve she had no desire for anything but escape. Leaving him brooding over the prospect of solitary tinned soup, she walked down Lansdown into town. At the crossroads where Lansdown and Broad Street met the Paragon and George Street, her miserable self-absorption was suddenly obliterated by the street vendor's board carrying the *Bath Chronicle* headline.

'I'm afraid it is true. I tried to ring you yesterday. How did you hear?'

'I saw it on a billboard. I had to find out from the bloody *paper*, Andrew! You should've told me.'

Andrew was taking Sara's distraught call from his small music room, where the desk opposite the piano had been cleared temporarily of its usual covering of cello music to make way for police files.

'You should've answered your phone. I did try. Look, Sara, I'd like to tell you more. And I've got to see you. You go back home now and I'll come straight over.'

Sara opened the door to Andrew and was immediately enveloped in his arms.

'Accident. Horrible, I know, but what else could it be?' he said.

Sara shook her head. She couldn't see what, but the arbitrary pointlessness of it was just unacceptable. She led him to the kitchen and began to put an unwanted lunch together, attempting to disguise the odd combination of grief and half-crazed lust under a veneer of domestic competence. She remembered a time, months ago, when she and Andrew had sat here and watched each other's mouths pulling and nibbling on the translucent shells and soft pink flesh of langoustines, and wanted to scream. Instead, she took several deep breaths and tried to concentrate on slicing the bread straight, wishing that Andrew would stop looking at her as if he were thinking about the langoustines, too.

'Leaking gas, followed by a match,' Andrew was saying. 'After the blast, a fire started. Looks like she was lighting a cigarette. Do you really want to hear all this?'

Her eyes were filling with tears. She didn't, nor would her mind accept the hideous coincidence, as the *Bath Chronicle* had reported it, of Jim's being away on the very day of a fatal gas leak. Usually he got her started on her work in the workshop himself before going to the shop. Ordinarily he would have been there and it would never have happened. She shook her head again.

'Sorry. It's messy, horrible,' Andrew said. He guided her to a stool at the kitchen table and sat down opposite.

'Poor, poor Adele. All because of a cigarette. I wonder she didn't smell the gas.'

'I gather it might not have made any difference. I'm getting the picture that autism might involve difficulty in processing sensory information. Even if the autistic person is aware of something like a smell, they may not process it as information that implies something else: danger from a naked flame in this case. The significance of the smell wouldn't be understood, so it wouldn't affect Adele's behaviour. Especially not her kind of ritual, rule-following behaviour. She went through the same routine every morning at the workshop, according to Jim. Shut the door, checked the work on the table, then washed the coffee mug, put the coffee in, lit the ciggie, filled the kettle, switched it on, when it boiled made the coffee. Only yesterday, we know what happened when she lit the match. I don't know whether it's hard to understand, or horribly easy.'

'What about the gas leak? How could the workshop suddenly become so dangerous? She was working there the day before, wasn't she?'

'That's the truly awful part. There was no leak, nothing faulty. It was some old gas cooker Jim's got down there. You know how Adele fiddles with switches and dials? Jim said she'd never shown the slightest interest in the cooker, so he'd never thought of it as a danger. She'd obviously turned one of the dials on the afternoon before, the very afternoon Jim wasn't there. Gas leaked into the room all night.'

'Obviously?'

'Nobody else was in the workshop that day, only Adele. Jim was in his shop until five and he went straight on from there to Salisbury for an auction the next day. And what's even unluckier is that if Adele had left more than one dial switched on, there wouldn't have been an explosion.'

Seeing Sara's mystified face, he went on, 'The cooker was taken away for examination. It wasn't faulty, so that's in Jim's favour at least. They discovered that just one tap had been left open. The dials were so damaged it was impossible to tell from the front. And then you apply a standard formula. Gas only explodes when it's mixed in a proportion with air of between five and nine per cent. Less than that and there isn't enough gas, any more and there isn't enough oxygen for combustion. The gas burners were standard, that's to say they emitted gas at a rate of 11.6 cubic feet of gas per hour.'

'So the volume of the room has to be – I suppose you know that?'

'Of course. It's – wait, I've got it written down.' Andrew pulled from an inside pocket a much scribbled-on piece of paper and unfolded it on to the table.

'Twelve by fifteen by seven. Feet, that is. That makes a total volume of 1,260 cubic feet, so there had to be between 63 and 113 cubic feet of gas. Given that, she could only have left the burner half on, emitting, say, about 5.75 cubic feet of gas per hour. It would take between about eleven and twenty hours to produce the quantity that would explode. So the dial could have been left on as early as half past one on the Wednesday afternoon. Or any time after that, before she left at four o'clock.'

'You mean if it had been full on, the room would have been too full of gas to explode?'

Andrew nodded. 'I've checked all the arithmetic myself.'

Sara put down the sandwich from which she had taken one bite, and stared into space. 'That's the day I went to Helene to find my music. To think, while we were chatting away, a few doors away Adele was fiddling with the cooker and gas was starting to fill the room. And we didn't know.' Suddenly she clapped her hand to her mouth. 'Oh, no! Do you think – do you think if I hadn't been there, Helene would have popped along to see her? Or would Adele have come back for lunch? If I hadn't been there, do you think—'

'No,' Andrew said firmly. He took her hand and brought it down from her face, gently stroking the wrist. 'Adele always did a full day uninterrupted. She took her lunch with her. She liked it, it was simpler and gave her less locking up and getting herself back and forth. And it freed up Helene's day too, of course. Wednesday was a perfectly normal day.'

Sara accepted this silently. About Adele there seemed to be no more to say, since there was no redeeming shred of consolation in the awful facts that either could offer the other. In the silence of the kitchen Sara cleared their plates away. Andrew watched her. The quiet of the house and the long afternoon stretched out, offering them their forbidden, longed-for possibilities. Sara wondered whether she should turn from the sink and say something but she couldn't bear to. And what, anyway? Anything would sound banal. Andrew was behind her now, his hands round her waist. She turned to face him, saw that his face was serious, intent, in a hurry. They were both breathing too fast for speech and in any case, everything had been said. Everything was clear and beautifully simple. Wasn't it?

'Wait. Wait,' Sara said, pulling away. 'She couldn't have left a gas burner on. She couldn't.'

'What do you mean?' Andrew's hands dropped to his sides.

'The clocks and dials. Remember the clock in Helene's drawing room? Have you ever noticed it's always at six o'clock? Because Adele fiddles with it, because she likes the hands symmetrical. Don't you see? Adele just *wouldn't* turn on a single gas dial.'

Andrew did not disguise his exasperation. He turned from Sara and tugged at his hair with both clenched fists. 'Christ, Sara,' he said through his teeth. 'Stop this! This was an *accident*—'

Sara's voice rose wildly. 'And you said it was awful luck Jim wasn't there. So someone else could have been there. Someone else could have done it!'

Andrew grabbed her by the shoulders and stopped her mouth abruptly by kissing her. 'Shut up. Shut up and listen,' he murmured eventually, both arms still wrapped tightly round her. She began to cry softly. 'Listen. Pointless, unpredictable things happen. They happen. I see quite a lot of them. I know you can't bear that. I know what you're doing. You're trying to find reasons for me, because you want me to clean up every case with some elegant resolution, so you can think I'm brilliant and that life won't sometimes be hideous. Even if you have to invent ludicrous theories to do it. Isn't that what you're doing?'

'No, I don't think so. Oh, I don't know. Maybe. Perhaps I am.'

'But you must stop, d'you hear? This thing does have to be accepted. And look, I know acceptance is hard, especially for you, especially since Matteo. But you'll drive yourself mad if you don't, because these things can happen. Oh, Sara, I do love you.'

With a burst of elation Sara reached up to Andrew's face and kissed him, drawing her breath in sharply but not loudly enough to drown out the sudden imperious knocking and plaintive 'Sara? Sara? Hello, your door is open, you are where, Sara?' from the hall.

Five seconds. Five lousy seconds were all they had in which to spring apart and fix smiles of welcome on nonchalant faces before Herve appeared in the doorway of the kitchen with a small suitcase in his hand.

'This is a surprise,' she said. 'Isn't it, Andrew?'

'Certainly is,' Andrew said tightly. 'Must be urgent.'

Herve hardly bothered to acknowledge him. 'Sara, I stay here.' He strode in and sat down squarely on one of the Windsor chairs, the suitcase at his feet. 'I am most upset, yes. That flat, I cannot stay there. And you say nothing, Sara. I am not happy.'

Andrew intervened. 'Herve, you look as if you've had a bit of a shock. Why don't you come in, sit down and tell us all about it?' He exchanged the merest glance of amusement with Sara who, desperate with mirthless tension, nearly burst out laughing. Or crying.

The irony was lost on Herve, who had looked at him critically. 'I *do* sit down. See?' He had had a shock. He had met Mrs Maupesson on his way out to buy himself something for lunch. She had shared the news of the explosion in the Circus. Mrs Maupesson had commiserated with him about the basement. Then she had gone on to explain about Miss Bevan, in graphic detail. How could he stay there now? Every time he thought about it, he couldn't work for worrying. He was the link! Camden Crescent, now the Circus; next, himself! He was Hungarian, could he just remind them. He had enemies, jealous people, to say nothing of politics. And what shocked Herve was not just the fact of his being expected to live in the flat above where a woman had recently met a violent death, but Sara's failure to inform him about it. How could she treat him like this?

'Herve,' she began, looking at Andrew, 'pointless, unpredictable things happen. They happen. You'll drive yourself mad, thinking up ludicrous theories.' Andrew was now making faces at her over Herve's shoulder. 'Won't he?' She felt suddenly like laughing, pointlessly. It was so unfunny.

'That's right. The letter-bomb had nothing to do with you. You weren't even here then,' Andrew said, coughing.

'Ha! You think that is the point? I tell you, Sara, you don't understand this world. My world.' Herve reached into his suitcase and pulled out a copy of *New Music Review*, the contemporary music glossy which Sara and Andrew had long ago agreed they found unreadable. He opened it and banged a page with the back of his hand. 'See! There – look there. This is what I suffer!'

Sara read aloud: '"An angry protest nearly prevented the French première of Herve Petrescu's opus 53 'Terpsichore's Nipple' for spectrally tuned grand piano, four trombones, four pre-recorded string quartets and soprano. Members of the Lyon Orchestre de l'Avenir du Peuple and the audience were showered with leaflets denouncing Petrescu as a 'subnormal intellect', accusing the European music world of being 'awash with pseudo-intellectual social climbers' and identified a cabal of conspirators controlling new music. Petrescu was unperturbed and conducted the performance as planned. It was confirmed by a spokesman for the orchestra that a subsequent performance scheduled for June had been cancelled." My God, Herve. This really happened, did it? There are some idiots about, aren't there?'

'And here! Look here!' He had delved back into the case

and was thrusting a back issue of the *New York Times* into her hands, open at the music reviews section.

'"We are told that doctors sometimes find it impossible to ascertain whether certain patients are in a persistent vegetative state, or clinically dead. I have hit upon a sure-fire diagnosis. Subject these poor unfortunates to Herve Petrescu's opera. Those who do not vomit violently within the first five minutes must be dead: time to switch off the machines. And death, while undeniably final, at least takes them beyond the reach of such rubbish." Hmm, not very favourable. Still, only a review. Just a bad review.'

Sara put down the paper. She did not dare look at Andrew who, she knew, would be trying not to laugh. 'Come on, you know as well as I do that a bad review is just a bad review. It doesn't mean someone's trying to kill you.'

'Ho, you think I am paranoid? Well maybe I am, a little. But this does not mean I am wrong, this does not mean I do not have enemies. And you put me in this flat which you know is dangerous!'

'Herve, I thought I was doing you a favour finding you anywhere at all. It's a beautiful flat. And if you won't stay there and you don't like hotels, what am I supposed to do? Where are you to go?'

Herve in his offended surprise merely looked down at his suitcase and back at Sara. He was not used to the matter of his comfort being regarded as a mere housing problem, and he did not like this new tone in Sara's voice. Sara was about to follow up with confirmation that he most certainly could not stay at Medlar Cottage when Andrew took charge.

'I do quite understand. It's not a pleasant thought, particularly upsetting for a creative artist.'

Herve looked at Andrew, considering. With a slight bow of the head in his direction, he murmured with the generosity of the prepared-to-be-appeased.

'But there's no link, I can assure you. We may be a provincial police force but actually, you know, that's one of our strengths. We can do things without being noticed, if I can put it that way, and questions relating to your . . . stature, I could say, well they're being looked into. And at the highest level.' He fixed Herve with a grown-up stare. 'I can't say more, you understand. This conversation never happened.'

Sara watched silently from behind Herve's chair, relishing the performance, adoring Andrew's nerve. She had seen this side of him before, his callous, brilliant handling of a weaker mind. Also known as lying through the teeth. God, but he was convincing.

Herve moistened his lips. 'You mean—?'

Andrew interrupted him, as if Herve's next words could place them all in the gravest danger. 'I think you know what I mean. Of course I am speaking off the record. But please do be reassured. The flat is *quite* safe.'

Herve turned first to Sara with a look that put her in her proper place and then back to Andrew. His face relaxed into an expression of comfortable self-importance. Sara wondered how she had ever found it attractive, let alone mesmerising.

'Yes, your word I can take,' he said.

'Did you come by taxi? I'm going back into town, so I'll take you. I just came out to talk to Sara about the Circus incident. It's all very much as we first thought, though we're talking to people who saw Adele most recently, just to get the full picture.' He took a step towards Herve and picked up his suitcase. Without irony, and ignoring Sara's incredulous face, he gestured towards the door.

'Maestro?'

With a last glare at Sara, the maestro swept obediently from the room.

In the hall Andrew turned to Sara and the look in his dark brown eyes almost scorched her. 'There are some areas we've barely touched on,' he said thoughtfully, tapping his lip. 'I'll contact you again, if I may.'

'You may,' was all she could say.

Chapter Twenty-one

Poppy took charge. Someone had to. When Helene had been persuaded to get into the bath she had run for her, she slipped into the sour bedroom, pulled apart the curtains, drew up the sash window and allowed in the first air and daylight for over two weeks. She whipped round the bedside tables with a duster, removed dirty mugs, glasses and empty bottles. She closed the albums of photographs of Adele and placed them in a neat pile out of obvious sight. She placed a vase of flowers (expensive, out-of-season irises and freesias, not funeral flowers like lilies or chrysanthemums) on the chest of drawers. A few shifts at the nursing home had stripped Poppy of any conscience about entering the territory of other people's bedding and clothing, so she dragged the covers off the bed and replaced them with fresh linen and a clean bedspread. Then she took from Helene's wardrobe a dark blue ensemble of skirt and long cardigan, looked out matching tights and shoes and placed them on the bed along with a set of what they referred to in the nursing home as undies. Next to them she put a pair of silver earrings, Helene's watch and a long silver chain with a chunky cross on the end.

Really, she thought, looking round at the prepared room while mild lapping noises, but no singing, came from the bathroom down the landing, it was like giving a massage only without actually touching the person. It was the same kind of care. By arranging for the washing, soothing, scenting and dressing of Helene's body, and at least visual order for her tired eyes in the shape of a tidy, beflowered bedroom, she was the dispenser of balm of a sort. She drew a small, narrow-necked bottle from her pocket and, uncorking it, scattered a few drops over the bedspread. Lavender, to promote peaceful thoughts. Poppy smiled with satisfaction. She could always choose the emollient to suit.

An hour later, dressed in her sober navy blue and pale jewellery, Helene appeared in the drawing room. In the dull light of a cloudy October afternoon she was diminished. She had lost weight and strength after too long on occasional biscuits, halves of sandwiches and cups of tea. Sleeping only the heavy sleep of a woman who has quieted herself with too much wine, the stained pillow of her face was downturned and pouchy. Her hair needed more than the shampoo she had given it to remove a look of matted, finger-dragged neglect. Deeper down, grief seemed to have robbed her of oxygen. She no longer seemed three inches taller than her height, with her arched eyebrows, lips, jaw and cheekbones arranged to assist the diaphragm in the sonic takeoff of the Voice. She no longer had lift. She was empty of air, energy and the will to fly.

Poppy bounced up from the sofa and went to her. Valerie, Phil and Cosmo, having all turned and taken her in at the drawing room door, began an ad lib chorus of murmurs of pity and admiration, to whose accompaniment Helene, led by Poppy, made her way slowly across the carpet. She sank into her wing armchair, saving for Poppy, who seemed to require it, a special look which spoke of gratitude for her help and slight shame that she needed it.

Helene looked round the room as if seeing it again after a long absence. She knew the others were watching and was conscious that her stage life had robbed her of the ability to behave without being aware of the audience. She did not know how *not* to open her eyes wider than strictly necessary, projecting further than the stalls, or how not to move her head in slow wonderment for the benefit of the dress circle. Without these people present, there would be no point in her casting from side to side wan nods and half-smiles of recognition and little looks to this doltish girl who appeared to believe she had acquired some rights in this house. But without resting her features for a moment Helene wondered if now it was their very presence that really was the point.

'Now,' said Poppy.

Cosmo coughed.

'Cosmo and I have been talking. There are things we both feel we want to express, like, it's obviously a really difficult time. Just incredibly painful. I mean, really, really bad, especially for you, Helene.'

Helene closed her eyes, blotting out the stricken faces and with a slight nod expressed concurrence.

'And Helene, well done you, for making it today. We all think that's brilliant, don't we?'

Failing to notice, quite, that they had suddenly become group therapy, everyone raised a voice in a yeah or a yah or an absolutely.

Poppy raised a hand. 'I mean, obviously, people can think whatever, but Cosmo and I thought that what Adele would want would be for the project to continue. Carry on and do the show, like a sort of tribute.' She looked slowly round and was nodding seriously as she said, 'Cosmo and I have been talking, and what we thought was Adele was like, well, here's someone that's not just really talented, but a really great person as well. Her own person. We honestly think she'd have wanted that.'

More murmurs rose. In the atmosphere of approval, Poppy repeated much of what she had said, in only slightly different words, concluding again, 'I honestly think she'd have wanted that.'

Helene took a breath and leaned forward, indicating that she was ready to speak. She paused. She looked almost kindly at them: hopeless Phil, narrow Valerie, weak Cosmo and dull Poppy. There was no point in any of them. The point, once, had been her own voice. Then all that had changed and Adele had become the point. How could they imagine it could be any other way? Yet she would go on. Over the past fourteen days, alone in her bedroom apart from venturing out to the sedated torture of the funeral, she had debated this with herself. She had actually had the top off the paracetamol bottle at one point. But the old trouper had won. She would go on even though for the moment she could see no point.

So instead, in a wavering voice she said, 'Thank you, so much, all of you.' It wasn't their fault. They had not been born for music, any of them, as she had been. What could they know of disappointment of the kind when a career collides with the needs of a disturbed child? And which of them had ever felt loss like this, as if every bone had been extracted from your body, leaving you in a meaningless heap? And what could they possibly have to say about hope, when none existed? Or about the exhausting battle, only beginning, that she would fight, just to carry on, growing old in its absence?

'I had hopes for Adele,' she began, but her voice and face collapsed and melted together, her grief liquefying away into wordlessness. She took the hanky that Poppy handed her, and hid her eyes. After a minute or two she blew her nose and looked up, with a sigh. No, they could none of them know anything. But already she had decided, or rather recognised, that she had to go on, because the audience was waiting. As long as there were people ready to react she would continue to act. She would go on with the show, envious of these others whose own pointlessness was hidden from them. She would be in every way splendid to these ever-diminishing, admiring others and pointless only to herself.

'Adele and I shared the healing power of music. In her own way, Adele had gifts. Those gifts were not wasted. The world was a better place because Adele was in it.' More murmurs arose, and for the first time since Adele's death Helene felt, with a flicker of warmth, that there were things that could be said about her daughter that would be both comforting and true.

'Where's Jim?' she asked.

Poppy settled a look of understanding on Helene and spoke with slow, rehearsed calm. 'Well, Cosmo and I were thinking about Jim ourselves. Naturally he's particularly upset, what with it happening in the workshop, but it would be the most terrible pity if—'

'But Jim wasn't even there. They said that, didn't they, the cooker wasn't actually faulty. Adele left the gas on the day before.'

'Well, he wouldn't come today. He didn't want to upset you.'

Helene stared into space for a moment and then sighed. 'He should realise,' she said wearily, 'that no one's to blame, unless I am, for thinking it was safe for her to work anywhere on her own.' Tears flooded her eyes again. 'What's the point anyway? Having someone to blame won't bring her back.'

Poppy looked down, nodding. It was only decent to conceal her relief. The opera could be rejigged to compensate for Adele's loss, but to try to carry on without the baritone would have been well nigh impossible. Thank God Helene was putting up no objection to Jim's reinstatement.

Cosmo took this as his cue to speak up for the project. He too was suddenly authoritative on the subject of what Adele would have really wanted. By the time he had finished it had become almost impossible to object to the project's going ahead without seeming to dispute that Adele had been a really great person. But Valerie tried.

'Look, I hear what you're all saying. But shouldn't it wait? I mean, do we really feel like it? Wouldn't it be a bit, well . . . *frivolous*, singing about Beau Nash? And what about Adele's part?'

Evidently Poppy had had ideas about that too. With a look from her, Cosmo moistened his red lips and began again. 'Well, we've had a bit of a rethink there actually. What's emerging is, ah, the *darker* side of Nash. Tragic, even. I mean, Poppy's been helping me see that seen from a slightly different perspective, Nash was actually a victim of his times. You know, the son of a bottle-maker getting to Oxford, unable to join the kind of society he is then exposed to. Being excluded. Not being valued or recognised for what he is. Feeling inadequate for

193

not being a gentleman, yet resenting the people from whom he craves acceptance. You know.'

There was silence, indicating that they did not.

Poppy broke in eagerly, 'And it's a story of such triumph! Because he ends up not just being able to belong in society, but actually dictating terms! We'll have to do that part of the story *real* justice.' She spoke as if it had been agreed that the opera was going ahead.

'So important that the audience really feels the tension there, don't you think?' Poppy asserted rather than asked the question. 'It's going to be very exciting, to hear that tension in the music. Once Cosmo gets an idea, he really runs with it. Don't you, darling? And so you see, Valerie, Adele's part would be less central. Juliana Papjoy, Nash's mistress, would be more a cameo role. Perhaps even you could do it.'

An enormous sigh escaped from Helene, whose attention seemed to be wandering off and returning to the community opera.

'You could, dear,' she sighed, 'with help.' Her concurrence put the seal on it. Valerie, converted, preened slightly in the faith Helene had expressed in her and in the prospect of a big part which would make Andrew sit up and take notice.

Poppy lowered her voice. 'And the community needs this project. I've been trying to fulfil my brief there and get people involved, like we agreed before . . . before everything happened. I've got smashing news there, everybody. The Iford Cubs are still really keen. I spoke to them and they're still on for three performances in the week before Christmas. We could still do it. The library are happy for us to use them for publicity, and I've nearly firmed it up with the Podium to do the performances there.'

'The *Podium*? The shopping mall? What, you mean, with all the escalators going and . . . and *people* everywhere?' It was not quite what Valerie had had in mind.

'Wonderful, isn't it?' Poppy's eyes were shining. 'Taking it right to the community. Opera, *people's* opera, right in the centre of their everyday, ordinary lives.'

The silence this time was dubious.

She went on, 'I'll fill you in when I've firmed it all up. The main thing for now is just to rally round Helene. Right now, she, like, needs us. You don't mind me saying, Helene? We're mainly here for her sake, Cosmo and me. We wouldn't dream of pulling out now and just leaving, it would be so terrible for her. She needs people around.'

Helene roused herself. 'What a marvellous support you all are,' she said, in something more of her old voice. 'Now, I'm sure we all need a cuppa, don't we? I wonder, Phil, could you? Yes, thank you, dear, you're a great help. You know where everything is. Before we start the rehearsal.'

Before the white face of Phil had withdrawn from the circle, Helene smiled and arranged her new facial expression. She gazed over them all towards the far horizons, somewhere through the window and beyond the Circus, with the lingering look of the diva as the curtain comes down after the big ensemble at the end of Act Two. It was a look designed to send the punters off to their interval drinks with the image, still burning on their retinae, of the human spirit triumphing over adversity.

Chapter Twenty-two

Sara had said that he may, meaning it. But Andrew did not contact her the next day, nor the one after, nor the one after that, sensing that if he were to telephone her he would want to see her and that if he saw her, nothing would ever be the same again. Perhaps if he had been able to think of his relationship with Sara as just an affair he would have found himself able to embark upon it, but it could never be just that. As his love for Sara had taken definite shape in his mind as the great life-changing force that he wanted it to be, and not a jokey little bit of adultery of the kind that he had watched so many of his colleagues amuse themselves with, the greater also had grown his sense of his huge, undeniable responsibilities to his children.

He had telephoned on the fourth day, unable not to, apologetic, eager and ultimately unavailing.

'Sara, I was stuck at home all weekend. Of course I wanted to ring, I simply couldn't. I'm at work now. I thought of you the whole time, Sara. When can I see you? Sara? Sara, please.'

'It's Tuesday. Why didn't you ring yesterday?'

'Sara, please. Be reasonable. I had to go Adele's inquest. It was opened and adjourned. I'm afraid Jim's in for a hard time.'

'*Reasonable*?' She was not going to be drawn away from what she wanted to say. 'All right, I'll be reasonable. Reasonable is seeing how stupid it is to get involved with a married man.

Reasonable is seeing that I'd always be waiting for you to have time to sneak out here, and you'd be so guilty and thinking about your wife all the time. Not to mention the children. Or do you think of them as "the kiddies"? *That's* reasonable, Andrew, not going along with this.'

'Sara, don't put us through this. We need to talk.'

'No, we don't. We need to not see each other, however much we want to. And I do want to. That's the trouble.'

'Sara—'

'I mean it. No visits, no lessons. I can't see you without wanting you, so I won't see you any more. I'm not being moral, I'm protecting myself. I won't be a *mistress*.'

He saw her, briefly and painfully, at Adele's funeral on 6 October. In the company of fellow mourners they had both looked quite wretched, perhaps even enough to raise in others some surprise at how the most unlikely people could be so affected by funerals.

That had been nearly three weeks ago. It was now 26 October and more than his relationship with Sara had frozen into a depressed immobility. Enquiries had been continuing among the known acquaintances of Brendan Twigg, a straggle of defiant underdogs that stretched halfway round Somerset and Wiltshire. Two or three whom they had brought in for questioning had not come up with the expected histrionic denials that they had clapped eyes on him for several weeks. That would have been a clear indication that he was, in police parlance, in the vicinity, staying with people for a night or two and rallying their support, under the anti-police banner that they all shared, in keeping a low profile. Instead they were getting vague murmurings that they had not noticed him around much recently, which meant that they probably genuinely hadn't.

It was a great pity, he thought, that something of the same torpor could not infect the opera project. The new momentum in *Nash!* (or *Beau!* – they had yet to decide) and in his own wife, by contrast, only added to Andrew's embarrassment in being associated with the whole thing. He still thought of it as fundamentally misguided but it now seemed to him, following Adele's death, also literally sad.

In the days before and immediately following the funeral, Helene had, to his surprise, turned to Valerie for nurture and sympathy, causing him to wonder briefly if there were qualities in his wife that he could not see. She had taken rather naturally to the role of comforter and, oddly enough, at around the same time, had found herself in demand in a similar role when an old friend, Linda, who had been Valerie's bridesmaid, had rung her up out of the blue, having been only in Christmas card touch for years. Linda was going through the most awful divorce, and was turning to Valerie. Andrew had never been able to stand her and had been given to understand that Valerie couldn't either.

'I thought you couldn't stand her. And why does she want *you* with her, after all this time?'

Valerie had resented the question. 'Linda was my bridesmaid. We go way back. It's not hard to understand. Most of their friends now are *his* friends. She wants somebody familiar, someone who's *her* friend. It's natural.' It was a sign of Valerie's new generosity with her time, as well as her surge in energy, that she had already allowed herself to be summoned away several times to Linda's house in Swindon, as fort-holder-in-chief. That Linda needed her she obviously took as a compliment, and was glowing in its warmth.

Then, nearly a week ago, coming round the Circus straight from work towards Helene's for the rehearsal, Andrew had heard the familiar sound of Helene's voice in a mounting arpeggio (ah – ah – ah – aagh!) followed by a scratchy imitation (er – er – ergh? – *ergh*?). So Valerie's condolence visits to Helene had become singing lessons. When Helene had answered the door she was practically trilling her little surprise. Dear Valerie was having proper lessons so that she could acquit herself in the new role of Juliana Papjoy and Helene was thrilled to be giving them because that was what it was all about, wasn't it, giving?

Valerie had been wearing one of his shirts with black leggings, a pen behind her ear and the facial expression of one upon whom everything depends. She had graciously assumed not only Adele's leading, although rewritten part, but also the mantle of the one who was almost single-handedly saving the show, and as the rehearsal had got under way Andrew had observed that with her new confidence there was a new energy which drew people's eyes to her, including his. He noticed that she was opening her mouth wider and not just to sing, and showing her bottom teeth when she laughed, which was more often. And he had not noticed before that she was fixing her hair so as to make it bigger, or perhaps it was just that she was tending to throw it back with a slight shake of the head, which drew attention to it. Although Andrew did not make a special study of these things he was pretty sure it had been done over with something to make it a bit redder. He liked the effect. In the moments when Cosmo was rehearsing others she had sat out with her legs studiously splayed or bent, ever poised, like a resting but eternally body-conscious aerobics teacher. She had spoken quite seriously to him over the coffee about the responsibility she felt for keeping Helene's spirits up, along with her sense of empowerment in finding her own voice and feeling that she had things to give as a performer. Helene had beamed her gratitude and spoken of Valerie as our saviour and Valerie had fussed reciprocally round Helene, substituting admirably for the still absent Jim.

Poppy had seemed a little left out. Perhaps she had been hoping to be appointed to the role of chief comforter herself, so Andrew had whispered something diplomatic about Helene perhaps needing the company of a woman who was also a mother and nearer her own age. He had felt sorry for Poppy, who continued to display a sort of dogged backstage stamina that got all the dull and thankless things done and for which they should all have been much more grateful than they were. While Cosmo sat at the piano every day like a chugging engine it was Poppy who was keeping him stoked from the library with biographical details, quotations and songs about Beau Nash, which she referred to as 'material'. Andrew had run into her once outside the Podium, laden with bags. 'Material for Cosmo,' she had said importantly, 'some more *fascinating* insights.' And off she had gone to fuel the refining fire of Cosmo's creativity with more votive offerings of photocopies and books with the relevant pages turned down at the corners.

Helene had also confided to Valerie, who passed it on to Andrew, that Cosmo was really getting on with the music now. He had commandeered Helene's drawing room and insisted on at least five uninterrupted hours every day. One evening, when Helene had ventured the observation that Cosmo had a very quiet way of working, she had been aware that the remark created a slight frost. But notes from the piano would reach her only seldom and were interspersed by long silences during which, Helene had said to Valerie, she liked to imagine Cosmo brooding at the piano or scratching on manuscript paper with a scowl like dear Beethoven's. He had grown more confident and, to everyone's relief, seemed to have clearer ideas about where the 'piece' was heading. And to give him his due, the music had not been too bad. What he had given them to sing were very nearly tunes; that was to say that after hearing one line, you would feel you knew where the second should go and then it didn't, but you got the knack eventually.

Only Phil, obviously trying diligently in his industrious way, had seemed nevertheless rather exhausted and disinclined to sing at all, unknowingly reflecting Andrew's own feelings. Andrew supposed he was having a busy time with his course. He was doing engineering or maths or some other thing, but he had never spoken of it except to say that it was fine. Perhaps he didn't have enough English to chat easily. Or perhaps it was just clumsy western thinking to mistake his intense quiet for unhappiness but, being anyway of slight build, Phil now looked smaller, as if the new reticence in him amounted almost to shrinkage.

Thinking all this at lunchtime in the canteen, looking out at Manvers Street and a concrete, East German-looking branch of Comet, and feeling as a result quite stupefyingly depressed, Andrew began to wonder if he could find an excuse to skip tomorrow's rehearsal. Last week he had understood from Poppy that big efforts were going to be made to persuade Jim to come back. We've all got to get Jim to *move on*, she had said, blinking when Andrew had said that yes, policemen ask people to move on the whole time. Quite apart from looming dread at having to play the joyless cello part again, he would much rather not run into Jim, less out of embarrassment than regret that he could tell him nothing that would be of any use or comfort to him. Andrew had made it his business not to know the detail of the case that was being built by the CPS and would have to say, were Jim to be present tomorrow and ask him, that indeed employment legislation can take a small business horribly by surprise. Jim's ad hoc workshop, only the spare room at the back was probably how Jim thought of it, was indeed a workplace and Adele, however informal the arrangement, had been his employee. It made no difference that nobody blamed him for what had happened if he could be found to have been negligent or even malicious in failing to provide a safe workplace.

Deliverance from the rehearsal came in the unexpected form of DS Bridger sloping in and standing over the table just as Andrew was finishing his sandwich.

'Sorry, sir, but Judge Ward-Pargiter is here, with his daughter,' he said, as respectfully as if the judge were standing gowned and bewigged behind him. 'He's asking to see you.'

Although Anna's face this time had the sleek, almost feline look of someone who is being both well and regularly fed and is always warm enough, she seemed cowed. The eyes behind the glasses were red and swollen again. 'Does the silly baggage ever stop crying?' was not Andrew's first question, at any rate not out loud.

'Well, Anna, have you got something you'd like to tell us?'

Adam Ward-Pargiter nodded towards his daughter. He looked weary and ashamed. 'Get on with it, Anna,' he said.

'Oh, I'm so sorry, I'm so sorry, I'm so sorry,' she blubbed.

Her father turned round to her. 'Anna, you know damn well it's a bit late for sorry. Nobody's that interested in hearing how sorry you are. Just get on with what Chief Inspector Poole needs to know.'

Anna gulped. 'I helped Bren. I gave him some money.'

'I found her building society book this morning. She gave him four hundred pounds. Practically all she had,' her father said, turning on Andrew a face that looked as if he had been kicked. 'Although it's not the money in itself that's at issue. It's hers, after all.'

'When did you do this, Anna?' Andrew asked.

'Over a fortnight ago. The date's in the book.' Anna fished the account book from a pocket and pushed it across the table. 'I took the money out on a Saturday, the tenth. Bren – he ran into me after school one day, you see.'

'*Ran into* you? Not quite accurate,' Adam Ward–Pargiter said stiffly. 'Don't make it sound like an accident. He's not stupid. He's vicious, and a manipulator and a coward, but not stupid. After all, he didn't risk showing his face anywhere near the school, or anywhere you'd be seen together. Did he, Anna?'

Andrew said, 'Anna, let's have the whole story. Will you please tell me in your own words exactly what happened.'

Anna nodded miserably and wiped her nose. She had come with her own supply of tissues this time, Andrew noted.

'On Wednesday the seventh I got the school bus home as usual. I'm the only one who gets off in Atworth. It's about two miles home from there so I come in on my bike and leave it at the garden centre, locked up next to the sheds at the back. When I went round the sheds to get my bike that day I found Fonz tied up there. Tied to my bike.' The tears started again and her father gave an exasperated sigh. Anna lifted her head. 'The dog. Bren's dog. He looked terrible. He was trembling all over and he had big scabs on him and he was even thinner than before. He was pleased to see me, though.'

'Just the dog? No sign of Bren?'

'Not straight away. I was so upset. Because of the state he was in. I'd just got him untied because I thought I should take him straight down to the vet in Box, and Bren appeared. He said he had to wait to make sure I was on my own. I was nearly crying about the dog and I started going on about how could he let him get like that. And Bren said it was all

right for me walking straight back into my cushy number and
my big house and poncy posh school and all that. He'd been
watching me come and go for weeks, he said. If I really cared
about deprivation and hunger and all those things I wouldn't
be part of the . . . you know, effing middle class that created
all the poverty in the first place. He was too poor to feed the
dog, he said.'

'Knew just how to get to you, didn't he?' her father said,
sounding almost gentle for the first time.

'And then he said he was being victimised and couldn't get
hold of any money unless I helped him.'

'Anna, didn't you realise that Bren was wanted in connection with a very serious offence?'

'But he didn't do it. I just know he didn't. He couldn't
hurt anyone.'

'He managed to hurt the dog, didn't he?'

'But that was because he hadn't got any money. That was
why I said I'd give him some. I know it was stupid. I do know
that, now. I'm sorry.' She looked so abjectly at her father that he
took her hand and squeezed it and smiled his almost-forgiveness.
Andrew watched without surprise, knowing how daughters
make you feel.

'I gave him what I had on me, so he could get some dogfood.
I said I couldn't get him any more till Saturday, till I could get
into town to the building society. We agreed to meet in Parade
Gardens, at the bit right down by the river next to the bridge.
It's a dead-end, nobody goes there and there are lots of bushes.
When I got there he hugged me and took my account book
out of my bag so he knew how much I had. He asked for all
of it, so he could get the dog's scabs treated properly. He went
on about helping Fonz, like he was really upset about him. He
was really caring, kind, like when we first met. He said I was
great.' Her voice grew quieter. 'So he waited while I went
and got the money. When I got back it was still only eleven
o'clock and I said let's get the bus to Batheaston because the
vet there has a morning surgery. Then he laughed and said no
way, he had to catch a train. He was laughing at me. He said

the dog would be all right anyway, the scabs didn't bother him. He needed the money to get out of Bath and was I really so stupid I didn't realise that.'

Andrew asked, very quietly, 'Did he say any more about where he was going? Where did he say he was going, Anna?'

Anna looked at him wretchedly. 'We'd got to the top of the steps out of Parade Gardens by then. You can see the abbey clock from there. I was saying, "Look, you've got to get Fonz better, he needs to go to a vet," and he just said, "Christ, is that clock right? I've got to get down the station." Then he started to drag Fonz off with him and he could hardly keep up. I grabbed his arm and I wouldn't let go. I said, "Wait, you can't, what about the vet?" He was trying to pull away from me but I was holding on. He said, "Shut the fuck up about that. I'll get him to a vet when I get there, okay?" People could hear us and everything.'

'Did he say *where*, Anna?'

Anna burst into tears, nodding. 'He was furious, he was trying to pull my fingers off his arm and I still held on. It was so horrible. He said to me, "What do I have to do to fucking get away from you? Let me fucking go, you rich slag and I'll get him to a fucking vet."'

'Anna?'

'I was crying and screaming, "When, when?" People were watching. He started running and I went after him and then he turned and shouted back, "When I get to fucking York." I let him go then.'

Adam Ward-Pargiter rose and took his sobbing, wounded, soft-hearted, over-privileged, immature daughter in his arms.

'I am very grateful to you, Anna,' said Andrew, with feeling.

Chapter Twenty-three

Sara had taken to running every day, letting her mind wander over the lives of other people, a mental tactic which partly deflected her from dwelling on her own emotional dead-end. She would not concede to herself that she missed the opera group, so she thought about them instead. It was Adele she thought about most, trying to grasp Adele's view of the world, a world where it made sense to switch on the gas before leaving work one day and return and light a match on the next. Had there been some significance for her in the hiss of the gas, or in the simple turning of one of the four dials along the cooker front? It still seemed wrong and inexplicable. Mixed with her dismay and grief for Helene was something like anger that Adele would do such a thing, which was gradually replacing her disbelief that she could have done something so destructive, yet so unknowingly. Andrew might have called it acceptance, but it was a more restless feeling than that.

The lanes through the valley were slippery now with fallen leaves and the wet hedgerows were darkening with the slime of dying grass; the season, being mild this year, rather disgusted her. The trample of her angry feet squeezed out the smell of composting vegetation into damp air that reminded her of warm cabbages. Three miles a day became four, then five. Anything to exhaust her body and fill her mind with feelings and thoughts not directly concerning Herve or Andrew. She left her answering machine switched off and answered the telephone only when she felt like it.

Brittleness entered all her dealings with Herve who was (and this did not help matters) virtually the only person she saw. He wondered that he had ever thought her flexible. Routinely now in their rehearsals he was irritated to waspishness, while she played with an expression on her face (a face, he marvelled, that he had once thought lovely but now more and more had the look of his mother in it) that was close to sneering. She had announced almost ten days ago that she would no longer come every day to Camden Crescent but only every other day, so Herve now made the journey out to Medlar Cottage on the days in between, resentfully carting his keyboard, synthesiser, amplifier, percussion deck and the day's music down the stairs of the flat, across the hall and out to a taxi with an unvaryingly hostile driver. At Sara's house he would even more resentfully unload his keyboard, synthesiser, amplifier, percussion deck and the day's music, carry them through the awkward narrow gate, up the steep stone steps, across the front garden, into the house and through to the large music room at the back. Sara would watch, occasionally holding open a door for him but making it clear that she wouldn't so much as push in a plug. And then he would go back to pay the driver. And approximately three hours later, after a morning's thankless work with the unaccommodating prima donna, he would do the whole thing again in reverse with the keyboard, synthesiser, amplifier, percussion deck and the day's music, which would all have doubled in weight.

Sara got back from her run one Monday morning at the end of October to find Herve (and his keyboard, synthesiser, amplifier, percussion deck and the day's music) sitting in the garden. It had been raining. When he saw her he jumped to his feet.

'Half an hour, half an hour I wait! More!' He thrust out his wrist as if she could read his watch from twenty yards. 'Forty minutes! And you not even here!'

'Why should I be? You're early,' she said. She could see at

once what had happened. But she was already enjoying his distress and deliberately prolonging the confusion because Herve's climbdown, when it came, would be the more humiliating if she gave him maximum rein to abuse her for her lack of punctuality and professionalism, as she knew he was about to. She walked past him into the house, hands loosely on her hips, with the languorous, well-toned swing of someone in very short shorts who has found a five-mile run no trouble at all and knows her buns to be worth looking at. Look, don't touch. Herve stared after her, his jaw working. She turned and came back to the door, rather impatiently.

'Are you coming in or aren't you?' With her eyes she took in all the equipment on the grass in its black vinyl, rain-spotted covers. 'I expect you can manage. I've got to shower and dress, of course, but you're welcome to come in and wait.'

She disappeared upstairs. Wait he did, pacing the music room after he had lugged in and set up the equipment, again single-handedly.

She reappeared half an hour later on the dot of ten o'clock wearing a black silk shirt and black Levi's, gleaming with demonic health. As she took the Strad out of its case, pulled out the end pin and tightened her bow, she noted with glee that he had gone almost beyond speech. Almost.

'What is this! This rudeness! So rude to me! Eleven o'clock! An *hour* late now. Sara, this is not right, not professional, this I cannot—'

'It is ten o'clock, Herve. Not eleven,' she said, calmly tuning up. 'The clocks went back on Saturday. The clocks go back one hour, for the winter.'

'So why do you not say? To inform me? How am I to know this? You tell me nothing!'

'I say nothing, Herve, because it is in all the newspapers, to remind people. It is on the radio. And the television. And if you'd been out once in the past thirty-six hours and bothered to look up once, you'd have seen it on the abbey clock, or the Post Office clock. Or the clocks in shops. Everywhere.'

'I do not see such things.'

'Fine. Suit yourself. You don't have to. But it's not my responsibility to see them for you.'

'All the time I am working, or I am thinking of work. And I have nobody to take care of these things for me. Now Helene does not ring me so much.'

'You're supposed to be a grown-up now, Herve,' she said in a mild voice. 'Not a child. But yes, it must be *inconvenient*, Helene grieving for her only daughter and not feeling quite so chatty. Not running after you.'

It was thrilling, making someone this angry. She wondered if she could make him lose his temper. He seemed determined not to. He merely shrugged with the discomfort of the thought she was burdening him with and switched on the tape recorder. It was a rough recording, but the sound that came eerily from the speakers was Adele's voice, intoning his wordless, witless notions.

'*What* is that?' Sara jumped up and switched off the tape recorder. 'Oh, how could you! How *could* you? She's dead! How can you use her voice like this?' She was angry enough to cry.

Herve was defensive. 'This for me is not the point. This is the sound I want.' He turned on the tape again and the strange inhuman voice floated around them again. Sara was struggling with tears. Herve gave an annoyed sniff and with a 'tch!' switched off the machine. 'Ach! No, maybe it's not so good. The acoustic. Too dead. The workshop no good for recording.'

'The workshop? You recorded that in Jim's workshop?'

'Yes, I don't want fuss, interference. So I visit Adele in the workshop,' Herve said loftily. 'Only one time. But, ach, the tape I cannot use.'

'I think that amounts to exploitation. You know quite well she should have been offered a fee, don't you? You can't just get people to sing for you for nothing, you know that. That's why you went to the workshop, so Helene wouldn't know. That's disgraceful.'

Herve shrugged. 'You react too much, like always. I will not use it, even, so what fee? What harm? And Adele is dead, yes, very sad. But just an accident. Death is everywhere. We must accept it.'

With a sniff he jammed the music on to Sara's music stand, with the clear message that he required her to start work straight away. Sara looked at it slowly without changing her expression of open contempt. Then caressingly she drew the cello against her, closed her eyes and as a slight smile settled on her lips, began to play. The grave, shiveringly rich sound of the Christiani cello of 1700 swept through the room, with a power that would have made salivating beasts lie down and turn over to be tickled. It was the first movement of Edouard Lalo's Cello Concerto: touchingly, achingly Romantic and Sara was playing it, to annoy him the more, with almost sexual joy.

Softly, she began to speak. 'Like it, Herve? This is the sound this instrument makes, when it's allowed to. Nineteenth century. Romantic, elegant. Grown-up music. It's about the big things: big, unmanageable, awkward human things. Do you have any idea what I mean? Listen.' She played on in silence for a while, not caring whether Herve was listening resentfully or allowing himself to be soothed. It really was up to him. She went on, 'People have died. Outrageously, it seems to me. Imogen Bevan died, and all you can do is think of yourself and cook up some nonsense about you being next, as if you were that important. And Adele is dead. So don't talk to me about "just an accident" and try to sniff it away like it was something stuck up your nose.' She drew breath, not wishing her anger to cut into the music. After a few moments she said, 'Their deaths require explanation, at least. Adele is lost to the people who loved her. Do you hear that now, in the music? It's about that pain, perhaps. Joy at what was. Loss, resignation. Mainly, it's about love. There would be no grief, without love. In the end, it's all about love. It's not about ideas. Not about *notions*.'

She should stop here, she knew, she'd said enough to wound him. But a slightly nervous, dismissive *pfaw!* from Herve made her look up, and the sight of his petulant face seemed to strike a match in her which ignited with sudden, destructive heat.

'And you know, Herve, it's not that I'm stuck in the

nineteenth century, although that's what you'd like to think. You think emotions in music are outdated, don't you? You'd like to say I'm just sitting in some cosy traditionalist time warp, wouldn't you? But I love lots of contemporary music.'

She stopped playing abruptly and put down her bow. 'Schnittke's First Cello Sonata, for example.' She played the opening few bars. 'It's wonderful. I can't play it the way Natalia does, of course. Natalia Gutman: Schnittke wrote it for her. But it's got emotions in it, all right. Wild, dangerous ones.' There was no response from Herve so she went on, 'So I expect it's way beneath you and your notions. Anyway, it was written in 1986, after all. It's over ten years old – how *passé.*'

There was a hellish silence, during which Sara must somehow, she realised afterwards, have made the decision to chuck the burning match into the dry gunpowder, although she was unaware of it at the time. For she said, 'No, it's not contemporary music I dislike, per se. It's yours, Herve. Your "music". Your pretentious, inhuman, self-regarding, tight-arsed—'

She got no further. With a wail and a spring towards her, Herve began to bang his fists up and down in the air. 'You! *You* dare to speak like this! *You* – you do nothing, nothing to make this music work! There is no collaboration! You are so . . . so head in air about those opera people, that Andrew – oh, I see all – and these dead ones, Adele and that other! They are dead! So you can do nothing! What about me? No, I am only game to you! And you accuse me! I need only some help from you, I get nothing. I travel all over, always alone, alone since my mother . . . my mother, she would be so angry at this. I have nobody now, I am alone, a stranger here, you put me in dangerous flat . . . I am so lonely . . .' He sank on to the sofa and burst into tears.

'Oh, stop that! Stop it! Don't be ridiculous!' she cried, more in desperation than anger, suddenly swamped with guilt. She grew flinty in her own defence. 'That is complete nonsense. You know it is! You've pushed me to the limit! Stop it now! If we are to work together I cannot, I . . . I *will* not put up with this kind of thing.'

Herve drew in a deep breath and got to his feet. He spat his next words, but with his Slav dignity restored. '*If.* Yes, indeed, if. For myself, I am sick, sick of it all. I phone taxi now.'

'Yes, do. And make them hurry,' she snapped. As a sour silence curdled around them, Sara put away her cello in its case and Herve began snapping cables and leads apart, rather as if they were Sara's neck. Unable either to stay in the room or say a civil goodbye she blurted, 'I'm going outside,' and stepped through the French window out to the garden. Almost before Herve had turned round to see the door swing shut behind her, she was lost among the dripping trees.

Part Three

And so thy thoughts, when thou art gone,
Love itself shall slumber on.

Chapter Twenty-four

Three weeks to the day after Adele's funeral the last of the leaves came down in the Circus. Then, instead of flurrying winds that would have sent them rattling prettily round the railings, and crisp sunshine to illuminate the residents' smart paintwork, rain came. It mired the ground under the plane trees and soaked the leaves in the gutters, so that people walking on the mulched pavements found their shoes claggy as if with wads of brown papier-mâché. The circle of wet, sulking house fronts looked out, one to another, with the suspicious disenchantment of hosed-down dogs.

Jim stared up at the weather from his basement kitchen window, beyond the still empty pot with its waterlogged compost, and tried to meet another day which had already looked him up and down with indifference. He felt overlooked. He had done all the necessary things. The shattered window and door of the workshop had been reinstated. The remains of the cooker had been taken away for examination and he had filled the space with an offcut of worktop. As soon as the room had dried out sufficiently he had had the walls replastered and repainted. He had bought some second-hand metal shelving and a work table from the classified section of the *Chronicle*. A surveyor came round and told him he was lucky that the structure of the building was still sound. Jim knew he should think himself lucky.

It was a relief, of course, to learn that Helene had been

coaxed out of her bedroom. He had walked past the closed curtains of her windows in the days following Adele's death and imagined them to be preserving a houseful of dark hatred for him. He supposed he was pleased to hear the opera was going ahead with, if anything, increased energy and commitment. But while Poppy had been round several times to try to reassure him that Helene was 'desperate' for his return to the group, he still had not heard as much, indeed anything, from Helene herself. And he would not accept that Helene wanted him back until that happened. Had he not made a big enough effort already? He still had some pride.

It seemed to him, walking home one day and hearing from Helene's drawing room the strains (in every sense) of Valerie's voice being coaxed up to a top G, that the shock of Adele's accident had propelled the others forward and further into their own concerns while he, to his own surprise, had halted in his tracks. It was not at all what he had expected to feel. Instead of looking forward, after a decent interval of course, to the proper wooing of an unencumbered Helene who might really need him now, he had been brought to a standstill by the sense of his own guilt. He found himself unable to resume the pattern of work that he had been used to before Adele. She had always arrived on the dot of nine o'clock, compelling him to settle her to her work and leave on the dot of ten past in order to get down to the shop and have half an hour's cleaning of the stock, ready for opening at ten. Without the spur of Adele's punctuality he was getting later and later opening up and lazier about the state of the stuff on the shelves. If somebody wanted a thing, should a little dust matter?

He must just get used to being alone again, just as he had got used to it after Audrey left him for Ronald Sweeting in 1968. But being left by his childless wife of seven years had felt, after the initial shock, like an unlooked-for luxury that was unexpectedly and suddenly his, like a raffle prize; it had made him realise that he already had spent much too long in her unsustaining company. That was not the same as what he now felt himself to be, which was lonely as well as guilty, for what he had done struck him now for the first time as wrong. And it made him lonely, even while he was trying to chat up punters, to think of the workshop at the back of the flat now sitting empty all day. He missed Adele's progress with the chandeliers, but he even missed knowing that she was there, as if her very presence warmed the place in his absence and left behind a sweet atmosphere of industry. Whether it was that or his guilt at what he had done that sometimes caused him to break down without warning, he didn't know, but it put the punters off just the same.

Chapter Twenty-five

Sara continued to suffer in the twenty-four hours following Herve's exit from her house. The sight of him suddenly in a state of weeping collapse on her sofa kept looming at her from the back of her mind, and she began to dwell almost obsessively on her contribution to his unhappiness. She began to believe that she might even have created it, and she tried to numb herself by practising unnecessarily for hours, although nothing, not even her guilt, could induce her to practise anything by Herve. Even after a marathon of Elgar and Dvořák on the Monday she was again the next morning taken by surprise, as if hit from behind, by great swamping waves of remorse. People were meant to be 'filled' with remorse, weren't they? Yet she felt somehow washed over and emptied by it, her well-being and self-worth leached away, leaving her with only an aching space in which reverberated, like an echo, the sense of her own hypocrisy. For it was surely hypocritical to be simultaneously capable of milking a piece of music dry of every last drop of emotion, and yet be deaf and blind to the real feelings of someone whose sufferings she could have allayed or even prevented. Life was falling short of Art in a big way, and although she did not elevate her misery quite to the height of philosophical discomfort, she was aware of the discrepancy and knew herself to be wanting. And on top of it all, like salt and vinegar sprinkled on ice-cream, the continuing absence of Andrew was imparting an inappropriate and increasingly bitter flavour to this day, as it had done to every other.

She rang Helene, who thanked her for the letter of condolence she had written weeks ago. Sara had not attempted to say in it that she understood how Helene must feel but had said simply and truthfully that she was thinking of her. But Helene was claiming in a brave voice that she had appreciated it very much and also that as she was making an effort to get 'back into circulation', was Sara free for lunch?

'Well, yes, I am. I was hoping I could see you. As a matter of fact I want to ask for your help with something. Someone, rather. Herve. I'll explain.'

As Sara turned from Bennett Street into the Circus the sun came out. She was early, and now paused on the pavement. Benches were sparse in the Circus, but she could see that one of the few set out at the edge of the plane trees had room for one more person on it, so she made her way over and sat down. The two people beside her – surely tourists, Japanese or Korean – took no notice of her whatsoever. It was almost the end of October, chilly for sitting about on benches, and Sara was glad that she had left her usual trenchcoat at home and put on a long coat made of hairy, burnt orange mohair. It had a wide shawl collar and no buttons, and she drew it round herself tightly. The tourists were in jeans and wearing only the lightest of short, bum-freezing jackets, but they seemed impervious to the damp cold, so absorbed were they by the architectural wonder around them.

Sara, looking round, considered it less a wonder than a peculiarity, this circle of houses with no focal point. Once you entered the Circus by any of the three roads that broke the circle at equal distances, the implied equilateral triangle within a circle, you found yourself in an exquisitely claustrophobic trap. The circle appeared to close around you because the architect, having chosen a fine site on a hillside from which you might have looked down over the city in one direction and out to the Royal Crescent in another, had then contrived matters so that, once inside, you saw nothing. Instead of four roads entering the Circus and criss-crossing round a central feature, so that you were offered, from whichever road you entered on, a view through the Circus and out across the other side, he gave only three roads at equal intervals. Once in, you had to search for a way out. The two tourists, without any apparent communication having taken place between them, rose as one from the bench and walked on with little steps around the inner pavement of the Circus, still gazing. Sara watched them go, then resumed her study of the three segments of houses which looked out upon nothing but one another.

Even in the autumn sunshine which so flattered the stone, the house fronts seemed reserved, almost bad-tempered, and Sara, knowing this to be fanciful, looked hard to see if there were anything in the architecture itself that could create this impression. Perhaps it was the excessively deep basement areas which gave the set-back houses a distrustful, moated air. By turning her head and searching along with her eyes she made out Helene's house, number 31. Its drawing room window was identical to all the others, and yet how unique they were, the lives that had been lived behind it. She had a sudden recollection of the rehearsal when she had stepped in for Andrew. Adele had been sitting in the window seat, engrossed in her star drawing, while the others in the room had chatted and clinked coffee cups politely, the ordered behaviour of ordered people in an ordered world. Two days later Adele had died. That had been just over a month ago. From where had the invasion come? Sara's eyes involuntarily moved seven doors along and found Jim's basement. It was as innocuous as the rest, any evidence of an explosion, had there ever been any here at the front, having been removed. It was as if a wound had suddenly erupted in a perfect skin, rendering the face so intolerably hideous that emergency cosmetic surgery had immediately been carried out. Beauty had been swiftly restored and the Circus could now offer its smooth façade for the visitors once more. Meanwhile, a girl was dead. And Andrew spoke of acceptance.

It was still a little early to go knocking at Helene's door, and she could hardly appear with her eyes full of tears in any case. Sara gave herself a shake and turned her attention to the doors. They were all painted white, probably in obedience to some bye-law. They were plain, bearing no architraves or embellishments. Sara imagined that this could be because of some stinginess at the building stage rather than a deliberate decision about the design, but the result was that the doors presented themselves as the purely functional means of ingress and egress; the very antithesis of welcome. Even the immediately noticeable decoration of the façade was in its way uninviting. The Doric frieze of carved masonic figures, objects and natural forms which ran all around, just above the tall ground-floor windows, spoke of a private iconography whose purpose was to obfuscate, not symbolise. They made the uninitiated feel exactly that: uninitiated. Unenlightened, left out. The obscure birds, fruits and faces, to say nothing of the gesturing hands, sickles, protractors, hammers and musical instruments spoke of meaningless, indiscriminate exclusion, like a petty playground game in which she was not allowed to join. She felt a sudden urge to stamp her foot and flounce away, because she didn't want to play by anybody's silly masonic rules anyway.

The thought of Adele came back to her. Perhaps being autistic was a bit like this, sitting in the Circus and trying to make sense of it. You are inside a circle which you cannot see a way out of. But the circle appears to make sense to other people, like those two absorbed visitors. It doesn't make them panic at all, but if you let yourself be, you would be frightened. Sometimes you are, so to stop yourself being frightened you blank out the confusing messages that you can't see the point of and then it is as if you see, hear, smell, or touch nothing that connects up with feeling or understanding. Then people think you are stupid. The two Japanese tourists were over on the far side now, still engrossed, now consulting a book. Sara looked from them up at the façade, in the direction in which one of them was pointing. On one level, of course, you see what they see, you see the same things. Sara took in again the curious carvings on the frieze: birds, animals, instruments. Of course she understood in one way: as objects they were all familiar enough. But while you could know what things were, they needn't mean the same to you as they appeared to mean to others, they needn't mean anything at all. And you might not come close to understanding what it was they meant to others. And they would certainly have difficulty understanding what things meant to you. Sara thought of Adele in the walled garden at Iford, her absorption in the symmetry of the paths and plants. Adele and her perfect patterns, her lists, her way of doing things, the things that had frightened her: had anybody understood? Perhaps, if you're autistic, what you are most aware of is that for some reason – no, for *no* reason you can pinpoint – you're out of it. You're excluded from the club where people know what things mean. You're not a member. And to top it all, you can't usually make them understand why you can't join. It's impossible to explain that it's because you just don't know the club rules and don't seem able to learn them.

Sara got up and walked round to Helene's house. Now judging the Circus to be the place she would least like to live in the whole of Bath, she was thinking that whatever one might make of Helene, she did not seem a Circus type. The Circus seemed to forbid the rumpled untidiness of even mildly problematical lives, let alone one stained by real tragedy. Helene was too unreserved, and much too genuine in her warmth. This architecture discouraged warmth and prejudiced Sara against its owners, too. Apart from Helene and Jim, Sara did not know any other Circus dwellers, but she had an impression, from the frequent fusses reported in the *Bath Chronicle*, that the Circus Residents' Association worked tirelessly to make it one of the least welcoming spaces in the city. It had always made Sara cross. Fancy buying a house in one of the most looked-at places in Europe, whose windows directly face the windows of your neighbours, and clamouring for privacy. And instead of being grateful that from their very doorsteps they could look out at the six most magnificent trees in Bath, some of them complained about the 'historically inaccurate' grove of superb planes in the grassy centre, as well as the tour buses and the crowds. She wondered if many of them cared as much about their neighbours as they did about crisp packets on the pavements.

Even less did Helene fit her idea of Circus resident when, a moment later, Sara saw her emerge from her door and make her way over the drawbridge across the basement area to the pavement, in order to welcome her in.

'I thought it was you, sitting out there in the cold! You should have come straight over!'

It was a fabulous performance, but Sara noticed the deep sallowness in Helene's face, and the sag that no determined smile could disguise. In a matter of weeks her eyes had taken the filmy look of someone much older. Sara was ushered in, divested of her coat ('how utterly gorgeous!') brought to a chair in the drawing room and given sherry. The room was warm and had the smell of well-maintained houses when the central heating first goes on, a mixture of hot paint and new carpets. It was entirely tasteful and rather restful in its predictability. The walls were painted white, the carpet was a deep rose and the furniture, much of it real, some of it reproduction Regency, was dark and slim-legged. The carriage clock on the mantelpiece was still stopped with its hands at exactly six o'clock. Only the baby grand piano, a well-used Broadwood with a loading of framed photographs, seemed to belong to a more personal history. Helene sat opposite in her wing chair and her hilarity subsided. She really could not keep it up for long.

Sara said, 'I was fine, really. I was having a good look at the Circus. It's curious, isn't it? So apparently logical, so open. But when you look, it's closed and secretive at the same time. I couldn't make head nor tail of it.'

Helene nodded. To Sara's dismay, the topic was not as neutral as she had thought.

'Adele loved it. The symmetry of it, of course, that satisfied her in some way. She would stare at it for hours. I *mean* hours. She was less fond of the trees. For myself, it's the trees that make it bearable. Thrusting upwards, leafy, reaching for the sky, defying control.' She sighed and sipped at her sherry. From anyone else it would have sounded ridiculous, but from Helene, because she meant it, it seemed like a perfectly moderate remark.

Hoping it was safe to say so, Sara said, 'I remember Adele in the garden at Iford Manor that night. She couldn't take her eyes off the garden, and the peacock. She was fascinated.'

'Obsessed,' Helene corrected her. 'One of her obsessions. Autistic people get these obsessions, odd things sometimes, things you couldn't imagine. And then their routines, that's another thing you have to accept.' She sighed again.

'It must be so difficult.'

There was a silence. Should Sara have said 'must have been', since they had been talking about a life that was over? No. Both were correct. For Helene it was still difficult and was always going to be, only now the difficulties were different. Sara reached across impulsively and touched Helene's arm.

'Oh, Helene, I'm so, so sorry . . .'

Helene was managing to smile. 'I know, dear, I know,' she said, more in the manner of the comforter than the comforted. 'You are so good. People are so good. But let's go down, shall we? I thought we'd have lunch downstairs. Much nicer.'

In the dining area of the L-shaped kitchen Helene had already laid out a lunch of cold meats, salad and bread. Soup had already been tipped into a saucepan and a bottle of red wine opened.

'I'm afraid it's all terribly simple,' she said apologetically, not realising how the reduction in her gushing, however tragically brought about, was making her much easier to like.

Helene ate little but drank some wine and kept Sara's plate generously supplied, like a practised dispenser of nourishment. Sara felt certain that she was the first person Helene had fed since she had given Adele her meals, and that she was in some way gratified by the familiar activity.

The kitchen revealed more personality than the drawing room, pointing to even quite contradictory tastes and preoccupations. Next to a bottle of olive oil on the worktop was a box of rice crackers. A copy of *New Statesman* lay under the *Lady* on the dresser. On the shelves above, *Music Therapy for the Autistic Child* stood alongside *Thinner Thighs in Thirty Days*, while a hardback edition of *Delia Smith's Winter Collection* lay on its side, almost invisible under a pile of cut-out recipes, opened envelopes, supermarket coupons, loose sheets of paper and a thick pamphlet of train times from Bath. Propped against a mug on a lower shelf was a miniature reproduction under a glass clip frame of a Sheppard drawing of Christopher Robin pulling on his wellingtons and Winnie-the-Pooh watching. Sara craned a little to read the caption, which was: 'Promise me you'll never forget me, ever. Not even when I'm a hundred.' Sara realised that her lips must have tightened with distaste because Helene said, 'Not guilty. Not me, it was Poppy. She gave that to Cosmo the other day. Oh, have another chorizo, dear, do.'

A little cautiously, Sara said, 'I wouldn't have thought that was quite Cosmo's sort of thing, somehow. He doesn't seem the Winnie-the-Pooh type.'

'He isn't, not in the least. But it's very much Poppy's.' Helene sighed and lowered her voice. 'I'm afraid she called it a "prezzie". A "little prezzie" to cheer Cosmo up because he was working too hard and getting too preoccupied. She plonked it up there, not him. I don't think he cares for it.'

'That's a bit sad.'

'Oh, it is. She said if she wasn't so fascinated herself, she would be "almost jealous" of Beau Nash. She's just trying to remind him she's here. If she'd asked me, I think I could have suggested better ways.'

The two women exchanged a look of amusement. Sara said, 'In my experience, "almost jealous" means gnawed to the bone with it. Poor Poppy.'

'Well, quite. And all this over supper, in front of me, as if I needed a little show of togetherness. But I suppose it takes my mind off other things.' Helene sighed. 'She goes in for little "prezzies" a lot, Poppy does. She got those for Jim. She's been round there quite a lot. They've obviously been talking container gardens.' She nodded at a Waitrose bag on the floor which had two healthy-looking plants in it. 'In fact, you could do me a favour, after lunch. On your way back, would you drop those off? She said she was busy and would I take them round but I'm not sure I feel up to seeing Jim.'

'Sure. If you want to avoid seeing him. I think I understand that.'

Helene considered. 'No, it's not that I need to avoid him, exactly. I really don't blame Jim for what happened. I just . . . don't feel up to it.' She paused. 'I'm not sure what I do feel. But since we've been so honest already, I think I'm really more bored by Jim than anything else. We were friends in a way, never more than that. Now Adele's gone and I don't need to be grateful to him any more for entertaining her or employing her, I just don't see the point. I don't mind him being in the opera, in fact I've told Poppy she can get on and invite him back if she wants to, but I'm taking a back seat. If that sounds very callous, it's too bad. I can't pretend I really care one way or the other about Jim.'

'I see,' Sara said, believing she did. 'I'd better not give him your love, then, when I give him these.'

'They're from Poppy,' Helene said firmly. 'Nothing to do with me.'

'What's it like, having Poppy and Cosmo here? Don't you mind? I can imagine wanting to be left on my own, after . . . such a terrible thing.'

Helene waved her arm in the direction of the dresser. 'Oh, well, I'm rather used to them. They've made themselves at home, certainly. I encouraged them to. What they don't realise is that I couldn't care less about the opera now. I really don't care one way or the other, though none of them guesses it.' She said this quite matter-of-factly. 'I suppose I was hardly thinking straight at the time, but I wish I'd stopped them going ahead. I was never convinced by this tribute idea. It doesn't mean anything.' Helene's voice had grown husky and tears began to run down her face.

Sara's eyes brimmed. Her own memories were not so far below the surface. 'Someone . . . someone I loved dearly, he died, nearly three years ago now,' she said. 'They did all sorts of tributes then. There's even a memorial fund. But you're right, it doesn't help, certainly not at the beginning.' She paused. 'In a way, that was an accident, too. He was ill, you see, but I didn't realise. Appendicitis. And I let him get on a plane. So it was hours before he got to hospital. Too late. It was too late, he died of septicaemia.'

Helene nodded. 'Matteo Becker the conductor, still in his thirties. I remember reading about it.'

'At first I thought it was my fault. I spent over a year convinced of it. But it was an accident. Like Adele.'

'Somehow I still feel I should have prevented it.'

'I know. But you couldn't. You have to realise that. Look, I don't mean to say it's just the same for you. I didn't lose a child. It must be worse to lose a child.' As she spoke she reflected that she must have changed. Was it possible that she could really countenance the idea that there could be loss greater than hers? That losing Matteo, her lover, partner, friend – and for a stupid, prosaic medical reason that proved fatal only through bad timing – could have even its equal in someone else's pain? With the years her grief had subsided but the fact of the loss was not altered. Was it then some shift in her understanding about what a child must mean to a mother?

'Loss is loss,' Helene was saying. 'People don't begin to understand unless they've felt it themselves. Good old Helene will rise above it, that's what they think. It's not as if Adele was even normal. So that's what I'll do, rise above it, because I always have. It's what I do. Oh, look, don't let me get all self-pitying.' Helene blew her nose. 'I'm all right. It's nice to talk to someone who does understand. You liked that drawing of hers you saw, didn't you? The one like a snowflake? I'd like to show you something.'

Helene rose and bent down to the dresser to pull out the deep bottom drawer, which was heavy and came slowly. It was full of artists' notebooks of varying sizes. Helene picked up the top three, straightening up stiffly, and brought them to the table as Sara moved the remains of their lunch to the side of the sink to make room. Helene softly rubbed her fingertips together and opened one of the books reverentially. The drawings were obviously Adele's. Page after page of the sketchbook was filled with finely detailed and shaded pencil drawings of architectural ornamentation: scrolls, festoons, swags, figures, shells and leaves and other solid, carved-looking patterns and abstract shapes of variously Baroque, Regency, Rococo, Art Nouveau influence. As Sara turned the pages, dumbstruck, she saw that all of them had been set down with the same unerring accuracy that revealed not a moment's wavering of certainty between hand and eye. They were not drawings of any whole buildings but more like designs for the ornamentation of doorways, windows, friezes, panels, columns, pilasters or fireplaces. And yet not so, because the artist had clearly been so caught up in creating patterns of intense, perfect symmetrical beauty that the designs, although drawn to look as if executed in plaster, wood or stone, were so detailed and fantastical as to be utterly unrealisable. Adele's perfect built world was one of possible and yet impossible beauty, too fragile to be fingered into shape in any earthy material, imaginable only as if spun from hair or moulded out of the clouds.

'They're all beautiful,' Sara said, turning the pages.

Helene was smiling. 'This is what my girl could do,' she said, more sad than proud. 'Books and books of it. Everything from memory. A faithful record of real things, all of them symmetrical, most of them based on buildings in Bath. Somehow her eyes took in all the tiny details without her being aware of it at the time, and she could draw them afterwards, as if everything was stored in some extraordinary visual memory.'

'Uncanny,' Sara said, feeling the word inadequate.

'I know. But it's not as if it made up for everything. You'd give anything for normality sometimes,' Helene said, eager for Sara to understand. 'Just to have the normal problems of bringing up a child. I thought I could cope with that, you see, and manage a career as well. We thought she was just a difficult baby.' Helene opened another of the books at random and gazed in silence at a drawing of a classical stone urn.

'Two seasons at the Met,' she said, leafing gently through the book. 'That's as far as I got. Supporting roles: Michaela in

Carmen, the maid in *Trovatore*. They might have led to greater things; I truly think they might. But by then Adele was having about a dozen tantrums a day. I couldn't keep things together. I couldn't keep a nanny. I couldn't even keep my husband.'

'What happened?'

'Oh, nothing dramatic, in the end. Edward was still trying to get noticed in opera, as a director. He did one or two good things, but nothing much was happening. Then he got involved in some film of *Don Giovanni* and met people, went to Los Angeles. We didn't go with him, and that was it, really. I can understand what an escape it must have been for him. In New York there was nothing but me, Adele, and no work. Nothing he wanted to come back to. He's been doing things in movies ever since, but I couldn't really tell you what. He's been good about money. He's still in LA. Called Ed now, of course.'

There was the merest smile on her lips as she said this, looking down and turning the last leaf of the book. Sara thought back to Helene's behaviour at the grim rehearsal she had sat through as Andrew's stand-in, and was wondering why she kept this slightly wicked intelligence concealed behind all the showbiz guff. But perhaps the real reason for all the opera-luvvie flannelling was to hide not her worldly intelligence, but the pain and difficulty of being Adele's mother.

Helene went on, 'I came back to England when Adele was five and then there were years of doctors, psychiatrists, psychologists. There was no question of school, she couldn't even sit still. Six years looking for a diagnosis, being told one thing after another. Nobody mentioned autism until she was eleven. A lot of the time I pretended to look on the bright side. My training helped. I always know what impression I'm creating. After a while you don't even need to pretend. You forget it's acting, and by then you've convinced even yourself that you're all right. Most of the time.'

Helene sighed sadly at these words. Sara said nothing. How could she claim to understand, how would being sorry help? Helene looked up and smiled again, rousing herself in the manner of people who have trained themselves out of self-pity.

'Coffee? Let's have coffee. I've gone on disgracefully, haven't I?' As she set about making it, Helene lapsed a little into the manner she had just been describing, feeling perhaps a little over-exposed by the confidences she had entrusted. 'Well now! So you've got a problem with Herve, have you? Fire away.'

Sara explained carefully, without maligning either Herve or herself, about the row. 'And I wondered, since the two of you do get on, if you'd just check up for me and see he's all right? I don't think he'd speak to me. I might even upset him again.' She hesitated and added quickly, 'But if he knew, you see, how sorry I was? It would make it easier. And I really am sorry. Not just that it happened, I mean sorry in case I helped cause it.' She stopped. It simply was not in her constitution to be any humbler than that.

'Of course I will. And I'll suggest it was just a clash of artistic temperaments, which I expect it was,' Helene said comfortingly. 'To be truthful, now I'm feeling more up to things, I'm even more curious about Herve. The wonderful Herve Petrescu. He is *rather* wonderful, isn't he? So distinguished-looking. In its way, it must be thrilling, working with him, apart from the row, I mean. How old is he? He's not married, is he?'

'He's fifty-two. Not married and not seriously attached, either. I actually wish he were. He'd probably be better organised and a bit less of a big baby.' Sara was surprised by the petulant edge in her own voice. Herve could make even her sound like a bit of a big baby too, damn him.

Helene seemed to think so as well because she said, confidently, 'Oh, you don't understand him. You're too young. I think a man like Herve—' She took a sharp breath and looked hard at Sara, considering whether or not to carry on.

'A man like Herve what?'

'Well, I think he's one of those men who are better off with someone older. It transforms them, an older woman. Look at Ivo Pogorelic. Herve's probably the same.'

'Oh, absolutely! He'd love anybody who's prepared to be a complete doormat and run around mothering him and treating him like he's the prince of light come down to walk among

233

us. Then *she'd* become the ageing hag who does all the tough stuff and he could carry on being the world's cherub. Oh, yes, Herve'd *love* that. The trouble is he seems to think that's what I'm here for.'

As Helene turned round from the worktop with the tray of coffee, Sara saw her face and could have cut her tongue out. It was too late; she could practically see the words 'ageing hag' bouncing off the walls and colliding with each other in the air above them.

'Well, you aren't,' Helene was saying smoothly, 'clearly you aren't. But perhaps a much older woman than you, more in sympathy with him, might do him a lot of good.' She sipped from her coffee cup and cast a swift, sly look at Sara, who knew exactly what she meant. Neither of them added aloud that this older woman might, by way of sharing Herve's international status as well as his money, be doing herself a bit of good, too. Whoever she might be.

Sara had expected Jim to be at the shop, so she was startled to see one of the two doors in the basement area swing open.

'Good gracious me, come in! I thought I heard someone coming down. Come along in, how delightful! I can't say I was expecting *you*!' The hearty welcome and the gratitude on Jim's beaten-looking face made Sara's heart lurch with sympathy. He led her into a small but neat basement kitchen with a small table and two comfortable old chairs. An iron spiral staircase led up from one corner. 'You'll have a cup of something? Tea? Coffee?'

'No, no, thank you, really. I've just had lunch with Helene. In fact I'm just delivering these.' She thrust out the bag with the plants in it.

'Oh, for me? Oh, how wonderful!' Jim drew the pots from the bag as if they were porcelain, and placed them on the table. There were tears in his eyes. 'A rose. A white miniature rose. And winter pansies.' His chin had started to wobble. 'I'm sorry, I think I'm a little overcome.' He pulled a large handkerchief from his pocket, sat down and began to weep quietly.

Sara could not leave him like this. 'Oh, Jim, I'm so sorry. The whole thing's just so awful. So sad,' she said, sitting down in the other chair.

'Oh, no, you don't understand. It's relief. I'm so relieved. And touched. I never thought she would, you see, and now these.' He gestured to the plants on the table. 'Of all the ones she could have given. Don't you see? White rose for "my love is unsullied" and pansies for "my thoughts are with you". The language of flowers. It's a message. She is thinking of me, with love unimpaired by recent events. I can go to tonight's rehearsal with an easy heart.'

His joy was appalling to watch, because misplaced, but Sara could not rob him of it.

'She just needed time, you see? I knew it. Perhaps she's beginning to see at last that she and I need each other.' Jim looked at her suddenly and clammed up, almost as if she had been eavesdropping and he had only just seen her. 'I've been so rude. I haven't even asked how *you* are. A death affects us all, doesn't it? How are you managing?'

'I'm all right, I suppose,' Sara said, unwilling to think about, let alone reveal anything to Jim about her many miseries. 'I just keep thinking there's something wrong . . . I mean, I know that theoretically Adele could have done something like this at any time. It was always a possibility, but still, I can't explain why, I'm finding it difficult to accept. It doesn't seem real.'

Jim shook his head. 'It's all too real to me. It happened, all right. I try not to think about it, or about the court case. My lawyer says it might even be dropped and meantime I must think positive. I've got the place sorted out again, at least. I should try and get on with some work, but I haven't found the heart.'

Sara hesitated. 'Will you show me? The workshop? I mean, I'm not even sure why I want to see it. But perhaps it'll seem more understandable if I do.'

If Jim was appalled at her curiosity he did not say so. 'Well, yes, of course you may. Yes, I'll show you round. No one's seen it actually, since the workmen finished, so perhaps it'll help me too. Look forward and all that. It's this way.'

Jim led the way back out of the kitchen door into the area and unlocked the smaller door next to it. A narrow passage ran straight down to another door at the end, which he also unlocked. 'This was a basement bedsit when I bought the place,' he said, stepping in and holding open the door. 'Separate entrance and so on, quite self-contained. I've got my kitchen, as you saw, and upstairs a decent-sized sitting room–cum–bedroom and a little bathroom. Quite adequate for just me. This house is typical Circus, all regular on the outside and mucked about on the inside.'

Sara was staring round the room. It was high and very light for a basement, about seven feet, and rectangular, measuring about twelve by fifteen feet. The only inappropriate reminder of its bedsit use was a thin corner partition with a cheap door, presumably with the loo and shower behind it. It was unremarkably functional, with its worktops, table and shelving, but it was cold and smelled damply new. The door had not been opened for days. No work in progress, let alone work completed or work to get started on, was anywhere in evidence. The one large window of opaque glass at the back was barred.

'I had plans to knock through from my kitchen when I moved in,' Jim said, 'but I changed my mind. That window's barred, and outside the garden's surrounded by eight-foot brick walls. And there are two doors into here, so it made it nice and secure for a workshop full of antiques.' His voiced tailed off almost to a whisper. 'Fine and secure, yes. That's what it was. Very private.' He closed his eyes against the mental picture of Adele with her skirt up, impassive on the couch, and swallowed. Nobody would ever know, now. So why could he not stop thinking about it?

He waved an arm towards the gap in a line of floor cupboards, bridged by a new piece of worktop. 'Adele never showed the slightest interest in the cooker. I only kept it there for heating glue and whatnot, for the ceramics work. And before she came I was so busy I usually worked over lunchtime and warmed something up. She only ever used the electric kettle. She only used warm soapy water for the chandeliers. I never dreamed it was unsafe for her here, I would never . . . I never thought . . .' He was fishing for his handkerchief again.

'Oh, Jim, nobody did. Nobody saw what might happen. It wasn't your fault.'

'I would have been here, you see, normally. Adele always locked up both doors and went home at four. I'd get back later and just check the outer door was locked; it always was. And next day I'd see her first thing, get her started and then go down to the shop. Only this time I didn't. I left straight from the shop the night before and stayed at a pub in Odstock – it's got rooms – because the sale in Salisbury started at nine and I wanted to view at eight. I gave up most of those terribly early starts when I turned sixty. So I'd left two days' work out. I'd done it once or twice before.'

'Jim, the cooker. It was just an ordinary gas cooker, wasn't it, with dials for the burners? How many? Where were they arranged?'

Jim collected himself. 'Well, yes, quite ordinary. Not terribly modern. There would have been . . . oh, six dials. Four for the top, one for the grill and another for the oven.'

'All in a row, along the front?'

'Good God, what's it matter where they were?'

He sounded irritated, like someone who has craved company but found it, when it came, disappointing. Sara thought that perhaps what Jim needed was not her troublesome and irrelevant questioning, but absolution which was not hers to give.

'Jim, you've done wonders here,' she said, turning towards the door. 'I'm sure you'll get things going again, once you're over the shock. Nobody thinks you were to blame.'

'Thank you, you're most kind,' Jim said stiffly. He was not of a generation that could weep openly and not afterwards be a little pompous. 'You are most kind. And now I mustn't keep you.'

Jim led the way out of the workshop, said goodbye in the area and returned through the other door back into his kitchen. At the top of the steps Sara turned to see if he might be at the window to wave her off. But he was too busy to notice her going, standing at the sink and watering the compost round his new plants from a milk bottle, smiling.

Chapter Twenty-six

'So, Phil, how's this fortnight been?'

Penny Meakins spoke with a smile in her voice, looked up to establish appropriate (neither tentative nor intimidating) eye contact, leaned back slightly to signal non-threatening but receptive body language and allowed the trained silence to prevail, during which she felt her jaw swell and sink as if someone were trying to shove a length of drainpipe down her throat. Her eyes were watering, but she would *not* yawn, although the effort of not doing so was making her swallow like a cat being made to take a worming tablet.

'Aw, it's been okay, really. Not feeling too bad last week.'

You could never tell, with this one, whether or not he meant it. Three interminable bloody terms coming every other Wednesday and he still behaved as if he thought it was rude to talk about himself. Self-effacement to this degree was an affectation that she did not have time for. She smiled with irritation.

'Tell me a bit about your work. How's that going?'

'Aw, it's been okay. I'm going to all my lectures. Mr Frewer gave me an extension, so now that also okay.'

'Okay. That's for his essay, is it? So you gave him the note I gave you, and he understood all the factors relating to the stress you were experiencing.'

'That's right. He said I could have a chat any time with him about it, no problem.'

'And have you?'

'Naw. He never in his room.'

'How about the' – Penny Meakins glanced at her notes – 'the, er, resit you only just scraped through. That result was making you very depressed in early September. We're nearly at the end of October now. Have you made any progress there?'

Phil appeared to have forgotten about what had been depressing him in September, the memory no doubt crowded out by the pressing demands of things depressing him in October. 'Er, well, that all okay now,' he said vaguely. 'I can done some more revision, my lecturer say. He say not to worry.'

How boring. Eleven years ago when she'd started here as a student counsellor it had been practically impossible to get any leeway out of the teaching staff. She had run workshops, introducing concepts such as stress loading, whole student wellbeing and unacceptable performance pressure to sceptical academics who had retaliated with expressions like cotton wool, old-fashioned hard work and thin end of the wedge. She'd fought some battles in the early days (in non-confrontational modes, of course) against that sort of prejudice. But now the academics were floppier than she had ever been. It was the lecturers who most often these days referred students to her, and they who were endlessly understanding of writing blocks, late assignments, and essay after essay being simply no bloody good. And that was just the ones who weren't clients themselves. She, on the other hand, had probably been in it too long; she felt all counselled out. A career move was in order, into running assault courses for middle managers or something. She could just picture herself shrieking at humiliated executives to grab on the ropes, the ones that would swing them straight into pits of shit-coloured mud. It was time for her to do some work on her own aggression, she realised, noticing that once again she was itching to tell Phil to go and get laid, or get some work done. She took a few deep breaths.

'And how about the social life? Last time we explored your attitude vis-à-vis some of the, er . . . social drugs.' Penny scanned her notes. 'You said you had been an occasional user, when you were out in a group. Are you still using recreational drugs from time to time?'

Phil shrugged. 'Haven't been out.'

'Right. Well, as you know, Phil, drugs are not really my area. Here's the Drugs Helpline number, if you need further counselling or advice. If there's nothing in general terms you want to raise with me.' She pushed the printed card across the table.

'Now,' she said brightly, 'what else? Still enjoying the, er . . . group?'

She could not remember the details of what Phil's group got up to. Two terms ago she'd sat and listened as Phil explained that campus life was not working out very well. He mixed, slightly, with the students on his course, but he was too worried about keeping up with the work to spend long socialising. He found his hall of residence depressing, and seldom went out. He didn't care for pubs and hadn't much money anyway. Well, she had suggested, could he not join something? What were his interests?

Mistake. It turned out that Phil's interests were opera and architecture. Really, he had wanted to study music or become an architect, but he did not have the talent for the first and his family did not have the means to support him through six years of the second. They were doing as much as they could to send him to Britain for a three-year engineering course. There was no university club or society catering for his other interests, Phil said. Penny had reflected that he was certainly right about that: real ale, paragliding, rugby, Nintendo maybe. So she had suggested he ask at the library and see if there was a club in the town he could join. Perhaps it would be good for him to get away from the campus environment and meet a wider group of people.

'Group's fine,' Phil said wistfully. Penny was appalled to see that tears had appeared in his eyes. She waited, giving the appropriate, non-judgmental space for him to cry. But must he do that here? She had another client in ten minutes.

'Group is fine,' Phil was saying, with difficulty. 'But there was a girl. She gone. I . . . loss her. I lost my girl.'

A few minutes passed as Phil whimpered and struggled to control himself. When he eventually emerged from behind a torn paper tissue, his face reminded her of a set of wooden Chinese dolls she had once had as a child, that fitted one inside the other. As they got smaller and smaller the painted flat faces looked crosser and crosser, until the baby's was screwed tight in infantile anguish. She said, 'It's very painful, isn't it? When a relationship ends. We feel pain. And we feel anger, too. Sometimes we turn that pain and anger upon ourselves, when in fact they are quite natural reactions to what's happened. That leads to confusion. And guilt. We blame *ourselves*, don't we? I expect that's how you're feeling now?'

Phil shook his head and sniffed. 'Naw. Dunno. I lost my girl.'

'We mustn't deny that guilt and anger, must we? Isn't that how you are feeling now, if you're honest?'

'Well, kind of.'

'You see, Phil, if you remember the anger work we did. You remember that we have to *own* our anger. And sometimes that means first of all we have to acknowledge it. Own up to what we're feeling. Sometimes we have to express it.' Christ, don't we just, Penny thought, her fists tingling. 'So you mustn't blame yourself. Of course you're feeling pain, if you've split up with someone. The pain and anger you are feeling are part of a process. A healing process. We tend to think we shouldn't be feeling these things. But we should. It's human, and natural. Will you think about that, Phil? Own your anger. Anger is natural. Anger is *good*.'

Phil nodded uncertainly.

'Anything else, Phil? All right now? Is there any more you'd like to talk about, or shall we meet again in a fortnight?' she asked, raising her voice against the scrape of her chair. She stood up to push Phil's notes back into her folder.

Phil had stuffed his tissue in his pocket and was reaching for his bag. Really, she should try to wind things up with this one by the end of term. It was doing him no good to spend all this time worrying about himself, and her no good either. A minute later she was grateful that Phil left the room too quickly for her to succumb to the temptation to call after him jokingly to get his finger out. That would not have been appropriate counsellor language, and she was a professional.

Chapter Twenty-seven

Herve telephoned that Thursday evening and enquired so contritely after Sara's health and general wellbeing that she told him the truth. She was fine of course in a way, but feeling very bad about what she did not call their row, but the 'last time we met'. To call it a row would beg the question of who had started it, and she had no wish to go into it.

'Oh, me also,' he said, a little breathily. There was a pause, during which neither of them filled the silence that each was giving the other in which to apologise, nor did either of them mention Helene.

Just before the silence became embarrassing, Sara said, 'So, when do we rehearse? Monday?'

Herve gave a non-committal murmur. 'Hmm, well, of course yes, but I wonder if we should meet tonight – not for playing anything, just to be friendly? But you are busy, perhaps?'

She wasn't, much to her own annoyance. Presumably Andrew was, since he had not answered the message she had left him at work, but she refused to speculate about what might be occupying him.

'No, I'm not busy. And yes, we should meet. Good idea.'

'So, good! So, you will come for me at half past six and then we go to Iford. Fine, good!'

'*Iford?*'

'Iford, yes. For Helene, for her opera. Tonight they have

an extra rehearsal. They go to sing with the little boys, the Scouts. Thursday is their meeting night. The boys are to be part of opera also. And Helene asks me to go. And I have no car, of course, but you can drive me, yes? And you will enjoy, too. Andrew, Valerie, all the group are your friends too, says Helene.'

'Yes, yes,' Sara capitulated, sighing, seeing how Helene had arranged for their reconciliation in the bosom of the opera group. 'Yes, my friends too. See you later.'

That evening Sara slowed down in Camden Crescent behind a parked transit van that was indicating to pull out. As soon as it drew away Sara nipped into the space and parked. As she locked her car she saw Dotty retreating from the top of the area steps back down to the basement flat.

She called out, 'Dotty, wait!' Dotty turned on the steps and looked up, her arms folded tightly in front of her. She seemed embarrassed. 'Oh! I, er . . . Well, er, hello.'

'Was that your van leaving just now? Is the flat empty, then? Did you find what you were looking for in the end?' Sara clattered down the steps and stood beside her in the area. 'It wasn't an earring, was it?'

Dotty sighed and tried to look past her. 'No, I . . . Yes, that was the van. The last of Imogen's things; they're going into a sale on Saturday. General household.' She lifted a weary arm in the direction the van had taken.

'I don't think you were looking for an earring at all.'

Dotty looked at her. 'No, no I wasn't. It wasn't an earring. It was just me being silly, I suppose.' She paused. 'I won't keep you. I suppose you're on your way upstairs to see your friend.'

'Yep. I'm in no hurry, though. We fell out, and now we're supposed to be nice to each other again.' She lowered her voice. 'I'm still curious to know what you were looking for. Call me nosy, if you like.'

'Yes, falling out's unpleasant, isn't it? People can be difficult. People can be so difficult and disappointing.' She looked at Sara. 'Look, you've been very kind over all this. I didn't like misleading you. Come in for a minute.'

Sitting side by side on the bottom stair, Sara listened and Dotty spoke, her voice booming in the empty flat. 'I do always try to be honest. The truth is, I've been looking for some letters.'

Sara waited.

'Oh, it's no good, I'm hopeless at this,' Dotty went on. 'I've never talked about this, ever.'

'What is it, Dotty? Can I help?'

'No. No one can help now, it's much too late. I've known that for years; it's so silly that it still upsets me now.'

Dotty seemed aware that this could make no sense to Sara. She turned to her. 'I was just looking for some letters. Some letters that I thought Imogen had, that were really mine. Oh, it was all years ago. And now I don't really think she did have them after all, she was just stringing me along.' She sniffed. 'No point going into it.' It was a brave attempt to sound sensible but Dotty could not sustain it. She sank her face into her hands and wailed. 'Oh, God, all these years! Oh, God, I feel so let *down*!' Sara placed a hand gently on her back and held it there until the crying subsided. Dotty raised her head, gave a more determined sniff. 'Look,' she said stoutly, 'I must seem like some neurotic old spinster to you, but I'm not, or at any rate I might not have been. What I mean is I'm sorry to have burdened you, but I'm fine now. It's been a rather emotional time, and I'm sorry.'

Sara nodded kindly. 'Are you sure I can't do anything? Do you, I mean, is it something to do with her death? Should the police be involved?'

'No! No, absolutely not, it's got nothing whatever to do with it!'

Dotty seemed to realise that she had made Sara too curious to drop the matter now. 'Look, it's nothing to do with that.' She took a deep breath. 'Remember I told you I met Imogen by chance about six years ago, after she'd retired?'

Sara nodded.

'I should go back a bit. When I first went to Combe Down Academy there was a young geography teacher there, Adam Hart-Browne. Canon now. I mentioned him, he took

Imogen's service. He taught geography and religious studies then. We were close. Not *lovers* or anything like that, we were both Christians. Anyway, people didn't then.' Dotty's eyelids drooped a little. 'I was so in love with him. Then almost out of the blue he got the chance to go to Africa for a year. It was a teaching mission and he wanted me to go with him. Only at that time Combe Down was smaller and everybody mucked in. It would have been hard to replace us both at short notice and only for a year, and Miss Bevan was furious. She called me in and gave me such a talking-to, it got me convinced I would be mad to give up a good job and go with him, at least just then. Give him a few months, she said. Let him prove himself, men need that. You can write, and then later if he still wants you to, you can go and you'll both be better for the separation. She made it sound as if it was all for our own good.'

'Then what happened?'

'He went. He didn't know exactly where he'd be at first, either in Botswana or Lesotho, and he said he'd write with the address. He never did. I never heard from him.'

'Weren't you worried? In case something had happened to him?'

Dotty nodded. Now she looked angry. 'Of course I was. Until after about six months he wrote a chatty postcard to all the staff, saying he was doing fine. I can still remember Imogen Bevan coming into the staffroom waving it about, all pleased.'

Sara did not know what to say except that the rejection must have been devastating.

'But he *didn't* reject me! Don't you see?' Dotty said. 'It was her!' Sara was getting rather lost. Dotty said, more calmly, 'Of course that was what I thought at the time. He'd just forgotten all about me, or changed his mind or even—' She shook her head. 'I even began to think he'd never had any intention of writing to me. I was so hurt, I didn't even try to contact him. I just tried to forget him.'

'So, you forgot him?' Sara asked gently.

Dorothy shook her head. 'No, I never did, although I tried. There was never anyone else. And then six years ago he came back to Bath. I read about it in the diocesan magazine. He was in his fifties, a canon, and married, of course. I went to hear him preach.' Her face lit up. 'I was hardly expecting him to remember me. But the first time he looked up from the pulpit, it was as if I was the only one in the congregation.' She smiled happily. 'I don't mind telling you, Sara, from that moment, it was a terrible performance. He kept losing his place, getting things wrong. I just sat there, feeling *wicked*. For the first and only time in my life.'

Sara smiled, well able to imagine it. 'He hadn't forgotten you, then.'

Dotty's face grew sad again. 'No. We met, of course. Over tea. And he told me he wrote to me for a year, at least sixty letters. He'd sent them to school, because I was living in, you see, as an assistant boarding mistress. Well, I knew at once what had happened. Imogen Bevan had kept them from me, so I wouldn't leave and she wouldn't have the bother of replacing me. All the post went to the office first, you see. So he never heard back from me, of course. He got ordained and then married, eventually. Well, a clergyman needs a wife. I don't blame him. They're not very happy, never were. He's still in love with me. Fifty-eight and fifty-three we are, grey-haired and past it now, and we never had our chance.'

'Oh, Dotty, Imogen Bevan kept his letters from you? What an awful thing to do.'

'I didn't meet her in Waitrose,' Dotty went on quietly, 'after she retired. When Adam told me all this I came straight round here and confronted her. I was so angry. She was old and I was very aggressive, but I didn't care. I was quite ready to strike her, to tell you the truth. She couldn't deny it. It would have been "extremely inconvenient and potentially destabilising", she said, to lose two key members of staff at once, after all the effort she'd made to appoint and train us. Inconvenient! She did it for the school, she said, she was building up the school and it was in desperate need of "administrative stability". And if faint-hearted Adam Hart-Browne had had anything about him, he'd have come straight back to marry me. Or I'd have gone off to Africa and demand that he did.'

'I suppose that's what she'd have done in the circumstances.'

'Probably. Adam and I are weaker souls.'

'Gentler, perhaps.'

'Anyway, after that Imogen kept dropping hints that I'd "get what was mine" eventually. She led me to believe that she still had the letters somewhere. That's why I kept coming to visit her. I wanted to see them so much, even though it was all too late. So much. Just to read what he'd said to me.'

'You didn't find them, then?'

'No. She can't have kept them. Heaven knows I've looked. No, she hadn't even had the decency to keep them. It probably amused her to think I was hoping she had.'

'The spiteful old witch.' But it did not help to malign the departed Imogen Bevan. Something in the air of the silent flat seemed still to taunt Dorothy's bowed head. 'Let's get you out of here,' Sara said, standing up. 'It can only hurt you, being here. At least – at least Adam's back in Bath,' she said, wondering if that did not make it worse. 'You can at least see each other, be friends. At *least* friends.'

'Yes,' Dotty said, rising. 'Yes, we are friends. We're tempted to be more than that, and we wouldn't be the first. We know that, but we never would. He's a married Christian priest.'

She made her way, exhausted, up the uncarpeted stairs. Sara followed. Near the top she turned and paused. 'And I aspire to be a Christian woman, but do you know, Sara' – her eyes travelled for the last time over Imogen Bevan's empty home – 'I hope she's roasting in hell.'

Andrew was grateful to have Phil in the back of the car because it made listening to Valerie unnecessary. While he drove, she sat at an angle with her right arm slung over the back of her seat, talking at Phil in an older-than-you yet coy tone of voice.

'Don't ever be stuck for a lift, will you now, Phil? If I can help at all, you're to get on the phone, all right? You've got the number now. I've got boys of my own, you know. Not quite as big as you of course! Only little, but they're a big handful! Though I'll bet you were never a handful, were you? Don't you miss your family?'

She didn't give a damn about Phil, Andrew knew that. Only two hours ago, the moment she had put the telephone down in the kitchen, she had started moaning about being put upon.

'That was Phil on a payphone. He wants a lift out to Iford, so he rang Helene. There's no room in Jim's car so she gave him our number. Cheek! I'm sure there's a bus.'

Andrew had replied mildly that it would hardly be a straightforward journey by bus and they were going anyway.

'That's not the point.' Valerie began to serve the children's supper, stabbing with distaste at an oven tray full of sausages, hacking them up on three little plates and pushing the pieces, which reminded Andrew of cigar butts, into defeated lumps of mashed, no, *mugged* potato. He'd noticed it before, the way she cooked with hatred, handling food as if it would do something awful to her unless she kept the upper hand. 'When I was his age I made my own way everywhere. You'd think he'd want to be independent. Well, I've told him to be at the bottom of North Road by twenty to seven. If he's not we'll just have to go on without him. We can't stop.'

Andrew did not bother pointing out that when Valerie was Phil's age she had made her dad run her everywhere and, about a year after that, Andrew himself. 'You're all heart, you are,' he said, swiping up the last unmutilated sausage from the tray, stuffing it in his mouth and leaving the room.

Valerie had turned back round to the front of the car now and was staring out of the passenger window, considering what she called 'doing the social bit' as done. Phil sat silently in the back, exuding all the personality of a traffic cone. Andrew allowed himself to lapse into thoughts of Sara, taking care that the expression on his face did not lift into anything approaching cheerfulness. Valerie would be on to that at once. Thinking about it, Sara really was all heart, all heart and passion, including sometimes rage, and quite unreasonable rage at that. But he loved even her anger, whether righteous or not, because it was rich and real, almost generous. Valerie was too sparse in spirit ever to feel anger like that, but she was annoyed practically all the time in some baseless, unfocused way. On occasion she could be pleased, but Andrew had never heard her claim to be happy. Valerie's emotions were a sort of surface irritant, an affliction like eczema, to be lived with or scratched at.

He drove on past the hill with the herd of deer, towards the set of lights at the viaduct, taking the bends gently. He did not want to have his train of thought interrupted by her voice complaining about his driving. And when he thought about it, he did not think that he himself had spoken once since his remark on leaving the kitchen. This was not because there had been nothing he wanted to say, but because he did not want to encourage any reply from her. He did not want to hear her voice at all. Automatically he cleared his throat as if to check that his voice still worked, and suddenly had a blood-freezing recollection of his own father. It was what he had always done. They'd be driving along somewhere with Andrew in the back. He knew every pit and wrinkle on the back of his father's neck, and every straight short stick of hair, just touching his mother's mauve or beige turtleneck, which had escaped the perms that whipped the rest up into the standard suburban fright-wig hairstyle that all the mums had. Going places, coming back from places, his parents in the same seats, always in complete silence. And in the silence, his father would periodically clear his throat. Andrew had always found it annoying because it was so obviously unnecessary. But Dad had just been testing his voice, chucking modest, experimental little pebbles of sound into his silent, stagnant marriage and now he, just past his fortieth birthday, had started doing it too. Not until this moment had Andrew realised what his father's little coughs had been for. Now that he did, it chilled him to his heart.

Poppy was out in the lane, unnecessarily directing cars in through the gates of the village hall. Although there were few street lamps the lighted windows of the hall lit up the entrance and car park perfectly adequately. Inside, the rectangular hall with its shallow stage at one end and its floor marked out for badminton was washed in fluorescent overhead lights. It was like walking into an over-lit crowd scene: dozens of dark-clad, uniformed boys in clusters, swinging, skidding on the floor and play-thumping together, Cosmo next to the piano in conversation with two stout uniformed women, clearly the *Uberfrauen* of the Scout troupe, and a half dozen or so other adults, mainly women in glasses. Jim, looking uncomfortable and on the edge, was there, not far from Helene, who was chatting and gesticulating to Herve. Bloody Herve was looking loftily down at her, and Sara was standing a little behind him, deliberately staying out of the conversation. *Sara.* How could Sara be here? She had seen him and now she was walking towards the three of them, concealing, as he was, the excitement that others must not see.

'Phil! Hello, Valerie!' she beamed. 'You're wanted over there, I think. Cosmo's trying to explain about the solo parts to the Scout lady. I think he'll want you two as well.'

As they moved away she turned and looked up at him and the smile evaporated. 'You took your sweet time. I've been trying to reach you.'

Andrew smiled over her head. 'Complaints, complaints. Is that all you do?'

Sara smiled back, more at his ear lobe than at him. 'I've got to talk to you about the case. And I've been here eight whole minutes already and I'm nearly dead with the tedium. Herve made me bring him and I couldn't refuse.' She hesitated. 'And I've been missing you.'

'I've missed you, too,' Andrew almost whispered, hoping he was managing to make her understand there was much, much more to it than that. But they were interrupted by the arrival of Poppy, who had come in from car-park duty glowing with the combination of cold and organisational zeal. Andrew and Sara moved themselves to the edge of the hall, as far from the piano as they dared, while Poppy clapped her hands and boomed that as they were already running late, could they make a start please, people? It was ten past seven.

At four minutes to nine Sara looked at her watch again and felt her neck expand with another swallowed yawn. Andrew was sitting with his back to her playing his cello, obediently sawing out notes under Cosmo's flailing conductorship from the keyboard. She had already exhausted the imaginative possibilities of staring at his broad shoulders and tapering back, picturing the beautiful flexing of the muscles under his clothes as he played, noting every lift and sway of the torso and arms. But unless by force of her will she could somehow make him put down the cello, stand up and stride towards her stark naked, there wasn't much future in it.

Poppy had a clipboard and a pencil behind her ear, so she was happy. The little boys had been marshalled on stage and pushed about first as Bath urchins, singing a very creditable medley of authentic-sounding street cries. After their squash and biscuits, at eight fourteen by Sara's watch, they had acquitted themselves a little less convincingly as invalids being brought by their attendants to the hot springs, marked out by a circle of rope on the stage floor. In the general collapse of their concentration a fair amount of chucking-in and drowning had gone on, after which they had been rounded up for a talking-to and a quiet game by Judy and Maureen, their now heavily sweating leaders. Now, in a mood of exhausted sobriety, they were stumbling back up on stage to be taken through the Assembly Rooms scene, in which they were to pretend to be squires in boots. Sara sighed and vowed to herself that, no matter how hard Herve might plead, she would not be present next week to witness the mayhem when they were joined by the Brownies (aka maids and ladies) and taught how to do a gavotte.

Valerie was up there now surrounded by her pygmy squires, nervously wetting her lips in preparation for her big number, with Jim by her side. Cosmo was thumping out the introductory music while Poppy bawled at the Scouts that they were meant to mingle *quietly* on stage until the singing started. Helene, who would not sing herself so soon after Adele's death, and had had her own part written out completely, was sitting with Herve. She was watching Valerie with the rapt attention of an

Olympic coach. Indeed, had she been watching a nine-year-old gymnastic prodigy insinuate herself into early spinal injury for the good of national morale she could not have given Valerie more complete concentration, so much so that she failed to notice, as had everyone else, that the ostensible star of the scene, Beau Nash, was nowhere in sight. After Valerie's thin opening phrases,

> Oh Beau, don't treat me so,
> Your Juliana's going bananas
> 'Cos you hurt her so!

the depopulated ensemble slid into a mystified silence as it became obvious that Phil was not there. And they only had the hall until a quarter past nine.

Cosmo popped up from behind the piano, looking cross.

'Phil! Where's Phil?' Poppy at once began slapping on her clipboard and calling 'people' to order, insisting that someone else could sing his part for now. Helene jumped to her feet and was joined by Herve, who had been following the score carefully and seemed annoyed at the interruption. Valerie turned round to scold the restive boys. Andrew was shaking his head and folding up his music, clearly having decided in his quiet way that he had had enough. Sara watched him, not wanting to accept that he would soon be driving home with Valerie. She wandered out of the hall.

It was too mild for frost, and outside the air hung still like horses' breath, grassy, warmish. Far away on the right past the village hall stood Iford Manor, aloof from the rest of the village which straggled off to the left beyond the cricket ground on the other side of the lane. Sara could just see the outside lights of the manor illuminating the prosperous gabled elevation of the house, but there was nothing to suggest that the sumptuous Italian garden which stretched up to the top of the hillside behind it, now asleep in the dark, was there at all. The garden was shut for the winter. Sara dithered on the lane, looking to left and right. It seemed unlikely that

Phil would have wandered off towards the publess village of mainly private drives and single-storey houses. It had the sort of This Is A Homewatch Area air of privacy about it which would make innocent wandering feel like snooping. Looking up, Sara set off along the lane towards the manor, wondering if Phil, curious as she now was, had ventured into the closed and out-of-season garden.

Coming towards the manor from the village side, Sara could not see the walled vegetable garden or Britannia on the bridge beyond it. Street lamps were fewer here and the lane was narrow. Passing by fields on either side, she was aware of the sensation of livestock, sheep probably, nothing more than an inkling of life close by, rather than the sound or sight of animals. As her eyes grew accustomed to the dark she became aware of heavy shapes in the fields. No cars passed. She stopped, and the lane seemed to vibrate with the sudden silence of her no longer sounding footsteps. Then from the far side of the lane the soft sighing of the slow river came to her, rising and mingling in the air all around, the sound directionless yet seeming somehow to sing a departing note. Then, through the sounds of water other sounds were reaching her, possibly from further away, a snuffling, a slight moaning. She had the impression that a shape was stirring, somewhere up in the field on her right. Sara moved on, walking on the grass verge now so that her feet were silent. She reached the corner of the garden's boundary wall, which at this point was broad and flat and less than four feet high. Just here a thick stand of holly bushes behind it, which created a far more effective barrier than the wall itself, was hideously lit by the last of the orange street lamps in the lane. Checking that there was no more than a shallow ditch on the lane side, Sara negotiated the thick growth at the base of the wall, climbed up on to it and began to walk along it, leaving the lane and heading upwards out of the light and into the darkness of the hillside, the garden on her left and the field on her right. About ten feet along the wall, between two of the holly bushes, a space had been cleared, apparently for a new compost heap. A smooth mound of leaves or grass cuttings was accumulating.

Sara jumped down and landed on soft leaf mould, skirted easily around the pile and came out on to the edge of the garden and stood quite still. What she had half heard above the shifting of the river was unmistakable now and not far away: the sound of human weeping.

Sara followed the sound past the cloisters, across the east lawn and into the rose garden, where she stopped. The rose bushes on either side of the path slouched shoulder-high, offering out the last few blooms which hung from their bones like encumbrances, late, uncomely children on the hips of mothers spent by parasitic, blousy offspring. Long before she reached him she could see that Phil was sitting on a bench, doubled over and sobbing. She took a seat beside him, not certain if he did not know or simply did not care that she was there, even less certain of what she could or should do. Gently, she rested an arm over his shoulder and waited. After several minutes Phil's crying subsided into muted gulps. Slowly, he lifted his head until he was sitting upright, and lowered his hands from his face. Sara withdrew her arm. He sat quite still, his throat occasionally convulsing in a pained hiccuping, and stared into the beds of roses whose petals shone either thinly white or yellow. In the unperfumed late October damp Sara thought they gleamed with the scentless sterility of all flowers which bloom out of their time.

'Phil,' she said eventually. 'Poor Phil. Please let me help. What's the matter? Is it Adele?'

Phil responded with a thin wail and a new outbreak of crying. Trying not to feel exasperated (but it would be so much easier if he would say *something*) Sara took this to be a yes. As he rocked to and fro Sara, without thinking, reached across and took him in her arms. She did not know anything for sure about his circumstances except that he was a student – and Andrew had said he was a loner – but he struck her suddenly as unbearably vulnerable. He was soft-bellied, unarmoured by anyone's concern for him. Indeed, Phil seemed utterly unclothed in love from anyone at all, and perhaps his grief had something to do with his being newly aware of it.

'Adele . . .' Sara had not planned what to say. 'Adele was lovely. And you miss her terribly. I can see.'

'Yes,' gulped Phil. 'She was lovely. My love. I love Adele, she was my girl.'

'I wish I could help, Phil.'

'I help her with things. We love each other. We could be together, I could look after her. Really helped her with everything, not hurt her. I would looked after her, for ever, I would not used her. With life, everything. I teach her everything. I want teach her *everything*. For love, not using. We could got married, she could even be mother. I won't *spoil* her, I love her.'

Of course. Phil's gentle presence, always close to Adele, watching her, helping her in her little routines without comment. It had seemed that he stuck to Adele only because she, almost mute, was less demanding company than the others. It must have been nice for Phil to speak better English than someone else for a change. But his bland calm had been something closer to adoration. Who was to say that because he and Adele said little to each other that they were not communicating? Phil clearly believed that they had understood each other on some other level. He was looking at Sara now, the black eyes shining not just with tears but with something like eagerness. His confusion over English tenses seemed for a moment to have obscured the fact that his generous, loving hopes for a life with Adele were now consigned to the past, the awful, aching might-have-been.

'Oh, Phil, I'm so sorry. I'm sure you would have taken great care of her. I mean, you *did*. You did take care of her, Phil. You couldn't have prevented what happened.'

Phil stared at her wildly. 'No! No! Someone *could*. Someone should. Adele should not be wasted like that! It make me so angry. Oh, you don't understand, nobody understand!'

'Phil, what do you mean, Adele wasted? What do you mean? Do you know something? What is it, Phil?'

But Phil's grief took hold of him once more and with a tighter grip. He almost fell forward on to the path, moaning,

'I lost her, I lost her. All just wasted. She shouldn't been wasted.'

Sara said eventually, 'Of course it's a waste, Phil. A waste of a life. Look, I don't know what else to say. Please don't torture yourself. Slowly, the pain will get less. It will.'

Several minutes later Sara was able to lead him, listless and exhausted, back through the unlit garden and down to the lane. Andrew was walking in the dark towards them.

'Nearly everyone's gone home,' he called. 'Are you all right, Phil? Valerie's waiting in the car.' Phil looked up, pulled away from Sara and ran off past Andrew in the direction of the hall.

'Don't go after him,' Sara said, before the astonished Andrew could speak. 'He's upset about Adele.' Cars were now turning out of the village hall in both directions and they walked back together in the glare of passing headlights. As they reached the gates Sara said, 'Andrew, I want to talk to you. About the case. When can I see you?'

Andrew gave a sarcastic groan and looked at her, it seemed almost coldly. 'When can you see me? Really? Oh, of course, about the case. Suddenly you want to talk about the case. Well, there's plenty I want to talk about too, and *none* of it's about the case.' He had already found his car keys and was walking away.

'Andrew, don't. Come to the cottage. Come and play some music, at least.'

He stopped and turned. 'Saturday afternoon,' was all he said before turning back and quickening his pace towards his car.

Chapter Twenty-eight

'Way too "magic of the opera" for me.'

'But *The Magic Flute* is magic. The whole story's meant to be magic, it's a fairy tale.'

'That doesn't mean you've got to have whizzbang stage effects in every scene. I thought it was meant to be a parable of freemasonry, full of symbols.'

'Oh, I see, you want whizzbangs with funny handshakes.'

'No, I want *implied* magic, not pantomime puffs of pink smoke and purple explosions every time the baddy comes on. I thought at one point you were going to hiss the Queen of the Night.'

'I was not. But you nearly called out "she's be-hind you!" to Papageno. Admit it.'

'Jeez, Sara, if you can really buy all that firecracker stuff, you must have the sophistication of a four-year-old at the circus.'

'Aha! I win. Your argument has just been reduced to the level of personal insult. Can I have some more of that?'

James cast his eyes to the heavens and poured wine into Sara's glass in a mock huff. Sara smiled peacefully and lifted it towards him.

'Anyway, we agree about this place. I love it here, don't you? Great to see you,' she said. 'I can't tell you how pleased I am you rang this morning. I haven't been to the opera for ages. But I thought you weren't going to be back in London till after you'd done the New European Composers series?'

'I wasn't,' James said. 'I can't really spare the time. I'm going back to Brussels first thing tomorrow. But I did want to see this production of the *Flute* and it finishes tomorrow. I only got tickets because they've asked me to go on the board next year.'

'Lucky old me, then,' Sara said. 'Opera and dinner, out of the blue. I love doing things on the spur of the moment. It's lovely to get on that train out of Bath sometimes.'

James looked at her sadly. He had rung her early that morning with the accurate suspicion that his beautiful friend was embattled and lonely.

'Tell me how you are,' he said gently.

'Shan't.' Sara smiled. 'Can't. Really, I can't. I don't know where I am with any of Herve's stuff. I'm drowning. And so many other complications, you don't know the half. You don't *want* to know.'

'I do.'

'You don't, believe me,' Sara said, shaking her head, 'and I don't want to talk about it.' She simply could not go into it, the mixture of dread and excitement at the thought of seeing Andrew the next day. 'This is the first time I've felt properly away from the place for weeks. I want to hear about you and the perils of new composers.'

'Ha! Don't get me started . . . Well' – James drew breath for a long speech – 'when they asked me to do the thing, it was a direct challenge. You know I've done a lot of reviews of new music in the past year or so?'

Sara nodded, with a wry face. James had been unsparing and all over the place: in at least two broadsheets and most of the specialist music magazines.

'That reminds me, have you had anything submitted by someone called Cosmo Lamb? I don't think he's had much performed.'

'Cosmo Lamb? Cosmo Lamb . . . no, nothing's been submitted by any Cosmo Lamb. Name's very slightly familiar, but no, I'm probably mixing it up with a recipe. The sort of thing you'd get here: cosmopolitan lamb, with tamarind, soy sauce, swede and anchovies. He any good?'

'Don't ask. It's just he's doing this thing in Bath, a community opera. Just one of the things I don't want to talk about. Sorry I interrupted.'

James groaned. 'A com-*mewn*-nity opera. Jesus. Anyway, well, I've done all this reviewing but I'd no idea I was becoming such a monster of the media. I've just said what I think on the whole, and apparently now I'm either impossibly hard to please, or the great debunker and ego-deflater of half a generation of living composers. Anyway, I was asked to judge this year's European New Composers Awards because this year it's for piano works. There was a piece in the July *New Music Review* about it, about me being asked to do it. Did you see it?'

Sara shook her head. 'I was away most of July. I only get it now and then anyway.'

'Well, they did this big feature, starting with the line: "Would *you* ask Brian Sewell to judge the Turner Prize?" I was furious. Comparing me to Brian Sewell! Have you seen how the man dresses?'

Sara laughed and looked for a moment happy, which was James's sole purpose in telling her.

'So, I get to choose the pieces and then do a couple of concerts of the winners. Most of the stuff's pretty unconvincing, some of it's dire. A *little*, I like. So I'm on Planet Contemporary Music Nightmare, I tell you, until the end of next month.'

Sara drank thoughtfully. Sadness had come over her face again.

'Good. I'll be glad of the company,' she sighed.

Chapter Twenty-nine

'Boo!'

Sara looked down at the three masked figures on her doorstep. 'Don't eat me!' she cried.

'Don't be silly. We don't eat people. We're ghosts,' came a muffled voice from deep inside the hood of the grim reaper. The mummy's head next to her nodded, making the hatchet embedded in its crown wobble slightly. 'I'm a jip-shin ghost!'

'Oh, ghosts. Is that all? Oh, well, that's all right then. You can come in if you're just ghosts.' She stepped aside and Natalie, Dan and Benji, draped in swathes of white sheet and black plastic, trooped past her into the hall, carrying with them a toy scythe, a broomstick, two pumpkin lanterns, a set of dracula teeth and a pointy hat. Andrew's faint voice, from the far end of the drive, followed them in. 'Kids! I said to wait!' A moment later he appeared on the doorstep with his cello case.

'What have you come as?' Sara said.

Breathlessly, he said, 'God, sorry. Look, I wouldn't have brought them, but they've got a party to go to later. I thought Valerie was taking them. She said she was. Then after lunch when I said I was coming here, she suddenly announced she'd booked a pedicure and was going to see her friend in Swindon, so I'd have to take the children. Sorry.'

'Doesn't matter,' Sara said, sounding more amused than she

felt. She turned to follow the small ghouls out to the kitchen. 'Let's deal with the little ghosties first.'

'As it's Hallowe'en,' she began, once Natalie, Dan and Benji, minus their props, had perched themselves on stools in the kitchen.

'Trick or *treeaat*, not hallowe'*een!*' they cried.

Sara shooshed them. 'Where I come from it's Hallowe'en. Always has been,' she said firmly. 'And you're guisers. You've got to sing me a song or say a poem or tell me a joke, and then you get something, like apples or nuts or sweeties.' She was drowned by derisive groans.

'Apples and *nu-uts*? Awww . . .'

'I got a joke! I got a joke – what do you get if . . . when . . . a cross sheep . . . and you . . . you . . . and a kangaroo . . . no, and a . . . a . . . if you put it . . .'

'What . . . do you get . . . if . . . you cross . . . a sheep . . . with a kangaroo?' translated Sara. 'Umm . . . no idea! Tell me!'

Benji took a deep, happy breath. 'A . . . a . . . woolly jersey!'

'Oh, brilliant! That's really good! A woolly jersey!'

Dan shoved at him and nearly sent him flying off the stool. 'Schoopid! A woolly jumper, schoopid!'

Cutting in through Benji's wails, Sara said, 'All right, no nuts and fruit. What about popcorn, then? Want to make popcorn?' She was on safer ground here. Andrew sat where he could watch while she got out a broad-bottomed pan, the oil and maize kernels. Sara's pan had a glass lid, which added to the fun.

When the children were settled in the drawing room with their popcorn in front of a video of *Men in Black*, which Andrew had brought with them, Sara and Andrew made their way to the music room. There being little else he could do in the circumstances, Andrew brought in his cello and tuned up.

'I've been looking at *Don Quixote*,' he said. 'I can't play it all, but I've been working on Variation 3. Let me just play you a bit before we talk about other things.'

'Number 3, The Adventure with the Windmills,' Sara murmured. 'Tilting at windmills. It seems appropriate, somehow.'

Andrew was in no hurry to reveal just how little progress he had made in the Bevan enquiry. In fact, if the truth be known, he was considerably prouder of his Strauss than of his abilities as a detective. He had just spent two days in York and achieved nothing.

He began to play, creditably, but with a slight lack of commitment which spoke to Sara of Andrew's preoccupation with other things. A little mechanically, she made a gentle criticism of his bowing. 'Less elbow, you don't need so much.' Mechanically, he corrected it. The truth, that neither of them was terribly interested in Strauss just at this moment, hung in the air unsaid.

'Right then,' said Andrew, drawing to a finish. 'The case. Fire away.'

'I'm not sure about this,' Sara began, 'and there's possibly nothing in it. Nothing at all.'

'But?' said Andrew. He had risen now, and placed his cello on its side on the floor.

'But this thing about the gas being left on.'

'The gas? You mean we're talking about Adele again? When you said you wanted to talk about the case I thought you meant the Bevan enquiry. That's the case I'm actually working on, if you remember.' He could not help sounding a little peevish. He had hardly seen her for a month and now it was sounding as if she had been thinking about Adele rather than him.

'I know, I know, of course I've been wondering about that, too. But remember you said that the volume of gas must have built up over several hours, a small amount leaking for a long time, rather than a huge leak over a short time, because only one tap was left on?'

Andrew nodded, turning over the pages of *Don Quixote* on the music stand.

'Don't you see? The gas switches all in a row along the front of the cooker. Beautifully symmetrical, the dials all pointing up, for "off". Adele just wouldn't fiddle with those switches. It would upset the symmetry. I know she wouldn't. And Phil on Thursday, he was so upset, he said something about someone wasting Adele. As if he knew something.'

Andrew shook his head hopelessly. 'Knew something? Like what? And if he does, why doesn't he say what it is?'

'I don't know. But someone else could have turned the gas on, couldn't they? There was no fingerprint evidence to prove it was Adele, was there?'

'Of course there wasn't. Half the cooker was blown across the room. God, I don't believe I'm discussing this. Look, Sara, what are you saying? It had to be Adele. Adele was the only one there that Wednesday afternoon.'

'But it could have been someone turning it on later that day. Almost anyone could have. You said yourself that the dial was damaged by the explosion; perhaps it had been turned on later and left on full.'

'Sara, that is pure fantasy. And for what purpose? Do you seriously think, on the base of some theory about what Adele would or wouldn't do, when we know that she was unpredictable and that she fiddled with switches and dials for no reason, that we should start thinking it wasn't an accident? Is that what you're saying? For what possible reason would anyone want to do away with Adele? What possible threat was she to anyone? Or do you think Valerie blew her up because she wanted her part in the opera?'

There was a silence. Sara said, 'Well, I did say I wasn't sure. I mean, I do know Herve visited Adele in the workshop, to record her voice. Other people could have, too.'

Andrew had turned to the Introduction. 'Shall I try this? Don Quixote Sinks Into Madness?'

'No. Play me Sara Selkirk Sinks Into Madness,' she said. 'You clearly think I'm going out of my mind.'

Andrew laughed. 'I can report progress of a sort. On Tuesday of last week we finally got a firm idea of where Brendan Twigg had disappeared to. York. So I set off up there straight away, as soon as we'd contacted Yorkshire police and got a trace on him. At first I couldn't believe my luck. They turned him up within minutes, via a check with Social Services. Brendan Twigg's name has been on the At Risk register there practically since birth.'

'Poor soul. But he's an adult now. He wouldn't still be on their books, would he?'

'Oh, his career goes way beyond being At Risk. Various youth offences. Many and various. Anyway, we got the name of his former foster mother, someone he was with for most of his teens. He was quite attached to her, did quite well with her for a time. So it seemed likely that that was where he'd be heading.'

'Only?'

'Only Social Services don't keep their records very up to date. I arrived at the woman's house to find it re-let. She died last year.'

'Oh, no. Do you suppose poor Brendan did the same? Arrived, not knowing? The poor boy.'

Andrew looked suddenly exasperated. 'Quite likely, yes. I stayed up there for a couple of days, followed up some old contacts of his. Nobody's seen him, or nobody's saying. You know, Sara, sometimes I almost wonder whose side you're on. Brendan Twigg killed Imogen Bevan. Almost certainly.'

Sara returned his look. 'And I keep wondering why you're so certain. You've no proof Brendan did it. No more than I can prove that Adele wouldn't have left the gas on. In fact, you have no proof the Bevan thing had anything to do with animal rights at all. And I just get this feeling it's something more personal, not about a big issue at all. I mean, where have you got to with any of this? The animal liberation lot hardly know him, do they? And these people don't work on their own.'

'Well, maybe not,' Andrew said defensively. 'But at least I'm pursuing a rational line of enquiry. Your feeling that it's something closer to home: it's just that, isn't it? A feeling. You've got nothing to go on, have you?' He wandered over to the French window and stood looking out on the bare garden.

'Not really,' Sara said, her eyes following him, trying to judge how much to tell him. 'But I wanted to tell you something else as well. Last night I saw Dorothy Price again. She wanted to tell me something. I listened, because there was something so sad about her.'

'Oh, *not* because your curiosity got the better of you? Again?' Andrew turned suddenly, smiling, from the French window.

Sara tossed her head grandly. 'An outrageous accusation, Inspector.'

'*Chief* Inspector.'

'Whatever. Anyway, after what she told me, I've got another suspect for you. But as long as there's no evidence, you won't pursue it, will you?'

'Certainly not. I'm not hauling anybody in for questioning just on the basis of another of your hysterical hunches,' Andrew said lovingly.

'You don't deserve me, Poole.'

'Damn right.'

'So?'

'So what?'

'So, aren't you going to ask me who it is?'

'No.'

Andrew came over and sprawled on the sofa opposite her.

'Because you're going to tell me anyway, aren't you?' How dare he look at her with that sceptical intelligence?

'Only if you promise not to believe me,' she said, 'which is all you do these days. Because if this person did it, I wouldn't blame them. Dotty Price had a boyfriend, you see. Well, not quite a boyfriend, and he wrote her dozens of letters which she never got, because Imogen Bevan intercepted them. So she and the boyfriend never got it together, and all these years later they're both miserable. That would be motive enough, wouldn't it? He's a canon, by the way, which does make it seem less likely. And I'd think it quite understandable if he had done it. I wouldn't want him caught, or even questioned. But I can't help wanting to know.'

'Come here, you nosy little wretch.' Andrew lunged out of the sofa towards her, planted his arms on the two arms of her chair, trapping her. He looked at her crestfallen face seriously for a moment, before bending to kiss her lightly.

'Better not,' Sara said glumly. 'The children are just next door.'

Andrew nodded unwillingly and returned to the sofa. He stretched out again and looked at her.

'I've still got a funny feeling about it all, the Bevan case,' Sara said. 'Something we're all missing.'

'Doesn't help,' Andrew said firmly. 'I can't go questioning people on the basis of your funny feelings. I'm bound by rules such as having reason to suspect, and in her case, I haven't.'

'So, back to the animal righters, then,' Sara said, defeated. She got up, picked up Andrew's cello and seated herself on the small high chair. She adjusted the tuning and Andrew watched her, loving the way she prepared herself to play, loosening her shoulders, arms, adjusting her straight-backed posture, arranging her feet, almost as if she were about to dance. She played a swift C major arpeggio starting on the open bottom string and in a winging crescendo travelling up and across the middle G and D strings to triumphant top C on the highest. It was not a great instrument, but it was good. Andrew was getting the most out of it. Really, he had almost reached the limit of what it would do and if he were to progress, he would need a better one.

'Yep. At least there's some circumstantial evidence, some motive.' Andrew paused, thinking about how very little 'some' was, only Anna Ward-Pargiter's account of the Oxfam shop incident and her denial of any knowledge of Bren's where-abouts on the day of the letter-bombing. 'So we haven't traced our Gentleman Twigg yet, not for want of trying. Trouble with the kind of circles he moves in, as soon as it gets around that the police want to question him, the more help he'll get to lie low. But he'll turn up, if only because he can't stay out of trouble indefinitely. He's had addresses in York, Bath, Glastonbury and three or four others in Somerset or Wiltshire. He might even be back down here now. He's been in with all sorts: road protesters, travellers, a couple of new age collectives. Never sticks around long. He'll be hanging out somewhere, probably claiming benefit using a false name, he's done that before. Even if he is outside our area we'll get him. Even if we don't actually find him, he'll get arrested again sooner or later for possession, petty theft, shop-lifting, something like that.'

'Hmmm,' said Sara, her head on one side, apparently concentrating on the sound coming from the cello, as she idled through, from memory, the first of Beethoven's Variations in F Major on a theme from the *Magic Flute*. 'Well now,' she continued softly, the cello notes like a pensive undertow to her words, 'of course it's only another of my funny feelings, not worth considering at all. But this Bren, you see, I have the feeling that if he is just what you say – a petty criminal, a guy who can't stay out of trouble for long – then it's odd you're after him for murder. It's a bit out of character for him, isn't it, to go sending letter-bombs?'

'Oh, maybe. Well, yes. Certainly, of course, perhaps it is,' Andrew blustered slightly, 'but you're forgetting that this wasn't necessarily meant to be a murder. The package had only a tiny amount of explosive, it wasn't actually meant to kill.'

'No, but even so,' Sara went on, 'this Bren drifts in and out of things, doesn't he? Goes with the crowd, whoever it may be for the moment. Has he ever been known to commit himself to anything, like animal rights, a cause? Enough to carry out a letter-bombing? It does seem out of character.'

Suddenly the door burst open and with a great waaagh!! three extremely solid ghosts hurled themselves into the room to give the grown-ups a good haunting. Andrew was saved from further consideration of Sara's funny feelings by Natalie landing like a bundle of weighted laundry in his lap. They had had enough of their video. Wasn't it time for the party yet? Wearily, and with a private look to Sara, Andrew agreed that it was.

Chapter Thirty

No, it wasn't too severe at all, not if she wore the earrings, Valerie thought, turning in front of the bathroom mirror to get the effect of the turban from all angles. Too theatrical and vain? No. In fact, it rather had the effect of 'hadn't a minute to do my hair, darling, so I just had to *throw* this on and *fly*.' She adjusted the black lycra folds so that her earlobes plopped out, and then clamped the two dangling flesh pillows in the bulldog grip of her new clip-on, Indian silver earrings. She gave a trial smile. It was amazing. She relaxed. Even in repose, her face now wore an expression of generous, high-minded serenity. It was amazing what a half-smile and eyebrows stretched a fraction by the tightening of the turban could do. Because it wasn't, Valerie had long ago worked out, the 'hands that do dishes' that took the brunt. It was on the face belonging to the hands that do dishes that the creeping patina of drudgery dulled the skin, where the downturn of expectation tugged the edges of the mouth and paled the eyes. It was the face, even as the hands did the dishes, that grew sadder before it grew older. And although she was aware that there would have to be more complex and profound tools in her resurrection than a new pair of earrings, a touch of highlighter and a turban, Valerie felt that she had suddenly been enrolled in a secret society. She had joined, along with the Faye Dunaways, the Shirley MacLaines and the Elizabeth Taylors, the discreet sisterhood of women who know that an £8.99 turban has much the same effect as a face-lift.

Lost on most of this lot, however, she realised an hour later, sitting in the window seat in Helene's drawing room. Helene had greeted her, she felt, a little thoughtfully and then turned most of her attention on Herve, who was gracing the rehearsal again. Helene was so pleased that he was now taking such a close interest in their little opera, even though it had to be without the thrill of Adele's voice. Valerie bridled silently. She was no singer, she knew that, not like Helene or Adele, but she had something. Herve certainly thought so.

Because Valerie had grown not just used to but fond of the sensation of others' eyes upon her during rehearsals. Herve looked at her too, although usually frowning, concentrating on every note of each rehearsal as if it were the most important music in the world. So it was curious, perhaps, that he and Cosmo still seemed to have so little to say to each other. Cosmo seemed more in awe of him than anybody, even frightened. But then, studying with Herve would be alarming, especially for a man. It took a woman to see what a kitten he was underneath it all.

Valerie sat tight in the window seat. Andrew, coming straight from work, arrived last. He was late, but looking over at her in a not unfriendly way, gave a slow smile and came to join her. They were both wondering what he was going to say about her new look. 'Nice earrings,' he managed, before Poppy boomed, 'Ah, Andrew, at *last*! We're about to get started, so chop-chop, people! Cosmo's ready for you.'

'Anyone know anything about Phil?' Poppy suddenly asked in a public voice, addressing the room. She had been busy with some dark material at the sewing machine set up in one corner. Heads shook, and people looked round as if he might be hiding somewhere. Poppy tightened her lips as if Phil's absence and the general ignorance of his whereabouts were deliberate slights. Valerie felt absurdly as if she had somehow let Poppy down.

'How *annoying*,' she said, turning back to the machine. 'I need him for his fitting. How can I fit the sleeves until he's tried it on? He was supposed to be here early for it. He's forgotten.'

Poppy was behaving more and more like the producer, not just the costume person, stage manager and general dogsbody. With a sigh of long-suffering, exasperated exhaustion she announced, 'Oh, *well*. Let's make a start, anyway. This'll need shifting for a start.' Helene's drawing room had become a little too small for rehearsing, now that they were doing all the moves as well as singing. 'Right! Come on, people. Er, 'scuse me, you'll need to shift.'

It was she more than Cosmo who was running rehearsals. Now she was bullying Herve off his chair and in a most inappropriate manner, as if he were an ordinary person, just because she had decided she wanted it moved. At least she wasn't asking Herve to move it, Valerie noticed, as Jim stepped forward in answer to her bidding.

Three-quarters of an hour into the rehearsal, Helene answered a ring of her door bell which donged through Jim's rendition of *'except they have no shoes!'*. A few minutes later she returned, looking worried, ushering Phil before her. Andrew's cello continuo halted abruptly, Jim's voice trembled away into silence, and Cosmo's jaunty gavotte on the piano lost its trit-trotting jollity and tinkled out after them both. Never one to make an entrance, Phil hesitated in the doorway long enough for everyone to see that he was unusually, noticeably dirty. The blue-black hair had the sticky matt look of a yard broom, his navy sweatshirt was stale and stained. His face, usually so white and smooth, had a greenish pallor and the suggestion of curds forming under the skin. And into the wool carpet and coffee aroma of Helene's drawing room he brought a pungent, cheaper scent which exuded from every cell, pore and fibre of his hair, skin and clothes: the smell of frying, beer and fags. It was attar of pub, distilled to a strength and purity achieved only by dedicated exposure. He had the puzzled, wrecked demeanour that reminded Andrew of lads arrested outside the clubs late on Saturday nights. He reckoned Phil must have been drinking since mid-morning. But drinking in the student manner – slowly – for he was not drunk, not swayingly, loudly so. Fixing his eyes on his destination, he made his way over the carpet to the other window seat on the far side of Valerie and sank into it as if he had crossed a desert to reach it. His head slumped forward almost to his knees.

'You're late, Phil,' Poppy said, with her arms folded, 'very late. I thought it was understood that discipline is part of what this project is all about? Discipline and responsibility.' Although it was not a question, Poppy clearly expected some answer.

Phil looked up and around, almost insolently unaware of the annoyance he was causing. He looked at Poppy steadily for a moment and raised his hands hopelessly. Then he shook his head and slumped forward again.

'Listen, Phil, this isn't good enough,' she began hotly, but Phil raised his head. This time his face was angry.

'Okay, okay! You shut your face, okay? You just shut your face!' He sounded cold sober, his voice louder and steadier than anyone had ever heard it before.

Helene jumped up. 'Oh now, Phil, that's not a nice thing to say! Poor Poppy's been working *so* hard, you know. Now why don't you come down and help me and—' Phil was on his feet now, staring round at them all, breathing in and out very fast with the effort of gathering more words.

Cosmo stood up, a frozen look on his face. 'Phil, I insist you leave this rehearsal. I'm the musical director, and I'm asking you to leave.'

Phil let out a shriek of frustrated rage and continued to stare from one to another, apparently immobilised by his inability to decide which of them to go for first.

'You all . . . so *stupid*! You all . . . don't care! Don't care at all! Hurting Adele and now you don't care. Using her, just using her! I know! I know what you do! She tell me all – she know things, you think she know nothing, but she know! She know everything, and she tell *me*! Only *me* she can tell, because I understand her, I know all about her. So I know all what you doing, using her, hurting her!' He was flailing with both arms, accusing the entire room, sobbing wildly. Of them all, only Andrew seemed able to move. He rose and came towards the trembling Phil, who held him off with a shaking arm.

'No, don't touch me! I go! I go now! Leave me!' And he ran from the room, almost knocking over Helene who stood nearest the door. He flung her restraining arm away, struggled noisily with the door handle and escaped into the hall and out through the front door, which banged shut.

In the silence that followed Valerie tightened her lips and looked dignified, which was easier in the turban. 'Drunk,' she said primly. 'How unnecessary.' Nobody agreed, or at least was not saying so. She looked round at the depressed group. It was obvious that someone was going to have to give a moral lead. 'We must rise above it, otherwise that kind of thing undermines us all.'

'He was upset, that's all,' Helene said, surprisingly simply. 'The poor boy, he hasn't any family here. It must be awful when nobody can make out what you're trying to say.'

'But that sort of rudeness is so uncalled-for,' sniffed Valerie. 'He was so rude to Poppy.'

'Oh, that's just stress. Stress is behind most people's aggression. When you know that's where it's coming from it's easier to cope with,' said Poppy, omniscient and all-forgiving. 'Phil obviously has to come to terms with a lot of anger. Maybe things aren't going well at college. He needs to relax,' she added comfortably. 'Cosmo does as well, don't you? We're all under pressure, in one way or another. I think there's far too much pressure nowadays.'

Andrew noticed that everyone, like sitting ducks, fell hungrily on the uncontroversial mouldy crust that Poppy had just tossed in the water. Cosmo, his stressed condition now out in the open, felt able to leave the piano admitting to tiredness and submit to Poppy's insistence that he take a Bach flower remedy. Helene judged it the right moment for coffee and commandeered a bewildered, servile Jim to help her. Herve was nodding in understanding; he knew all about stress, possibly aggression too. Valerie stood up, adjusting her god–awful headgear, and was now making her way over to Herve. Brave of her, Andrew thought. A month ago she wouldn't have done that. And the turban must have taken some guts, too, and it would look wonderful on her if it didn't err just slightly a fraction too far towards weird.

When the coffee arrived a little later, Andrew wondered if he was the only one who noticed that the task of taking cups round now fell to Jim alone. For the rest of the evening nobody mentioned Phil again, nor did anyone speculate, or at any rate not aloud, about who among them he had been shouting at, nor of what, exactly, he had been accusing them.

Chapter Thirty-one

So, what did she feel? Sara wandered away from the window through which she had just watched Andrew's car as it backed down the drive of Medlar Cottage, turned and disappeared out of sight. From here he hadn't been able to see her, but she knew he knew she would be at the window. What did she feel? She made her way into the kitchen, switching on lights. It was only a quarter to four, but it got dark so early now. She wasn't hungry or thirsty, not really; aware of appetite, but for the moment lacking any. She was completely relaxed and simultaneously as wound as a spring. Adele's mirror-images and opposites came to mind. She felt like that. Happier now than she had felt for years and, conversely, also more anxious. Totally, intensely close to Andrew and at the same time, watching him leave, unutterably abandoned. Again, or rather still, yearning for him.

It had been, in the end, so easy. No farcical interruptions, rows or misunderstandings. Andrew had arrived for a lesson, walking straight from the door to the music room where he had set out his music on the music stand and turned to open his cello case. Something, although she was sure she had not said anything, had made him look up at her standing in the doorway. The look they then exchanged told them that they both knew precisely what should happen next. Without saying anything she had gone back and locked the door, switched on the answering machine and led him upstairs. Or perhaps he had led her, but it had been if not unhurried, then not frantic. As if they had both decided that now, finally, making love was an imperative that must be given all the time and space it demanded, they had undressed deliberately and in silent agreement, saving their first words – a breathless whispering of names – for the moment when they first touched each other naked. Sara stood in the kitchen and smiled, the memory of it like gentle, playful licking. Now they could never again make love for the first time. Or the second, she reflected, remembering the slow, sweet time later, after they'd lain and talked, stroking and gazing, as the afternoon stretched away in a delusion of timelessness. The surprise was just how shockingly, wonderfully right it felt to make love with Andrew, and how wrong it felt that he was actually someone else's husband. And there, she recognised, was the anxiety.

She wandered into her music room. It was just as he'd left it, music on the stand, cello case and more music on the floor. She switched on the lamp behind the chair they used for playing on and collapsed on the sofa, determined not to feel lonely yet almost luxuriating in the first minutes of his absence, when she was free to think about him. The place where he could be sitting now playing to her was empty. Stupid to switch on the light, it merely emphasised his not being there. Her eyes glanced over to the music on the floor, Strauss's *Don Quixote*, lying open at Variation 9: The Combat with the Two Magicians. On the music stand was a single sheet of music which, with the light shining through it, she could read from behind. She read music as other people read words; not since she was six or seven had she had to stop to work out a relatively simple line. She could see that the music on the stand, with the light shining through it, was Herve's four notions. Funny of Andrew to be playing those was her first thought, until she realised that of course he couldn't be, because nobody but her had ever seen the music. It came straight from Herve's hands to hers. But of course, as she realised in the next second, she was reading from behind, she was reading it backwards. So she read the notes again, realising that it couldn't be Herve's music at all, and indeed the phrasing was all different, the rhythms and note values were altered. Except – sitting up now, she checked again – those intervals between the notes *were* Herve's. Nobody could know them better than she (she knew them better than she cared to) and there they were: his four blasted notions. She grabbed the music off the stand, turned it over and studied it properly. What she was holding in her hand was Andrew's cello part for *Nash!* Sara gasped, took the music over to the piano and played it through. Yes, it was the cello music, it was Cosmo's unconvincing, unreliably melodic drivel all right; she'd played it herself. What she was now hearing, for the first time, was that all it was was Herve's stuff rearranged and played backwards. Fiddled with somewhat, some notes longer, some rhythmic alterations to fit the words, but Herve's music all right. She held the page up to the light and played the notes as they appeared from the other side. No doubt about it. The work was Herve's.

Indignation washed over her. Of course she'd always known Cosmo had no real talent, but for him to be a cheap little plagiarist, to take Helene's money, to masquerade as a composer, to deceive everyone. For months now he had been deceiving everyone except . . . Oh, Christ, no, please no. All at once, worse thoughts were beginning to crowd in. Conscious that she must slow her mind down, she stood up and, with the music still in her hands, slowly paced the floor.

Adele's drawings. Every line and feature of Adele's creations, effortlessly drawn in razor-sharp pencil, was symmetrically perfect. It was as if she had been mesmerised by the notion of equilibrium, or rather comforted by it, in a world she could make little sense of. Adele could not make sense of the world's garbled, difficult messages about the purpose of objects, the meaning of language, the reasons people had for things and their puzzling demands on her. Perhaps her compulsive systems and ordered behaviours were attempts to hold down the world and get it to wait in line, to stop all the messages banking up, clogging the waves and bombarding her. Within the rectangle of her blank page of drawing paper, using her perfect pencil lines, she could create order, make the world behave predictably. A perfect, glittering chandelier must have been another contained, perfect world; small wonder she had taken such a delight in them. And – Sara stopped pacing and felt her heart begin to pound – Adele, with her perfect pitch and memory for music, did the same thing with the music she heard. The distressingly uneven message when a line of music reached Adele's ears could be smoothed out and perfected, made sense of, only when she sent it back, the same line inverted, transformed into its mirror-opposite, to finish the message and complete the circle.

Suddenly Sara was back in the walled garden at Iford on a sunny late September evening. Adele sat next to her on the white bench, staring down the path, crooning softly the four atonal, difficult phrases of Herve's that she had heard Sara play in the performance. Then, a pause, and four new phrases. Four new ones which, Sara now realised, had been Herve's original four simply sung backwards, as effortlessly as Adele could with a pencil draw a mirror-image, or with her eye spot a misplaced crystal on a chandelier. Four phrases that now formed the entire musical basis for Cosmo Lamb's 'opera'. Andrew had said that night at Iford that Cosmo had not written a note. And following that evening he, still bereft of any ideas of his own, had obviously been getting Adele to sing Herve's notions to him parrot-fashion, then backwards, while he copied it down, messed about with it and passed it off as his own. She now recalled his flubbery, discontented mouth, the bored, shut-down eyes which did not conceal the man's self-glorious ambition. She sucked in her breath with distaste and wrapped her arms tightly around herself. She still had to face the worst part of the truth.

Poor Adele. Sara now saw her, in her mind's eye, in her mother's drawing room, looking wide-eyed from Cosmo to Herve, her finger swinging from one to the other as she declared, 'Backward! Forward! Backward!' Sara herself by that point had been sunk in an atrocious temper and had been too sour to pay much attention to the effect this had had on Cosmo, but that must have been the moment at which he had realised the risk represented by Adele. Until that point he would have believed that he would be safe. After all, Adele had very little speech and was ordinarily disinclined to use what little she had. Cosmo had made the plagiarism less blatant by embellishing and manipulating the notes. And when he embarked on his deceit he could not have known that Herve himself would be in regular attendance at rehearsals. But another outburst of that kind from Adele and Herve might twig and Cosmo would be finished. Perhaps it occurred to him only at that point how stupid it had been to pick, of all contemporary composers, Herve Petrescu to steal from. Herve had the reputation, clout and ego to nail Cosmo and his shabby trick in the courts, the music press and the whole, gossipy, international music business. Cosmo would never work again, far less go on to higher things and make any kind of reputation, if Herve caught on to what had happened. So two days later Cosmo had slipped into the workshop, either when Adele was there alone, taking care that Adele did not notice, or later, knowing Jim to be away, and had turned on the gas, knowing exactly what Adele would do the next day. It was no accident. Cosmo had murdered Adele.

There was no answer at Helene's door. There were no lights on. Sara walked back from the door to the pavement and looked up, as if contemplating the house from a distance would reveal signs of occupancy. It now seemed to her an added outrage that Cosmo should be out, probably on some banal errand, and thereby avoid her confrontation. At that moment a fizzing noise erupted from somewhere high above her, and she looked up in time to see the orange tail of a rocket shooting through the sky behind the bare branches of the plane trees in the centre of the Circus. Of course, 5 November. Somehow the actual date had been obscured in the huge significance of the day's other big event and in her angry haste to find Cosmo Lamb. Now she thought of

Andrew's reluctant leave-taking in the coming dark of the late afternoon. He would not go, he said, unless he could see her later. She had shaken her head, knowing that they had managed to stop the clock for a few hours only and now they had to let it start ticking again, with all the arrangements and obligations that took no account of how much they might want to be left alone and together. Andrew must go. Had he forgotten? He had to be with all the other members of the opera group at the Boy Scouts' bonfire and firework party at Iford. Then he had wanted her to come too, to turn up separately in her own car of course, but she could not face it. It would be too confusing, she told him, to have to make polite conversation with his wife, over a hot dog round the bonfire, so soon after, well . . .

Walking briskly back to her car from Helene's dark house and looking up from time to time as, from back gardens all over the city, fireworks whooshed up and cracked open the sky above her, Sara thought that confusion of that sort was nothing in comparison to the turmoil she was feeling now. However squeamish she felt about coming face to face with Valerie, her knowledge of Cosmo's evil act must be conveyed to Andrew. She must go straight out to Iford and find them, explain things to Andrew. Cosmo must be arrested at once.

Chapter Thirty-two

She joined a line of cars snaking through the single-track lane that narrowed down into the valley where the village of Iford lay. It was not hard to be patient, she found, as her car trickled down behind others between the hedges. She needed time, because the sudden appearance of the truth shining through that single sheet of music on the music stand had been, in her mind, like a bike slipping its chain. She must get her head back in gear. As she edged forward, her headlights lighting up the bare hawthorn and twiggy dead grass in their turn, she tried to concentrate.

This time it was not Poppy but a trio of lads in fluorescent jackets who waved her into the car park surrounding the village hall. She parked, got out and stood by the car, wondering where Andrew would be. She felt out of place, alone and with dire things on her mind, among the calling-out and door-slamming of couples and kids getting wellies from the boots of cars, remembering their sparklers, insisting on gloves, putting hoods up and hats on. Naked white light from the swinging doors of the hall sliced on and off the surface of the car park with the coming and going of people buying drinks and food inside. They stood around in dark clumps, or stepped out of the glow from the hall in twos and threes to join a straggly line of darkening, thickly clothed figures, like a medieval procession to Calgary, which swung slowly round the side of the building, through the gate at the back of the car park and up into the high field behind. At the top, the Scouts' bonfire stood waiting behind its barrier of rope. Sara reckoned there must be over a thousand people here. In the dark out on that field, what hope had she? Any number of them could be Andrew. Or Cosmo.

'Gosh, *hi*!' Poppy's voice was like a small explosion four feet away. '*You're* here!' Can in one hand and food in the other, she brought with her the scent of fried onions with a sharp top note of ketchup.

'I was wondering where Andrew was,' Sara said, glad of the dark which must at least partly hide the horror of running into the girlfriend of the man whose arrest she had come to arrange. 'Loads of people, aren't there?' she said, as if surprised.

Poppy nodded, looking round and beaming, before sinking her face back into a paper-wrapped burger the size of a side plate.

As casually as she could Sara said, 'Have you seen him around?'

Poppy said, chewing and pointing with the hand holding the can, 'Near the gate. He's waiting for Valerie. You should get one of these,' she said, taking another bite. 'Anyway, may see you up there. Got to help the boys with the guy. Bye!' She disappeared into the dark, leaving a fried-onion cloud behind her.

Andrew, with his arms crossed in front of him, stood in the dark, almost behind the hedge, by the side of the gate leading into the car park. Cars were now arriving intermittently, their headlights arcing in the same predictable swing across the lane, over the stone gatepost and along the tarmac in front of his feet. The three car-park lads stood in a group on the verge on the far side of the lane, having a fag. Sara ran to him.

'Andrew!'

'Sara! Sara? I thought you weren't coming! Dar—'

'No, listen! Listen! You've got to listen! I've found something out. I know what happened now. I know. That music you left, I've seen, your cello part, I've got to tell you . . .' But to Sara's alarm, from somewhere in the dark behind Andrew a rustling noise began softly and grew louder. Someone rather heavy was making his way out of the long grass behind the hedge and coming nearer. Cosmo loomed out suddenly and appeared unsmiling at Andrew's side.

'Don't recommend the bushes. Nettles. At a very awkward height.'

Then he turned to Sara with his usual expression of recognition untouched by either welcome or curiosity. Sara could not recall ever having heard him say hello to anyone.

Andrew said, 'Cosmo's been waiting here with me. I'm stuck here waiting for Valerie. She's coming in her own car. What was that were you saying just now?'

Sara thought quickly. How much had Cosmo heard? If she led Andrew away to speak to him privately, he could easily slip away. But perhaps he hadn't heard anything, or hadn't cottoned on to what she meant; he certainly looked calm enough. Shivering slightly, she turned her face up to Andrew. Her heart was thumping and her voice was shriller than she intended it to be.

'I wanted to talk to you first, Andrew. About Adele. There are things you don't know. Aren't there, Cosmo?' Cosmo swallowed hard and stared at her, shaking his head, pretending not to understand.

Through the gate from the lane now came a metallic trundling noise at which they all turned. Half a dozen duffle-coated boys, accompanied by Poppy, were pushing along a large wheelbarrow which held a life-sized guy dressed in breeches, frock coat, at least two jumpers, gloves, boots and three scarves. A pair of boxer shorts flapped out of one sleeve like a dandy's handkerchief. It lolled rakishly in the wheelbarrow, its whole head bandaged and wearing a plumed tricorn hat, as if it were being carted home from a marvellous Hogarthian piss-up rather than towards its scorching demise. As they rolled by, one of the boys looked up. He waved. 'Thanks for the old clothes! It's really brilliant!' Cosmo, transfixed by other concerns, did not respond. Poppy called out a loud 'Hey!' and waved as she went past. Sara, who had been staring at the guy, looked at Cosmo.

'Whose old clothes? Whose old clothes are they?' she asked.

Brightly, as if relieved to be asked a question he could answer, Cosmo explained, 'It's just some old stuff of ours. They hadn't got much to dress the guy in. We found some extra clothes for it, that's all.'

'Sara, what is all this about?' Andrew sounded confused. 'What's this thing I'm supposed not to know?' She turned away from him, wishing that he would do something, anything, rather than just stare in that puzzled way at Cosmo and back at her as if he weren't sure who to believe.

She looked hard at Cosmo. 'Look, Cosmo, you might as well admit it. Look, I *know*! I know all about it! Admit it! You used Adele *shamelessly*, you abused her and then you . . . you've been cheating Helene, cheating us all! Haven't you! Haven't you!'

But he would not admit it. Even in the raw November night air he was managing to blush patchily. He was shaking his head with a stupid search-me look on his face, while from his greasy lips came lying platitudes. 'Ah, sorry, I'm just not with you. I'm not getting this at all, I'm afraid.' Either the cold or her anger was making her shake. Whatever it was, it was unstoppable and she could hardly speak.

Andrew placed a hand on her arm and spoke softly. 'Sara, it's not altogether clear what you're saying. Slow down.'

She snatched her arm away. 'Ask him, Andrew, ask him! He knows! He knows what he's done! She's dead!'

Cosmo was shaking his head now, and with a shock Sara realised that in his gesture there was more than a suggestion of pity. 'If, ah, Poppy was here, I'm sure she'd say that you're terribly tense,' he said, almost smoothly.

'I am not!' Sara shrieked, her fists clenched and her body rigid.

Andrew's arm came heavily round her shoulders and he held her tightly against his side, his hands gripping her upper arms. 'Steady on,' he said, almost in her ear. He went on holding her easily, despite her attempts to free herself.

'Andrew, let *go* of me, you've got to listen . . .'

'Just . . . steady . . . on,' he repeated. 'I will listen, when you're calm.'

Impatiently, Sara took a deep breath, and then another. Andrew's hands relaxed a little, but he did not let her out of his embrace. Nobody spoke. Another car turned in, the first for several minutes. Faint tinned chunks of the Royal Fireworks Music being tannoyed from the back of the hall up to the bonfire site reached them from across the tarmac. Over by the door of the hall sparklers were being lit and swirled in the dark. Sara stared. She blinked. The mirror-image of the silver scribbling in the air appeared on her retinae as streaks of dripped green paint, her own private Jackson Pollock. No one else sees what I see, she thought. She opened her eyes.

Andrew began, 'Sara, let me take you down to the hall. Cosmo's right. You are very stressed and—'

'Andrew, shut up,' Sara hissed, her voice trembling. 'I'm fine. There's nothing wrong with me. I have something to say.'

'She thinks she's fine. That's a classic symptom,' murmured Cosmo dolefully to Andrew, 'of mental breakdown.'

'Well, Sara?' Andrew said.

'Adele knew what you were doing,' Sara said to Cosmo in a hard voice, 'didn't she? You were stealing Herve's musical ideas, getting her to sing them to you backwards so you could pretend the work was yours—'

'I was *not*,' gasped Cosmo.

'You thought she'd never understand it herself, let alone be able to tell anyone else, didn't you?'

'How dare you? That's utter rubbish,' said Cosmo.

'Then she nearly came out with it at that rehearsal. Forwards, backwards. Remember, Cosmo?'

'No, I don't,' he said sulkily. 'You're mad. Adele was always saying odd things.'

'Well, Sara, is that it? Satisfied now?' asked Andrew.

Sara began to shake again. 'You did, you did! It . . . it must have been you,' she whimpered. Had she expected a climb-down, an admission? She had not anticipated that Cosmo would sound so convincingly aggrieved and she felt suddenly uncertain. Andrew placed his arm round her shoulder again. Expecting to hear his voice speaking some soothing thing to her, something about wrong ends of sticks, she was surprised to hear his voice suddenly raised.

'Wait. Phil. He knew something. Where is Phil?' he demanded. 'His outburst at the rehearsal. When he was late. Wasn't he supposed to have a costume fitting? He knew something. He said Adele had told him everything. She must have told him. He was enraged, upset. She must have told him. *He* knew, too. So where is he now?'

There was a silence while Cosmo went into his mystified headshaking routine again. Sara had not seen the outburst at the rehearsal and had, in the confusion of her discovery over the music, almost forgotten Phil. Poor Phil, weeping in the rose garden for love of Adele. Of course Adele would have told him.

'If Sara's wrong, he's quite safe, isn't he? Isn't he, Cosmo? Nothing to worry about,' Andrew said. It was a challenge.

Out of the dark at the top of the hill came the sound of the crowd cheering.

'The guy! The clothes! The costume! You dressed the guy!' screamed Sara, breaking out from the shelter of Andrew's arm, pointing a shaking hand at Cosmo. 'The guy! It's Phil! They're burning him! Phil!' She tore away, making for the dark field. As she reached the end of the car park she looked up. Ahead, through the dark moving shapes of people she could see the flames of the bonfire just beginning to take hold.

Chapter Thirty-three

Andrew overtook her easily, turning and shouting back to her that he was running ahead to get the marshalls to douse the fire. She must come up as fast as she could and find him at the top. The incline was gentle but long. When Sara got to the top a few seconds later, the crowd had already parted to make way for the man who had just burst through, shouting that he was a police officer and demanding to see the person in charge. Sara could see him being directed towards a hut behind the rope barrier, at least ninety feet from the fire. He was still running but he was going to be too late.

She turned to look at the fire. It had been built broad and low, roughly circular, about twelve feet in diameter and eight feet high. It had been lit from behind and flames were now ripping up through the back in pale gashes. Wood splintered and sank lower, bedding down for extinction. She saw that Phil, trapped in layers of clothes that covered every bit of him, his entire head swathed in white bandages with a comic face drawn in black marker, and the ridiculous hat on top, had been perched right on top at the front. He lay on his back, his legs and arms crooked over the criss-crossing net of planks and branches. Sara looked frantically over to the hut. If they waited any longer, Phil would be dead. Of course he could be already, but she hadn't time to consider that now. She slipped under the rope barrier and ran across the safety area of no-man's land towards the fire. The marshalls, diverted by

293

Andrew, were nowhere in sight but she bolted fast, fearing that someone from the crowd might stop her. People called out to her.

The heat and rush of the fire were in her face now. She blinked against its unbearable brightness and her eyelids almost stuck in the heat. Sucking in a breath, she felt her throat fill with sharp hot sparks. Yet she was still running, and a loud roaring sound from the fire, or perhaps it was her own terrified breathing, surrounded her.

'Phil! Phil! Oh, my God! Phil!' She was screaming at the top of her lungs, wasting the breath she needed to run. She took one last, hot gulp of breath and threw herself at the wall of black wood, clambered up four or five feet easily and grabbed Phil's foot and pulled. He stuck. She pulled again, and this time one side of his body came easing down towards her with a rush of crackling like gunfire. The other arm was still hooked over a branch at the top. She steadied herself, and with half of Phil's body draped over one shoulder she pushed higher, stretching out with her one available hand to free the trapped arm. No, she had to reach even further. She strained upwards again under Phil's crushing weight and heard herself groan. If only she could get another breath. A crash and a scream sounded together as a branch under her foot suddenly snapped. Others beneath it were giving way. Below her, rags of flame were weaving upwards trying to bind her feet, and sparks shot up to meet her face, finding her skin. As she fell backwards under Phil's body she was aware of the smell of her own hair burning.

Fractions of a second or whole hours may have passed, she wasn't sure. But at the same moment as she realised that the huge, heavy weight that had thumped her hard in the back was the ground, she was aware of Phil's silly tricorn hat rolling past her across the cold grass. His head was still in it.

Chapter Thirty-four

It was not a bad place to be. It was too bright, and the thing she was lying on was too high, but it was padded. Nice blanket, too. Not out of curiosity, for it did not seem to matter where exactly this was, but more for something to do, she moved her eyes. She could see mainly ceiling, dominated by the long glaring strip light. There was a door, light switches. Her eyes travelled down the wall and across to the notices pinned up there.

LAST PERSON IN HERE LEAVE SINK TIDY AND SWITCH OFF LIGHTS — THIS MEANS *you*.
Toilet rolls ect in cupboard see caretaker for key

She could still read. That was good, so it was quite odd, really, that she should now burst into tears. She struggled to a sitting position and found Andrew next to her, helping her up. For the next few minutes she sobbed noisily into his chest, until slowly she fitted together her presence in this room and in this state with the last thing she remembered.

'Phil? Oh, Phil . . .' she wept.

Andrew's tone of voice was the one he used when he had been, but was no longer, extremely angry. 'Sara, the thing you pulled off the fire was the Scouts' guy. It was just a guy, made out of stuffed tights, sawdust, bits of wire and old clothes. You could have got yourself killed. Rescuing a dummy.'

This was clearly not designed to stop her crying. 'I'm

sorry, I'm sorry, I'm sorry,' she repeated, through the stinging tears and snails of mucous that she was catching in Andrew's handkerchief.

Andrew sighed and was silent for a few moments.

'All right, all right now,' he said, more kindly. 'I'm angry with myself, too. You swept me along with you. I didn't stop to think. Let's just try to calm down now. Look, I've made you a cup of tea. Here.'

Sara took the cup and sipped. Her lips felt new to the activity. Swallowing helped, although it made her aware of how raw her throat was. Andrew moved away and sat down at the table, and poured himself tea from a huge aluminium teapot with Iford WI written on it in nail varnish. Sara was beginning to breathe normally. She swung her legs round and let them dangle over the edge of the high first-aid couch.

Andrew said, putting down his cup, 'Don't you dare. Don't you dare move. I can't cope with you on the loose just yet. I love you, you crazy bitch.'

Sara couldn't cope with forgiveness. She gave a short, gasping half-laugh, and at the same time more tears began to fall. She wiped them away. 'I'm sorry, I really am. I just suddenly felt sure. But I hadn't worked it out.'

Andrew shook his head. 'You sure hadn't. And I shouldn't have gone along. But supposing it had been Phil, and I hadn't done anything . . . Anyway, it was a ridiculous idea.' Andrew went on, 'Christ, Sara, how crazy to think that anyone would kill someone by dressing them up as a guy and getting them burned, or even dispose of a body that way. It'd be impossible to keep it concealed, wouldn't it, to say the least? Even if it was possible to do, with dozens of Boy Scouts running around, which is highly unlikely.'

Sara nodded meekly. 'I'm sorry. I think I got everything a bit mixed up.' She rubbed her head. 'I really do feel quite unwell. Can you take me home? Where's Valerie?'

Andrew looked at his watch. 'Of course I'll take you home. Valerie's not coming. She rang to say there's some new crisis with Linda the divorcing bridesmaid and she's gone to Swindon till tomorrow. Her mother's with the children. It's only half past eight but I'd better not be late. I want you to stay here and rest a bit longer.' He glanced at the door. 'I managed to stop them calling an ambulance, but I'll have to give some explanation and then I'll get you home quietly. I guess that's what you want?'

'Who's they?'

'Poppy, for one. She's very concerned, she's telling every-body it's a sign of hypertension. She won't shut up about the risk of thrombosis if it isn't treated. Helene. The organisers. And about half the crowd, probably.'

Sara sighed and thought. 'Tell them I was making a protest. About the ritual effigy burning of Catholics in the late twentieth century. My religious sensibilities deeply offended or something. That'll do, I expect. God, I do feel a fool.'

'You deserve to.'

'But, Andrew, there is the question of the music,' she began, sitting up properly. She was talking fast and feeling her heart begin to thump again. 'I'm not mistaken there. Cosmo *has* plagiarised Herve's stuff and he's got to be stopped. Exposed for what he is. And Adele did . . . I mean, she did, well, I'm pretty sure she—'

'Don't make me say it,' Andrew broke in, rising from his chair and coming towards her. 'Don't make me say I prefer you unconscious.' He took her in a huge hug. 'Cosmo seems to have made himself scarce for now. But I will go and see him. I'm not sure it's a police matter, but at the very least he mustn't go on hoodwinking his patron. Helene ought to know. All right?'

Sara's head was giving her trouble. She had begun to cry again. 'Please can I go home now?'

Chapter Thirty-five

She marched along, hands jammed in her coat pockets, feeling oddly calm about her first ever dawn raid. It was just after eight o'clock, but since she had been awake since half past two this did not register with her as early for visitors. Indeed she considered she was being generous in waiting until morning. When she had finally worked out the truth, at around four o'clock, there had been mixed with her self-congratulation a certain delight in solving the matter for Andrew, and she had nearly telephoned him there and then. But, she had thought, with the receiver in her hand, he would probably be maddeningly calm about it. He would ask her for evidence or – what was that awful phrase of his? – 'reason to suspect'. Much better if she saw it through herself and presented Andrew with the whole thing cut and dried with a full confession, because it was a certainty that, once confronted, there could be no denials.

She smiled. After enduring a night with the sky bursting inexplicably with showers of exploding chrysanthemums and filled with loud alarming bangs, Herve would probably be quivering indoors now, thinking the revolution had come, as unaware of this annual pyrotechnic madness as he had been of the end of British Summer Time. He would probably think she was doing him a favour, coming to explain that the end of civilisation was not as nigh as he might fear.

Not up yet, Sara noted without surprise, pressing the

299

outside buzzer and looking up at the closed drapes of 11 Camden Crescent. The curtain moved as she waited. So he had been easy to wake. But no reply came. She buzzed again and waited, still looking up. This time the curtain was still. She pushed on the buzzer again and kept her finger there. After a very long time a slow, groggy voice rasped quietly through the intercom. 'What? Who is that?' He was pretending that he had been asleep.

'Herve, is that you? It's Sara. Let me in. Sorry if I woke you, but it's very important.'

'Sara? I don't ... what is important? Now is not so good.'

'You'll understand. It won't take long.'

'No. Not now. Now is not good time.'

'Herve? It's important. Please let me in for a minute.' There was a long pause filled only by the faint whistle of the intercom.

'*Herve?* Look, it's freezing out here. Will you please let me in for a minute? It *is* important. Let me in, Herve.' There was another long pause and then with a click the door lock was released.

Herve opened the door of the flat dressed only in a short towelling robe.

'Hello, Herve. Sorry to appear unannounced,' Sara said, feeling a stab of retaliatory glee for the occasion when he had burst in on her and Andrew. She marched past him into the drawing room. He had not asked her in, but he would not want to stand out at the door dressed only in that. She turned. 'I am sorry. You look as if you were about to have a bath.' He looked in need of one too, she couldn't help noticing. His long hair looked mussed up and then pasted down, his skin had the faint sweaty shine that is produced by overheated rooms in winter. The room was not only warm, but seemed to have been sucked empty of breathable air. He did not invite her to sit down.

'Herve, this is important. Look, I know what you've been doing.'

'Doing? I? Of course you know what I am doing. We are doing together, new piece for keyboard, cello and recorded tape. And you say you have important thing to say. This is not good time, Sara, really.' Herve had arched his eyebrows defensively and was already making for the door to show her out.

'But I do have important things to say! You're a plagiarist. Fooling around with other people's work. Pretending to write music when all you've done is copy someone else's stuff!'

'Plagiarism?'

'It's so dishonest! I mean, just writing something backwards, calling it your *own* music when you don't care what it actually sounds like, it just means you've written something down . . . you can't call that composing. I don't see how you can call it music. It's shameful. Isn't it?'

Herve gave a shrug and folded his arms. 'True music is about process. It is the idea that is all. The material is not important, it is the composer's mind that supplies the musical landscape, his idea. It is the idea of the music that matters.'

'Oh, no matter what it sounds like?' Sara challenged, then collected herself. Wishing more than anything in the world that she had not gone into this alone she said, slightly hesitantly, 'Look, this isn't the point and you know it. It's what else you did. When you went to the workshop. You turned on the gas to make sure Adele wouldn't give you away. You killed her, didn't you? You know what you've done . . . You know . . .' Suddenly the truth, or perhaps the heat of the room, her lack of sleep or the events of last night, possibly all of them, were going to make her faint, or be sick . . .

Herve moved impatiently, shifting his weight on to the other hip. He glanced over Sara's shoulder, then back to her. Gulping hard, Sara looked swiftly behind her at the door that led to the bedroom and its attached bathroom. 'I need to use your bathroom. I need to . . . Sorry, but . . .'

But Herve was blocking her way. 'No, you cannot,' he said quickly, and openly annoyed. 'But this is not the time.

You may not go there. You go now.' He was steering her towards the door of the flat.

Sara made her way to an armchair and sat on the edge of it. 'Wait. I feel dizzy. I'll go in a second,' she said. She took a few deep breaths. 'I know what you've done. I'm getting the police. You killed Adele. You know you did.'

Two things then happened, and Sara was not sure in which order. A loud, explosive sound burst from Herve's nose and mouth, a combination of a derisive snort, a laugh and a 'Haa!'. The door to the bedroom opened and a woman appeared, newly woken, wearing one of Herve's shirts with only one button fastened. She was opening and closing lips that looked as if they had been rubbed with sandpaper, and her hair looked like an exploding firework. Sara drew in her breath.

'Hello, Valerie,' she said.

Chapter Thirty-six

Sara made her way shakily back to her car, trying to expunge the picture of shagged Valerie in the doorway of Herve's bedroom. Yet she had to hand it to the woman. Even half asleep and half naked, Valerie had been almost dignified. Once she had woken up sufficiently to realise who she was looking at, she had gone on staring for several seconds, then looked at Herve.

'What's all this?'

'Sara is making another little scene of hysterics.'

'Valerie, get dressed. You've got to come with me. Valerie, I'll explain—'

'Sara thinks I am murderer.'

Valerie had then raised her head, taken a deep breath and stared again with hostility at Sara. 'Oh, please. How utterly typical. I suppose Andrew's in on this?'

'I tell you, Sara, I think at last you are out of mind totally.'

'Valerie, I know it looks odd, but—'

'You've got a nerve, haven't you? I'm going nowhere with you. Now just get out, will you?' Then, as if having considered what else she might say and concluding that after all, no, there were no more words appropriate to the occasion or at least none at her command, Valerie had simply turned and walked back into the bedroom, closing the door.

Driving out of Bath back to St Catherine's Valley Sara felt at least two emotions, even two judgments at once, which collided badly and yet coexisted in her now fairly jiggered head. For hadn't Valerie and Herve looked a bit stupid and tawdry? But then, perhaps other people's adultery always seems so, while one's own is always perfectly understandable, inevitable even, and of a purer, rarefied kind. Was she so certain that it must be flabby, middle-aged lust that drew Valerie and Herve together, whereas she and Andrew were in love as well as in better shape? She could not predict how Andrew would feel about it, beyond realising that he could not, any more than she could, take the moral high ground. Neither of them was in any position to judge Valerie at all, having so happily and only yesterday done exactly as she had. Should she not even acknowledge a glimmering of gratitude towards her, for Valerie's perfidy surely excused Andrew's and hers? She tried to tell herself that the questions that now arose concerning Valerie and Herve, never mind Andrew and herself, would all have to wait, because Herve was a murderer. Yet, of course, it was not going to be that simple, for how could she now contact Andrew to tell him that, without going into the other? Andrew might even go straight round to arrest him. What should she say then? Oh, and I should just mention, Andrew, your wife's also there, wearing a silly grin and the murderer's pyjama jacket? She felt angry with Valerie, not liking to think of Andrew as a cuckold and at the same time not wanting him to care. She wanted him too besotted with herself to get territorial about Valerie, but however he might feel about it, the matter of Andrew's reaction begged the question: how was she going to tell him? *Was* she going to tell him? In any event she had to get home first.

Andrew had solved the last of Sara's problems by having his mobile phone switched off. Sara sank, almost grateful for his unavailability, on to the sofa in the drawing room. All she could do was wait a few minutes and keep trying; for the moment her head was swimming too much and her thinking too ragged to do much else. She was exhausted enough for sleep. But when her second try at Andrew's number was interrupted by loud knocking at the door she found she still had enough energy to swear.

'Well, I'm glad I followed my instinct to come out to see

you,' Poppy said, stepping past Sara into the drawing room. 'I was so worried about you last night. You still don't look good. Sleep badly?'

Sara nodded. 'Actually, Poppy, I've got a few things I must do. Then I really must have a rest. It's very kind of you, but—'

'Oh, I don't mind! Acupuncture'll do you a lot more good than a rest. It's after nine, anyway. You can't go back to bed. I've brought everything with me.'

'Poppy, I . . .' Sara raised a hand to her head and had to sit down again. 'I really don't think—'

'Oh, you'll see the light about acupuncture,' Poppy said warmly, placing a friendly hand on Sara's arm. 'I think sometimes it takes a thing like last night to let us know we need help. Sometimes, something just gives way. Hypertension's just extreme tension after all, isn't it? I must say you do look tired.'

'No, well, I have a lot on my mind.' Sara smiled wanly, trying not to let her impatience show. 'Look, I have to make a phone call.'

'No, fine, you carry on,' Poppy said gaily. 'I can wait. I'll just set up next door. This way, is it?'

'Poppy . . .' Sara began. But Poppy had gone. She tried Andrew again. The mobile was still switched off. She tried Manvers Street Police Station and was told he was not yet in. Nervously, she dialled his home number and got no reply. Andrew, maddeningly, was still unavailable and also was failing to provide her with an excuse to get rid of Poppy. From the music room Poppy's cheery voice was calling, 'Ooh, what a super room! Nearly ready!' Sara sighed. All she could do was to keep trying, and in the meantime, perhaps she really didn't want to be alone. Acupuncture might even help, and it certainly couldn't hurt.

'He had your name and phone number on a scrap of paper in his breast pocket. Lucky, that,' said the Welsh duty physician over the top of his glasses. His good humour had a half-hysterical edge, like a lunatic's. 'You and your wife's. Only we'd have been contacting you lot anyway, for a case like this.'

'I'm not on duty,' Andrew growled. 'If I were, I would have pinned you down long before this.' It was just after nine o'clock in the morning and he had been waiting to see the doctor, with the patience required of a private citizen, since a quarter past seven.

Dr Hugh nodded towards the mound in the bed, attached to drips and respirator. 'Thing is to keep his fluids going,' he said with the hilarity of the seriously sleep-deprived, 'though he's not out of the woods, of course.' He turned back to Andrew. 'Why do they want to do it to themselves, that's what I want to know.'

'Definitely drugs, then?'

'Oh, he's a user, any road. Blood samples not back yet, of course. They'll confirm it, though. Got a drink in him too, I expect. Thought we'd got an ecstasy overdose first off. Student in a coma after a party, first thing you think of, but the scan didn't look that way. No brain swelling. Well, he might not still be with us if there was.' He gestured ruefully towards the bed.

'So how do you know he's a user? Did friends come with him, tell you what he'd been taking?' Andrew had not been able to talk to the paramedics directly. But the reception staff had been able to tell him that an ambulance had been called to the hall of residence, where a fire crew was already in attendance. They'd gone expecting firework injuries, but it had been a false alarm of a kind. Some students, at around three in the morning, had been larking about with fireworks in one of the corridors and had set off the fire alarm which automatically triggered the call-out. There was of course no fire, nor any burn injuries. But Phil, missing from the roll-call, had been found comatose in his bed.

'No, he was brought in on his own. But he's been injecting. Not very good at it, actually. New to it, I suppose. Have a look.'

Andrew looked at the tiny raised pinpricks on the arms.

Raising one shoulder very slightly from the pillow, Andrew scanned the pale skin.

'You think he injected his own shoulder blades, do you?'

On the other side of the bed Dr Hugh said complacently, 'Funny that, isn't it? Can't say I have worked that one out. Full of surprises, my job.'

'Yes, half the fun, I'm sure. These are acupuncture marks,' said Andrew with weary patience.

'*Oh!* So that's what they are, is it?' Dr Hugh exclaimed, with the glee of the newly initiated. 'I never knew that. Don't come across it, you see. But look here.' He drew up the sheet and cotton blanket from the bottom of the bed, exposing the feet. 'Here. On his left ankle.' Andrew came round to look. The puncture mark was bigger and had been made into the vein. 'That one's not acupuncture now, is it? Made with a syringe, that one. Must have been injecting something.'

'You said he wasn't very good at it,' Andrew said, after a pause. Dr Hugh looked puzzled. 'Suppose he injected some air? Would that account for the state he's in?'

Dr Hugh gave Andrew a look which told him he couldn't fool him. 'Well now, he'd hardly do that now, would he?'

'By accident, I mean,' Andrew said wearily.

'Oh, well, you tell me. Depends how much. Less than a fatal amount; well, it would depend.'

Andrew tried another tack. 'Assuming he survives,' he said, looking back at the bed, 'and he might not, I understand that, but assuming he does, what's the outlook?'

'Oh, can't say. It's wait and see time, isn't it? Might just wake up with a headache. Might be damage, though, affecting any number of things.' He counted them off on his fingers. 'Depression, epilepsy, loss of speech, use of limbs, eye coordination. Or PVS. That's persistent vegetative state, for the layman.' Dr Hugh smiled and seemed physically to swell with the power to enlighten.

Andrew shuddered at the thought that this man could be in charge of a scalpel.

Dr Hugh nodded again at the mound, remembering something he'd heard on a course once about connecting with patients at a human level. 'He's Chinese, is he? I'm from Swansea, myself.'

'I'm ready for you no–ow!' called Poppy. Sara shambled through to the music room, too tired to resist. Perhaps afterwards she would sleep better. Poppy's good hands had certainly helped Andrew, she recalled.

'I don't feel I've had the chance to get to know you properly. I like to get to know people if they're doing anything like this to me,' Sara said mildly, once she was lying comfortably on her back on Poppy's folded-out table. 'It's all right if I chatter, isn't it? Won't disturb your concentration?'

'Oh, no,' Poppy said. 'Trust's very important. You just relax and chat away. Whatever helps.' Expertly, she was checking that Sara's loose trousers and shirt would allow access to the necessary acupuncture points. 'I'll be working here and here first. Then here, and then up here. Last ones down here. All right? You just relax and let me do the work.' She arranged a light blanket over Sara's lower body.

'You're amazingly skilled,' Sara said. 'Multi-talented. I can't believe you know all about this *and* you do stage management as well. Not to mention all the night duty at the care home. Cosmo's jolly lucky. I hope he knows it.'

'Hmm-hmm,' Poppy murmured, as if it were all rather boring. 'Look, you're still jolly tense. I think I'll start with a short cranial massage, just to get you relaxed. Okay?'

'Did I tell you I saw your *Magic Flute*? You did stage effects for that production, didn't you?'

'That's right. Of course I wasn't there for the run. We were in Bath by then. I just helped get the production ready.' She reached into Sara's long hair and began to knead her scalp. Sara groaned at the delicious tingle that suddenly burst through her body and wondered if her fingertips were going numb.

'You just upped sticks then, and came with Cosmo? That was selfless. You do such a lot for him, Poppy.' Unable to see her, Sara could nevertheless sense Poppy's smile. The kneading continued, spreading out around the back of her skull. Sara's eyes grew heavy.

Poppy's voice was so soft as to be nearly inaudible. 'I like to. He needs me. He's in a very tough business.'

'I'll say,' Sara sighed quietly. 'Very tough.'

There was silence as both women brooded privately about just how tough.

'Really cut-throat, at times. So many jealousies,' Sara murmured, almost asleep. It was wafting in and out of her mind that Cosmo could not have told Poppy about her mad accusation last night. She owed him thanks for that at least, as well as an apology for getting things so wrong. Cosmo was quite a gent, after all.

'It's so difficult for him,' Poppy agreed. 'It's so difficult just getting performed, let alone commissions. And getting reviewed. Critics can be so cruel.'

Sara opened her eyes and said suddenly, 'Oh, I've just thought of something. I know someone who does a bit of reviewing. James Ballantyne – the pianist. D'you know of him? Ow!' Poppy's hands were gripping her head rather. Sara struggled on to her elbows. 'Look, do you? Because Cosmo really should send him some work.'

She lay back down, sensing that Poppy was a little annoyed that she had broken her concentration.

'In fact, I've got a piece on him somewhere. Let me get it now, before you get started again. I'll probably forget later.' Sara slipped off the massage table, went over to a tidy pile of magazines and papers sitting on the floor beside the sofa and began to rummage.

'Yes! Here it is.' She pulled out the *New Music Review* and began to leaf through it. 'The July issue, James told me it was in here somewhere. I haven't even read it myself. Herve left this copy behind. He's in it, too. Ah, yes, here we are.'

Sara, her head in the magazine, had not noticed that Poppy was looking less than enthusiastic. 'There's a whole profile of James. I won't read it all: "none better qualified to judge the

European New Composers Piano awards, with homes in Bath, London and Brussels"; "pre-eminent recitalist and accompanist"; "Ballantyne's star is no less bright today than it was twenty years ago" blah blah. And then at the foot of the page it says, "Ballantyne reviews for *NMR* page forty-two." So, on to page forty-two—'

'I know all about page forty-two,' Poppy said sharply. 'Stop it. Are you doing this on purpose? I never thought of you as unkind.'

Sara lowered the magazine in astonishment. 'Unkind? But I'm not,' she said. She had now found page forty-two.

'Go on, read it,' Poppy said bitterly. 'It's Marthe Francis's Wigmore, isn't it? I know it by heart anyway. How does it go? "The decision to include some contemporary repertoire in the second half was commendable if not understandable. Francis failed to convince that Cosmo Lamb's mercifully short 'Musica Spiritua Mundi' was worth a performance. But on the basis that we should all be able to sustain an open mind for eight minutes, I listened. It took rather less than that to decide that if I were given the choice of playing lacklustre Lamb or nothing, I wouldn't touch a piano again."'

'Oh, Poppy,' Sara said gently, putting the paper back on the pile and coming over to place a hand on her shoulder. 'I'm sorry, but you must put it in context. One bad review, that's all it is.'

'Yes, well, most of the time they know absolutely nothing, anyway. At least Cosmo never saw it. He was still in Prague.' She brightened. 'You're right. One bad review, that's all it was. And there's no need for him ever to see it. Why not hop back up now? Then I can finish your massage.'

The pressure of Poppy's hands again sent tingles across Sara's tired body. Her fingertips were now working around Sara's ears, almost stopping her jaws from moving.

'They don't realise,' Poppy said, 'do they? Critics.'

'Oh, they're much too powerful. And you can't answer back, that's what's so frustrating.'

In the silence that followed Sara's eyelids drooped. With a

huge effort she went on, 'It's harder for the partner, of course. The artist or composer, whatever, they have this sort of inbuilt belief in themselves. They have to, if they're going to survive. Nobody realises it's the partners who suffer most, trying to shield them from it. They take the brunt. You took the brunt over that one, didn't you?'

'I certainly did! I was sending his work all over the place for him. Anyway, as you say, it's only one horrible review,' Poppy said, trying to sound easy about it. 'Your critic friend just had it in for him, for some reason.'

'And you're so *helpless*, aren't you?'

'It's quite wrong, just one person standing in someone's way like that. Having it in for them. Anyway, doesn't matter. That was before Bath. We've put all that behind us now.'

'You are so good. You really care, don't you? You'd do anything for Cosmo, wouldn't you? Shooting a few critics mightn't be a bad start!'

Poppy laughed jerkily. 'Just that one, maybe!' Her hands were working fast now. 'Now! That's it for the massage. That should settle things down ready for the acupuncture. Stay nice and still, or only move very slowly and gently.'

But, turning to the case of acupuncture needles sitting open on a chair behind her, Poppy's own movements were anything but slow and gentle. She caught the lid with her arm and sent the whole thing on to the floor. Needles skeetered across the floorboards with a pretty tinkling noise. She wailed. 'Oh! *Oh!* Bother! Oh, look, how awful of me. Just when you should be getting nice and relaxed. Don't move. Stay there, I'll get them.'

When all the needles had been recovered Sara said, 'I suppose those'll have to be sterilised again, won't they? I'll show you where.'

'Well, yes. Yes, really, I suppose they should be . . .'

Sara climbed off the table for a second time and led her into the kitchen. 'They have to be boiled, I guess? Do you want a saucepan?'

But Poppy had already found the kettle. She filled it and

switched it on. 'Steam's better,' she said cheerfully. 'And quicker. You go back now and get warm under the blanket. I'll be along in two ticks.' Sara lingered, listening to the rising groan of the kettle as it came to the boil. Poppy turned and busied herself with the needles, holding them in a cloth and turning them in the steam which was now clouding one corner of the kitchen. Sensing that Sara had not moved, she turned back and smiled. 'Go on. Don't want the effects of the massage to wear off, do we?'

'No. No, course not,' Sara said mildly, and returned to the music room.

Cosmo unlocked and opened the door in his dressing-gown, blinking in the light but quite unsurprised to find Andrew on the doorstep. Andrew followed him down to the kitchen, where Cosmo released the window blind. He turned from the window and blurted, 'Okay, I'll tell you the truth. About last night. I want to get the record straight about what I did. I don't want anyone else accusing me, do you see? But I don't want Poppy knowing.'

Andrew raised his eyebrows enquiringly. 'Quickly then, if it's relevant,' he said, sitting down at the table. 'That's not actually why I'm here.'

Cosmo sat opposite, drawing his thin polyester paisley dressing-gown around him, because he had lost the cord. He wet his lips. 'Okay, right, I couldn't admit to anything last night. When Sara started on about . . . doing something with Adele, I thought she was talking about something else. You know.' He blushed and licked his lips again. 'I'm admitting it, all right, but only to you. I was, you know, seeing her.'

'Seeing her?' Andrew asked sternly. '*Seeing* her?'

'Well, you know, we were . . . er, you know. We were, er, having, ah . . . relations. Sexual relations. Look' – Cosmo raised both hands in front of him, as if warding off a blow – 'it's not what you're thinking, not what Sara was going on about last night.' Seeing Andrew's face, he went on quickly, 'Look,

I didn't force her, not at all. I didn't exploit her. I mean Adele
– I mean, she enjoyed it. She really did. She even made the
running. In a sense. Honestly.'

'What? I don't believe you. What do you mean, "made
the running"? She was practically a child. You're disgusting.'
Andrew's voice was low with anger.

Cosmo leaned forward, desperate to be understood. 'Look,
I'm telling you the truth. She came to my room one night,
when Poppy was away working. She was . . . willing. More
than willing. After that, well . . .'

'Oh, after that, don't tell me. You went to *her* room, am I
right? Every chance you could get, I'll bet.' Andrew closed his
eyes for a second. The effort of not actually hitting Cosmo was
making him nauseous. He opened his eyes. 'But don't you *ever*
try and say it wasn't abuse. You exploited her. You exploited
a girl who didn't understand the consequences of things. You
took advantage.'

'I took precautions,' Cosmo whimpered. 'She wasn't a child.
She wasn't *innocent*.'

Andrew jumped to his feet, grabbed Cosmo by the lapels of
his dressing-gown and hauled him up across the table. 'Christ!
You say one more thing in your own filthy defence and I'll
break your fucking neck. You're a piece of scum!'

'But she liked it . . .' Cosmo was trembling.

Andrew stared at him. 'Christ!' he exploded, and shoved
him backwards so that he landed heavily in his chair.

Practically weeping, Cosmo said, 'Don't. There's more.
About the music. About Prague.'

He took Andrew's revolted silence as permission to carry
on. He shrugged his shoulders and turned his head extravagantly
once or twice, in the manner of someone who seems to feel that
dignity can be restored only when he has checked that his neck
fits properly.

'The, ah, material that I'm currently developing for the
opera is based, both substantially *and* substantively, on sound
sketches dating from an earlier, ah, creative period.'

'Oh,' said Andrew savagely. 'You mean it's old.'

Cosmo turned an appalling colour. 'Mozart did it! He was always reusing things!'

Andrew dismissed this with a disgusted grunt. 'Look, you're pathetic. Fucking pathetic. There's really nothing else I can say. Where's Poppy?'

'No, listen, please. There was nothing else I could do. Look, everyone thinks Herve's some sort of mentor of mine. Well, he isn't! I hate him. I was desperate to study with him, but that was before I found out what he was like. I thought once he'd heard my stuff he'd want to teach me, so I went to Prague and more or less forced myself on him, to be honest. It sounded so great – studying in Prague with Herve Petrescu – doesn't it? Only it hardly *was* studying, I only saw Herve three times, less than once a month. He gave me less than half an hour and just sent me away to rethink things. The second time he asked who I was again. The last time he lost his temper and told me I was wasting my time and his. He threw my sheets of music all over the place, then stormed out and just left me there. So I started picking them up, and there was this note on the piano. Sara's note to him. About this opera group in Bath needing a composer. So I grabbed it, left half the music behind. I reckoned he owed me that. That's how I got here.'

He looked hard at Andrew's scornful face and raised his voice plaintively. 'That's all I did wrong! Only since I came back I haven't been able to write anything, I just haven't got the courage! He's taken away all my confidence. So I had to pretend I was writing stuff for the opera. What else could I do? With everybody expecting something and Poppy never leaving me alone. I just brought out the old stuff from Prague, bit by bit. I didn't steal any music. Herve stole *mine*.'

It was easy to imagine Herve's cruel dismissal of this unattractive, dull man. Andrew gave a short sigh. He could see how it had happened, but that didn't make what Cosmo had done right. But by now Cosmo had warmed up thoroughly to the idea that it was he himself who had been grievously wronged.

'And it was horrible for me to find out Herve was in

Bath, too! I've had an appalling time, wondering if he'd say something at a rehearsal, about the music being old stuff. But then I realised. He doesn't even remember it. Now that he's stolen it and changed it all round, it's like the original doesn't exist. *My* music doesn't exist, oh no. It's *his* music that'll get all the credit and the London premières . . .'

Andrew roused himself. 'Look, Cosmo, there's plenty I could say about all of this. You probably haven't committed a crime, but you've nothing to be proud of. That's not why I'm here. I'd be grateful if you'd go and wake Poppy, please, and tell her to get dressed and come down.'

Cosmo wet his lips and shook his head. 'Can't. You just missed her. She's not here.'

'What? Where is she? She's not working, is she?'

'No. Well, sort of. I think she's gone off to do an acupuncture session.'

'She's *what*? Where?'

Cosmo shrugged, wondering why Andrew was suddenly so agitated. 'Don't know. She woke me up as she was going off. She had her black bag.'

Andrew was already at the door. 'Oh, Jesus. Jesus Christ. I know exactly where she's gone.'

When Poppy returned to the music room with a gleaming handful of long needles, Sara was already lying back up on the table. Humming softly, Poppy busied herself in returning them to their places in the racks of the open case and Sara, flat on her back and seeing her upside down, watched. She moved her eyes across the room to the shelves on the opposite wall where all her sound equipment and CDs were stored. She hoped Poppy would not suggest soothing music, but mentally prepared a convincing refusal, just in case.

'Now,' Poppy was saying, sitting at Sara's side. 'I really want you to relax. Probably best if you close your eyes, as it's your first time.'

'Oh, but it's not the first time! I watched Andrew's, remember? That was amazing! And I've got no problem with seeing the needles going in. No, I'm really curious.' Sara was conscious that she was babbling in her effort to stay alert.

Poppy pressed her lips together. 'All right then, just to start with. But you'll relax better with your eyes closed,' she murmured. 'Lie down properly at least. Arms by your sides.'

Sara obeyed and a moment later was aware of a tingling sensation in one arm. 'No, actually Poppy, I was just thinking about your *Magic Flute*. I thought it was marvellous. It must have been difficult doing all those lovely little flashes and bangs. How's it done?' She half sat up to watch Poppy selecting her next needle.

'Do lie down,' Poppy said mildly.

'No, but how?' Sara said, propped up on her elbows.

'Gosh, you *are* tense,' Poppy said, rising and rearranging the blanket. Sara's eyes were still asking the question. She sighed. 'I'll tell you if you promise to lie down. And I was just helping out, remember. You take a charge and a tiny, *really* tiny amount of explosive. Then you just set it so that it goes off when it's meant to. That's all. Do try to relax. Empty your mind.'

'On whatever the cue is? Like right at the beginning when the serpent tries to attack the Three Ladies, or when Papageno touches the forbidden food, or when Tamino first tries to enter the temple, or when the Three Genii step on to their cloud to wave farewell?' Sara rambled.

'That's right. Now, no more talking. Re-lax.'

'Okay,' Sara said, settling herself. 'And when Sarastro opens the book of wisdom, or whatever it was?'

'Hmmm,' Poppy said, as Sara felt another strange tingling surge which seemed, perversely, to be pulling strength out of her. She breathed in deeply and exhaled slowly, feeling her head pounding. Another needle went in. This time Sara could not have said exactly where. She took another deep breath and began.

'No, but, it would be terrible, wouldn't it, to be doing so much for someone, like you do for Cosmo, and then find out it was all for nothing?'

There was no reply. Sara felt another tingle. Or two. Her

body seemed to be answering stimuli that nobody was giving it. She recited the alphabet swiftly to herself, only fairly confident she was getting it right.

'If they were being unfaithful, for example,' she blundered on. 'If, for example, someone else was just turning their heads somehow, and while you were slogging your guts out, they were sleeping with them. And you could see it was all leading to disaster. Ow!'

'Oh, sorry. Maybe you really should stop talking now. I wasn't really following you anyway, to tell the truth.'

'Of course,' Sara went on soothingly, 'these things are seldom straightforward. You wouldn't necessarily know who to blame.'

'You're really not making much sense to me, I'm afraid.'

'Cosmo preferred Adele, didn't he?'

'Please do lie back down. Right, that's it. It's important to lie still and not tense up.'

'Poppy, I know that Cosmo was being unfaithful to you.'

There was a silence, followed by Poppy's voice, all-understanding and womanly. 'Oh, that! It wasn't anything. It wasn't his fault if she came on to him. Artists hold a certain fascination for some people, even for someone like Adele. But I'm the one he needs. What makes you think so, anyway?'

'So it's all right as long as they don't shove it in your face?' Sara murmured. Another tingle somewhere near her hips sharpened into a sting. 'You don't think that.' She tried to raise one hand and found she couldn't.

The merest edge entered Poppy's voice. 'Oh, her and that autism. It was mainly put on, you know. And her drawing. I don't blame Cosmo a bit.'

'No, I don't suppose you do. You probably think it's your fault he strayed, don't you? For not being tiny and blonde and undemanding? So you just have to remove her from the competition and keep Cosmo's little foible a secret, so he never knows you found out? That's what you thought, I expect?'

To Sara's relief, sensation and power seemed to have returned to her hand. 'Because you can also suddenly see that Adele could actually destroy him completely. And you too, of course. She could undo everything you'd done for him. Everything.'

Poppy folded back the blanket away from Sara's feet. Her hand brushed gently over the ankles. She had clearly decided she hadn't heard. 'Now this time, you might feel one or two of the needles. Just let me finish and any slight discomfort will all melt away.'

Sara was struggling to sit up. Poppy, with her back to her, now had a firm hold of one ankle.

'And supposing then, supposing you found out a new thing? Something even *worse*?' Her voice was rasping now. 'Suppose, Poppy, you found out you'd got it *wrong*? That there was no reason, no reason at all to protect Cosmo, because it wasn't Cosmo who stole Herve's work, but the other way round! What *then*, Poppy?'

Sara drew up her free leg and kicked forward with all her strength into the middle of Poppy's broad back. Poppy shot forward and fell sprawling on to the floor. Winded only for a moment, she crawled away to the wall where she cowered, white-faced.

'What are you doing? Stop it! Just stop it! Stop saying these things!'

Sara was struggling to free her feet, caught up in the blanket. 'It's true! You killed Adele for nothing, you know. You thought the same as I did, didn't you, that night when Adele got so agitated about the backwards, forwards thing? You thought Cosmo had been stealing Herve's ideas and turning them round?' With shaking fingers she tried to stop the blood welling out from her ankle. More came. 'It was you who took those sheets of music from my case, wasn't it, Cosmo's and Herve's, so that you could check it for yourself?'

Poppy was still on the floor but sitting up now, aghast. 'It *was* the same music. I didn't get it wrong! Cosmo couldn't help it. He works hard, but sometimes nothing comes. You were all waiting for something, expecting something. He doesn't know I know. He did it for both of us.'

Sara had made it on to her feet now. 'Poppy, are you listening? You killed her for nothing. It was Herve who stole music from Cosmo. Understand? Don't you see? You got it wrong. And it would have made Cosmo's career. If you'd just waited for the première of Herve's piece you could have exposed him. And here's Cosmo Lamb, the one the great Herve Petrescu steals from? Think of the attention he'd have got. You could have made him. Missed a trick there, didn't you? You screwed up again. Just like you screwed up with the letter-bomb. You're crap, Poppy.'

A hideous wail escaped from Poppy's mouth and she was having difficulty drawing breath. 'Oh, no, no . . . how did . . . ? When she shouldn't even have . . . it wasn't even address— I don't believe it . . . I can't . . . oh, no . . .'

Sara walked over to the sound system, clicked off the machine and removed the tape. 'I'm going to ring the police.'

But since, when she turned to leave the room she was surprised by a scream and Poppy's full weight landing on her back, she didn't, after all.

Chapter Thirty-seven

Andrew, though the effort nearly killed him, slowed the car down on the approach to Medlar Cottage. He parked quietly on the lane below the house and came up the side to avoid being seen from any of the front windows. Banking on Sara's persistence in her bad habit of not locking doors, he tried the kitchen door. It opened noiselessly and he stepped in, sensing not only that the room was empty but that the air in it was utterly still. He stopped, listening to the house. No creak, no sigh of feet on carpet, no voice came to him. Disturbing the unbearable quiet, he strode into the drawing room, terrified of what he might find. A sound outside the door brought him into the hall to see, stepping through from the music room and locking it, Sara. She had clearly been struggling. She turned, sank against the door and stared, breathing hard.

'You took your sweet time,' she said, sliding down the door. He ran to her, brought her into the drawing room and got her on to the sofa.

'Christ. Where is she? What happened?'

Sara took a moment to answer. 'She's in the music room. In a bit of a heap. She hit me. I hit her back. Here.' She held out the cassette tape.

'Oh, my God! You lunatic! You should have rung me before she even arrived! How did you know, anyway?'

'Well, no thanks to you, I'll say that,' Sara said. She sighed. 'I didn't know, not clearly. Not when she arrived. But I was awake most of the night, going over things. All right, I got it all wrong about the guy. Other things too. I think I've got it right now. I didn't see till this morning how crazy she really is.'

Andrew stopped her. 'I'm going to get officers out here now and have her arrested and charged with the attempted murder of Phil Leung.' He pulled out his mobile phone.

Sara interrupted with the small amount of energy she had left. '*Phil?* I thought Phil was safe? Not Phil, too? Oh, God.'

From where he stood Andrew could see that both her eyes were bloodshot from last night's fall. On her cheek and forehead were two angry red patches where sparks from the fire had touched her. He had pulled from her head flakes of white ash and crisp wisps of burned hair like brittle black straw. She had been lucky to escape so little scathed, yet the signs of even this little damage almost physically hurt him. He made his call.

As he turned away from her to speak Sara closed her eyes and let her head fall back. Her eyes were beginning to hurt. Tiredness like a sickness spread through her. She yawned. Andrew finished speaking, switched off the mobile and came to her, standing over her.

'You're exhausted. Look, they'll be here in a few minutes. I'm going in there now just to see she doesn't need any urgent medical treatment and make sure she stays there. She'll soon be in custody, then you can relax. I want you to see a doctor. And you must try to get some sleep.'

'Oh, you,' she murmured, opening one eye. 'Just trying to get me into bed, aren't you,' she said, holding up her arms.

Chapter Thirty-eight

The following Tuesday Andrew left the Royal United Hospital and drove straight to Medlar Cottage. He walked in by the kitchen door and went silently through the house, across the drawing room and out to the passage that led to the music room. There he stopped, knowing that if he went any further he would be seen, and he did not want her to stop yet. She was playing. Andrew closed his eyes, listening and thinking. If she had been only a little more cowardly and less clever, this sound would never have been made. He would have been too late to save her, and on Friday morning her life would have been extinguished, one way or another. Instead of standing here now listening to her, he might be arranging her funeral. Even worse, he might be feeding her porridge in a hospital, her huge eyes like stones, her limbs already locking into rigidity and the hands that were capable of making this music seizing up into rigid claws. He still felt his throat tighten at the thought of it. Part of him wanted never to let her out of his sight again.

A yearning melody that he did not recognise drifted from the music room. There seemed to be in the music today the deepest sadness, and not the slow serene ache of grief accepted. She was drawing out of the phrases an unbearably beautiful sobbing, like raw suffering, new grief undamped by the passing of time. He stepped quietly towards her as the piece ended. She raised her head as she lifted the bow away from the strings, and smiled.

'I knew you were there,' she said, reaching out a hand. He bent and kissed her.

'That was beautiful. Especially beautiful. You're beautiful.'

Sara got up and began to loosen the end pin of the cello. 'I was thinking of Phil. How is he?' She carried the cello to its case, standing upright against the wall. Andrew did not answer straight away. She turned, alarmed. 'How is he? He's all right, isn't he?'

Andrew opened his arms and she came over to the sofa and settled against him, using his chest as a pillow.

'He's awake,' Andrew said. 'He's in a neurological ward. There's no obvious paralysis or brain damage that they can see. They think he's all right, but they're keeping him in a bit longer to do more tests. He was able to talk, but he couldn't tell me very much. He remembers Poppy arranging to come and do his costume fitting and coming to his room. He remembers her measuring him and trying on various hats. Then she said she'd noticed that he seemed rather stressed, and acupuncture would help release tension.'

'Oh, God, where have I heard that before,' Sara groaned, burying her face in Andrew's sweater.

'She made him some sort of herbal tea, very sweet, he said, and made him drink it all. That's undoubtedly how a high dose of tranquillisers came to be in him. He doesn't remember anything after that. He doesn't remember any of the treatment, though she must have done some, there are the marks. Anyway, what happened next is that she took a syringe, no doubt taken from the nursing home, picked a nice big vein, and filled it with air. Induced a thrombosis, effectively. She knew he'd been hitting the booze and drugs, and very likely his death would be passed off as an overdose. Couldn't be traced to her, anyway. Tragic, sudden, but the things kids do to themselves . . .'

'Oh, it's ghastly. And she was planning to do the same to me.'

'With your high blood pressure, that quite a few people knew about, coming in handy. Tragic, sudden, but the way these artists work themselves . . . Yes, horrible. What she didn't get right, thank God, is just how much air is needed to kill someone. You'd probably need over two hundred millilitres to be certain. The syringe she had with her here on Friday was only sixty millilitres. Even if she got the lot in, and she can't have done in Phil's case, that would probably result in permanent brain damage rather than death.'

'What a comfort you are.'

Andrew squeezed her tight, and they were silent for a while.

'What I still haven't worked out is how you knew you were in danger. When you didn't even know about Phil.'

Sara had been waiting for four days to be asked this. Slyly, she said, 'Oh, I just worked it out. How in the end it all came down to Imogen Bevan.'

'What?' Andrew sat bolt upright, almost dislodging Sara from her comfortable position. 'Stop right there. Imogen Bevan?' Andrew sighed heavily and settled again in the sofa. Sara lay back again complacently. 'Let's hear it,' he said weakly, closing his eyes.

'Well, I admit I got the whole thing wrong about Cosmo and the guy. I spent most of the rest of that night thinking. The way Cosmo denied stealing the music made me want to believe him about that, at least. But the music *was* the same. Then I remembered that Cosmo had been in Prague, and realised that Herve could easily, well, *must* have taken the material from Cosmo, and killed Adele to keep it quiet. He'd been down to see Adele in the workshop, after all, when he recorded her voice, and could have seen the cooker then. He knew about her smoking, too. So I was sure Herve had done it.'

Sara hesitated. She had not, despite four days in which to think about it, decided what she was going to say about her visit to Camden Crescent. 'Andrew, has Valerie . . . I mean . . . do you . . . ?'

'Do I what? Why are we suddenly talking about Valerie?'

'Oh,' Sara said. 'No, you're right, it'll keep.'

'We will settle all that stuff,' Andrew said gently. 'We have to, now. But go on.'

'Right. So, er, that's what I was thinking when Poppy arrived. I was trying and trying to get hold of you. I didn't know she was going to do me any harm because I didn't even know about Phil at that point. No, what really put me on to Poppy was Imogen Bevan. And Dorothy. When Poppy and I had our chat about critics, and I read James's review . . .'

'I should have known your fixation with Dorothy would come into it. You wouldn't let up about her, would you? I suppose I should have listened.'

'I'd been thinking about Dorothy as well, in the night. There was something missing in the way she talked about all those letters. She wasn't surprised. When Adam Hart-Browne told her that he'd written her dozens of letters, she knew immediately why she hadn't got them. She knew it wasn't anything to do with the post, even though they were sent from Africa. "I knew at once what had happened," she said. "I went straight round to confront her." Not once did she say how outrageous it was in the first place. The only question was whether Imogen had kept them or not. She was sad and angry, not surprised. She really was used to her, you see. Taking and opening other people's letters must have been Imogen Bevan's kind of thing.'

'Yes, but all that was what, over thirty years ago. I suppose you're going to say people don't change?'

'Well, there's no *evidence* that she'd changed, is there? Nobody else could stand her. Now, remember her kitchen? She ran out up to the street after the explosion, leaving the kettle on. She'd had the kettle on even though breakfast was over and done with. I'd wondered what she was wanting hot water for after she'd had breakfast. It was when I was watching Poppy sterilising the needles, standing there in all that steam, I suddenly thought, you don't always put on a kettle for boiling water. Sometimes it's the steam you want. I think Imogen had been steaming open the letter-bomb, because it wasn't addressed to her. It was addressed to James. There wasn't enough of the wrapping left to tell, was there?'

'No. Oh, Christ. We hadn't looked at it that way. Oh, Christ.'

'That was when I got frightened. And then I thought what a bore you are about evidence, so I thought if I could just get something out of her, maybe not a full admission, but at least something to go on, and it would have to be recorded, of course.'

Andrew sucked in a breath and tried to sound furious. 'You were mad and stupid to attempt it. Bloody insane. Don't you dare *ever*—'

'Shut up and listen to the funny part. So I nipped back to the music room and set up a tape to record, right? Not a blank tape, though. Herve's tape. His newly finished, final, pre-recorded tape for the new piece. I recorded over it.' Sara exploded with laughter. 'The one and only master. He'd given it to me to copy.'

'And then,' Andrew said, when their laughter was fading, 'you drew Poppy into discussion about making all those little explosions in the opera. And she showed that she knew how to.'

'Yes.'

'Wait, wait. Go back to the bit about the critics.'

Sara sighed, lying back and pulling Andrew's arm more tightly round her. 'Well, I'd asked James if Cosmo had submitted anything for these awards he's judging and he hadn't, which I thought was slightly odd. James also told me that he didn't know Cosmo's music but his name was vaguely familiar. He'd forgotten he'd reviewed this short piece. He does tons of these things.'

'And he can be quite a wasp.'

'Exactly. And Poppy couldn't take it. I could see that from the way she reacted when I found it in the magazine. At the time Cosmo was in Prague and she was doing all she could to get him performed and recognised. The European New Composers Awards are big, and she would see that after such an awful review Cosmo would get nowhere as long as James was judging. She was working on these stage effects when the thing came out and she must have seen how easily it could be done, setting the charge the same way and using more explosive, but still only a small amount. The profile says he has a house in Bath, and he's in the phone book. She could make sure that someone would have to replace James as the awards judge and also make sure he didn't touch a piano again. All those crazy ambitions for Cosmo are just as much for herself. Anyway, of course, James wasn't even in Bath, and Imogen Bevan opens the post. So James stays in Brussels oblivious, and of course Poppy doesn't submit anything of Cosmo's for the awards. Hard to know if she cared about damaging the wrong person.'

'Destroying a pianist's hands? That's sickening,' Andrew said. 'But also hard to prove.'

'You could start with the stage effects department at the Coliseum,' Sara went on. 'They have to be careful with explosives, don't they? They should know if even a little's gone missing, shouldn't they? Anyway, I don't suppose she thought of herself as a murderer at that stage,' Sara went on. 'I think she was just so desperate and furious. She might even have regretted it. But since Imogen Bevan died, I'm sure it was easier to contemplate getting rid of Adele. Adele had to be stopped from exposing Cosmo's plagiarism. It would just be a matter of setting the scene, like a stage manager does, because Adele's routines meant that she carried out the same actions in the same order as predictable as a scene in a play, the same moves every night. Poppy would have seen that, she knew all about the morning cigarette in the workshop.'

'But it's Herve who's the plagiarist, I thought? Herve who was using the stuff Cosmo left behind in Prague?' Andrew's voice was making his chest rumble under her head.

'Oh, you are so stupid. Poppy didn't know that *then*. After that rehearsal when Adele was upset and saying "backwards, for-wards" she came to the same conclusion that I did, that Cosmo was the plagiarist, getting Adele to sing all the Herve material she remembered from Iford and then setting it backwards. So

Adele had to go. Oh, and of course that was also the night she found out that Cosmo had been sleeping with her.'

'*What?* How on earth did *you* know that? How did you—?' Andrew sighed and gave a short laugh. 'No, no, I should know better by now. Just tell me.'

'Adele's drawing, the one she did that night. Some sort of star, wasn't it? An exact copy of something she'd seen. Poppy saw the drawing too. It was the snowflake on Cosmo's boxer shorts. Poppy did all their laundry at the nursing home. So Adele could only have seen it if—'

'Wait, *wait*. How the hell do *you* know about the pattern on Cosmo's boxer shorts?'

Sara laughed. 'Remember the guy? Cosmo had given the Scouts some clothes for the guy. The guy had them up his sleeve. I remember staring at them, thinking they were familiar but knowing they couldn't be. It was the pattern.'

'And you think Poppy realised when she saw the drawing that Cosmo must have been sleeping with her?'

'Yes, and that was another reason for killing her. It could even have been the main one, as far as Poppy's actual feelings were concerned. She'd be suddenly so jealous, possibly enough to kill her. Poppy needs Cosmo. Nobody else can have him, that's for sure. And if it ever got out about him and Adele, think how she'd be humiliated. Adele was in the way, badly.'

'Used by Cosmo and then disposed of by Poppy.'

'Not that Cosmo knew about the disposing part. He may still not even realise that Poppy knows about the sex.'

'So going on to last Thursday, when she tried to kill Phil earlier that day it was because she still thought Cosmo was the plagiarist? And Phil knew, because somehow Adele had told him before she'd died?'

'Yes. Poor Phil.'

'And she thought you knew too, which is why she wanted to kill you, too?'

'I wonder if by that stage she knew *what* she thought. It was all getting a bit out of hand, rather, wasn't it, by then? But what I did at the bonfire must have struck her as too dangerous to forget about. She knew I was frantic about Phil, and why would I be unless I knew something? Even though I didn't get it right.'

'Christ.'

'So most of the night after the bonfire, I was awake, thinking, and I still got most of it wrong.' Sara paused.

'Poor Adele. Poor, poor girl.' Andrew gave a growl and thought a little longer, gloomily. 'It'll still be difficult. There's next to no evidence.'

'Well, there's the thing about the gas tap. You said if it was turned on by Adele it couldn't have been turned on full. If it had been on full it would only have taken about ten hours to fill the room with the right amount of gas for an explosion. And you said that it was desperately *unlucky* that the proportion of gas to air was perfect for an explosion. But it wasn't luck or unluck. It was planned and it had to be someone with technical knowledge, mustn't it? Someone who could do the calculation about the output of a standard gas burner, the size of the room and the mixture of air and gas? Like the highly practical daughter of a "heating engineer", perhaps, which is just a posh name for a gas fitter, isn't it?'

'Poppy was working the night before the explosion, wasn't she?'

'Yes. And she had an arrangement with one of the other staff. She could skip off to do her washing and the other one would have a break later on. She'd been to the workshop, calculated the size and done the calculation – how much gas had to be let in and for how long. It was obviously going to be easiest for her to come in at night and turn it on, which meant a relatively small amount escaping for between eight to ten hours. One of the gas taps turned on full would do it. I bet she went off to do the laundry around eleven that night and slipped out while the machine was on. She could have been there and back easily within fifteen minutes, especially if she already had Adele's workshop key with her. She'd slip down and turn the gas on full. It's pitch black in the Circus, there are only about three street lamps, and the trees mean you can't even see across it. She'd walk home as usual at the end of her shift and put the key back before anyone was up.'

'We went about it quite the wrong way,' Andrew said miserably. 'Assuming it was an accident, done by Adele herself, and then working out that there had to be less gas escaping over a longer period. We thought we were dealing with an unlucky combination of circumstances.'

'Through lack of evidence, I suppose you'll say.'

'Look, the night after the bonfire. If you were awake all that time believing it was Herve, why didn't you ring me then?'

'What? Me? Ring you in the middle of the night? I wouldn't *dream* of telephoning you at four o'clock in the morning. Would I?'

Chapter Thirty-nine

'Uh? Hello? Andrew? Happy New Year. God, I'm shattered.'
Sara, woken by the ringing telephone on New Year's Day from
deep, partied-out sleep, reckoned as she finished speaking that
she could just about feel her lips.

'Happy New Year of course, but I'm not ringing for that.
In fact it's nothing festive. Meet me out at Iford, would you?
Quick as you can. Bad news.' He may have said something else,
but he was obviously speaking on a mobile phone and in the
dips of the hills round Iford the sound was lost.

It was only a quarter to ten. James and Tom would not
stir for a while yet, but when they did their expectation of
a large late breakfast would be unfulfilled unless they made it
themselves. She smiled at the thought of last night's dinner,
which they had cooked in her kitchen squabbling happily in
the way of people dedicated in almost equal amounts to each
other and, for the moment, their delightful foodie tasks. They
had allowed her to set the table and she had prepared the dining
room lavishly, since she used it less than half a dozen times a
year, in the way she might bring out a Versace dress and take
two hours getting ready to step into it. New candles the colour
of buttermilk were set in the wall sconces. Along the sideboard
she placed a dozen more, and instead of using candlesticks she
stood them in Victorian glass dessert dishes which were far too
gorgeously fragile for actual puddings. From the garden she cut
holly and ivy and left it in long swirls down the centre of the bare

polished oak table, curling round the stems of two plain pewter candelabra. She had busied herself with these little attentions for much of the evening, setting a single Christmas rose at each place, to avoid missing Andrew. Then the three of them had spun out the long minutes to midnight with a dinner of several delectable small courses eaten slowly between pauses for stories and gossip. They all drank enough wine to discuss the murders as if they had happened long ago.

'You don't think Poppy's going to get off, do you?' James asked. 'She's bloody dangerous.'

'No, not "off" as such. But she's pleading guilty and claiming diminished responsibility in both cases, Imogen Bevan and Adele, so she might get off with manslaughter. They're still waiting for psychiatric reports. But she's been a model of cooperation, according to Andrew.'

'Ah, the power of love,' Tom said facetiously. 'Is Cosmo really standing by her, then?'

'As long as she admits to everything. Cosmo's conditions. You know he got a job at Duck Son and Pinker flogging amplifiers after Helene threw him out? I saw him in there, we had quite a long chat. He seems to like the shop and he's got himself a room somewhere in Twerton,' Sara said. 'He said he was quite happy.'

'How heart-warming. So Cosmo's "found" himself as a result of his girlfriend destroying two other people, and herself. That makes it all right, then,' James slurred. 'There's one good thing. At least he's stopped trying to write music.'

'I know. I couldn't tell whether he felt some responsibility for what Poppy did or was just enjoying the moral superiority.' She glanced at Tom and caught his eye. 'But he hasn't stopped composing. Oh, no. He's writing an opera based on what happened,' she said. 'The whole story. We're all in it.'

'And James is being played by a girl, didn't you say? A mezzo?' Tom asked. 'A trouser role?'

They sat back to watch James explode, which he did to their satisfaction. After a full ten minutes' rant, he paused for breath.

'*Jeez*, is there no limit? He's fucking unbelievable! How can he – God! How . . .' His voice faded again as he took in the look on Tom's face. He glanced at Sara.

'You . . .'

'Just kidding,' Sara said.

'Don't take on so, pet,' Tom cooed.

'Bastards,' James muttered into his glass. '*Bastards.*'

Sara sighed. 'But none of it's funny,' she said. 'It all seems so wrapped up and finished with, but it's not, is it? They're still dead. And there's Brendan Twigg. I wonder what'll happen to him in the end.'

'Who the hell's Brendan Twigg? Is this another wind-up?'

'Andrew's first suspect. An awful character, according to Andrew, exactly what you'd expect him to be given what people did to him practically from the minute he was born.' She sighed again. 'All that fuss and effort to track down Brendan Twigg. Now Poppy's in custody the police aren't interested in him any more, of course. Nobody cares where he is. Nobody wants Brendan Twigg unless they think he's done something wrong. That's why I got Andrew to check with all the vets in York, unofficially.'

'You *what*?'

'Oh, it's complicated. I just always hope there's good in people somewhere, I suppose. Andrew was sceptical, he did it just to prove me wrong, and I wasn't. A vet in York did treat a dog called Fonz in October. The owner answered Brendan's description exactly. No address though. He spent over two hundred pounds on treatment, paid in cash.'

'Sounds like a Britten opera. *Billy Budd, Albert Herring, Peter Grimes, Brendan Twigg,*' James said.

'Raise your glasses to Brendan Twigg!' Tom said, picking up and waving the bottle.

As they did so Sara silently, sincerely wished him well.

Andrew was standing halfway along the long path between the cloisters and the summerhouse, looking down, watching for her car, motionless. He stood as still as the garden itself; the light swirls of his breath vapourising in the frozen air were all that moved. She had parked by the wall of the manor. Seeing him up there, she waved. He may have nodded his head, but he did not wave back. As she climbed the frosty steps she glanced up from time to time to see if he would come towards her. He did not, not even when she reached the far end of the path he was standing on. She began to make her way along the frozen gravel, and only then did he turn and begin to walk slowly, unsmilingly, to meet her. Above the crunch of her own feet Sara heard voices, from a direction she could not determine. There were other people here. So they met without kissing. Andrew's face was drawn, cold and pinched with waiting, but there must be some other, awful reason for the remoteness in his eyes.

'This way.'

He strode ahead. She followed, walking briskly but finding she was always just slightly behind him. He was making for the rose garden. As they entered the quadrangle of rose bushes, reduced to black barbed spikes, the knot of people assembled at the far end dispersed as discreetly as undertakers.

Orange tape hung between metal spikes in a rough half circle round a flattened patch of earth between rose bushes, on the edge of the long border.

'This is where they found him. Phil. His body. This morning,' Andrew said flatly.

'Oh, no. No. How? Andrew, how?' Sara pulled at his arm. 'Andrew?'

'Suicide. No doubt about it, there's a note. A long note.' Andrew stopped suddenly, raised his face towards the sky and took a deep breath. Sara could see that he was trying to stop tears gathering in his eyes. He turned back towards her. 'Overdose. The really pathetic thing – no, just one of the pathetic things – is that in the note he gave the name of his student counsellor for us to contact when he was found. His *counsellor* —' He broke off again, wiping at his eyes savagely with a gloved hand. 'Not a friend. Not me. Not you, or any of us. His counsellor. Along with apologies for inconveniencing everyone.'

Stinging tears were running down Sara's face. 'What else? What else did it say?'

Andrew stared at the patch of earth as if he hadn't heard. 'Can you imagine the temperature out here last night? He hitch-hiked out here. Got a lift with a man who lives just down there, next to the hall. He picked him up along the A36. Says he told him the garden was closed, but he wanted to come out this way anyway. Still, as he pointed out' – Andrew's voice was bitter – 'not as if they celebrate like us, is it? Got a different calendar, haven't they? Don't even celebrate Christmas.'

Sara touched his arm. 'Andrew . . .'

He jerked away from the contact. 'So what if a bloke in his early twenties in a catatonic depression wants to be dumped on his own in the countryside at eleven o'clock on New Year's Eve in minus six degrees? Free country, innit? Christ, I'm so ashamed.' He turned from her, his eyes tight shut, his face twisted in an expression of pain. 'He didn't come to any of us for help. And we didn't take care of him. Any of us. We just didn't notice.'

Sara reached again for his arm, this time firmly. She tugged him round and led him slowly along the path away from the insultingly jovial orange tape. They walked slowly and Sara, with an arm through his, held on tight. She tried to remember the latest she had heard, weeks ago now, when she had bumped into Helene and Jim in town. After he'd come out of hospital in mid-November, Phil's sister had come over from Hong Kong and he'd gone back to lectures after three weeks. The opera had not been mentioned.

'His counsellor's a bitch. Pointed out that her responsibilities towards students applied to term-time, not the holidays. Phil was being treated for depression and anxiety, following his discharge from hospital. She was seeing him regularly. His concentration was affected. His work was going downhill. He overdosed on his tranquillisers.'

'Is that what his note says?'

Andrew shook his head. 'No. His note doesn't mention work. It's all about Adele. Yet another thing we got wrong.

His outburst at that rehearsal wasn't about Adele being exploited over the music. He didn't know anything about the music being sung backwards or forwards. Adele hadn't told him that at all. The thing he'd realised was that someone there: Cosmo, or Jim, or Herve or even me, had been having sex with her. Phil and Adele weren't exactly lovers, not in the straightforward technical sense, though it was fairly physical. The note says Phil wanted to wait till they were married. He really believed he would marry her. Anyway, something she did – it's all in the note – made him see she was experienced, sexually. That was less than a week before she was killed. He's been haunted by both, the death and the fact he thought she had been unfaithful, ever since. He couldn't stop thinking about it. The poor boy didn't consider that the concept of fidelity might have meant nothing, or just something else, to Adele.'

'And it was all too much, in the end?'

'Oh, his counsellor's got it all explained, of course. Another student suicide: anxiety about work, fear of letting parents down, isolation, money worries. But in the end, none of that explains Phil.' Andrew drew his arm from hers, took off his glove and found Sara's hand. They walked on, their hands clasped in Andrew's coat pocket.

'Phil loved and lost,' he said.

'He lost, all right.'

Nor could it by any reckoning be better, Sara thought, that the tormented Phil had become a frozen, drug-filled corpse in the rose bushes, than that he never should have loved at all. They stopped on the path and looked down at the white meadow across the dark slice of the river. A crow on the head of Britannia watched the water. Black-fingered trees pointed haphazardly into a sky full of snow at the far limits of the fields. From here she could see across the brick tops of the wall and into the square vegetable garden. A few obedient lines of twiggy brassicas stood in the rimey squares of empty soil. Sara looked back across at the crow, its feet apparently frozen on to Britannia's head, and back into the walled garden. She realised suddenly that she was standing now in the very spot where Phil had stood that evening, as she had hesitated on the bridge. She had been standing down on the bridge next to Britannia and had seen him stand just here, very still, in his pale yellow shirt. She looked back across into the vegetable garden and now she saw it: the space where Adele's white bench had been, against the far wall, exactly halfway along. It had been taken in for the winter, of course, but she could see the interval in the espaliered fruit trees against the wall where it belonged. Phil had been standing just here on that warm September evening, watching Adele as she sat softly singing on the bench. He had been standing here, surely sensing, if not quite understanding the deep happy peace with which she had surrounded herself and which he must disturb if he tramped down and in through the garden door to be with her. His beautiful Adele. He must have felt something like contentment then, Sara thought, to be young on a golden evening, loving and watchful, keeping his beloved safe in her perfect garden before the world burst in and spoiled it all.